ALSO BY DAN FREY

The Retreat
The Future Is Yours

DREAMBOUND

DREAM BOUND

A Novel

DAN FREY

NEW YORK

A Del Rey Trade Paperback Original

Copyright © 2023 by Moon Media, Inc.

Published in the United States by Del Rey, an imprint of Random House, a division of Penguin Random House LLC, New York.

DEL REY and the CIRCLE colophon are registered trademarks of Penguin Random House LLC.

ISBN 978-0-593-15824-1
Ebook ISBN 978-0-593-15825-8

Printed in the United States of America on acid-free paper

randomhousebooks.com

2 4 6 8 9 7 5 3 1

Book design by Elizabeth A. D. Eno

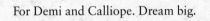For Demi and Calliope. Dream big.

DREAMBOUND

CHAPTER ONE

HANDWRITTEN NOTE

Dear Mom and Dad,

If you're reading this, I've already left. I'm going to the end of the world and beyond. I won't say anything more, because you won't believe me and I already know what you'll say. Dad, you'll say that I should live more in reality, and Mom, you'll say that I should take deep breaths and not make hasty decisions, but I have no choice. I have to go.

Maybe this comes as a surprise to you because you think that on the surface I seem fine. But surfaces can be deceiving. I feel like I am meant for something more. I'm sorry because I know this will be scary, but I don't belong here. I promise I'll try to come back in the future. Maybe then I can make it better for all of us.

Sincerely,
Liza

This note was found the morning of March 20, tucked between pages 11 and 12 of a well-worn copy of Fairy Tale Book One: *The Wishing Well.*

EXCERPT FROM FAIRY TALE BOOK ONE: *The Wishing Well*

By Annabelle Tobin. Published by Rotterdam Press, 2004. Pages 11–12.

. . . and as Ciara wandered out beyond the edge of her town, she happened into a field. It was an ordinary field that she had passed through a thousand times before. Only this time, it was different. For at the center of the field, there was a well.

Ciara walked closer, inspecting the old-fashioned water well. It looked ancient, with a rotting wooden roof, a fraying rope attached to the pulley, and lichen-covered stones at the base. *How curious,* Ciara thought as she looked about. Was it possible that she had never noticed it before? Or that she was crossing a different field than she thought?

She approached the well, peering over the lip into the abyss. Far below, she could see the silvery shimmer of the water. But it did not make sense to her that it was *silvery.* How could moonlight shine upward from a well so deep?

Perhaps it is a wishing-well, Ciara thought, and the instant the notion occurred to her, she felt it to be true. Ciara was twelve years old, and hardly prone to such fanciful thoughts, but this one fit her like a glove. Such was the pain of the fight with her mother and such was her desire for escape that she leaned her head into the cavern of the well. The sounds of the world were drowned out and she was swallowed up by the echoey swish of the water lapping down below.

"I wish I could escape this world," she whispered into the void, and then shouted, "I wish I were gone forever!" The words reverberated . . . then evaporated into nothingness, like every other wish she'd ever made.

She sighed in resignation and started to push herself back up. But in the process, a stone came loose on the ancient well and fell inward. Ciara's weight oofed down upon it, and the wall crumbled, sending Ciara tumbling awkwardly into the hole.

Down and down and down she fell, splashing into the water below. The air was knocked out of her lungs and she became disoriented, not sure which way was up or down. Thrashing in her heavy clothes, she felt certain she was going to drown. She churned the dark water desperately, seeking the light. When she glimpsed a glimmer, she swam toward it and gasped to the surface.

Only, it was not the surface she expected. For surfaces, as she would soon learn, can be deceiving.

Once Ciara's head emerged from the water, she realized she was no longer at the bottom of a deep, crumbling well. She was bobbing on the undulating waves of a lake, its water dappled by the pure silver light of a radiant full moon overhead. As she spun around, trying to orient herself, she discovered there was a *second* moon, this one crescent-thin, hanging at the opposite end of the sky. Ciara looked back and forth between the two, marveling at the impossibility.

She dragged herself up onshore and found herself at the edge of a dense, dark forest. A shape zipped through her periphery— a bird, she presumed, judging by its size and speed. But as she tracked it with her eyes, she saw that it was not a bird at all, for birds do not have purple wings and arms and legs and silvery crowns on their heads. And a bird would not stop midair, studying Ciara with a quizzical gaze. A bird would not laugh and shoot off into the canopy trailing dewy bubbles in its wake.

Her eyes followed the creature, and she was disappointed as she lost sight of it amid the branches overhead. But when she looked closer, she realized that the branches were swaying, not with the wind but with a deliberate sense of purpose. Some reached for each other and clasped twigs as though holding hands.

As her gaze traced back down the trunks of the living trees, she found that two of those in front of her were stepping to the side by slowly lifting their roots from the dirt, finding new purchase, and scooting away in opposite directions. . . .

All to make room for a massive redwood, its trunk thick as a house, striding forward and towering above her. Ciara watched, awestruck, as a huge hollow in its bark opened, forming a mouth that spoke to her in a warm, deep baritone:

"You. Are. Ciara?"

Her mouth was too dry, and her lips too violently trembling, to vocalize a response. But she was able, with some difficulty, to nod. To her surprise, the redwood's mouth curled upward into a grin as it spoke again: "Welcome to the Hidden World."

EXCERPT FROM POLICE INTERVIEW WITH BYRON KIDD

Boston Fourth Precinct Police Station. April 18, 9:55 A.M.

DET. CORDOBA: The note she left . . . you said you found it inside a book?

BYRON: Yes. Her favorite one. Tucked between pages like a bookmark.

DET. CORDOBA: And you think she wanted you to find it there?

BYRON: Definitely. On that particular page. What's happening in the story—the main character is a girl who runs away and gets whisked off to another world.

DET. CORDOBA: And you think that's the reason Liza ran away.

BYRON: Inspired by this. Obviously.

DET. CORDOBA: How about you walk me through the day your daughter ran away again. You had an argument . . . ?

BYRON: I didn't even talk to her the day she left. She's very independent. We let her make her own dinner sometimes, and I was under deadline, and . . . we just missed each other.

DET. CORDOBA: The last conversation you *did* have, then. The day before?

BYRON: That was . . . not an argument, but . . . she was upset.

DET. CORDOBA: I see. And why was that?

BYRON: She asked me for money, for a costume. These books and films she's into, there are people who dress up as the characters. It's ridiculous, how much they spend on things.

DET. CORDOBA: So you said no.

BYRON: You have to have boundaries. Rules.

DET. CORDOBA: And what did she say? When you refused her.

BYRON: She's a twelve-year-old girl who didn't get what she wanted, what do you expect? She was mad. Saying that . . . I don't support her choices. Don't believe in her, and never did, and . . . yeah, that was the last thing she said to me.

DET. CORDOBA: Is it true? That you don't believe in her?

BYRON: What kind of . . . How is this supposed to help my daughter?

DET. CORDOBA: Based on my experience, when kids run away, it's not about what they're running *to* so much as what they're running *from*.

BYRON: What are you suggesting?

DET. CORDOBA: Nothing, sir, I'm just saying—

BYRON: She's been gone for almost a month, and you've got *nothing*. Except for her cell phone used once, out in California, and you haven't even gone out there to follow up on that!

DET. CORDOBA: Sir, we're confident that the cell phone was stolen.

BYRON: But you don't *know* that.

DET. CORDOBA: I find it extremely unlikely that a twelve-year-old girl traveled across the country, from Boston to Los Angeles, in less than three days, without using her phone once. And then used it ex-

actly once, in L.A., before shutting it off permanently. We've had the
LAPD check out the last-known-use location. It's a dead end.

BYRON: So now you're trying to turn this around on me, like it's—

DET. CORDOBA: Not at all, I'm just . . . I find it unlikely that a book
is to blame here, even if it did have special meaning to her.

BYRON: Special meaning would be an understatement. These books
were her *life*. She had toys and T-shirts and books about the books,
and . . . you know what she wanted for her birthday last year? She
wanted me to paint the Wishing Well on the inside of her bedroom
door. And I did! My wife insisted. It didn't look great, I'm not much
of an artist, but Liza acted like it was the best present I ever gave her.

DET. CORDOBA: That's very sweet.

BYRON: It was a mistake! I wish I'd told her to forget all about it.
Listen, she was . . . Do you have kids, Detective?

DET. CORDOBA: A son. He's six.

BYRON: Well then, the Fairy Tale books aren't a big thing for him
yet, but they probably will be. You're teaching him to read now,
yeah?

DET. CORDOBA: Of course. Doing our best.

BYRON: Liza learned early, and . . . I used to write out sentences for
her to read out loud. Watching her acquire new words, one by one,
getting faster and faster—those were some of the best times we ever
spent together. She'd get so excited when I'd make up sentences about
her. *Liza is reading. These are the words that Liza can read now.* And
then I'd make them longer and more difficult after a while. *Liza is a
precocious young scholar. Soon, Liza will be capable of thoughtfully
analyzing long sentences.* She'd get them right and get so excited and
proud.

DET. CORDOBA: Sir, I don't see how this is—

BYRON: But eventually, her appetite kept growing, and my work got busier and busier, and I'd be at the editorial office late. So she stopped reading sentences written by her dad, and then it was just . . . whatever she could get her hands on. I tried to get her to read nonfiction, the kind of thing that I write. Not the news, but . . . there's plenty of fun nonfiction out there.

DET. CORDOBA: Mr. Kidd, we're not asking about her reading habits, we're—

BYRON: Kids aren't interested in nonfiction. There's something in them that's just wired for make-believe. And once she found the Fairy Tale books, those were everything to her. It was like a whole other language. I figured it would be a phase she'd outgrow . . . but no, she took them more and more seriously every year. She devoured the books, and when every movie came out she was first in line. And she's been nonstop obsessing over when the final volume's gonna be released.

DET. CORDOBA: I'm sorry, sir, but . . . what's your point?

BYRON: I know you're trying to pin this on me now because you're out of explanations. I've written about enough of these cases to know, if something awful happens to a child, it's usually one of the people closest to them. It's never a stranger in a van, it's a parent who lost their temper. But I'm not that guy.

DET. CORDOBA: Those guys all say they're not that guy.

BYRON: Then I'll tell you who I am. I'm the guy who can't sleep, wondering what I did wrong. Wondering how I could have possibly prevented this. Wondering if I made a mistake by teaching her to *read,* or giving her those stupid, dangerous books.

But I'm also the guy who's gonna find her. Because it's crystal clear that you're not gonna do it. Whoever or whatever took her away, I'm gonna find the truth. If I have to go to the end of the fucking world . . . I'm gonna bring her home.

CHAPTER TWO

EMAIL

From: bkidd@gmail.com
To: Valeriekidd@sltpartners.com

Val,

I hope it's all right that I'm emailing you. I trust that it's better than a phone call. I know the last time we spoke, we both said things we didn't mean, so I know it might be hard to get back on the same page right away.

I'm continuing to look into the circumstances around Liza's disappearance. I know we agreed I'd stay away for a bit so we could both get space, but I wonder if I might come take a look at some of her things. I know the police have been through it all, but I have some new leads I'm working. And I'd be happy to do so while you're at work. Let me know. Thanks.

Byron

REPLY

Byron,

Hope that you are doing well and finding your own ways to process our loss during this time apart. I appreciate your effort to respect the boundaries I've tried to implement.

If you feel that coming to look at Liza's stuff would be helpful in your process, I can accommodate that as long as you're willing to do me a favor. I've been meaning to clear out her room for a month now, but I find it too triggering. The only way I can do it is by fully detaching, which Martin (my new therapist) warns can be a dangerous step backward in my journey. So please, feel free to do so, as long as you take it all with you when you leave.

Thanks,
Val

REPLY

Val,

Clearing out her room? What are you gonna do, put a home gym in there? We still don't know that she's not coming back. It's only been six months. Are you really so hard up for space that you need to get rid of all the things that are meaningful to her? And look, I know you don't want to get into it, that's the whole reason I'm emailing you, but do you have to be so cold and clinical about all of this?

REPLY

Byron,

   I'm not trying to be cold, I'm trying to be precise, in the hope
that we can both avoid saying things we don't mean.

   Clearing out Liza's room was one of Martin's strongest recom-
mendations, and based on some of the books I've been reading, it
is a common and useful exercise during the grieving process. (If
you were willing to see someone, you'd get the same advice.)

   While I know that your personal attacks are coming from a
place of hurt, they are nonetheless hurtful. It is of course not
about needing the space. It's about the fact that every time I walk
past her room I glance inside and think maybe I'll see her sitting in
bed, leaned up against the wall, head buried in a book. It's about
the SILENCE that I think might be interrupted by her voice yelling
for me to make her a smoothie, which annoyed the crap out of me
a year ago and now I feel like I'd trade anything to hear it just
once.

   Having her posters and clothes and furniture in there makes
me feel like she still lives here. Which she does not.

   I want to speak from a place of clear intention, but I would
remind you that it was YOUR decision to move out. I believe we
both know you couldn't have stayed in this house one night longer.
It wasn't just our growing differences, it was your own unexam-
ined emotional pain surrounding her loss.

   So by all means, come look at her stuff, and take it with you,
please. I will be at the office all week; I stay until 6 these days.
Whatever is still around this weekend, I'll donate to Goodwill.

Warmly,
Val

CATALOGUE OF THE CONTENTS OF LIZA'S BEDROOM

ACCESSORIES:
- Blacklight tubes
- Lava lamp
- Wire antique birdcage with a small stuffed bird on the perch
- Casio electric piano (Liza was self-taught, and decent. Should've gotten her lessons.)

POSTERS:
- Billie Eilish looking creepy
- Lana Del Rey looking glam
- Some red-on-black image that looks vaguely like a person with wings, no text
- Movie poster for Fairy Tale Part Four: *The Crystal Palace,* featuring the face of the young actress Melody Turner in front of a glowing tower
- Framed art print of Dalí's melting clocks

CLOTHES:
Too many to catalogue. Still-dirty inseparable from the clean. Jeans, various degrees of ripped. Several pairs of overalls and several hooded sweatshirts. Notably missing: the red hoodie that was a second skin to her, which she was likely wearing when she left.

COSMETICS:
- Cherry lip balm. That sweet, chemical smell, inextricable from her.
- Makeup: lots of black, lots of red, lots of glitter
- Palette of brightly colored face paints, labeled "for Flutterseek"

BOOKS:
- Schoolbooks for all of her subjects
- Sketchbook full of colored-pencil drawings

- Yearbooks going back several years
- The full boxed set of Fairy Tale books, as well as multiple Fairy Tale books with alternate covers from other countries
- Various other fantasy books: Ursula K. Le Guin, Patrick Roth-fuss, Terry Pratchett
- The Jon Krakauer volumes I gave her; looks like she didn't get far with them

SCHOOLWORK:
Notebooks full of her handwriting (sloppy) on photosynthesis, the American Revolution, etc. At the top of the pile, a recent graded assignment:

SCHOOL ASSIGNMENT

THE LAST BATTLE BY C. S. LEWIS
A 5-Paragraph Book Report by Liza Kidd

This book is not very good compared with the other books of Narnia, in fact it is terrible. The reason this book is terrible is there are many things that do not make sense. *Chronicles of Narnia* is the story of the Pevensie children and many magical creatures especially Aslan the lion. But half of this book does not have Pevensie children and there is a fake Aslan and it is hard to follow what is happening. Susan is not there because she does not believe in magic anymore, which is the saddest part.

I online researched and learned that the writer C. S. Lewis in this book is saying a secret message about the end of the world. He is telling the same story that is in the Bible about the end of the world. This is probably why the story makes no sense. He should have made an original new story not the same old one of the Bible.

Most likely this was the reason my dad did not want me to read these books. He is opposed to religion. Personally I am not opposed to all religions but I do not like it when the author has a message that they are trying to get across but they do not say what he means. If a person is a religion they should tell you if they're trying to get you to be too. It is also funny because this book is written 70 years ago but today Christian people are opposed to there being fantasy with magic and witches in it.

I also learned some of the other parts of the Narnia books are the same as the Bible too. But those parts are still good. When Aslan comes back from the dead in the first book this is because Jesus comes back from the dead in the Bible. But it is better because Aslan is a lion who fights the witch's army not just a ghost like Jesus who doesn't do anything. In general it is a good story element when someone dies to save someone else's life, but not if it's predictable like Jesus.

In conclusion, you can compare and contrast this to another book that is partly about the end of the world which is the Fairy Tale book series. Even though I have been told I should not do book reports about these books it must be said where they are better. In those books when Ciara goes to the end of the world it is a real place it is not a secret message. This would be a better approach and C. S. Lewis could learn some lessons but he is dead now and has been for a long time.

EMAIL

Val,

Check out this essay I found in Liza's stuff. I got a big kick out of it, thought you would too. Laughed so hard it took me a minute to realize I was crying. Nice reminder of how, in addition to all the unconditional parental love, I actually really *like* her too. I like how she thinks. I like how she seems to think a book report is a book *review*. I like how she calls out Lewis on his overly didactic allegory and even slams the inclusion of an explicitly religious text in the school curriculum. Hell, I even like how she passive-aggressively shades her teacher, and still somehow managed to get a B+ anyway.

The part about me not wanting her to read *Narnia* . . . do you remember me saying that? I was always trying to get her to expand beyond fantasy, sure. And to be honest, I'm proud of her for hating the book.

But here's what I really wanted to share with you, the phrase that caught my eye: *The end of the world.* The same one that was in Liza's note: *I'm going to the end of the world and beyond.* She mentioned that it was in the Fairy Tale books as well. Could that help explain her reasons for running away?

I did a quick Google of "The end of the world Fairy Tale books" and found a fan article that pointed me to a particular passage, which I looked up in Liza's copy . . .

EXCERPT FROM FAIRY TALE BOOK THREE:
The Valley of Shadows

By Annabelle Tobin. Published by Rotterdam Press, 2010. Page 155.

Gloverbeck's forces pursued Ciara relentlessly. She crashed through the forest, slashing at thick vines with the Ruby Shard, cutting a path—but the fey troops giving chase hemmed her in on all sides, flying beside her and above her and behind her, filling the trees with the rushing thrum of their wings.

Finally, Ciara burst through the tree line and found herself stumbling onto the white sand of a beach, the likes of which she had never seen. Inky-black water lapped at the shore. Ciara stared at the waves, contemplating the undulating darkness.

"Welcome to the end of the world," said Gloverbeck as he hovered beside her, his spearpoint mere inches from her flesh. "That is the Sea of Nothing."

Ciara backed away from Gloverbeck, moving closer to the dark water, and the faerie soldier smirked. "Simply touch the water, and it will rob your memories. Submerge yourself entirely, and you will be forgotten entirely. Even if you do survive a swim, no one will know you ever existed. Not even you."

Ciara turned and stared out at the frothing waves of abyss. A shiver of terror at their dark power coursed through her veins.

Then she charged madly across the sand and dove right in.

RESUME EMAIL

To me this seems like nonsense. And disturbing. How am I supposed to read this passage if not as a veiled metaphor for teen suicide? Fuck these books.

Of course, the character survives, and her memory is restored for some sort of Chosen One reasons I cannot make sense of from the summary.

Does it mean anything useful? Maybe, maybe not. I called Detective Cordoba to share it with him and as usual found him astonishingly unhelpful, but it was an opportunity to finally get him to email me the exact location of Liza's last cell-phone-tower ping.

It's in Venice Beach. Right ON the beach. For an East Coast kid looking longingly across the country, Venice might as well be (you guessed it!) a sea at the end of the world. Just like the one the girl in the books dove into.

So I think that Liza DID go there. And even though it's been six months . . . I'm going after her.

Byron

REPLY

Byron,

Thank you for cataloguing Liza's stuff, which I know can be a beneficial part of a grief journey, especially since directly engaging with emotionally sensitive material can be challenging for you.

However, when I see how far you're going down the rabbit hole of investigation and recrimination, I have to ask: Why would you put yourself through this? This strikes me as a form of self-flagellation. I can't imagine that you're going to solve a mystery the police could not. To what end are you pursuing this?

Martin has reminded me repeatedly that grief manifests differently for everyone, that the Kübler-Ross stages don't happen in a neat, sequential order—so I'd like to give you the benefit of the doubt and assume that Denial is simply keeping its claws in you longer than it does for most. But that is absolutely what this is. Denial of the tragic reality: she's gone.

I recommend that you find someone to help you manage your emotional journey. Martin has been invaluable, and I'd be willing to share his contact info if you're amenable.

Warmly,
Val

REPLY

Fuck Martin. I get that you are trying to cope in your own way, but asking "To what end" I would search for our LOST DAUGHTER is the most ridiculous question imaginable. The end is simple: finding Liza. Or in the absence of being able to do so, finding out what happened to her.

Now, look, I've been inundated with statistics about how many teenagers go missing every year. I am not denying the awful possibilities. But take away those fleeing abuse, those with substance-abuse issues (their own or their parents'), those kidnapped by family members, and how many are left? How many kids from happy, healthy homes, with middle-class means and reasonably well-adjusted social lives, go missing with literally no sign of what happened? Not many. There is something strange going on here, and I will not rest until I find out what it is.

REPLY

Oh, Byron, I truly have nothing but love for you in my heart, even if every word you write is clarifying of the ways in which we have grown apart. But I must say, if you insist on communicating in such a toxic and aggressive manner, I won't engage. I sincerely hope you are able to take a fraction of your power for scrutiny and turn it inward on yourself and find some self-actualization, or at the very least, self-acceptance.

Warmly,
Val

CHAPTER THREE

REDDIT POST

FROM U/LILJONTHEREVELATOR
CODE BLACK: 3 NEW CASES

Through my research and government contacts, I have recently found an additional 3 missing-persons cases with undeniable connections to the Fairy Tale books. Use this thread for discussion.

- Miriam Yorin, 14, in Florida, vanished from her high school with left-open copy of *Fairy Tale Book Three: The Valley of Shadows* on her bed at home.

- Joseph Atuwunde, 11, in Johannesburg, South Africa, did not make it home from school; well known to be an avid fan of Fairy Tale film series.

- Smitta Agarwal, 15, in London, made social media post about Fairy Tale and then "went for a walk," never seen again.

We need to tell these stories since Mainstream Media is deliberately NOT reporting on the truth here. This community is the only hope for these kids. Help us Save the Children!

REPLIES

u/Dedditordie: Yes absolutely, I will discuss this on my YouTube show tomorrow.

u/Power4Words: We need to act quickly, FairyCon is next week in Los Angeles, huge gathering of fans, could be used for mass-kidnapping.

> u/Chemtrailblazers: this is an important point. Look at the Convention Website. There's an entire panel exclusively for "Young Fairy-Fans." We need to place operatives on the inside to monitor closely.

u/QualityQAlly: Look at how this is connected to Deep State intelligence operations. My research shows that all of the kids were in school and ALL had strong academics. Possible they're not being killed but being brainwashed and recruited.

> u/MKUltraDude: This is a great point, one of the first identified victims who disappeared was enrolled in Academic Decathalon, kids are being ID'ed and targeted for their smarts.

> u/Blazeitupnow: This whole thing is about kids who were into a book series of course it's going to be "smart" kids, there's no connection there.

u/PearlPopper: MSM is turning a blind eye the question is WHY. Could be suppression by global elites, could also be an active mind-control campaign underway.

> u/RobbinRobinHood: You guys need to get a grip this is ba-nonkers.

u/ByByronJames: I am a reporter working within mainstream media. I can agree that no one is talking about this, but I am interested in changing that. My own daughter is among the missing. If anyone in this community has any information at

all about the case of Liza Kidd, I would be greatly apprecia-
tive. And I am happy to help out in any capacity. PM me to
discuss further.

> u/PearlPopper: Everyone DO NOT respond to u/ByByron-
> James, we CANNOT trust operatives of MSM, recommend
> BLOCK him from the sub, he is spying.

EMAIL

From: bybyronjames@gmail.com
To: hwwesting@atlanticmag.com

Holly,

Hope you're having a good Monday. Attached please find my
proposal for the new investigative piece I'd like to undertake. I'm
very passionate about this and think this is important work that
could make a big impact. Looking forward to your thoughts.

Thanks,
Byron James

ATTACHMENT

THE TRUTH ABOUT FAIRY TALES:
Global Disappearances Connected to Children's Book Series

It was a warm May evening in Southwest London when 15-year-old
Smitta Agarwal logged on to her family computer. On TheQueen
dom.com, a popular message board for fans of the bestselling
Fairy Tale book series, Smitta made her final cryptic post: "Áine is
calling. My time has come!" She then told her parents that she was

going for a walk, left the family flat wearing a small backpack, and never returned.

Two weeks later, Smitta posted a single enigmatic photo on Instagram, standing in front of a spray-painted mural in Los Angeles, which creates the visual impression that ten-foot-tall fairy wings are sprouting from her back. But her expression looks haggard and vacant. That photo is the last known evidence of her young life.

The mystery of Smitta's disappearance raises questions. Readers of the bestselling Fairy Tale book series will understand that the "Áine" of her final message refers to a fairy queen character, but why is she being referenced? Why did Smitta leave? How did she get to Los Angeles? Who took that final photo, and what became of Smitta after it was taken?

Most troubling of all . . . why are there so many remarkably similar stories from around the world?

There has been an epidemic of global disappearances in recent years, all connected to the Fairy Tale book series. Exact numbers are hard to pin down, but I have identified at least 26 different cases—half in the United States, half abroad—that fit the same fact pattern. Diehard fans of this fictional world, whose ages range from 8 to 18, have vanished without a trace. Prior to their disappearance, each victim engaged in online communication regarding their fandom. And at least 21 of the cases have some connection to Los Angeles, which is both the home city of Fairy Tale author Annabelle Tobin and the site where the movies are filmed.

Are the cases abductions? Runaways? Something else entirely? An in-depth investigative article could get to the truth.

For context: The Fairy Tale book series has captivated young audiences around the world since 2004. The story started modestly enough, with protagonist Ciara visiting the Hidden World— a fantastic parallel universe inhabited by fairies and other magical beings. Tobin's book drew upon centuries of folklore and spun it together with the modern trappings of YA fantasy-adventure to create a distinctly optimistic form of escapism, with an underlying message about embracing individual uniqueness.

The series resonated with Millennial and Gen-Z readers, whose interest rocketed the books to the top of bestseller lists. Subsequent film adaptations amplified the popularity of the series to incredible heights around the world and spawned a cottage industry of merchandise, costumes, and online speculation. The annual FairyCon convention in Los Angeles (which is being held two weeks from now) typically draws tens of thousands of rabid fans.

But few have considered the dangers that might be inherent in this type of widespread, immersive escapism. Researchers have noted that the books are sometimes embraced so strongly that young fans can fail to recognize the content as fiction. According to Mary Weiss, a child development researcher at Boston University: "Prior to complete development of the pre-frontal cortex, which typically doesn't happen until 20–25, there can be a blurring of the line between fantasy and reality. We usually associate this with young children, but adolescents today are coming of age in a world where the 'virtual' spaces they occupy are just as real, maybe more so, than the physical ones. Understandably, the generation growing up with these books might be seduced into believing the stories are real—at least as much as their online lives."

A growing digital community of independent nonprofessional investigators has begun to gather evidence for how the books might be related to the disappearances. One popular and frightening theory contends that Fairy Tale fandom is being used by sexual predators to lure young victims into compromising positions.

Vanessa Brink, 15, of Bridgeport, Connecticut, was an avid collector of Fairy Tale figurines who went missing in March. Her parents reconstructed her communication through an online forum with another collector who was offering to sell her a rare figurine, and it appears likely that she went to meet him the night of her disappearance.

Another theory contends that Fairy Tale fans, perhaps stirred by discussion in online communities, end up leaving home in an effort to reach the Hidden World accessed by the main character of the book series. In so doing, these runaways could be getting lost or hurt, or simply electing not to return. This seems to be the case with Karl Weiller, 17, of Stuttgart, Germany, who participated in online conversations about ways to access the Hidden World and informed friends that he was traveling to the Black Forest in July to seek a possible "portal." He never came home.

One key source that needs to be investigated is the books' author, Annabelle Tobin. But Tobin has been absent from the public eye for years, and her book series has remained incomplete, with only five of the promised six volumes released. Speculation abounds that she is finally close to finishing—and I believe that, with the backing of the magazine, we could make a compelling case for her to agree to her first interview in years.

Whatever the cause of the disappearances, it is undeniable that they are united by a single common thread: a popular children's book series. This raises important questions. Can a book be a threat to public safety? Can an author be accountable for the harm her work might indirectly generate? And as the publisher prepares to release the sixth and final volume of the series . . . should they be allowed to do so?

REPLY

Byron,

In all the years we've worked together, this is the longest and most in-depth proposal you have sent me, written with more care than you sometimes bring to first drafts of your actual articles. So it is not lightly that I say we will pass on this, and encourage you to move on to another subject.

There is simply not enough "there" there. Your reputation has been built on fact-based reporting, and you do it better than most.

But in this proposal, you are linking the most tangential anecdotes from around the world in a way that makes you look like Charlie Day at the whiteboard. You refer euphemistically to "a growing digital community of independent nonprofessional investigators," but let us be clear what that means: the QAnon conspiracy-nut crowd on Reddit and Facebook. They've moved on past Adrenachrome, and this is their next frontier. Please, don't get swept up in the insanity.

By our magazine's standards, this article will always feel hopelessly incomplete without the voice of Annabelle Tobin, and I can guarantee she won't talk. Your well-earned reputation as a bulldog who asks hard-hitting questions hardly positions you to coax a reclusive fantasy author out of her self-imposed media blackout.

I have a couple other long-form topics that could use the help of someone with your research and reporting skills, so let's chat about an alternative assignment.

Best,
Holly

REPLY

Holly,

Thanks for your feedback. I understand some of your reticence here, as I know that you have both the magazine's reputation and legal liability at stake. But I can assure you, I will undertake this investigation with the utmost rigor, and we will not move forward to publish until we have an ironclad case to make.

If Annabelle Tobin is open to an interview, it will be valuable to include her voice—but even in the absence of her involvement, this is a vital story. There is a legitimate danger here, and we have a responsibility to shine a light on it. Both for the sake of the children who have disappeared already—and may yet be saved—and for other children who may be endangered by this phenomenon in the future, whatever the ultimate source of the threat may be.

With the magazine's support and a modest travel budget to attend the FairyCon event in Los Angeles, I am confident that I can make some real progress. If I fail to show undeniable results in a couple weeks, we'll pull the plug. I eagerly await your response.

REPLY

Byron,

I appreciate your passion, but it does not change my mind.

Now to say what I did not want to bring up before: even if this were an article we would consider pursuing, you are patently not the one to write it. We are all aware of the loss you have suffered, and it is understandable that you want to look for answers. But this is not the way to find them.

You cannot pretend to possess anything resembling objectivity here—and objective, fact-driven reporting is exactly what has distinguished your career. Your personal connection is a liability, as it would discourage your subjects from talking with you.

Best,
Holly

REPLY

Holly,

Very disappointed to hear all of this. In my tenure as a reporter, I have never once needed to print a retraction or had my credibility questioned. I've been a good soldier, tackling every topic you assigned. When I did the campaign-finance piece, I was the one who held back publication on my own article, and it was *my* fact-checking that saved us from a costly error.

Yet as soon as a piece comes along that I have any personal connection with—a connection that will only fuel my passion to get to the truth—you impugn my motives and cast doubt on my ability to be objective.

I would also point out that I have conducted my entire career under the pseudonym of Byron JAMES for exactly this reason—so that when a story comes along that demands my anonymity, I can tackle it without risk that my personal life will jeopardize the investigation or vice versa. There was barely any coverage of Liza's disappearance—here is the most widely viewed article, and as you can see, it is VERY brief (too brief in my humble opinion), makes no reference to my pen name or occupation, and includes no photo of me. Every other article online follows the same pattern, so I don't see how I might be compromised.

I hope you will reconsider and I look forward to your reply.

LINKED ARTICLE

"Watertown Parents Expand Search for Daughter," published April 14

Watertown, MA, resident Liza Kidd, age 12, disappeared from her home the night of March 19th. She remains missing and is considered endangered.

At a press conference last night, her parents, Byron and Valerie Kidd, reiterated their commitment to finding their daughter and asked the public for support. A $25,000 reward has been offered for any information that leads to her recovery. "We just want our little girl to come home," said Liza's mother, Valerie. A tip line has been set up and posters are being distributed widely, both online and in the greater Boston area.

Liza, pictured below, is physically slight for her age, just under five feet tall, with dark hair midway down her back. She is described as shy and socially reserved. At the time of her disappearance, it is believed that she was wearing a red hooded sweatshirt, dark blue jeans, and black Converse shoes, and was most likely wearing a backpack with numerous decorative patches.

"Liza was a quiet girl," according to one of her classmates. "She was nice to people when she did talk, but she was mostly just off in her own world." Other classmates noted her infatuation with fantasy literature and films.

While police report that she left behind a note suggesting that she was running away, her father has voiced fears she may have been induced or even threatened. "She never would've just left and not come back," said Byron Kidd. "We're a happy family."

REPLY

Byron,

As your editor, my answer is simple, straightforward, and easy to give: No. I don't feel the need to explain myself beyond the reasons I've articulated, except to point out that even if you DID succeed in reporting this story without your personal connection being discovered, it would undoubtedly come out when we went to press—which would be just as much of a problem.

Now, let me also address you as a friend and say: Let this go. Please. My suggestion would be to take some personal time. I know that Corporate approved three months' paid leave for you when the disappearance first happened, yet you were back in the office within two weeks. I understand wanting to lose yourself in work to move on, but perhaps the moment has come to take the time you need.

Best,
Holly

REPLY

I will take you up on the use of my approved leave time. But I cannot, in good conscience, let this go.

REPLY

Byron,

I wish you solace and recovery during your leave and look forward to continuing to work together in the future.

Best,
Holly

CHAPTER FOUR

INVESTIGATIVE JOURNAL OF BYRON KIDD

October 22

Touched down 8:00 this morning. Flying west is like being frozen in time. You land the same time you leave. ~~That's how I've felt ever since Liza disappeared: stuck in time. It's like~~

Focus. Who what where when why.

Rented a car. If I know one thing about this ~~godforsaken~~ city, it's that you need a car.

(Just the facts. No gods, no forsaking.)

It's a Chevy Impala. It's a piece of shit. (That's a fact.)

Warming up, finding my way. Be clear. Clear writing is clear thinking. Clear thinking leads to the truth.

Currently writing this at a maddeningly wobbly table at a dingy café with a misty view of the Pacific Ocean. Started a fresh notebook for this new investigation, leaving space at the front to drop in some of the supplemental materials re: Liza's disappearance.

Need to be thorough. Bulletproof. Document the process.

How I got here: the last ping from Liza's cellphone. Location-triangulation puts it in Los Angeles. Makes no sense really: there are no other pings between our house in Watertown, Massachusetts, and this random spot all the way across the country. This is why the police think it was stolen.

But the data is the data, so I headed to where the phone was last used. Drove up from LAX. There's traffic on the freeways here at 11AM; ~~where are all these idiots going?~~

This city sprawls and glows and hums with useless hamster-wheel energy. Billboards everywhere—a mix of movie stars pouting at the camera and plastic surgery clinics where you can try to look like them. ~~This city's affinity for illusion is written all over its face.~~

(Don't get cute. Just the facts.)

Location data puts the phone signal on the beach in Venice, which is only a short distance north of the airport. So I headed there first without waiting to get settled.

Gloomy morning, marine layer hanging low, no tourists out on the sand. I parked at a meter a couple blocks away from the beach, but the fog had rendered the sea ~~into a vast, ghostly abyss~~ almost invisible.

Liza always loved the beach. We never visited California, but we'd take her down to Florida every couple years. She would build sandcastles for hours; always did so in the wet sand at the edge of the surf, crafting elaborate turrets and defenses. She'd tell me about the people who lived there, how their whole lives were spent preparing for the monumental attacks from the sea. Then a big wave would come in and wipe out everything, and Liza's invisible little sand people would despair. Nonetheless, they'd set about rebuilding their walls before the next catastrophe rolled in, and they'd spin myths about the reasons they had angered the sea monsters, and Liza would ask me to step in as a benevolent god who could protect her people.

Yeah, she was a ~~weird~~ interesting kid.

(Relevance. Stick to the story.)

(It IS relevant. <u>Who she is</u> is relevant. Whatever happened, she wasn't abducted in the night. She left. Her choice. Part of the mystery is HER.)

As I approached the location pinned on my phone's map, it was clear that it used to be a hip neighborhood for artists but had gone to seed. Zoomed in tighter on the pin. It was not out over the sprawling sand but in the middle of the Venice Boardwalk.

The boardwalk, these days, is ~~disgusting~~ remarkably dense with homeless persons. Cups of change jangled at me aggressively as I passed. A few still busk, filthy fingers strumming shitty guitars. A couple artists peddle psychedelic graffiti art. Another sells handmade hemp dolls. But mostly it's just rows of tents. Acrid smell of smoke and body odor. Urban poverty, herded toward the beach.

The businesses that remain open are hanging on for dear life. T-shirts with dirty jokes and California flags. Head shops, tattoo and piercing stands. Sunglasses and beach toys. A "float lab" where you can get in a sensory deprivation tank for a dollar a minute. The world's sketchiest yoga studio.

All of it: the remnants of a countercultural mecca that became a tourist trap, then eventually collapsed into a decimated shell of its former self. ~~Proof of the unsustainability of dreams as an engine for~~

Graffiti everywhere, running a wide gamut of quality. A 5-story forced-perspective mural on the side of a hotel: a rendering of a graffiti artist drawing a mural on that very same building—a picture within a picture, a meta-commentary on itself. Alongside various bathroom-wall-worthy scrawls, unintelligible and profane. FTP. ACAB. And a message on the ground: "The end is nigh."

Well, that's what I came for. "The end."

I followed the location data to the middle of the boardwalk, placing myself where Liza's cellphone was last used. I looked around, trying to see this place through the eyes of a 12-year-old girl. Wondering if all this might excite a tween who'd grown up in an East Coast suburb. Wondering if she might see the impoverished and drug-addicted denizens here as ennobled, free-spirited bohemians. If the grime might look, to her, AUTHENTIC.

But as I attempted to look through Liza's eyes, I saw a man selling goods laid out on blankets, and my heart sank. Knockoff designer handbags alongside stolen electronics. Including cellphones. ~~Fuuuuuuck.~~

That felt like ~~the nail in the coffin~~ proof that Liza had never been here herself. It all clicked into place, exactly as Detective Cordoba had predicted: her phone was stolen, turned off, passed along across the country, ended up here for sale. Someone probably turned it on to test that it worked, and the SIM card pinged the cell tower. Then the wary seller had the good sense to pull the card before completing the transaction.

What a fucking waste of time. My entire trip here had hinged on the certainty that Liza herself had actually BEEN here.

I was tempted to rush forward and pummel the small, hunched-over man who was calling out, "iPhone! Two hundred! FaceTime! Just like new!" But I knew he was only ~~a cog in a larger machine of urban injustice~~ trying to get by.

I turned away ~~in disgust~~, ready to head back to the car, perhaps back to Boston. Perhaps Val was right, Holly was right, the police were right, Liza was gone, and I was ~~tilting at windmills~~ desperately ~~digging for scraps~~ clinging to false hope in the face of an unacceptable reality.

But then I saw it: "The End of the World Museum."

~~Holy shit.~~

The small storefront had a carnival quality to it, a freak-show promise of illicit or dangerous sights inside with a flashy sign promising "Lost Treasures, Exotic Lifeforms, and Forbidden Antiquities!"

This must be the place Liza had been drawn to. What she came for. ~~I don't care what Val wou~~ The coincidence was impossible to ignore.

I stared at the building, nestled between a tattoo parlor and a sex shop. Pulled out my phone to look up whatever information I could get. But the museum wasn't even listed on Maps. Googling the name yielded nothing.

OK, so this was some off-the-grid, top-secret attraction. The type of place a 12-year-old girl would have been thrilled to learn about, even if it seemed a bit cheesy to me.

The ticket vendor was a woman in her fifties. Her skin had the leathery quality of having spent decades in the sun, with once-colorful tattoos that had faded into shapeless bruises. I approached and asked for a single ticket; she informed me that admission was free and waved me inside.

I passed through a glass door into a tiny antechamber, barely five feet wide and ten feet long. It was pitch-dark, and I could faintly see images painted on the walls. Suddenly, I heard the woman's voice crackle through an intercom speaker overhead: "Stand against the wall." My eyes were still adjusting to the near-complete absence of light, but I did as instructed. "The other wall," she corrected. Again, I complied, though I was thoroughly confused—until I saw the tiny pinpoint gleam of a camera lens, poking through a cut-out hole.

"Neutral face," she said. "I'm going to photograph your aura."

"Oh, I don't need that," I said aloud, but the crackling speaker interrupted again: "Not optional. Hold still."

There was a flash, which momentarily revealed the walls of the tiny room. They were painted with an immersive mural showing a verdant forest landscape, sparkling with fireflies. But it was visible for only a fraction of a second, then gone completely. No doubt the image was designed as a backdrop for the photos, but it was hard to imagine why they had painted all four walls when only one would be seen in the picture.

"Twenty dollars" crackled though the speakers. So much for free admission. But as the next door buzzed open, and the ticket-taker greeted me on the other side, I grudgingly paid the toll.

I pushed through the glass doors into the cramped little "exhibition hall" of this "museum." It was absurdly dark everywhere except for the exhibits that lined the walls in brightly lit glass cases. A bluish glow illuminated just enough of the sticky cement floor to find my footing as I browsed the "collection."

To call the museum eclectic would be an understatement. A couple dozen exhibits featured a mix of antiques and supposedly historical objects. I paused at a raggedly ancient leather-bound book, open to a page with writing in an indecipherable alphabet.

THE CODEX OF GALBRAITH

This text was discovered washed ashore in the mortal world (1105 BCE) and provides the only surviving evidence of the written language of the trolls.

The object was obviously a fabricated prop. But in the dim light, the illusion that this book was three thousand years old was reasonably compelling.

An employees-only service door opened and the ticket-taker came through, keeping an eye on me as I browsed.

I still wasn't sure what to make of this place. Was it all ironic? Or were the exhibits asking for genuine suspension of disbelief?

Regardless, I was impressed with the ingenuity of some of the creations, especially a "fountain of youth"—a water feature that appeared to flow backward.

Other objects surprised me simply with the audacity of their labels. A ratty knot of hair hung suspended inside a glass box with a placard claiming it had been shorn from the head of Joan of Arc and was imbued with her Wiccan power.

As I studied various "exhibits," I imagined how this might have aroused Liza's curiosity, assuming that she had indeed made it inside. ~~My revulsion at the manipulative spectacle turned to a deep pang of~~ ~~longing for her excited eruptions of joy upon~~

Just the facts. She was here. What did she see?

I moved on to an exhibit that would have particularly drawn her interest. In one of the center cabinets, I discovered what looked like the taxidermized remains of a fairy. Perhaps a foot tall, its body was desiccated like a mummy's, with shriveled parchment-like skin wrapped tight around an angular skeleton. Its wings were delicate filigree, remarkably detailed. A plaque read:

SIR PALMEROY OF THE FEY
This noble squire of faeriekind traveled back to our world as the companion of an itinerant bard and was stranded by the closure of his portal.

I caught the eye of the ticket attendant and gestured toward the "fairy" display, then asked, "If I clap my hands and believe, will it bring him back?"

She frowned but said nothing. And I was about to move on when suddenly—

WHUMP-WHUMP!—the display-creature's wings flapped twice against the glass. I was certain I could hear the creak of the simplistic animatronics in action, but it scared the hell out of me anyway.

The ticket-taker cackled, and it was my turn to frown. "Who made all this?" I asked.

She shrugged. Then I heard a faint click sound, and she walked away, returning to the wall beside the employee door. I peered between the exhibits to watch what she was doing. She approached a small metal slot in the wall, and a photo-booth style picture dropped down. My "aura photo," clearly. The ticket-taker took it out—making a cut with a pair of scissors and pocketing half. Then she returned and handed me the photo.

It was the size and shape of a baseball card—a flash-soaked image of my head and shoulders, while behind me, the trees of a towering forest loomed all around. Points of glowing light appeared to flit through the air. A full moon glowed brightly in one corner of the image—and a second, smaller crescent moon was faintly visible through the trees. I had to concede, the effect realistically conveyed the impression that I was standing in some sort of "enchanted forest" at night.

The space above my head was clouded with an optical effect, a pattern of dark spots on the image. The "aura" that this photo was purported to expose. I asked the ticket-taker, "What's that mean? Good fortune?"

She studied the photo for a moment. "Means you're closed-off. Heart and mind. So you're not going anywhere."

I turned my attention toward the rest of the exhibits while she headed back toward the ticket booth. But as I looked at a faux-crystal dagger, I remembered that the photo had been duplicated and cut. Before the ticket-taker went back through the door, I called out: "Hey. Where do you put the other half?"

The ticket-taker pretended not to know what I was talking about, but I pressed her. "I saw you. There were two photos."

"It's *our* camera," she snapped back at me, then softened. "If you want the other one, you can have it for ten more."

I shook my head. "I want to know where you keep them."

She shrugged. "We just toss 'em."

I do not have great "people skills" in general, but I have one that is impeccably refined. I know when people are lying. It happens on a gut level. I don't decode specific clues of how their eyes move or their voice shifts. I simply KNOW, and I'm never wrong.

"We just toss 'em" was obvious bullshit, and I told her as much.

She shrank from the accusation, and I could see she was clamming up. I tried to disarm her. "I just want to see the rest. Please. The ones from March?"

She studied me with a level gaze, as though truly seeing me for the first time. Then she dug my second aura photo out of her pocket and stared at it, searching for meaning there. She snorted with a derisive semi-laugh, as if discovering something amusing. "Suit yourself," she said, and beckoned me to follow as she disappeared through the staff door back toward the ticket booth.

The door opened into a long service hallway that ran parallel to the "photo booth" where my picture had been taken. The hall was soaked in a darkroom-esque red glow, and as my eyes adjusted, I could see the walls were lined with photos, showing an array of faces, all posed in front of the enchanted-forest image. The pictures were like floor-to-ceiling wallpaper, all taped up, edge to edge. An eerie visual catalog of everyone who had passed through this place.

"Why do you keep all these?" I asked.

"Our benefactor insists on maintaining a visual guestbook," was her reply, with an air of finality. Naturally, I asked who the museum's benefactor was, but she told me she didn't know.

"It's public record, I'm sure. So why not just tell me and save me the trouble?"

"If I did, I'd be finished here."

As frustrating as that answer was, it was clear that I wouldn't get any more information, so I didn't press further. I believe that I got the spirit of her words right, though I must confess, I am reproducing what she said from memory, and I wish I could go back and hear it again.

Regrettably, I had left my audio recorder in the car, which I vowed not to do again. Need to be prepared for an interview at any time.

The ticket-taker added my photo to the end of the line, which was only a couple rows short of completely covering every inch of the walls of the hallway.

My breath caught in my throat. If Liza had come here, her image would be on this wall. But there were so many.

I started to scan through the pictures. Tried to do a quick estimate of how many photos were here. Twenty rows vertically. Twenty feet horizontally. Six photos per foot. Two walls. Almost five thousand photos, ~~an impossible haystack into which the needle of my heart had been~~

It would take forever. That was fine.

I realized I had a way to make it go faster and asked how long this place had been open. "This summer was three years," the ticket-taker told me.

OK—that meant about sixteen hundred visitors a year. And if Liza was here approximately half a year ago, she should be one-sixth of the total way back through the sequence of photos. Based on that rough calculation, I started scanning through the same wall where my photo had been posted, midway up.

So many faces. Some smiled, some wore expressions of strained longing. Every child I saw gave me pause. Made me wonder at the circumstances of their coming, and the events that followed their departure.

The ticket-taker watched me for a while, then grew bored and could tell from the intensity of my search that I was not about to move on. She returned to her ticket booth.

I looked and looked and looked. No Liza. Hundreds of times over, not-Liza.

And then, I collapsed to my knees. Because there she was.

My girl. The hood of her red sweatshirt was scrunched up around her neck. Her long hair was swept to the side of her face. Dark circles under her eyes; I worried she hadn't slept in days. Her expression was haunted and distant, as though she didn't realize a photo was being taken.

In the space of the image above Liza's head were a series of glowing reddish spirals. The optical effect was beautiful, with a surprising sense of DEPTH. And a quick scan of the surrounding images revealed none that matched it. I didn't know how these "aura" effects were achieved, but hers was especially impressive. ~~Or perhaps I was just so enraptured by the sight of her that my heart was inflating the magnitude of~~

I started to pluck the photo from the wall, but immediately the intercom speaker crackled: "No touching."

I left the picture in place, but my finger lingered on it, like I might somehow lose the thread of her if I lost physical contact.

I weighed my options. The photo PROVED that Liza had been in Los Angeles. That her single cellphone ping had not been an aberration. She had somehow gotten herself here and turned on her phone exactly once. But how and why were totally mysterious.

I studied the photos to the left of hers. The first few appeared to show a family that had come together and all had their pictures taken in sequence. To the right, just AFTER her, apparently, a teenage couple photographed together. Not sure what I expected—some leering old predator, perhaps? No such luck.

There wasn't anything else I was going to learn from this wall of photos, but I didn't want to leave yet. I softened my gaze, letting the sprawling mosaic of faces melt together.

But then one among the mass rose to the surface of my attention. I focused on the image, several rows above Liza's—probably three or four months earlier, based on my best estimation.

For a moment, I could not place the woman. But her penetrating gaze was singular. Her sharply angular features and oddly sensuous lips, curled into a smirk, were familiar. Where had I met this person? I struggled to put my finger on it. . . .

Then I remembered where I'd seen that face. On the back flap of books that had been left all over our house, above a brief biographical blurb:

"Annabelle Tobin is the author of the Fairy Tale book series, which has sold over 100 million copies and been translated into more than fifty languages. She lives with her cat and her son in Los Angeles."

My eyes burned with cold fury as I stared at Annabelle's image. I could swear that she was staring back.

I knew this wasn't the sort of evidence the police would be likely to act on, but it was a puzzle piece that could be useful. So I snapped pictures on my phone of both photos (Liza's and Annabelle's). They were difficult to capture in the low light—the flash glared, and it was hard to keep the camera steady enough for an unlit exposure. But I eventually succeeded and made my way out to the glaring light of the boardwalk.

I looked back at the grimy façade of the End of the World Museum. It seemed pathetically inconsequential . . . but Liza had crossed the country to visit this place. To figure out why—and more important, where it had led her to next—I needed to understand what she was looking for. What she had hoped to find.

I suspected there was only one person who might be able to answer that. And I knew she would not be easy to get to.

CHAPTER FIVE

EMAIL

From: sg@rotterdarnpress.com
To: a.q.tobin@gmail.com

Annabelle,

Hope you are doing well. How's progress coming on the draft? Just want to see if we can pin down a pub date.

Don't want to interrupt the creative process but have to ask, have you been tracking any of the online chatter about the disappearances? I'm concerned this is getting widespread enough that it demands a response from you. When we release Book Six, we want the conversation to be focused around the triumphant conclusion to the greatest fantasy series of our generation, not for it to be hijacked by this nonsense.

Yours,
Stanley Gottheim
Senior Editor (he/him/his)
Rotterdam Press

REPLY

Nice to hear from you, Stan. Been a minute, has it not? No time for pleasantries these days I see. Not to worry, I can assure you I'm staying on track to deliver Book Six very soon. I know you're nervous after all the delays, but trust me, this is happening, and it will be in your hands soon.

As for the business about the disappearances . . . as far as I can tell, it goes no further than Twitter and a handful of fear-mongering newspaper articles. Are we really going to humor this insane, baseless conspiracy theory? The fact that reputable publications are even mentioning this trash is absurd. Delete, ignore, move on.

A.T.

REPLY

Annabelle,

I could not be more aligned with you about the reality of the situation. Unfortunately, this does not change the fact that there are serious repercussions we have to confront. The story has gained enough traction that "no comment" will be construed as callous disregard for missing children.

I know you don't want to hear this, but you may have unwittingly created the conditions for this to flourish. While I fully understand and respect your reasons for retreating from the public eye, an individual of your stature staying out of view through the last book release and last two film releases creates a vacuum, one that will be filled in *some* way—if not with your voice, then with pernicious deceit.

Fortunately, I have in mind a remedy. Perhaps now is the perfect time for a long-form journalistic piece, which could allow the public a more personal and private view into your life and your process. The piece would be a sensation, especially after years of silence and speculation. I believe that overnight we could transform you from "secretive recluse" back into "beloved voice of a generation."

Sincerely,
Stanley

REPLY

The last time I let a reporter get close to me, it was a total hatchet job. In case you've managed to block it out, let me remind you of this particularly winning quote:

It is not uncommon for a children's author to subject her young characters to struggles no child should have to bear. But Annabelle Tobin has advanced this trope to such an extreme, one wonders if the books are born out of a deep-seeded hatred of youth. The most fantastical element of her stories is not any of the magical runes, enchanted swords, or otherworldly creatures she has invented. It is the protagonist, Ciara, a caricature of tortured adolescence who endures trials that would give any hardened soldier PTSD, yet she bounces back with aplomb every time. Tobin's treatment of her heroine as a vessel for torment is borderline sociopathic.

Yes, it was insinuated (in *The New Yorker* no less) that my writing demonstrates that I *hate children* and am a *sociopath*. So I hardly think I'm being paranoid here. Doing an interview now seems like a big risk, and I don't understand what there is to be gained.

REPLY

Annabelle,

What happened with *The New Yorker* was an utter travesty, there is no disputing that. I understand you might be gun-shy now, but I'm fairly confident that writer was in Tom's pocket and it was all part of his smear campaign to get as much as he could out of the divorce. Those days are behind you now. And to be blunt, the imbalance of that article may owe, in part, to your categorical refusal to participate.

Now let me address "what is to be gained." The short answer is . . . a great deal. Sales have dropped precipitously, and I think much of that may be connected to the fact that you've stopped promoting the films and engaging with fans. They don't only love the fairies and the Hidden World—they love *you*. I'm confident that your reemergence in the public sphere would greatly benefit the new book's popularity, likely to the tune of a six-figure sales difference easily, perhaps even seven.

Even if you are unmoved by commerce, please consider the reputational benefits here. Right now, your work is being tarnished and overshadowed by a public conversation that we've lost control over. I believe that you and I both want to see this through and get Book Six out into the world the way it deserves to be seen. I think this is the perfect next step.

Sincerely,
Stan

REPLY

Appealing to my ego and my pocketbook—you know me well. I do want my son growing up feeling proud of his mother rather than shrinking from the association. So yes, of course, I'd like to set the record straight.

The question is: Who's the writer to do the job? Who could I trust at this point? I burned most of my bridges with the literary press long ago.

REPLY

Annabelle,

Glad that you asked. There's a writer who's recently gotten in touch with me, and while normally I bat these requests away, his appeal was uniquely compelling, and I think he might be just the one for you: Byron James. He's not famous by any means and not the type desperate to make a name for himself—just a journeyman from *The Atlantic* with a reputation for solid, fact-based reportage.

Based on early conversations, I'm confident that Byron is trustworthy and willing to play ball with us. No one will grant full editorial approval, but he's content with 100% quote approval and a tacit understanding that this can't be any sort of slam piece. It won't be pure puff either, but I'm certain that it will humanize your image, and at the very least will debunk the ridiculous allegations regarding the disappearances.

REPLY

Stan,

Interesting recommendation. It's clear that Byron has a solid reputation as a journalist, but his articles (at least the first ones that appear on Google) seem to be a far cry from the arts and culture beat. I actually recall the exposé he did on data-harvesting making the rounds a couple years ago.

The writing is strong, but I worry he may be a bit . . . confrontational. Surely we could find someone a little more, shall we say, agreeable?

REPLY

Annabelle,

I understand your reticence, but I think James's approach is exactly the reason he's a good choice. There will be plenty of time for softball interviews and late-night appearances, but the first step here is to *clear your name,* which can only be accomplished through the pen of someone respected for his objectivity. Other journalists will follow his lead, his article will restore some sanity to the discourse around your work, and it will be downhill from there.

He's asked me if he could reach out directly . . . would you be amenable to at least hearing from him?

REPLY

Fair point. And I suppose it can't hurt to hear him out.

EMAIL

From: bybyronjames@gmail.com
To: a.q.tobin@gmail.com

Ms. Tobin,

I'm writing to you after Stanley Gottheim passed along your email address, which I'm grateful for. I appreciate you entertaining my request to profile you. I don't want to pitch you the story I'm going to write because, to be honest, I don't yet know the truth about your life, and any effort to sell you on a story I haven't found would be disingenuous. Instead, I'll try to explain who I am, and why I believe I'm right for the job.

Let me first be transparent: I am not a fantasy fan. I identify as a journalist because that word carries prestige, but I am at heart a reporter. I report the truth. I have a sacred duty to be honest, thorough, unflinching. There are no doubt fancier writers out there who would swoon at the opportunity to interview you for a story, but it would be just that: a story. And based on the state of journalism today, the stories they concoct might be every bit as fantastical as your books.

What I will write is the truth, as you have lived it. As I'm sure you're aware, truth is hard to come by these days. Socially, politically, spiritually, even medically—the world is filled with deceit and deceivers, and it almost seems like the extent and volume of the mendacity is so vast that it hardly matters anymore. But it matters to me. And if your reputation has been damaged by lies, then getting the truth out there will matter to you too.

The reason I am particularly attracted to your work is simple: my daughter loves your books. Like so many girls her age, she became obsessed with the world you created—and by extension, with you. I was happy for her to find a hero in a successful woman who made her way by her wits, not a mindless social-media celebrity.

I would not seek out this opportunity if it were merely a way to fluff your pillows. For me, the more pressing issue is how you are perceived by your young readership and my daughter in particular. For many kids, including her, news stories about the connection between your fiction and child-trafficking is not only frightening, it is traumatic. So, if the truth can restore your reputation, then it can assuage my daughter's fears, and those of a million other girls like her.

Sincerely,
Byron James

REPLY

Byron,

Thank you for your email. I generally don't have the highest opinion of journalists for the very reasons you pinpoint; insofar as their lies have damaged my family, I am unforgiving. But if you are as honest as you say, perhaps we might find common ground.

If you wish to meet toward the goal of writing a piece, very well. I am willing to be more open than I have recently been regarding my work and my life. But I have one firm and inviolable boundary: my son is off-limits. As an interview subject *and* as a topic of the article. You may refer to the fact that I am a parent, but I will not allow him to be dragged into the public eye any more than he has been already. As a parent yourself, I trust that you can understand my protective instinct.

Let us start things off with a conversation. Meet me on the 25th at Chateau Marmont, say 1 P.M.?

A.T.

EMAIL

From: bkidd@gmail.com
To: Valeriekidd@sltpartners.com

Val,

Hope that you're doing well. I'm writing to share that I'm in Los Angeles now, and I believe I've found a connection between Liza's disappearance and Annabelle Tobin (yes, *that* Annabelle Tobin). I don't have it all figured out yet, but it's clear there is a link, and I intend to get to the bottom of it, as part of a story I'm working on. I have secured an in-person interview with Annabelle, which is something of a feat since she hasn't agreed to one in years.

I'm reaching out to you because I'm conducting this investigative piece independently, though I'm confident I'll be able to sell the article when I'm done. As such, I don't have the usual institutional resources of the magazine, so I could use your help. I need to draft an agreement for her to sign at our first meeting, just to confirm her assent to publication, use of quotations from her books, etc. I can send over the bullet points it needs to hit, I just need a bit of legalese to make it legit.

B

REPLY

Byron,

At an earlier time, I might've responded quite bluntly—but I'm attempting to communicate more intentionally, so I will instead try a practice that my therapist Martin employs: mirroring. I'll reflect back what I'm hearing, so hopefully you can come to your own sensible conclusions.

I hear that you have traveled across the country on your own dime, and you are now conducting an unsanctioned investigation into the most famous and reclusive author in the world. That you are trying to connect her to what happened to Liza, based on a series of online conspiracy theories. You pride yourself on rationality, but does that sound like rational behavior?

I am very sorry to hear you're not on staff anymore. I hadn't realized The Atlantic let you go. But surely you should take that as a sign that you need some time for self-care to gain perspective.

Warmly,
Val

REPLY

Val,

I haven't left *The Atlantic,* so don't worry, I still have insurance coverage and won't need to go on yours again. That said, I might leave in the future, because I don't want to work there if they don't have the courage to back me on an important story like this.

And just so you know I'm not totally off my rocker, check out the pictures I've attached.

Even setting aside the connection between Liza and Annabelle (which I can't fully explain yet)—this is PROOF that Liza was HERE, in L.A., at this weird tourist attraction in Venice. That alone merits investigating, does it not?

B

REPLY

Byron,

This is your evidence? These pictures are so grainy and blurry I can't tell who they're of. One might perhaps be Annabelle Tobin. The other, I would say with a reasonable measure of confidence, is not Liza. I support just about any coping mechanism you might need, but not if it's harmful. And the fact that you would send this image to me, in the hope that I would share in your delusion, is both troubling and hurtful.

REPLY

Val,

The picture is her. I know it is. When I look at the image on my phone now, I can see that yes it's not as clear as I thought at first, so maybe I need to take another one to prove it to you.

I'm still near the museum, so I just walked back over to get a better image. Had to pay to get back inside again. But guess what? The pictures are gone now. Both of them have been removed. Which only confirms my suspicion that something strange is going on and someone doesn't want me to know about it.

You call this a coping mechanism? Fine. Excuse me for coping by trying to find out the truth. Like your therapist said, everyone deals with things in their own way, and my way is by actually DOING something useful.

B

REPLY

Byron,

You sound more unhinged with each new email you send. And that's not exactly what Martin said. He said everyone GRIEVES in their own way. Grieving is about finding closure. Moving on. And what you're doing is going backward, not forward.

I'd like to share what moving forward looks like for me. It looks like packing up Liza's room of everything you left behind . . . apparently everything that didn't quite fit with your crackpot theories. It looks like taking that blue Guess jacket we got her for Christmas, which was a little baggy but I said she'd grow into it, and donating it because now I know she's never going to fill it out. It looks like breaking down and crying in the parking lot of Goodwill.

THAT is moving on. And it's hard. But I will choose that, even though it hurts, over an aggressive regimen of self-deception any day.

REPLY

Hey Val,

I'm sorry you had to do all that. I honestly tried to take everything with me, but I guess I missed a few things. When I was going through the contents of her desk, I totally lost track of time, and then suddenly it was half an hour before you were going to be home, and as much as I wanted to see you, I equally wanted to not-see you, and I got what I could as quickly as possible and took it with me.

I understand not being able to look at Liza's stuff right now— I've broken down just from finding her gum wrappers in the back- seat of the car. I lugged a bunch of her stuff out here to L.A. because I'm hoping there might be useful clues, but I'm not sure I have the courage to look through it all. And that makes me wonder if there were signs before she disappeared. Maybe we missed them because maybe we didn't want to see.

I understand if you need to deal with things differently. But from my perspective, you're the one burying your head in the sand. I have identified more than two dozen cases that are shock- ingly similar to Liza's. I have no doubt that there are other victims already, and the list will continue to grow if someone doesn't get to the bottom of this.

Grief is for a loved one who is gone. Who is DEAD. But we don't have any evidence that applies to our situation. So "mourn- ing" as you've described it could directly PREVENT us from sav- ing Liza's life.

REPLY

Byron,

I'd rather not get drawn into debating conspiracy theories with you. But to put on my legal hat for a second: there are millions of worldwide fans of the Fairy Tale books, many of whom take its fictional world very seriously. There are also thousands of children who go missing every year. Naturally, there is bound to be a large overlap between those two groups. Dozens, if not hundreds, of possible cases. If I presented those correlations as causation in a courtroom, I'd be thrown out, if not disbarred.

Even if there IS some nefarious child-trafficking ring preying on young fantasy fans . . . do you honestly think Annabelle Tobin is involved? And that she's going to consent to be interviewed by, of all people, the father of one of these missing children?

REPLY

I think Annabelle Tobin knows more than she's letting on, and I think her books are dangerous. I suspect she will be the gateway to the truth.

As for the other question . . . of course I have not told her about Liza, and I don't intend to. As far as she knows, I'm Byron James. My entire body of work is under that pen name, and my personal life is none of her business.

Now can you help me with the agreement or not?

REPLY

Byron,

I've attached the agreement you asked for, mainly because I've learned that with you, the path of least resistance is sometimes the best one for my mental health. But I hope you realize this is not bringing us closer together, it is alienating us more than ever.

When I talked about this with Martin, he had an interesting theory, which I know you won't want to hear, but too bad. In doing this, you are probably going to destroy your career, and maybe that's actually WHY you're going through with it. To punish yourself. Because you know that no matter what sort of exposé you could conceivably write, it will never bring her back.

Warmly,
Val

REPLY

I won't know until I try.

CHAPTER SIX

INVESTIGATIVE JOURNAL OF BYRON KIDD

October 22 (Cont'd)

After visiting the strange museum in Venice, I spent the rest of the day holed up in a coffee shop near the beach, getting the story down while my impressions were still fresh, and sending emails. They proved to be effective—both in securing the interview I wanted and getting the legal document I needed from Val—but the responses I received were also infuriating.

~~What is wrong with Val? Why is she so desperate to believe the worst possible outcome, when we don't have any evidence to~~

The café where I sat provided a window into the inner lives of the city's dreamer class. The baristas were absurdly attractive young people, gossiping about their auditions between latte pours. The tables were filled up with laptop-pounding thirtysomethings, and of the screens I glimpsed almost all showed screenplays. ~~Terrible ones, I'm sure~~. All these grown adults spending a weekday afternoon crafting made-up stories no one would ever read, much less film.

I hadn't intended to eavesdrop, but the conversations taking place within just a few feet of my table were all held at a volume I could hardly block out. One seemed like a breakup in progress, until I realized it was two actors practicing a scene. Another was a filmmaker pitching a time-travel story to a disinterested producer who barely looked up from his phone. The room stank of desperation, and I felt a desire to somehow proclaim that my own work was rooted in something REAL. But no one cared.

I was eager to get out of there, but I stuck around to finish my emails and wait out the traffic. The room I'd booked in Hollywood was only twelve miles away from Venice, but at 4PM Waze said it would be a 90-minute drive. What the actual fuck. By the time I got on the road around 7:30, the estimate was down to an hour. Still, it felt like I could've gotten there faster by literally crawling down the 10 freeway.

Once I headed up La Brea into Hollywood, I started seeing bright lights, theaters, hordes of tourists. Then into East Hollywood, shitty stepcousin of the real thing, an ungentrified working-class neighborhood, predominantly Thai and Mexican demographics. Every shop here is plastered with some hollow reminder of the vague proximity to money and fame. Starlight Cleaners. Lights, Camera, Deli! A diner with old movie stars' images plastered on the windows. Plenty of payday lenders in between.

Eventually reached the inauspicious motel where I'd reserved a room: The Starlet Inn. Seedy as hell; rates are cheap, parking is expensive, rooms are shit.

While carrying in my bags, I encountered a homeless man in the parking lot. Sixty years old, white guy with long dreads, oversized coat to the ground, and a ratty top hat. As I approached he was singing nonsense that sounded vaguely like a sea shanty: "Come hear me and heed me, come feed me your love. Your fate is my burden, your faith is my blood . . ."

Then the song abruptly ended and he fixated on me, told me he'd been waiting for me and asked what took me so long. Offered to take me to "the Dreamvale." I declined.

At that point the encounter escalated, to say the least. The homeless man drew a large knife, more than a foot long, that I would almost characterize as a small sword. The metal had a reddish patina, which I hope was rust and not blood.

Fear instinctively bubbled up, of course . . . but I sensed that the man was not prone to violence, despite the apparent threat. So I asked what he was upset about.

Instantly, he parroted the question, like a child repeating what I'd said. I asked if he was going to repeat everything, and he repeated that too. Charming.

"Wanna tell me your name?"

"Wanna tell me YOUR name?"

"Byron," I said.

Apparently deciding enough was enough, he pointed to himself and said, "Mr. Echo."

I laughed at that, since I took it to be a joke. But the homeless man frowned. He stepped closer, eyed me with suspicion, and asked if I was a Hollowbody.

"Not sure," I told him. Before I could even ask what that meant, he became agitated and told me to get away, and swung his sword wildly in my direction. He was still several feet away, but the blade cleanly sliced the side mirror off the rented Impala.

Welcome to L.A.

He ran off, and I called to report the incident to the police (who never came) and the rental company (now I have to pay the insurance deductible and drive all the way back to the airport to swap out for a new vehicle).

One interesting takeaway: The encounter demonstrates that the language of the Fairy Tale books (Dreamvale and Hollowbody are references I now recognize) has so profoundly permeated the popular imagination, it is saturating the delusions of the mentally ill.

Couldn't remember what a Hollowbody was, so once I got inside, I opened the suitcase full of Liza's things I had taken from her room. Pushed aside her notebooks and some odds and ends until I found the Fairy Tale books and flipped through until I found a reference . . .

EXCERPT FROM FAIRY TALE BOOK TWO:
The Bridge of Dreams

By Annabelle Tobin. Published by Rotterdam Press, 2007. Page 398.

As Ciara followed Blueblossom down the twisting path, she thought she saw her own shadow moving unnaturally, out of sync with her movements. She flinched. Then, realizing it had been nothing but a trick of the light, she shook her head and resumed her stride.

Blueblossom had witnessed Ciara's reaction and asked what had given her pause. She relayed what she'd seen and told Blueblossom not to worry. But Blueblossom froze in her tracks, scanning the ground fearfully. "We need to hurry. It could be a Hollowbody taking form."

As they double-timed down the path, Blueblossom explained, "From every living thing that casts a shadow, a Hollowbody can be summoned. They are ravenous, insatiable spirits, and when they take corporeal form they will suck the life force from you if they get hold."

Ciara wasn't sure if her new companion was overreacting until her own shadow distended and slid across the path before her. She stared at the flat shape on the ground for a moment, puzzled.

Then the shadow began to bulge, extruding from the earth and taking form—a pitch-dark doppelgänger, like a Ciara-shaped hole in the universe. It stepped toward her, reaching for her throat.

"RUN!" Blueblossom exclaimed, and Ciara did not have to be told twice.

RESUME JOURNAL ENTRY

Right. Shadow monsters. Hollow, hopeless, desperate. ~~Mr. Echo had a point.~~

I have two days before I meet with Annabelle. Need to find some dots to connect, figure out the how and why of it all.

Remember: She's missing. Not dead. She's somewhere. She came to this city. She needs you. Don't get lost in self-pity. Just the facts.

Need to focus. Turned to a collection of Liza's things I'd brought with me. Hadn't had the courage to go through most of the personal stuff before I left Boston, and wasn't feeling up to it now. But I needed answers. So I walked down to a liquor store on the corner, got a couple twist-off bottles of red wine, and by the time the first one was empty, I was able to take a look.

Started with some notebooks, but they were too opaque to provide much. Some moody poems, some notes for school, some things I couldn't make sense of. Nothing resembling a journal with any coherent narrative, just scraps of thought and whim.

There was Liza's sketchbook also, full of colored-pencil drawings. As an artsy kid, Liza tried her hand at every non-performance-based form of creative expression, and her drawing skills were impressive. Flipping through the notebook, I was unsurprised to find that every picture was fantastical, probably Fairy Tale driven. Mostly characters from the films: fairy queens, knights in armor, unicorns, and other magical beasts. Many of them looked familiar, and they were incredibly well-rendered.

But studying them filled me with frustration—that her talent had been entirely consumed by her obsession with this stupid fantasy world that had somehow taken her from me. Set the sketchbook aside and moved on to . . .

LIZA'S YEARBOOKS

Liza had been very private for the last couple years, and I wondered if I might get a better sense of her life from the school yearbooks. The ones from a few years ago—3rd grade, 4th grade—were jam-packed with signatures from friends, but in the newer ones, the signature pages were drying up, just a few short messages inked in the corners, proof of a dwindling social circle.

I focused on the most recent one, 6th grade, the end of elementary school. There were sweet but generic notes from a few girls whose names sounded vaguely familiar, and then a message that filled me with rage: "Idk what to say to you but HAGS! —Marley Brinkman."

Marley was such a bullshit cool-girl name. And HAGS, Liza had explained to me once, was an acronym for Have a Good Summer, which seemed here to double as an insult.

Val and I had been called in for a parent-teacher conference near the beginning of the year along with Marley and her parents in the wake of an online bullying incident. Marley had posted something on Instagram mocking Liza. I'm not sure why we four parents were all brought into one room, unless the teachers were taking bets on whether I would lose my cool and punch the other dad. I did not, but only by force of will.

Yet in the aftermath of that incident Liza had nonetheless asked this Marley girl to sign her yearbook, and Marley had barely deigned to write her name. It made me sick.

I flipped to Liza's yearbook photo—sullen, barely smiling, slightly off-axis. Her expression was incisive but unamused. It had been taken when she still had her braces on and you couldn't pay her enough money to open her mouth for a photo. I flipped through activity pages, wondering if Liza had been involved in anything. Apparently not. Her life at school had been as minimal as she could possibly make it.

I turned to her laptop. No password for the device, a rule in our house, not that I'd ever actually looked through her things before. Maybe I should've. Opened it up, confronted by an utterly chaotic desktop, overflowing with school assignments and bookmarks and photos, mostly obscuring a desktop image of a symbol that vaguely resembled a figure with wings. (Saw this symbol recently. Poster in her room. Interesting.)

Needed clues as to where she might have disappeared to. So start where kids get lost these days . . .

BROWSER HISTORY

Liza's History tab showed the sites she'd visited for the two years she'd had the computer, all the way up to the night she disappeared.

Skimmed through her last few weeks of activity. Some research for school. "Manifest Destiny." "James K. Polk." "Isosceles triangle." Wikipedia pages. Nothing helpful.

Then there were the social-media sites, visited often, which seemed promising but turned out to be dead ends. All required username and password to access. Liza had been diligent about logging out. A quick search of her computer didn't yield any document that contained her passwords. Her security protocols were more rigorous than mine; clearly digital privacy was of paramount importance to her. Maybe a generational thing. Maybe there was a lot she wanted to keep secret.

The site I was least familiar with, but which was visited the most often (and the most recently, even the day she disappeared), was one whose name I'd heard her mention. Its connection to the Fairy Tale books piqued my interest: TheQueendom.com. Turned out, it also required a login, with name and password prompts. With nothing to go on, I couldn't begin to guess what Liza's might be, so I gave up. For now.

CATALOGUE OF LIZA'S PHOTOS

A couple thousand photos. The "ALL" archive was too overwhelming, but fortunately Liza's organization was meticulous, with everything sorted neatly into a folder. That's my girl.

<u>SELFIES</u>
The largest folder. Hardly shocking for a twelve-year-old girl. The images are heartbreaking in their transparent self-consciousness. A sequence of twenty variations of the same neutral expression, apparently

taken at slightly different angles to minimize the profile of her nose. ~~Who was this girl?~~

Liza was beautiful to me, of course, but I knew she had none of the beyond-her-years sultriness that so many of her peers awkwardly mustered in an effort to attract male attention. Some dad part of me was glad for that, proud of her for not needing to be sexualized at her age.

But I also knew it was connected to her isolation. As long as "popular" had been a category that meant anything in her school, she had been decidedly NOT. The indifference she had affected around that reality was undercut by the care with which she picked out her clothes and the days she came home from school in tears.

Looking at the selfies, I saw that the only ones that featured makeup were clearly not intended for public sharing. They were more childish and outlandish than anything her peers would post. A series of them showed her face painted with glittery red swirls and thorns, like tribal tattoos if they were done by Barbie. Another series catalogued a darker look—deep green and blue hues, applied so thick it was like her face was the canvas for an oil painting, adorned with abstract shapes that echoed hieroglyphics. Her hair was tightly and elaborately braided.

So . . . this is what she was doing when her door was locked.

FAMILY

Many of the images were older here, and I was touched that she'd even saved them. Opening presents at Christmas when she was eight. Boogie-boarding in the Florida waves during a vacation two years earlier. The oldest image: Liza and me reading together in bed while Val snapped the picture surreptitiously. And the book, of course, was one of the Fairy Tale volumes. I grimaced at the thought of how that early innocent moment might now be implicated in the unraveling of her life.

The more recent photos of our family, the ones she had taken herself, were much more prosaic and domestic (unsurprising, as it had been more than a year since we all took a vacation together). There was our spaniel-mutt Greta, tongue lolled out, grinding joyfully against the carpet. A couple of Val, making faces for Liza's benefit. And one of me, lit by the glow of the laptop, which I did not remember her capturing. ~~I felt accused by the image, as if it were documenting my~~

MEMES

Why had she saved so many images taken from the internet? Or had she generated all of these herself? I squinted at them, trying to make sense of the inscrutable mashups of pop-culture imagery with text. One showed Melody Turner, the lead actress from the Fairy Tale films, with tears streaming down her face, captioned by the text: "TFW you find out your friend is a Crimson." Some were even more opaque, with references piled up on each other, forming an indecipherable collage.

PORTALS

I opened the folder and was greeted by a grid of a couple dozen seemingly random, artsy-ish photographs that smacked of a kid wondering, "Could I be a photographer someday?" No human subjects in sight, only captured details of the urban environment: A dark drainage tunnel, dripping into a ravine. A ripped opening in a chain-link fence. The sun reflected in an iridescent puddle.

I squinted at the images, trying to imagine what Liza saw in them. Portals, of course, but to what? Something she was searching for. Behind and inside and underneath the surfaces of the city. The images were not overly dark, but their lack of human subjects felt lonely, and when I imagined her stopping to take them, I felt a tightening in my chest. This was how she spent her time?

Then: one that made my blood freeze. A portal as well as a selfie. It showed a cracked window of a seemingly abandoned warehouse, sunlight glaring off the glass and rendering it reflective. Liza had snapped a self-portrait in the window, with the cracks in the glass fragmenting her image, like fissures in reality. In the background, some dark ~~energy~~ shape appeared to hover over and behind her. She looked haunted. Troubled. ~~A cry for help.~~

How had I not seen this sadness in her? She had hidden it. But as I stared at the image, I felt as if her eyes, meeting the lens of the camera, were in fact staring right back at me. ~~Accusing.~~ Intense. (Don't over-personalize. Stay objective.)

I reached out. ~~Touched her face, through time.~~ Touched the screen.

The image darkened. The shape hovering over her seemed to expand. Bled outward. I pulled my finger back, watching the effect in real time. Not like the picture was being edited, the contrast turned up or down—more like an actual spot of darkness inside the 3-dimensional space the photograph represented, spreading like cancer, ~~suffocating~~ erasing the light, ~~erasing Liza in the process~~, until all at once, darkness consumed the entire image.

Then it was gone. And I was back in the "Portals" gallery, staring at all the other photos of city life, wondering what just happened. Had I imagined that photo? Had I somehow deleted it? ~~Had my touch somehow crossed time and~~

Panic tightened my chest. One more piece of Liza was gone. Maybe it was somewhere else, another folder, the trash, but the thought of searching her computer for it only filled me with more dread. I looked at my fingertip, as though the darkness that penetrated the image might've come from me or might be spreading across my hand and erasing my body. Nothing, of course.

Looked at the wine bottle beside the laptop. Second of the night and two-thirds empty. For fuck's sake. Lost in the reverie, I'd been oblivious to how quickly it was going.

Slammed the laptop shut. Put it back in the suitcase and zipped it. Worried that my intervention might destroy everything. Needed some rest. Rest of the bottle was empty by the time my head hit the pillow, room was spinning.

Couldn't stop thinking about the image. As cars drove by outside, headlights through the shitty blinds conjured shifting shadows on my walls. ~~The darkness was alive.~~

INVESTIGATIVE JOURNAL OF BYRON KIDD

October 23

Woke this morning hungover. Incident with the photo felt like a dream. No doubt a mix of sleeplessness, adrenaline, and wine. Stick to the facts here. Can't let myself fuck things up like that. Who knows what useful info I might end up destroying if I don't take better care of things. Should back up all that data anyway.

Instant coffee first, splash of cold water, and then Liza's laptop. Opened on the flimsy little table, Photos program still running, still on the "All Photos" album . . .

But it was empty.

Clicked around, trying to understand what had happened. The "Portals" folder did not exist. The other folders either. The complete archive contained 0 images.

Clicked over to Finder, looking at data about the actual drive folders that housed the info. Empty. Nothing. And that's when I realized . . .

Everything was empty. The basic apps were still there, but Liza's cluttered desktop was devoid of content. The Documents folder, the Music folder, the Trash folder they should've been held in . . . all were empty. Everything except the bare minimum out-of-the-box basics . . . gone.

My skin went cold with panic, but I fought to stay calm. Think straight.

The data on her computer had been corrupted somehow. Just like the pictures I took at the museum, which, I swear, were far blurrier when I emailed them than they had been before. Now an entire hard drive of useful data evaporated overnight. I'm not great with technology, but this is ridiculous.

Need to understand what's going on.

Theory: When I touched the image, it created ~~a glitch a virus~~ an anomaly that spread and deleted all the data.

(OK, I'm not some cyber expert, but I do know, that's not how it works. My finger could've messed up the display but not corrupted the data.)

Theory: Some sort of self-destruct sequence? Programmed by Liza? She wasn't exactly a computer genius either, but maybe something she picked up online.

(Weird that she wouldn't password-protect her system but would implement such an advanced security measure.)

Theory: A hacker. Someone remotely monitoring the computer. Saw I was using it, intervened, deleted everything. Maybe the computer getting turned on sent out some sort of alert?

(This makes no sense.)

~~Theory: Someone came into the room after I~~

(Nope.)

I stared at the laptop. Empty husk. Twelve hours ago, it had been a library of her life. Now . . . nothing. I'd just lost her all over again. I felt the familiar welling up of despair, suffocating, but—

No. It's just 1's and 0's. It's a loss, but it's not THAT much of a loss unless I never see her again. As long as I find her, it hardly even matters. Need to believe that. Need to make that happen.

Opened the internet browser. Entire history, gone. Was there anything useful I could remember? Flipped back in my notes, found the name of the website she loved, and decided to look at whatever was publicly available. Anything that could be helpful. Background. Context. Trying to understand her.

HOME PAGE OF THEQUEENDOM.COM

NEWS   FANFIC   SIGHTINGS   FORUMS   ABOUT US

WELCOME TO THE QUEENDOM—YOUR GATEWAY TO THE HIDDEN WORLD!

The Queendom is more than a website. It is a community for Fairy Tale fans around the world to *connect:* to share words, ideas, images, stories, and experiences. We have been here since before the books became a global phenomenon, and we will be here long after the sextet is complete. All races, creeds, and orientations are welcome, as long as you are willing to accept the core of Queen Áine's teaching:

"My beloved brothers and sisters are not merely those with wings, but those with *dreams*."

—Queen Áine

FROM "ABOUT US"

Founder: Misha Pimm

Misha Pimm is a culture writer whose work has appeared in publications including *Harper's, Digital Humanities Review,* and *Buzzfeed* (yes, she is proud of all of them). Her essay *You Don't Own Me: Authorship in the Digital Age* became a viral sensation in 2021, and landed her interviews on CNN and MSNBC. Currently, she lives in Los Angeles with her girlfriend and her Cavalier King Charles and is pursuing a PhD in Media Studies at UCLA.

RESUME JOURNAL ENTRY

Founder of the website. Based in L.A. "Media Studies" was something you could get a PhD in? Fine. Perhaps a worthy sherpa into this world I clearly do not understand. Reached out online. In my email I shared the basics of the story and teased the fact that I had secured an interview with Annabelle Tobin, hoping that would catch her interest. Had a reply within minutes.

Making real progress now. A direction to go, at least.

~~So why this crushing sense of dread? Why do I feel like I'm being watched?~~

CHAPTER SEVEN

INTERVIEW WITH MISHA PIMM

Location: Graduate student office at UCLA Taper Center for Humanities. Fishbowl-style room with windows on all sides, grad students at desks arranged around the outside. Misha's desk is a mess. Numerous toys on display—robots, fairies, a unicorn. Hard to believe these are not embarrassing to her in an academic setting. Collectible cards taped to periphery of her monitor. Interview conducted at her desk; other grad students present, curious and listening in, but subject appeared free of self-consciousness.

Subject: Misha Pimm. Late 20s. Short hair, semi-spiked, dyed electric blue. Nose ring. Warby Parker glasses. Somehow making a button-down shirt and slacks look too hip for me. Effusive would be an understatement. As would "talks with her hands." And "overcaffeinated."

TRANSCRIPT OF AUDIO RECORDING

MISHA: Hi! I'm Misha.

BYRON: Byron. Good to meet you. You're OK with me recording this?

MISHA: Of course, hundred percent. I'm so stoked to be part of it! Mind if I ask what's in your notebook?

BYRON: Not much. I'm just getting started, so—

MISHA: It looks like you're writing a whole book in there!

BYRON: (*Sighs*) Yes, it's . . . I don't just take notes, everything from the investigation goes in this notebook, in order, as I collect it. Transcripts of the interviews, as soon as I complete them. Relevant articles and excerpts, when I encounter them. And most important, a journal of my experiences, narrated as objectively as possible.

MISHA: So it's kinda like you're already writing the story as you go along.

BYRON: Sort of. When the investigation is complete, I spend a lot of time editing, often restructuring. But I find it necessary to capture the story as it unfolds. Most writers are so taken with a single narrative, they fit the facts to the story. The facts should *determine* the story, not vice versa.

MISHA: Don't you think that's a little bit . . . not how humans work? I mean, there's a lot of psychological evidence that shows our perceptions are actively shaped by the internal narratives we believe.

BYRON: I think you're making my point. I do my best to be a blank slate, so that I can accurately convey the truth. Now, if we can start the interview, I'd like to ask you about Annabelle Tobin.

MISHA: Totally, totally, first I just have to ask . . . how'd you get her to agree to an interview?

BYRON: Good timing, I guess.

MISHA: Wow, OK. That's it?

BYRON: That and my winning personality.

MISHA: (*Laughs*) Was that a joke? Sorry, you're kinda hard to read. I just want to say, for everybody in our community, the fact that she's doing an interview at all is going to be *huge*. She's a hero for so many of us.

BYRON: A hero? For writing some books?

MISHA: I mean . . . you have to know it's more than that. For girls, especially ones like me who didn't fit in when we were growing up, having a self-made-millionaire literary-genius nerd-chick to look up to was incredibly formative. And yeah, considering all the philanthropy she's done, I'd say she's a hero.

BYRON: OK then.

MISHA: Come on, you're a writer. When you were coming up, you're telling me you didn't have someone you looked up to?

BYRON: It's not relevant to this interview, certainly. If we could—

MISHA: No, no, no, dude, no way. This has to be a two-way street! You want me to open up, you have to get a little naked too. So tell me. Just one person, one story. Who made you want to do what you do?

BYRON: (*Sighs*) Hunter S. Thompson.

MISHA: Ha! For real?

BYRON: What can I say, I was a teenager. I thought his whole gonzo thing was so cool. Putting himself into his stories. Blurring the line between fact and fiction.

But then he shot himself. While he was on the phone with his wife, and his daughter was home to discover his body. And when I heard all that, I realized what a sad, bitter man he must've been. And how reckless his way of "reporting" really was. It almost made me drop out of journalism school. All because I made the mistake of putting someone on a pedestal.

MISHA: That is the most depressing origin story of all time.

BYRON: Calling someone a hero blinds you to what's real. And sets you up to get hurt.

MISHA: Starting things off on a real up-note here.

BYRON: Just telling it like it is.

MISHA: All I'm saying is, whatever you call Annabelle, she means a *lot* to people, including me. OK? I wasn't like the type of kid who exactly fit in where I grew up.

BYRON: Right. Because you were just *so* quirky and unique.

MISHA: What, are you gonna call me "snowflake" next? Dude, I grew up in West Texas, going to a church where I was taught that people like me are "an abomination." The first girl I ever kissed had a change of heart the next day and told me I was going to hell. And when I came out to my mom she straight-up threatened to disown me if I told anyone else.

BYRON: . . . Oh. I'm sorry, I was just . . . Can we start over please? I think I messed this up, and I really do need your help.

MISHA: Fair enough. I'm Misha. Founder of the Queendom.

BYRON: Byron. Recovering Hunter S. Thompson fan.

MISHA: And judgmental asshole?

BYRON: Those two kinda go hand in hand.

(*Misha laughs.*)

BYRON: Why don't we talk about your site . . .

MISHA: Right. You want, like, my little talking-point spiel? Queendom is the biggest online Fairy Tale fan community in the world. I mean, the official one that the publishing house runs has got all the fancy graphics and a mobile game and everything, but daily traffic, user count, we are light-years ahead of them.

BYRON: And why do you think that is?

MISHA: In a nutshell . . . authenticity? To go back to when I started it, I was, like, sixteen, and I was writing fan-fic, and—

BYRON: Sorry, I've seen the term on the site, but—fan-fic?

MISHA: Fan fiction. When fans write their own stories about the world and characters of the story. Sometimes called slash-fic, when it involves relationships between characters, which mine did, because . . . well, I was seventeen, and, like . . . working some stuff *out*. That first story is still on the site, even though now it is totally cringe to me. . . .

EXCERPT

From the short story "Wings of Desire," by Misha Pimm
Published on TheQueendom.com fan site

Ciara admired Applebaum's gossamer wings, marveling at their delicacy. She asked the ancient fairy, her voice trembling, "May I touch them?"

Applebaum informed her, "It is forbidden for mortal kind to make contact with those of my race," and Ciara flushed with embarrassment, cursing herself for a fool. But Applebaum continued, "So you will have to keep it a secret." Ciara met the fairy's gaze, finding it fiery and intense, looking deep into her soul.

Ciara started at the top of the left wing, stroking the surface, finding it dewy, slightly sticky to the touch, but not unpleasantly so. Her hand glided down, down, down, until it grazed the fairy's rump—as firm as the fruit of her name.

Ciara feared she had gone too far, but she saw that the fairy's eyes were closed now, as she whispered breathily, "Don't stop."

RESUME TRANSCRIPT

BYRON: So these stories you made up . . . they weren't based in . . .

MISHA: Canon? No way. But I'd argue that a queer reading of the character is a valid one. The whole point of fan-fic is for people to imagine themselves into the story in new ways. And for me, the story of Ciara, this girl who escapes a drab, boring life where she's misunderstood into a world of wonder and magic, where all the old rules are out the window, where she can be anything she wants—that changed everything.

So naturally . . . I wanted to share what I was creating with other people. And at first, I was just too freaked out to put my stuff up on any of the bigger fan-fic sites, sometimes the criticism you see in the comments there is brutal. So I taught myself HTML to build Queendom on my own, and started putting stories up there every day. I had a lot of free time.

I thought my stories were crazy-weird. And I imagined they'd be mostly just for me, but kind of shockingly, people resonated with them I guess, and I started getting requests from other people to post. So I opened it up for user submissions, and it tapped into this whole community that was looking for a real *home,* because it took off insanely fast, and the scope kept expanding.

Now I've kept it going for . . . God, over ten years now. And a lot of the day-to-day maintenance gets done by a volunteer team, but I'm still in charge of moderation and overall direction, even while I'm going to grad school full-time.

BYRON: Uh-huh. And your users . . . you have access to information on each one? So you could see what someone has posted, or . . . who they've talked to?

MISHA: Technically yeah, I have access to the back-end data, but it's all anonymized.

BYRON: I see. So just for example, if I gave you the name of a particular person who used the site . . . could you give me the information from their account?

MISHA: Well . . . A, I'd need their username, which may or may not be linked to their email, and B, no way, that would be a huge violation of our privacy standards, which are seriously *sacred* to me. I never sell or share data, no cookies even.

BYRON: But if the police requested that user data—did they ever come to you with a warrant or a subpoena . . . ?

MISHA: Whoa. No. Why would they?

BYRON: In connection with any of the disappearances.

MISHA: Ohhhh. (*Laughs*) I don't take any of that stuff very seriously. I mean—sorry, it's very serious, what's happened with all those kids, but . . . no, to answer your question, no police have ever reached out to me.

BYRON: I see. Can I ask you about the "Sightings" section?

POST TO THE "SIGHTINGS" SECTION OF
THEQUEENDOM.COM

"HOLLOWBODIES IN EAST L.A."
Posted by Eduardo Ortiz, age 11

Today I witnessed I think a Hollowbody trying to cross over. It was dusk and I was walking home from music practice after school (I'm in 5th grade at Renaissance). It gets dark here by 5 so the shadows were all the long dangly kind. I was walking down Cesar Chavez Road it got all quiet and I think the wind had whispers in it like Ciara was hearing in Book 3 in the Living Labyrinth. I looked back my shadow was bending weird. Then I felt something grabbing me on my shirt and trousers.

I turned around nobody was there. I started going again and this time I could see my shadow moving, not just the normal way but like it was shrinking, and I felt like I was getting pulled into the ground. There were scratchy things pulling at me and then there were sounds like flapping and screeching which if the Hollowbody was pulling me through could've been sprites on the other side ready to eat me. I tried to yell but it was like the sound was sucked into the black of my shadow. It grabbed onto my viola case and jerked hard trying to drag me in. I let go and that got me one second of surprise, my feet were free and I ran, but I could hear it behind me its voice was angry.

I never found my viola it's gone now and of course my parents don't believe me that anything happened to it. I got in trouble but I don't even care I'm glad I'm alive. I do want to cross over but not with a Hollowbody like that.

Has anyone else seen similar? Any other sightings in East L.A.? I'm on the lookout.

(412 replies)

RESUME TRANSCRIPT

MISHA: I think of the "Sightings" section as an organic outgrowth of the fan-fic component, one that's accessible to everyone. Even if you don't have the stamina for a full story, you can probably generate one of these little microfiction snippets. And instead of being full, in-universe stories, it's people blurring the lines with these quasi-docu-style reports, you know? It's a new phenomenon. Honestly, I'm very excited about it, and as a cultural anthropologist I'm eager to include it in my research for my dissertation.

BYRON: Uh-huh. Your dissertation about . . . what, exactly?

MISHA: Well, it's . . . I mean, I haven't firmly landed on one topic exactly, I've been circling a few different ones. My first couple years I was focused on marginalized community representations in both traditional folklore and contemporary fantasy, but then I started to feel like there was a lot of work happening in that space already, so I started developing a thesis that revolved around identity signifiers, comparing traditional tribal structures with modern fan communities, but I dropped that last year 'cause I just feel like semiotics is *over,* so I'm kinda on the hunt for a new idea now.

BYRON: I see. That's . . . a lot of years, without picking a clear direction.

MISHA: Uh, did my dad send you? Chill out, I'm paying for all this with fellowships and working as a TA.

BYRON: Don't you worry that some of your audience—especially younger kids—might take the reports of these "Sightings" literally?

MISHA: I mean, not really. And besides, who's to say they shouldn't?

BYRON: Well . . . I would say that, for one.

MISHA: OK, but, you don't have proof to the contrary, do you? There's a free-speech principle too. If people want to write this material, then it deserves to be online.

BYRON: I don't understand the appeal.

MISHA: I think you need to pop out and look at the Fairy Tale phenomenon more holistically. Why are young people so drawn to this? It's not just that there are fun fairies with wings and skirts. These books are incorporating elements of multicultural folk stories, synthesizing them all into an original mythology. And people—kids especially—they're hungry for that.

My generation, and the Zoomers even more so, we're growing up with an apocalyptic worldview, a total spiritual void, zero trust in our leadership . . . it's a crisis of faith. So these books—which teach values we admire, with stories that move us—they're giving us something to believe in.

BYRON: But if that belief is in something that doesn't exist . . . that's dangerous.

MISHA: I think you're assuming an overly simplistic definition of what does and doesn't exist.

BYRON: I'm honestly not sure if you're messing with me or just neck-deep in academic BS.

MISHA: It's not BS, it's . . . epistemology! And metaphysics! Platonic ideals. Look, every great story eventually takes on a life of its own. What I'm talking about is accepting a paradigm of truth and existence that's not so explicitly bound to Enlightenment-era rationality.

BYRON: Gotcha. That's gonna be super helpful to all those missing kids.

MISHA: I'm just saying, if you want to understand Annabelle, you're gonna have to dig deeper on how she created this world and what went into it. And she hasn't talked about any of this stuff in *years,* but she used to be super open about her life and her process and everything.

There's this clip that used to be on YouTube from the first-ever FairyCon, which I was at, by the way, cosplaying as Gloverbeck, who's the lead sentinel of the court of the fey. Want to see a pic?

BYRON: I do not. You were saying, the video clip . . .

MISHA: Right, I was saying—FairyCon 2010. By the way, are you going to FairyCon? It's next weekend, here in town. I kind of assumed that was part of the timing of your article, but not sure when it's coming out. I can get you passes if you need them, I used to be—

BYRON: Misha. Focus. The origin of the books . . . ?

MISHA: Yes! Sorry. I'm a little neurodivergent, and I get kinda tangential.

Anyway—there *used to be* this clip online of Annabelle talking about the origins of the series. I think it got taken down a while back, but if you dig that up, you might start getting some understanding of what she's all about. I'll see if I can find a link for you. Now I gotta get to class, you can't be late when you're leading the section, but—just promise me, this all stays between us. I'll help you as much as I can, but, ya know . . .

BYRON: What are you afraid of?

MISHA: Oh, nothing, nothing, there's just rumors. Stuff happens to people that go after Annabelle, or the books in general. Curses, magic, angry ancient gods, all that fun stuff. Probably nothing to it, but better safe than sorry, right?

CHAPTER EIGHT

INVESTIGATIVE JOURNAL OF BYRON KIDD

October 24

Last night: tried to make sense of what I've got so far, which admittedly is not much. Picked up another two bottles of pinot on the way back to motel. Finished them by 9 PM, walked to get one more. That was a mistake. Two is good, sweet spot. Forgetting Liza just enough to focus. The one-more brings her back. ~~The one-more opens up the wound, and~~

No time for self-pity. Just the facts.

When I booked this room I stipulated that I wanted to be on the ground floor. Been afraid of heights since I was a child. But I regretted the decision this morning when I was awakened at 5 AM by the sound of loud banging on the window of my motel room. Went to see who it was. Peeked through the blinds. No one there. Back to bed. More banging. Went outside.

Same homeless man from yesterday, Mr. Echo, carrying the same knife as before, now strapped to his belt. I asked if he was gonna try to cut my arm off again. He seemed to find that quite funny at first, said it would be no problem for the Ruby Shard (he's named his knife, apparently). Then he got very serious and said he'd have no choice if I was a Hollowbody.

I asked why he thought I was a Hollowbody. He said he can tell I don't belong here because he doesn't either. Fair enough. I told him not to wake me up at 5 AM anymore; he put the accusation back at me— "Don't wake ME up at 5 AM!"—waving the knife.

I said I'd call the police if he did. He said he's killed a troll before, the police aren't gonna scare him. Then he said he had to get back to the Kingdom of Echoes, turned and ran off, and almost got nailed by a truck before he disappeared down Sunset Blvd.

This fucking city.

Goal for today: Prep for interview with Annabelle tomorrow. Find the clip Misha mentioned. See if it leads anywhere.

INTERVIEW WITH ANNABELLE TOBIN

October 25, 1:06 P.M.

Location: Lounge café of Chateau Marmont. Swanky Hollywood hotel, up in the hills, beautiful view of downtown. Valet-only parking. Decor is faux-Victorian: gaudy velvet sofas, exposed brick walls, bare lightbulbs. Seating areas discreetly separated. $20+ cocktails and appetizers.

Subject: Annabelle in person is striking, even more so than her author bio photo, which is more than a decade old. Strong jawline. Late forties and rail-thin, bordering on gaunt. Icy makeup tones. Never removed her ash-gray cashmere sweater, despite the warmth. Midway through a black coffee when I arrived. In conversation: probing, evasive, difficult to pin down, seemed to regard the whole thing as a game she had been forced to play.

TRANSCRIPT OF AUDIO RECORDING

BYRON: Hi, Ms. Tobin. I'm Byron.

ANNABELLE: Like the poet?

BYRON: Not really the Romantic type.

ANNABELLE: I see. Well, thank you for meeting me here.

BYRON: Fancy spot.

ANNABELLE: I suppose it's a bit ostentatious, but the coffee is good, and they keep the photographers out.

BYRON: I could meet you at your home next time if that's easier.

ANNABELLE: Inviting yourself over already?

BYRON: Just trying to make you comfortable.

ANNABELLE: You look like you haven't slept much.

BYRON: Still a little jet-lagged. And the light here doesn't agree with me.

ANNABELLE: Everyone from the East Coast loves to hate on L.A., so get it out of your system. The traffic, right?

BYRON: I can handle traffic.

ANNABELLE: But sunlight disagrees with you.

BYRON: It doesn't feel like a real place. The Egyptian Theatre with those fake hieroglyphics—straight out of Vegas. I mean, look at this hotel. "Chateau Marmont"? Are we supposed to believe there's anything remotely French about it? The style is more faux-villa than chateau.

ANNABELLE: L.A. is a place that requires some imagination, to be sure.

BYRON: I'll get off my high horse. I'm pleased to interview you.

ANNABELLE: And I am . . . tolerant.

BYRON: I'm recording—just want to be upfront about that. And I have an agreement here for you to sign, if you don't mind.

ANNABELLE: I'll take it home with me to review. Would you care for a drink?

BYRON: Bit early for me.

ANNABELLE: I meant coffee. And from the looks of it, you're still metabolizing the ones from last night. It's interesting that you say you're such a realist, yet you make a habit of retreating from reality.

BYRON: I don't retreat. Drugs are escaping from the world; booze is just turning down the volume.

ANNABELLE: Whatever helps you sleep.

BYRON: How about if I start with the question everyone's dying to know the answer to.

ANNABELLE: You don't even have to ask it. Book Six. I've always said it'll be out when it's good and ready. But—I trust that you will not divulge this until the article comes out, all right? It will be finished *very* soon. I almost declined this interview because I'm on the cusp of completion, but my editor, Stan, assured me this bit of publicity, at the moment, was more pressing. With a rush order, the title will be on shelves next spring.

BYRON: Wow. That should come as welcome news to your fans. Could you speak to the reason for the delay?

ANNABELLE: Yes, well . . . I had a few false starts. As much as the fans are clamoring to have it right away, they will be vicious if it is anything but perfect. And I need to figure out how to satisfyingly bring it to a close.

BYRON: So the ending—it's not something you had planned from the beginning?

ANNABELLE: Oh, lord no. I'd love to tell you that it was, but when I was twenty-six, I hadn't a clue that I'd be writing a second book, much less finishing a whole series. And honestly, any author that tells you otherwise is lying through their teeth. The crippled kid becomes king? Please.

BYRON: Well, if you think—

ANNABELLE: Sorry, would you mind striking that? I don't think I'm supposed to say "crippled," and . . . I don't want to be seen as . . .

BYRON: It's all right. My goal here isn't to show the world how un-PC you are.

ANNABELLE: Appreciated.

BYRON: I'm more interested in your creative process. Where the idea came from.

ANNABELLE: Where it came from, twenty years ago? Oh, who knows . . . I was only a few years past being a girl myself, so I think perhaps it came from childhood fantasies. I'm sure you've done enough research to know my back story. Abusive household, abject rural poverty. Fairies and magic must've been my escape.

BYRON: I see.

ANNABELLE: You seem skeptical.

BYRON: Well, you gave a very different answer back in 2010.

ANNABELLE: Did I?

BYRON: Here—I can show you a video to refresh your memory.

EXCERPT FROM PUBLIC Q&A AT 2010 INAUGURAL FAIRYCON

Annabelle's answer to fan question following reading from forthcoming Book Three

ANNABELLE: Where'd the idea come from? That is certainly the question most writers profess to hate the most, but I'm happy to talk about it, as long as you don't mind a bit of a story.

This all started perhaps three or four years after I'd moved to L.A., and I was trying to find my footing still. Well, to be more accurate, I was lost. I had tried being an actor for a bit, a musician, a screenwriter—basically all the things people come to L.A. for, only I wasn't particularly good at *any* of them. What I didn't realize at the time is that I was just hungry to *connect* in any way, and I was still looking for the method that best suited me.

I was wandering, looking for a purpose, a home, a community. I was in an acting group, but after I dated two or three of the guys in there, it became pretty toxic. I tried some yoga, some transcendental meditation, honestly I could've gotten sucked into Scientology if they hit me on the right day. But none of it was clicking.

So I decided to go to, of all things, a bookstore. I wasn't even a big reader, but I knew I needed something. Odyssey Books, up on Cahuenga in North Hollywood. This dusty little independent shop in the Valley. It was empty, and the owner, Marcus, he greeted me when I came in and asked what I was looking for. And—poor man—I just poured my little twenty-six-year-old heart out to him about how very *lost* I was in the world. He listened and then he brought out this old copy of a book from the late nineteenth century called *The Hidden World*, by one Sir Henry Raleigh.

It was leatherbound and ancient, and even worse, it was some sort of collector's item priced at over a thousand dollars. I was skeptical— even more so when I flipped through it and I could tell it was full of fairy stories. For a young woman wanting to be taken seriously as an artist, that was not particularly appealing. But he told me it was not exactly, or not *only*, a book about fairies. It was a compendium of world folk tales. It would've cost me two weeks' worth of shifts at the cocktail bar where I'd been working, but Marcus said something about how the book wanted to be with me, and graciously offered me a deal, the sad-lost-wanderer discount, I suppose.

I took it home, and then I just took it everywhere. I read it on the bus, in the kitchen during my breaks, everywhere I got a spare mo- ment. I was *obsessed*. It was like my childhood love of magic and fairies was clicking in with a more rigorous academic scholarship, and my mind was swirling.

But . . . not with the idea for Fairy Tale, not yet. It was . . . gosh, this is almost embarrassing to admit, but—the thing I was really looking for was spiritual guidance, not an idea for a book. I had no desire to write fiction. In the stories of *The Hidden World,* I found some hint of a mentor. A guru, perhaps. Not the author, but an entity, whose name I don't want to say. So I decided to seek guidance from—I'm not joking—the forest.

Now, living in the middle of North Hollywood, my idea of "the forest" was Topanga Canyon, so that's where I went. I drove in and parked—not at a hiking trail or anything, just at random—and I marched out into the trees with the book in my hand. And I got to this great big sycamore, and I leaned against it, and I asked for help. In life, mind you, not in my writing.

What came to me was an image of a girl walking out of the city, into a field, and finding an old, crumbling well. And I could tell, this well was her gateway, and . . . that was it. It wasn't a full story of course, but I could see the character so clearly in my mind. That day, sitting at the base of that tree, I just started writing in a notebook. No plan, no outline, nothing. The first piece of fiction I'd ever attempted. And I wrote the first two sentences, unchanged to this day, sitting there under that tree.

"Ciara was lost, for the first time in her life. Or rather, she was aware of being lost for the first time, though she began to suspect that she had been lost for quite some time."

It's strange to think that now there are grown women tattooing those words on their bodies. But it was very special to me. That opening . . . and that moment . . . and that book. And while I know I risk the world's derision for saying it, perhaps there really was a bit of magic.

RESUME TRANSCRIPT

(*Sound of YouTube clip ends. Long silence.*)

ANNABELLE: Where did you find that?

BYRON: Took a bit of digging. For some reason, the official video posted on the FairyCon channel was deleted years ago. I've inquired about why but haven't heard back. The convention's archives didn't have any record. But there's a girl who was there, who posted a three-hour video of her time at the convention, and . . . if you're patient, you can find this little nugget in the middle.

ANNABELLE: Impressive.

BYRON: I'm curious why you don't talk about this anymore.

ANNABELLE: Honestly, I haven't thought about it in a very long time.

BYRON: Forgive me for saying so, but that forgetting seems almost . . . deliberate. This book, *The Hidden World,* seems to have had a very important role in your creativity. At the very least, it provided the name for your fantasy world. But now . . .

ANNABELLE: My connection to that book was more than just intellectual. It was, as I indicate there, almost spiritual. But that part of me is very personal, so . . . I've elected to keep it to myself.

BYRON: Meaning . . . keep it secret.

ANNABELLE: I wouldn't say "secret." I'm not opposed to you knowing about it, per se. But I'd rather not discuss it any further. It's a fraught subject for me these days.

BYRON: Is that why you became estranged from the man who introduced you to it?

ANNABELLE: . . . You talked to Marcus?

INTERVIEW WITH MARCUS HOLLAND,
OWNER OF ODYSSEY BOOKS

October 24, 11:16 A.M. (The previous day)

Location: Musty book shop in the San Fernando Valley, north of Los Angeles. Neighborhood is a mix of auto-repair shops, industrial-looking film-equipment outlets, and large complexes of cheap apartments. Shop is sprawling and understaffed for its size. Mix of new and used titles, poorly organized. We sat on couches that hadn't been cleaned in decades; clouds of dust puffed up into the air as the fabric absorbed my body.

Subject: Marcus is 70ish, tall, professorial, Black, spectacled. Wears a vest and corduroy trousers. Speaks frustratingly slowly, but always thoughtful and amused.

TRANSCRIPT OF AUDIO RECORDING

BYRON: For starters, why don't you tell me about the day Annabelle Tobin came in here?

MARCUS: Certainly. She was a scrawny little thing, I recall. Most of the actresses are. They're usually looking for books on Stanislavsky or Marilyn Monroe, but Annabelle was undertaking a search of a different sort. Most striking was that she was simply . . . wide open. Many people ask for a recommendation, but few actually take you up on it.

BYRON: So you recommended this book, *The Hidden World*?

MARCUS: Indeed. It was an old first edition that had been out of print for quite some time. A novelty for collectors. The sort of rare book that falls between the cracks—old and uncommon enough to command a high price but obscure enough that it's difficult to find a buyer.

I read it myself, or at least gave it a skim, and found it intriguing, though rather difficult to follow. Perhaps because it was never completed.

BYRON: What do you mean?

MARCUS: Well, the text is from the late nineteenth century, peak Victorian, when Brits were sticking flags all over the world. I'm not sure how familiar you are, but this was the age of the "gentleman scholar" in England—rich lords traveling far afield, studying nature and local cultures and bringing it back home with them. Rationalism reigned supreme, yet this was also the time when Spiritualism had its peak, and interest in the *supernatural* flared. Arthur Conan Doyle was having séances, and even believed in fairies. Tried to prove their existence with photography.

Anyhow, the author of *Hidden World* is another lord, Sir Henry Raleigh. He was a rich heir who got the notion in his head to travel around and record local fairy stories. First it was only Britain and Ireland and Scotland, but then he began going farther. Scandinavia, Germany, Russia, even the Orient—that's what he calls it, not me— getting the local tales of fairies and trolls and all manner of "hidden folk." He did it for years, and the book is a compendium of the mythic narratives he collected. In his commentary, you can see him sketching out something of a master theory for what these beliefs all have in common. But he never finished it.

BYRON: He died?

MARCUS: Most likely, on one of his voyages. It's not recorded. The book sat around for a spell, but then there was a resurgence of interest in these things—*The Golden Bough* and all that—so his daughter Constance edited the manuscript into a somewhat coherent form, and then Oxford picked it up and published a small run. Never caught on much, but it's a curiosity.

BYRON: Seems like a strange choice to give to a twenty-six-year-old struggling actress.

MARCUS: I suppose that's a fair point. But perhaps it was meant to be! The book had only recently come into my possession. Maybe a couple days earlier. It was donated by an odd-looking fellow who dropped it off and didn't ask a penny for it. Must've been eager to get rid of the thing and didn't know the value of what he had.

At any rate, I was happy to take the book, and I put it in the collectors' case in back. But collector sales had been slow, and I had no prospects for unloading it anytime soon. And then, less than a week after I acquired it, Annabelle came in, and on that day, for whatever reason, it was right up here on the front counter. Almost like magic. Must've been a customer considered purchasing it and then left it there when he saw the price.

Truth be told, I was eager to be rid of it. I discounted it steeply and might've seen in Ms. Tobin an opportunity to unload it. I would probably feel some guilt, if the book hadn't inspired a billion-dollar franchise. Maybe I should've just kept it and seen what it might've inspired in me!

BYRON: Have you had any further interaction with Annabelle through the years?

MARCUS: Not for some time. She used to come in on occasion, even did a couple signings here, for Books Two and Three. That was helpful; sold a lot of books at those. So I've tried to reach out, keep up the relationship, but . . . she's become hard to get hold of. I suspect she's outgrown us, especially now that the movies have put her in another category entirely.

BYRON: What do you make of the controversy about the disappearances?

MARCUS: Oh, all that is a bunch of, pardon my language, hogwash. The individual cases are tragic, but connecting it back to her, the books . . . that's not right, and there's not one credible explanation for any of it. You think this is any different from the Satanic panic around Dungeons & Dragons? Or videogames and school shooters? It's the same type of thing. People—especially parents—they want someone to point the finger at. But it's time for them to take a look in the mirror.

BYRON: I see . . .

MARCUS: If I've poked a nerve in some way, I didn't mean to—

BYRON: Last question . . . do you have a copy of *The Hidden World*?

MARCUS: Not on hand, no. They've been hard to come by, ever since Annabelle talked about the book publicly. It was never so popular that it merited reprinting, but there was enough interest to drive up demand. I got my hands on one a couple years back on behalf of a client who was looking for one, and guess who it was? Melody Turner. That's the young lady who plays Ciara in the movies. Researching the part, I suppose, and she wanted to go to the same source as the creator. Wasn't easy to find one for her, and she certainly paid for the privilege.

BYRON: I'd love to talk with her as well . . . do you think you could put me in touch?

MARCUS: Oh, I don't give out customers' info, especially someone famous.

BYRON: I understand. I'm sure I'll be able to get in touch through her agent, it's just that it'll take ages. If you could save me some time, I won't mention where I got her contact info from.

MARCUS: I'd love to be helpful, but . . .

BYRON: If you'd be willing to, then I'd be happy to repay the favor with an explicit mention of your store in the article. Could be good for business, just like when Annabelle mentioned you before?

MARCUS: . . . That *could* be quite helpful. . . .

RESUME TRANSCRIPT OF INTERVIEW WITH
ANNABELLE TOBIN

BYRON: So why have you distanced yourself from Marcus and Odyssey Books?

ANNABELLE: It's nothing personal. I used to live around the corner from there and now—depending on the traffic—it's nearly an hour away. And I used to be able to go browse a bookstore and plop onto a couch and not be inundated with fans wanting selfies. I'm grateful for the fans, of course, but . . . celebrity is not what I signed up for when I tried my hand at writing a damn book.

BYRON: I asked Marcus about getting a copy of *The Hidden World,* and he mentioned how hard they were to come by these days. I did a little digging and I was able to find records of online sales of a few copies over the years. Some going for nearly ten thousand dollars.

ANNABELLE: Goodness, that's absurd. Glad I got mine when I did.

BYRON: The buyers have all been anonymous, which isn't entirely unusual in rare-book deals. But it appears that every one of the sales I could find was to a collector living in Los Angeles.

ANNABELLE: And to think that our fine city has a reputation for never reading.

BYRON: That suggests a single collector is buying them all up, which is highly uncommon. Do you happen to know who the collector is?

ANNABELLE: I couldn't say.

BYRON: Couldn't, or won't?

ANNABELLE: Byron . . . I feel like we're straying rather far from the topic of my creativity, don't you think? If there is some *theory* here . . .

BYRON: Only questions, I promise.

ANNABELLE: Good.

BYRON: How did you feel when Melody Turner got her hands on a copy?

ANNABELLE: (*Sighs*) If it helps her with her goddamn "process" in preparing for the role, more power to her.

INTERVIEW WITH MELODY TURNER

October 24, 4:19 P.M.

Location: Twelfth-floor condo in Santa Monica with ocean view. Glass and stone and bamboo everywhere. Decorated with expensive New Age paraphernalia: a massive mandala, crystals and geodes, a woven dreamcatcher. Interview conducted on her balcony; I retreated from the edge, tried not to look over, but was nonetheless gripped with vertigo every time I even thought about how high up we were.

Subject: Actress Melody Turner, instantly recognizable from the posters of all the Fairy Tale movies and numerous talk-show appearances. Shorter than anticipated, barely over five feet tall. Looks incredibly slender and delicate; hard to believe this is an adult. Head-to-toe Lululemon, appeared to have recently completed a workout. Personal assistant, a woman five years her senior, brought Melody a green juice concoction and then lingered just inside the glass doors the whole time.

TRANSCRIPT OF AUDIO RECORDING

MELODY: Are you OK? You want a spinach smoothie? Adrienne will whip one up, no prob, let me just—

BYRON: I'm fine. Just not one for heights.

MELODY: Have you looked into where that comes from?

BYRON: Probably a mix of evolution and common sense.

MELODY: No, no, no, you have to look deeper. I've got a spiritual guide who does past-life regression. You might have been—

BYRON: Let's get started, if you don't mind.

MELODY: For sure. I love, like, long-form conversation-type interviews. I was on Maron last year, and—

BYRON: This isn't gonna be like that. I just have questions I need answers to.

MELODY: Oh. Sure.

BYRON: You play Ciara in the Fairy Tale films. That must be quite a responsibility, given the intensity of the fandom.

MELODY: Yep! Huge honor. I just hope Annabelle finishes Book Six soon! I want to be *in* the sixth movie, and—I'm twenty-six now, actually, the same age Annabelle was when she wrote the first book, which is wild to think about, but Ciara at this point in the story is still only sixteen. I mean, I'm told I can play sixteen convincingly, I was in a high school thing on Netflix last year, but it's not, like, my first choice. And if there ends up being another big delay, I mean, the movies take a few years to do, and I can't be, like, *thirty* and out there promoting a movie about a teenage girl, you know?

BYRON: Makes sense. Now, I want to ask you about a specific part of your research. About the book *The Hidden World,* which you secured a copy of. Can you tell me a little about how that came into your life, and what it meant to you?

MELODY: Yeah, totally! I got the book from the guy at Odyssey, obviously, because that's where Annabelle got it. By the time I was cast, I was already, like, a superfan. I mean, the series didn't instantly take off, so Book Three had just come out, and I was, I think, fourteen? I did movies one and two, but I was just a kid then.

Then, when we were getting started on movies three and four—we did those two back-to-back, 'cause one and two were so huge—I had this feeling that I needed to go deeper on Ciara, and this whole world. And I was growing—ya know, not just as an actor, as a *person.* I understood it on a deeper level. And my agent negotiated a producer credit for me, and I took that seriously, so I wanted to be more involved with the whole process. I did a big dive into the mythology, and part of that was—yeah, I felt like the *Hidden World* book was maybe this kind of secret key to unlock the mystery behind it all.

BYRON: How much did you pay for the book?

MELODY: I dunno, maybe five grand? I forget exactly. But it was so worth it, not just to get to read it—I mean, it's surprisingly hard to read, I haven't, like, cover-to-cover finished it or anything—but just to have this ancient manuscript, you know? It's from, like, over a hundred years ago, and to read the same words that Annabelle herself read and learn what she learned . . .

BYRON: What sort of things did you get from the book? Was it . . . inspiration for your character?

MELODY: I mean, it put me in touch with the Green Man.

BYRON: Sorry, who?

MELODY: The Green Man. He's an ancient pagan spirit who crops up in all kinds of world folklores and mythologies. Almost like . . . the god of the Hidden World. Not capital-G God, but *a* god, you know? Annabelle doesn't talk about all this anymore, but he's the true origin of the Fairy Tale series. He was in the first three books, as sort of an abstract background figure, but not the last two. And the whole idea of even mentioning the Green Man got cut out of the movies.

BYRON: You're saying . . . you discovered a spiritual connection with . . .

MELODY: Look, I don't want to talk about this too much. I've had journalists try to make me look stupid before, taking things out of context. I know I'm just, like, some woo-woo L.A. chick to you, but I take this stuff seriously.

BYRON: I have no desire to make you look stupid. I'm honestly just trying to understand in an arena where I'm out of my depth.

MELODY: OK, well . . . I'm not saying I believe any of this, but the idea is that there's an ancient, noncorporeal being who can bridge into our physical universe.

BYRON: You're talking about . . . portals?

MELODY: Sure, that's one word, and it's a concept that Annabelle explores in Fairy Tale, in a fantastical way. But what's more interesting is how, like, maybe *stories* can be portals too. I mean you read something great, you're "transported," right?

BYRON: Metaphorically, yes. But . . . it's interesting that you bring that up. Because—I'm sure you've heard some of this—there are numerous reports of children who love these books and have gone missing. Literally.

MELODY: And where they've gone is still a total mystery, right?

BYRON: You're suggesting . . . what exactly?

MELODY: No, no, I'm not suggesting anything, I don't want to try to draw any conclusions here. I'm just generally of the opinion that there are larger forces at play that we might not rationally understand.

BYRON: Forces like . . . portals. That can transport children into another world.

MELODY: I didn't say that, but . . . I mean, is that so much crazier than what people are saying—that there's some global conspiracy of, like, pedo kidnappers? Maybe the better question we should be asking is, like, why are these children leaving home in the first place? And if they're disappearing, what if they're going to a better place? What if they know more than we do? I'm just pointing out—if the disappearances are a mystery, where they're going is a mystery, and it could be that they're entering a spiritual realm, somewhere ancient and special and joyful.

BYRON: That is . . . possible, I suppose.

MELODY: I mean, don't get me wrong, it's super sad, especially for the parents. But maybe if they were providing for their children's needs, maybe the kids wouldn't feel like they have to leave.

BYRON: You don't know those parents. You don't know anything about that.

MELODY: No, but . . . look, I don't just mean physical needs, I mean spiritual needs, you know? Our modern capitalistic culture is so spiritually depleted, and adults don't even notice or care, but the kids, they're the ones who feel deprived, and they're hungry. For meaning, for connection, for a *tribe*. The world is burning, and everything is unfair, and so, yeah, what's so wrong if kids these days want somewhere they can escape to?

BYRON: That's an interesting perspective. To be clear, you think they're going . . .

MELODY: I think it's a mystery where they're going. But there are forces beyond our understanding. There are gateways to other dimensions of reality; this is not just hippie-dippy stuff. This is quantum physics, and it seems likely that the Green Man might be an entity who transcends the normal divisions between some of our usual binaries, like . . . here or there, dead or alive, fantasy or reality. You're looking at me like I'm high out of my mind, which I promise, I'm not.

BYRON: Well, these ideas are just . . . unfamiliar to me, so . . . I'm wondering if maybe, to support this perspective a little further and to help out, could I have a copy of the book? I could borrow it, just for a couple days, as part of my research. It's extraordinarily hard to come by.

MELODY: Um . . . I'm not sure. I don't remember where it is, exactly, and . . . it's pretty special and personal to me, so . . . I'm sure you can find one online or something.

BYRON: I've tried, and I can't. I know it's valuable, I can assure you I'll take the utmost care and have it back to you in just a couple days.

MELODY: Yeah . . . I don't think so. Sorry.

BYRON: But don't you think it would be helpful to me? It would help me get to the bottom of what's going on. And your sharing it with me, that would probably be beneficial to . . . how you're portrayed, in the story I'm writing.

MELODY: What do you mean?

BYRON: I mean, right now in this interview, I have you on the record saying, essentially, that the kids who disappeared—maybe they're better off that way.

MELODY: That's not what I meant.

BYRON: I can tell you, the studio isn't going to love their lead actress victim-blaming these children. . . .

MELODY: No, I didn't mean to victim-blame anyone. . . .

BYRON: And the *parents* of those missing kids, they're not going to love that quote. . . .

MELODY: You're taking me out of context.

BYRON: When I look at a twenty-six-year-old millionaire, who's been beautiful her whole life and famous since she was fifteen, who is literally the most privileged person I've ever met . . . I'd like to try to be a little forgiving. Because however much you care about your career, and your fans, and your Green Man, and your costar boyfriend . . . you have never cared about *anything* a fraction as much as those parents care about their kids.

MELODY: I'm . . . sorry.

BYRON: I think that readers will want to know that you were . . . *helpful.*

MELODY: Of course! I love making a difference.

BYRON: A perfect way to do that would be helping me get access to the book. I'll even mention in the article how you went out of your way to help me get to the bottom of this. And I'll neglect to mention the victim-blaming and minimizing.

MELODY: I guess . . . I mean, I'm not actively using the book right now, so . . . just for your research process . . .

BYRON: I'll have it back to you in no time.

RESUME TRANSCRIPT OF INTERVIEW WITH
ANNABELLE TOBIN

BYRON: You're not opposed to others reading the book, are you?

ANNABELLE: Of course not.

BYRON: Good. Because I'm wondering if you could help me make sense of it. . . .

(*Sound of bag opening. Thump of book onto the table. Long silence.*)

ANNABELLE: Where did you get that?

BYRON: This is Melody Turner's copy. She lent it to me.

ANNABELLE: . . . All I can say is, you should be careful.

BYRON: What do you mean?

ANNABELLE: Have you shown it to anyone else?

BYRON: I've barely had time to look through it myself.

ANNABELLE: You should return it to Melody and forget you ever saw it.

BYRON: I don't understand.

ANNABELLE: Good. Because by the time you understood, it would be too late.

BYRON: Too late . . . for what?

ANNABELLE: Do you like horror movies, Byron? Personally, I can't stand them. Not because I don't like being scared, although I don't. It's because there's always a moment, around the end of Act One, when the couple moves into the steeply discounted house, or the teenagers decide to take the trip, or whatever, and some batty old crone or lost-his-mind scientist appears and tells them not to do it. But of course they do it anyway, because otherwise there wouldn't be a movie.

My point is, I can't stand to see people ignore a sensible warning. After that, everything that happens to them, I can't help but feel like . . . they asked for it.

BYRON: Ms. Tobin, are you threatening me?

ANNABELLE: Not in the least. I'm trying to help. To give you the warning I never got.

BYRON: Warning about . . . what?

ANNABELLE: (Sighs) Well, this has been delightful, but I think that's all we have time for today. I need to pick my son up from school.

BYRON: It's not even two o'clock yet. Perhaps we could order some food?

ANNABELLE: No, no, I need to be going. I have a child to mother, a book to write.

BYRON: If I said something to offend you . . .

ANNABELLE: You couldn't if you tried. Honestly, Byron, I'm impressed with you. I think you're a good writer. But that won't save you from what's coming if you continue down this path. In fact, it'll probably make it worse. Now, take care of yourself.

(End of recording.)

CHAPTER NINE

INVESTIGATIVE JOURNAL OF BYRON KIDD

October 26

Liza is out there. Alive. Probably in danger. ~~Possibly hurt.~~ (No need to speculate.) What matters is she needs me. She needs her dad. And yet I'm just poring over the words of some obscure book of fairy tales, like Liza might be hidden between the lines. Useless.

Yesterday's interview with Annabelle did not go as planned. I came on too strong. Or maybe not strong enough. It's clear she's got secrets. Not so clear if she's playing games with me or simply struggling with paranoid delusions. ~~At least I'm not the only one~~.

She knows more than she's telling me. Maybe I should just ~~grab her by the throat and~~ come right out and ask her where Liza is. But it's not clear that would do any good. Not like she's hiding them in her basement. Or like she'd cop to it if she were.

Focus. Just the facts.

The fact is I'm angry. Need to keep it under control. Can't help that I'm inside the story, but I have to minimize my role. ~~Love for Liza might be what drives me but it also~~ Emotion clouds perspective, obscures objectivity. Only way I'll ever find her is to negate myself.

After the failed interview, I went for a drive. Headed west. Needed to clear my head. Big mistake, doing so late-afternoon. Soon as people started getting out of work (happens around three here apparently) I

got trapped in traffic like I've never seen. Baking on the freeway. Looking around, through the windows of the other cars, into all the little
bubbles. Everyone on their phones. Everyone in two worlds at once.
Who needs a world of fantastic stories when nobody's really living in
this one anyway?

Got off the 101, dipped back down to Franklin, and started grinding
back toward the motel. Saw the imposing façade of the Scientology
headquarters, gated-off like it's the Forbidden City. The massive tem-
ple of a failed sci-fi writer's made-up religion, towering over a row of
acting workshops and storefront theaters. No doubt all the would-be
movie stars start out sneering at the much-maligned religion across the
street, but after a few years of failure soften them up, who knows how
many wander in there, looking for anything, anyone to give them answers. . . .

This is a city of searchers. No wonder it's where Annabelle landed.
Is she so different from L. Ron Hubbard? Her fans are practically aco-
lytes, her books are treated like sacred texts.

A few more lights and I found myself in front of a place called Alad-
din Liquor. Melody Turner would call that a sign from the universe.
Skipped the wine, picked up cheap bourbon. Once I pulled into the
motel, didn't even wait till I was inside, drinking from the brown paper
bag. No better than Mr. Echo, who was back in the parking lot. Left me
alone this time, singing his boozy lullabies.

Once inside, I got to work reading through the Hidden World book
and making my way through the bottle. Trying to decipher what about
the stories might hold such meaning for Annabelle. The stories were
difficult to read; first, owing to the appearance of the text, which is
faded and printed in an old-fashioned font that's challenging to parse.
Even before the whiskey kicked in, it felt like the letters were ~~drifting
across the page~~ hard to focus on, and I struggled to keep my eyes—
and my mind—engaged with the task at hand.

The antiquated Victorian style and diction didn't help either; deliberately obtuse. Most difficult of all is the disorganized presentation of the
tales. The book is a compendium of folk stories, as promised. But some

stories feature lengthy introductions, others none at all; some are par-
tial or incomplete; the author insinuates himself liberally at times, disappears entirely at others. It's difficult to determine when one story
begins and ends or to separate the authorial commentary from the text.

Also, I'm not at my best. Haven't been for a long time. Here's the
thing no one tells you about ~~grieving~~ ~~losing someone~~ dealing with a
disappearance: it makes you stupid. Because a corner of your mind is
always consumed with the person who's gone. And as long as you
don't know what happened to them, that corner grows and spreads,
colonizing your brain. The slightest association consumes you. The act
of trying to read makes you remember THEM reading.

Liza read everywhere. Curled up in the backseat on long drives.
Sitting on the bench during her softball games. She even brought a
book with her when we all went out to dinner, held it under the table, so
she'd be looking down like she was staring at the menu. I yelled at her
for that one time, when we were out with Val's brother and his wife. I
lost it and lost my temper and Liza cried, she was a sensitive kid, and
she ran off to the bathroom. Then I realized she'd brought her book
with her to the bathroom, and I wondered how much she might've exaggerated the tears or invented them entirely, and I didn't even care, I
laughed when I realized she'd gotten just what she wanted. She was
different from me in so many ways, but like Val said, "the willful part,
that's all you."

Point is: I'm not operating at 100%. 40–50 tops. And as a result, I
made more progress with the booze than the stories and got no closer
to comprehending what was going on with Annabelle, much less finding a clue that might help me get to Liza. ~~Passed out~~ Went to bed
around 10:30.

Woke at 3AM. Startled. Heard something but couldn't say what.
Only silence when I listened. Trouble focusing my eyes. Groggy and
still somewhat inebriated. Hate to say it, but it's important to note since
so little of what happened next makes sense.

Shadows moved across the walls, cast by the yellow streetlamps
outside. Could not determine from what. One shadow ~~formed into a~~

~~shape~~ looked like a person, with an ~~impossibly~~ exaggerated long, thin body. ~~Darker than the darkness.~~

(Reporting the perception here, not the reality. Just the facts. Is perception a fact?)

Went to the window. Looking for the source. Closed the blinds.

Then . . . someone grabbed me. From behind. ~~All over.~~ Didn't get a good look. Arms wrapped around me, pinned me, squeezed me. I fought back but couldn't see. Flailed. Tried to strike back against the body, but the person moved aside, judo-style, took me down.

Felt arms wrap around my neck. Chokehold. Tried to shout for help then but couldn't breathe. Arms felt thin but incredibly strong. Driving me down, grinding my face into the floor. ~~The harder I fought, the more the energy drained from my body.~~ My muscles trembled. Started to lose consciousness.

Suddenly my attacker relented. Heard a ~~bone-chilling~~ loud shriek. Took the opportunity, rolled away, backed up.

In my room, I saw the homeless man from the parking lot. Mr. Echo. Oversized coat flapping ~~like a cowboy's duster~~ like a superhero's cape. (Just the facts) Holding his big, reddish knife, which ~~seemed to glow~~ gleamed in the faint light. Still swiping and slashing at the air. At what, I can't say.

I backed away, fumbling for a weapon. Brandished the lamp like a club. Mr. Echo squinted at me. "I'm not here for YOU."

I saw that the door was open, which it had not been before. A huge gash slashed into the wood, as though the handle had been carved out by his blade. Not the interaction between rusty knife and thick door I would expect.

Was it possible that someone ELSE had been in here first? And that Echo had indeed come to my rescue? I looked at him—but abruptly, something changed in his eyes, and he hurled the large knife at me.

I flinched, ducked, covering my face uselessly with my hands—but it went past me, and when I turned, I was surprised to see it was stuck hilt-deep in the wall. An impossibly expert throw. "Got 'im," Echo muttered. And while there was not anyone else there, I did feel confident that he was not trying to hurt me.

As he retrieved the weapon from the wall, he spoke again. "Keep an eye. They got your scent, somehow."

When he told me this, my eyes glanced instinctively toward the Hidden World book that I'd left open on the desk. Echo caught my gaze and followed it.

Echo went over to the book. He ~~caressed the parchment~~ touched the pages. Entranced. ~~A deep well of emotions~~ He seemed to recognize the book, so I asked him, "You've heard of this?" He nodded vaguely, ~~as if distant recollections were replaying a movie in his mind's eye~~. Then he started flipping through the pages, a half-smile playing across his face. Glanced to me, then back to the pages. "If you want to understand, start here."

He left the book open, turned away, sheathed the knife on his belt, and ran out the door. I still had a million questions. Staggered to my feet, went and looked out into the parking lot.

He was gone. ~~Vanished completely~~. I felt my mind spinning with confusion~~ . . . but more than that. With wonder~~.

Working theory: Someone (other than Mr. Echo) broke into my room, having learned (how?) that I possessed an expensive and rare book. I woke up in the middle of the break-in. When I went to the window, they attacked. Echo, alerted to the struggle in my room, came in, frightened them away with the knife. Probably the book doesn't actually mean anything to him, but he became convinced it held some divine purpose.

After the attack, I considered calling the police again, but what was I going to report? Break-in, assault, attempted robbery, miraculous salvation by a mentally ill vagrant who was gone now? Nothing was taken. Unlikely a police report would yield much. ~~And for some reason I felt like it would make me even less safe.~~

So I went to the book. Mr. Echo had left it open to a story called "The Leanan Sídhe." No idea what that meant. Several reads later, still don't.

Now it's 6:30, and I'm sitting in a shitty linoleum diner booth with a "No Sleeping" sign on the table and a view of Vine. The clientele is a 50/50 split of long-night revelers ending their debauched nights out and early-morning workers filling up before long shifts. The coffee is kicking in, mercifully, and my greasy food should arrive any second. Hopefully it'll help ~~ground me~~ settle my nerves, and maybe then I can start to wrap my mind around why he pointed to this particular story.

SHORT STORY

From *The Hidden World: On Faeries, Fauns & Other Creatures of Folklore,* by Sir Henry Raleigh. Published 1889, Oxford University Press.

THE LEANAN SÍDHE

This tale came to my ears from the lips of one Lilian O'Connell, a reputable woman from Derry and mother unto seven youths, narrated this 16th Day of January, 1873, and faithfully set unto ink.

There once was a man named Martin Gallville, himself a dairy farmer of a goodly personage. One day, Martin bid his wife and daughters farewell, and, bearing a multitude of fine cheeses upon his horse-drawn cart, he set out across the Pike Road that traversed the Bailiwick Forest to exchange his goods in the village of Cornwall.

It was a voyage of three hard days, and Martin began to play upon his lute, so that its jolly sound would frighten away any mischievous and malevolent sprites of the wood and help him to pass the time.

Traveling thus, he came upon an elderly woman of diminutive stature and ill bearing, wearing a cloak and humming to herself. She waved him to a stop. "Your skill upon the lute, good sir, is formidable to hear. Wherefore do you play?"

"Only to pass the time," he replied.

"Your skill deserves to be improved!" she told him. "And I am bless'd with a certain power, which can elevate your ability far beyond mortal talents. For my breath is made of inspiration! All it will take is a kiss."

The woman was haggard and crook-nosed, yet her promise did tempt Martin, as he was always eager to improve his skill. So he hopped down from his cart, and drew close to the woman, and overcoming his aversion to her powerful stench, he planted upon her lips a kiss, whereupon she did exhale unto him a great breath, which filled him to the core. The old hag thus bade him farewell and continued down the road.

While Martin Gallville continued his three-day journey to Cornwall, playing the lute to pass the time, he felt a spell of guilt for kissing a woman other than his wife. But his suffering was dispelled as he found that now he could play with such skill as he had never before. And lo! The sun had nary reached its apex in the sky, when he came upon the edge of Cornwall—for his playing had so passed the time, he had already attained his destination.

With utter delight, he hopped down from his cart, and sold all of his cheeses at a fair price. He bought himself a suitable meal for celebration and hopped back into his cart, for such was his speed with this new skill upon the lute that he knew he would be home before nightfall.

So he played and traveled quickly back across the land and again did he encounter the old hag he had seen before, and stopped to give her thanks.

"No thanks are required, good sir," she said. "My talent is only to amplify skill, I cannot give it from nothing. Now, what else do you wish?"

Martin wondered just how well he may be able to play with her blessings. He exclaimed, "I would be the greatest lute player in the world! That any who hear my tune would be utterly transported!"

"A suitable wish," the old woman said. "But to have it granted, you must suitably avail yourself to me, and lay with me as a lover, here in the back of your cart."

Martin knew he ought protest, for his wife would never abide such a transgression. But he reasoned that she did love to hear him play the lute, thus this brief betrayal would in fact do her benefit.

So he lay with the old woman in the back of his cart, turning his face from the sight of her crooked nose and the scent of her wicked breath.

When the deed was done, she once again exhaled and filled him with an even greater breath that stretched his lungs till he nearly burst. "You are now bless'd with the power for which you wished."

Martin Gallville got back into his cart, and headed home at a rapid pace, playing the lute with even greater skill than before. And indeed he was home before the sun dipped below the horizon.

When he attained sight of his cottage, his wife and his two daughters ran out and embraced him, marveling at the wonder of his travel in a single day. And that night he set them down in the parlor and played for them his lute with such skill that they were filled with rapture, and exclaimed what a wonder it was that he had been so gifted. Never before had Martin Gallville slept so soundly.

But in the morning, he woke in an empty bed, and was much alarmed to find the bed of his daughters empty too. It was a cold and empty cottage now, and Martin was filled with dread at what knavery had taken those he loved.

So he set out in his cart upon the road he had yesterday traversed, and he found the old hag at the same crossroads. He lamented what had befallen him! He cursed her treachery!

"You wished to play with such skill that any who heard would be transported!" the woman replied. "So marvelous was your song that they were indeed."

For the old woman was none other than Leanan Sídhe, muse of the forest, faerie ambassador to those who dream of greatness, and punisher of those who reach too far.

And so at night, to this very day, Martin Gallville sits upon his porch, and from his lute pours forth songs of such enchanting beauty, any would be loath to turn away. But come too close and listen too long and you will be transported, too, never to again be seen.

EMAIL

From: bybyronjames@gmail.com
To: m.pimm@ucla.eng.edu

Misha,

Got my hands on a copy of the *Hidden World* book and wondering if you can help me make sense of what the fuss is all about. Took photos of pages to send you one of the stories called "Leanan Sídhe," which is attached, and which might have special significance for Annabelle Tobin. Is there anything you're seeing here that I'm missing?

—Byron

REPLY

Hiiiiii Byron,

OK whoa first off this is SO. F-ING. COOL. Can't believe you got your hands on the book. How'd you manage it? I've been trying for years and coming up empty. Any chance I could see it sometime? Briefly borrow it? It's basically the Holy Grail for scholarship in my tiny area of study.

To be more specific (and start making my way toward an answer to your question): I'm studying the commonalities between folklores across different cultures, with an eye toward how similar characters, symbols, and images seem to emerge organically in geographically and temporally disparate societies. You look into all this stuff—it's beyond Jungian archetypes. The tropes of a virgin birth, a ravaging flood, a shaman who moves between two worlds . . . these stories are somehow universal.

This story represents another one of those tropes. Leanan Sídhe is a source of inspiration, like the Muses in Greek myth, or the voice that spoke to Daniel in the Bible, or the Hindu goddess Saraswati.

But it's important to note that these figures of supernatural inspiration are not always pure of heart and intention. You don't want to piss off one of the Muses. Which brings up the other dimension of this story: it's a classic wish-comes-true-turns-into-worst-nightmare. A Monkey's Paw, where the character gets what they want but there's a horrible price to pay. You see this in Grimms' Fairy Tales, in 1,001 Nights, in the Panchatantra. What's the point of these stories? It's not just "be careful what you wish for." It's reinforcing a karmic sense of the universe, one where energies are balanced, and whatever you gain freely will result in suffering and hardship down the line.

Since you come at this from looking into Annabelle, there's a parallel to a chapter from Book Five: The Forgotten Abyss, where Ciara makes a deal with the Illuminator, and she gets the magical Boon of Persuasion. As a result, people do whatever she says—but then it backfires when she tells her friend Palmeroy, "Get out of here," and Palmeroy leaves the Hidden World and can't find his way back. That's the closest similar story I can think of from the books. Hope all that is helpful!

—M

REPLY

Misha,

Interesting but a little academic. I'm trying to go a step further in terms of what it all means about Annabelle. Or perhaps any connection we might be able to ascertain between these story elements and the rash of missing children connected to the Fairy Tale series. Looking for something tangible and actionable here. Any thoughts?

Byron

REPLY

Byron,

On the first point—connection to Annabelle—it's a bit of a reach. Perhaps she identifies with the story in the sense that she was inspired when she was younger and paid a price for it when she got older and became uber-famous and unable to live a normal life. But it seems silly to map that backward onto her life and imagine that's why she was drawn to it in her mid-20s.

As for the other part . . . I can't imagine what connection might exist between the disappearances of the children and this old fable. Again, I think the whole premise you're acting on is flimsy at best. Are you planning to make the conspiracy theories a major part of the article you're writing?

—M

REPLY

Misha,

I agree, the story might not be clearly connected to the disappearances—but the connection between ANNABELLE and the disappearances is probably stronger than you realize—and you might be in the best position to help me reveal it to the world.

I want to come back to something we talked about earlier: your website, Queendom. I'm hoping you might be able to give me limited access to the back-end user data. I trust that helping missing children is important to you, and it's worth a look to see if the key to their safety and freedom is right under your nose.

Byron

REPLY

Byron,

No. Way. Sorry to be blunt, but was I not clear about this? The integrity and privacy of the Queendom community is my sacred responsibility, and I'm not going to compromise that for a flimsy conspiracy theory. Honestly your insistence is lowkey freaking me out. I'm happy to be helpful in the capacity of an academic consultant but we need to set some limits around what's appropriate here.

M

REPLY

Misha,

I would not be so insistent if it were not a matter of life and death. So I'm going to take a chance here and share something with you, which I'm trusting you to keep in confidence.

This article (LINK) is about one of the missing children whose disappearance is connected to the Fairy Tale series. But it is unique from all the others in one important regard: Liza Kidd is my daughter. (Byron James is my pen name; my legal name is Byron Kidd.)

I'm trying to find my daughter. And I'm stuck. I have evidence that she was here in Los Angeles, and I'm confident Annabelle Tobin is connected to what happened to her. I know for a fact that Liza used your website every day, including the night she disappeared. I have nothing else to go on. I need your help to save her. Please.

REPLY

OK dude, I'm honestly super sorry to hear about what happened to your daughter (if that is even true), but seriously wtf did you think was gonna happen when you told me all that? And that you straight-up LIED to me? Have you never heard of boundaries?

The answer is NO. I don't break the rules of my community, and I don't F around with middle-aged lurkers who try to manipulate me. Plus it's not even fair for you to lay a guilt trip on me like that. I'm full-on blocking your ass, and if you get near me again I'm gonna call the police.

TEXT MESSAGE EXCHANGE

BYRON KIDD	VALERIE KIDD

11:22 P.M.

Val i need your help with ome more thing.

The website Liza was using the queendom.com is important

could be the only source of infomation of what she's doing the night she used it last.

She has to have things on there that we can help.

you can write a court order or something right?

12:11 A.M.

Val?

VAL VAL VAL VAL.

I still love you val.

I still think we can save our family.

I'm going to get Liza back.

You don't believe me you never believed in me

Thats OK i wouldnt either

but im gonna get her back

do you remember disneyworld?

i fucking hate disneyworld.

but liza in the teacups

round round and round, again again agiln

have u ever seen anyone happeri?

and i promised her wed go back when she was big enough to ride space mtn

i dont lie so we have to

find her save her back to disneywrold promise me

6:04 A.M.

                                      Morning Byron.

                                      Late night huh?

8:52 A.M.

Sorry about that.

It was a long day.

I haven't been sleeping very well here.

You free to talk on the phone?

                                      I'd rather not.

You want to access a website's user data? Good luck.

If the company doesn't want to give it up, you'll have to sue for release.

That'll take at least a year.

And I'm not going to continue to enable you by helping out.

I see.

                                Please don't drunk-text me again.

I won't, I promise.

It was just a bad day.

                              Are you open to some feedback Byron?

Always.

                            You only have bad days these days.

Perhaps you ought to consider that the source is internal, not external.

Please I've been having bad days for the last seven months.

Gee what's been going on during that time?

       Please don't pretend your drinking was caused by her disappearance.

              That's been going on for two years, at least.

Once in a while, maybe.

But this is different.

Don't pretend that nothing changed.

Things weren't perfect but we were happy. Right?

    Jesus christ you are honestly hilarious, you act like everyone else is self-deluded when YOU are the one telling yourself a story that's total bullshit. About how her disappearance turned you into a miserable drunk. Wrong. You've been a miserable drunk for years, and it's not bc of Liza or bc journalism is dying or bc the world is getting worse, it's bc that is WHO YOU ARE. And if there's any cause-and-effect here it goes the other way, it's you being a miserable drunk that made our home a horrible place and drove Liza away from us

Oh.

9:33 A.M.

              I apologize.

       That was more than I meant to express.

You wouldn't have said it if you didn't think it.

             Good luck, Byron.

          I'm sorry I can't help you.

      I hope you can start being honest, at least with yourself.

CHAPTER TEN

INVESTIGATIVE JOURNAL OF BYRON KIDD

October 27

Dead end. No idea where to go next. Misha was my best lead, fucked that right up. ~~Can't believe how callous and condescending Val has become, acts like going to therapy makes her~~

Focus. Resentment is a distraction.

Back to Liza. Back to the source. Back to what I have: her things. A few tokens of her existence. Painful as they are to look at, that's where I needed to turn my attention.

Flipped through her notebooks again. Utterly disorganized. Random fragments, a mix of reminders and fleeting notions.

- Soc studies project due Mon.

- NK Jemisin

- Renew library books

- What would happen if gravity stopped working?

- I before e except after c or when sounding like A as in neighbor or weigh

No useful information. Maybe that's the problem. Maybe all I'm looking for is information but I need to look deeper, need to see what she saw, if I'm ever going to understand why she left behind ~~a good life with~~ her life.

Opened her sketchbook. Started going through her drawings. Slower this time. Making myself really see them. Intricately detailed. Hard to imagine the hours that went into each one. All those hours alone in her room. All those hours away from everyone. Away from me.

First page was some fearsome magical creature. Tentacles and claws and fangs, roaring. Sure it's from the books. Is this an expression of how Liza felt? Rage?

Next: a tree on a hill. A man sitting at its base. Shaved head, beard. Eerie image. Lonely. ~~Wondered what dark corner of her mind~~

Flipped forward more. Fairies. Lots of them. A queen on a throne, a mischief-maker carrying a potion. But they were not flitting about in action. The drawings were all close-up portraits, exquisitely detailed. Capturing emotion. One looked pensive. One gazed longingly toward the horizon. One seemed nostalgic.

I was amazed. Liza's technique was far from perfect; shading was amateurish, perspective often distorted. But the way she captured subtle emotion was incredible.

And many of the faces looked vaguely familiar. Assumed I'd seen images from the films, and that's what Liza was using for reference.

But then I paused on one. A fairy, yes, with blue skin and wings spread wide, but also: a soldier. Clad in gold armor with a helmet obscuring part of his face, a spear in his hand. I studied the expression, the grim, joyless curl of the lip, the ferocity in the eyes. This was a villain, for sure. A threat. The emotion: bitter anger.

And beneath the helmet, the face was familiar. It was me.

I googled "Fairy Tale soldier with spear" and pretty quickly was pointed to the character of "Gloverbeck." A fan wiki informed me that he was the head of Queen Áine's army; he chased down and captured Ciara, imprisoning her in the Crystal Palace.

Most of the images of the character were stills from the film series, and I saw that the actor who played him didn't resemble me in the slightest. Which meant that Liza had cast me in this role in her mind. The role of her captor? Her jailor? ~~Her enemy.~~

I was gutted. Stared at the fierce expression she had drawn. That was how Liza saw me? I wasn't even that strict of a parent. But the armor . . . maybe I did have armor. How could I not? ~~Maybe Liza should've had armor too. Maybe if~~

I couldn't afford to dwell. An idea was triggered, and I started going through the other images, looking for other correspondences. Now that I had a goal, it was not hard to find them.

I quickly discovered an image of a kindly older fairy in an apron, whose face was instantly recognizable as Val. Cast as "Cloverpea," a renowned baker of magical treats (there was even a branded cookbook available online). ~~This equivalence hardly seemed fair to me, since I did just as much cooking as Val did; the simple fact that Val baked Liza a birthday cake every year had apparently qualified her as~~

More important, I found Annabelle's face on the body of Queen Áine, the matriarch of the fairy realm. Annabelle's features were rendered even more dramatic than in real life. She was wrapped in flowing robes and seated on a crystal throne, looking down with an enigmatic but benevolent smile. I was not surprised but felt infuriated that Liza had bought into Annabelle's self-mythologizing. The reclusive genius.

There were other, younger faces I didn't recognize, which I assumed were some of Liza's classmates, cast into various roles from the films. One that I DID recognize was Marley, the girl who had mocked Liza online. She was featured as a fairy with fins, a tail, and a sharp-edged seashell bodice—like an S&M mermaid. "Sylkie" was the character's name, I learned. But in the books, Sylkie was not overtly villainous. And heartbreakingly, Liza's drawing did not betray fear or hatred of her so much as . . . infatuation? Admiration, at least. Sylkie was sensual and powerful.

As I stared at it, I saw the bullying incident in a different light. Saw Liza in a different light as well. Couldn't help but wonder, just how little did I know my own daughter? I flipped through the other female faces, noting how many were idealized. Long, curving necks, plump lips, gleaming eyes.

Then I came to a familiar face with a shock of blue hair. It triggered a mix of irritation, anger, and . . . jealousy. ~~She was featured positively in Liza's imagination? Being a parent really is the most thankless job in~~ But eventually, as those unhelpful feelings subsided, an idea took shape.

HANDWRITTEN LETTER

Left in the Graduate Student Mailbox of Misha Pimm

Misha,

First off, I am sorry that I lied to you. And I'm sorry to be leaving you this letter, when I understand the reasons that you had to block me. I know that you don't have kids, but I hope you will understand and perhaps forgive a parent for doing anything that might help his missing child. Especially a child as special as Liza. I could proudly regale you with her academic accomplishments (which are formidable) or her athletic achievements (virtually nonexistent), but that would hardly scratch the surface.

Instead, let me share a bit of her Fairy Tale fandom. I recently discovered Liza's sketchbook, featuring pictures of various characters drawn with the faces of people she knows (or doesn't know, but knows of). Every image in that sketchbook is special to me, because every one represents hours of her life and imagination.

But I feel like you should have the one that I've included in this envelope because, as you can see, it is a picture of you. And Liza has drawn you not as a soldier (like me) or a goddess (like Annabelle). But instead as Ciara, the protagonist of the whole story. You would think that Liza would see herself as the protagonist, but she has instead cast you in the role. An aspirational surrogate for herself maybe? Or perhaps, to use another word . . . a hero. I believe I've made known my feelings about heroes, but if my daughter needs one, I greatly prefer that she look up to you than Annabelle Tobin.

So even if I never see you again, I want you to have this drawing. I hope it shows you the responsibility you have to your audience—to the impressionable young people who look up to you. I think Liza would want you to have it too. And if this small gift does slightly thaw your heart toward me, I'll be waiting in the coffee shop across the quad until the end of the day. If you're open to talking again, you know where to find me.

Sincerely,
Byron Kidd

2ND INTERVIEW WITH MISHA PIMM

October 27, 4:14 P.M.

Location: Campus coffee shop at UCLA. Public health posters on the walls, open-mic stage, study groups huddled in every corner. I chose a seat against the wall—far enough that any conversation would not be overheard but out in the open enough that it would hopefully inspire a sense of security.

Subject: When Misha saw me this time, she scowled, but came over anyway. Usual infectious enthusiasm was replaced with wariness, and her body was visibly tense. Sat down and I was already recording.

TRANSCRIPT OF RECORDED INTERVIEW

MISHA: So. How'd you know?

BYRON: That you'd come?

MISHA: That I don't have kids. Lots of gay couples have kids now. Shelby and I have talked about it plenty.

BYRON: Just a hunch, I guess.

MISHA: Don't think I don't see what you're doing. Super manipulative. And it's hard to take your word for any of this when you've done a *ridiculous* amount of lying since I met you.

BYRON: The important parts are all true. I do want you to have the picture. And I really am just a dad who will do anything to get his daughter back.

MISHA: Yeah, yeah, good excuse. You ever see *Finding Nemo*?

BYRON: That the fish one?

MISHA: Uh-huh. Single-dad fish loses all his thousand babies, except for one. And then the one gets lost, and he goes on this crazy mission across the ocean to get him back. It's great.

BYRON: You're saying . . . I'm like Nemo.

MISHA: Nemo's the kid fish. You're Marlon, the dad. And that story trope of the dad who goes off to rescue their runaway kid—it's in a million movies. *Taken* is the Euro-sex-trafficking version, but there's *Commando*, *Die Hard 4*. *San Andreas* is the Rock versus an earthquake. Mel Gibson did two—*The Patriot* and *Ransom*. There's even an all-on-computer-screens version that was surprisingly good. And every single one of these movies has the same plot—unhinged dad will do anything to save his kid—just a different setting.

BYRON: So? Seems like dad-saves-kid is one of the most basic stories there is.

MISHA: Here's the thing: having studied hundreds of myths and legends, this trope isn't all that common, historically. There's a whole genre of *rescue stories* for sure, with different permutations of who saves whom. Lover-rescue stories, from *The Iliad* to Orpheus and Eurydice, and all the prince-rescues-princess fairy tales like "Snow White." There are tons of brother-rescue stories, sister-rescue stories, even animal-companion-rescue stories.

But there aren't that many parent-rescues-child stories. There are more of the other way around! In "Beauty and the Beast," it's Belle that rescues her father, and in the Grimm story "The Carnation," it's the son who rescues his mother. But dad-rescuing-kid is all over the movies of the last thirty years. So the question that interests me is . . . why? What changed?

BYRON: Maybe us modern dads are just better. More connected to our kids. And we like to imagine that if shit went down, we could save the ones we love.

MISHA: I kinda think it's the opposite. That modern dads are full of guilt, 'cause they all work too much, and modern kids all feel abandoned.

You have to remember, stories are fantasies. Dreams of what you don't have. And the real wish-fulfillment isn't for the dad in these stories. It's for the kid. The audience is the proxy hostage. We all feel helpless and lonely in the modern world, so we perpetuate stories of crusading fathers with a particular set of skills and the willingness to kill a gazillion bad guys because we want to believe *our dad* would do that. We want to believe he's on his way and he's not taking no for an answer.

BYRON: I'm guessing . . . you would've liked that.

MISHA: (*Sighs*) My dad was a jazz guitarist. Never made any money, but he was super cool. He just didn't want to be a dad. Certainly not to me. When I was ready to come out, I knew he wouldn't judge me for it. My mom was the uptight, religious one, but my dad was a total libertine. He was happy for me, and I guess I should be grateful for that. But it wasn't enough.

BYRON: You wanted him to protect you?

MISHA: Yes! From my mom . . . from the world . . . Instead he just fucked off and went on tour, and I've seen him twice in the last ten years. So someone who's willing to do anything for his little girl . . . maybe I can give him another shot.

BYRON: What you're saying is . . . I've got Big Dad Energy.

MISHA: (*Groans, then laughs*) Oh God, that was *terrible*. If I'm gonna help you, no more dad jokes.

BYRON: So you'll help me?

MISHA: I'm not doing this out of the goodness of my heart, all right? I want something too.

BYRON: Anything.

MISHA: *The Hidden World*.

BYRON: You want the book? For yourself?

MISHA: I think it's a reasonable ask.

BYRON: It's yours. Full disclosure, it doesn't technically belong to me, but—

MISHA: Ugh, you are exhausting. Let's just get to work.

BYRON: Thank you.

MISHA: Look, after I talked to you last, I went and did a deep-dive into some of the Queendom data. A meta-analysis of the "Sightings" section, based on geographical tags. Turns out, Sightings are seven times more likely to happen in L.A. than anywhere else.

BYRON: Which means . . . ?

MISHA: Maybe there're more Fairy Tale fans here, on average. Or maybe something else is going on in this city.

BYRON: Not sure I follow.

MISHA: Your daughter, she ran away because she *believed*, right? In the Hidden World, the portals . . . she ran away to try to get to another realm.

BYRON: As far as I can tell, yes.

MISHA: But *you* don't believe any of that.

BYRON: You're asking . . . if I believe in magic portals?

MISHA: I'm just trying to understand what you think.

BYRON: I think that a twelve-year-old girl doesn't vanish into thin air. Not without someone else being involved. So someone has to be taking advantage of this whole idea of the Hidden World to lure kids away.

MISHA: And you know for certain that Liza made it to L.A.

BYRON: Her cell phone was used exactly once after she left home. At a place called the End of the World Museum in Venice. And in case there was any doubt it was her, there was even a picture of her on the wall.

MISHA: Oh yeah, I know the place. And the weird picture-wall thing. There's one of me and Shelby up there too.

BYRON: Seems like a strange spot for a date.

MISHA: I liked it. Shelby not so much. She's much more . . . like you.

BYRON: Sane?

MISHA: Literal. About everything. So a museum full of artifacts of questionable provenance wasn't exactly her bag.

BYRON: "Questionable" is a stretch.

MISHA: Whatever, dude, I don't think we're gonna see eye-to-eye here. How about we get to how you think the site can help.

BYRON: I need access to Liza's account.

MISHA: All right, for starters, I'll need her email address. If we're going to look up her info, we need to figure out her username first.

BYRON: Thank you. It's Lizathekidd—that's "kid" with two *d*'s—at gmail.

MISHA: (*Typing*) Liza the . . . Let's see . . . Sorry. I don't have it in the system.

BYRON: I know she was using the site.

MISHA: It's common for people to use a burner email when they set up their account if they want to be anonymous.

BYRON: She's not some computer hacker, she's—

MISHA: Kids grow up with this stuff now. Point is, email is the best way to find her username, and I need her username to be able to look up anything.

BYRON: Maybe it's Lizathekidd for that too.

MISHA: (*Typing*) Nope. I've got a few Lizas, but if she's going to the trouble to anonymize, she's not likely to make her username include her actual first name. It's common in our community to pick the character you identify with the most. So I've got like eight thousand usernames that start with Ciara . . . but if you think there's another character she might vibe with, that could help.

BYRON: None of her drawings were of her, they were all other people as the book characters. And I don't know the characters all that well anyway.

MISHA: Don't you think you *should,* since your whole theory seems to hinge on the books being involved in her disappearance?

BYRON: I know the basics, OK? And I've tried to read the books for anything that could be a clue. I've got Liza's copies here with me in L.A. . . . but every time I open them, I just picture her reading them over and over, and think about what happened, and—is there a word for an angry version of a panic attack?

MISHA: OK, well, maybe we can figure this out together. It's like Guess Who of the Hidden World. The Fairies are members of

Enclaves—sort of like different tribes—so we can narrow down which one she'd be part of if we just know . . . what was she like?

BYRON: I mean, she was . . . a twelve-year-old girl.

MISHA: Having been a weird one myself, I can assure you that category is not particularly uniform.

BYRON: She was imaginative. She loved reading. Not just the Fairy Tale books. Older fantasy stuff like Tolkien. *Dracula,* even. She loved *Dracula,* it got her on this whole horror kick. She tried the scary-story stuff they had at the book fair, but that wasn't doing it, so she started branching out on her own. I wasn't thrilled about any of it, but Val kept pointing out that at least she's reading. She even read *The Shining* at one point. We wouldn't let her read that stuff, but she got it on her e-reader. (*Chuckles*) We only found out because when she couldn't sleep she came into our room in the middle of the night, woke us up crying, afraid some woman was gonna crawl out of her bathtub.

MISHA: OK, so, I like her already, and I'm guessing she's a little bit . . . dark?

BYRON: For her age, maybe. But she's also kind, and sweet.

MISHA: I'm not judging, I'm just trying to get a read on her. She was probably drawn to the Violet Enclave—they're the darkest fairies. Anything else we can go on? Was she, like . . . adventurous? Risk-taking?

BYRON: She was . . . not very popular, at school. She got teased, sometimes. Which is brutal, being the parent . . . wanting to go in there and yell at the other twelve-year-old girls who have no idea how much power they have. But Liza told us not to worry. That was her, taking care of *us.* She said she was just . . . still looking for her people.

MISHA: That's pretty vague . . . was there any character she wanted to cosplay as?

BYRON: Yes! She wanted money for . . . I dunno. A costume. Wings. Four wings, like a dragonfly?

MISHA: That narrows it down to all the *fae* characters, of which there are about a hundred.

BYRON: You know . . . there were these photos I found of her, with crazy makeup on her face. Lots of glitter, and red swirls on her cheeks, and the design was . . . like they were thorny vines or something.

MISHA: Ohmygod, of course! Flutterseek!

BYRON: Flutter . . .

MISHA: It makes total sense. Flutterseek is the one fairy that isn't part of *any* enclave, that got left out of the Choosing. Those markings are a birthmark because she's Rose-born. She's a pretty minor character and not super popular because she doesn't participate in any of the big battles or court intrigue, but she helps out Ciara in Book Three. She's dark, she's lonely, she's a bitter introvert. . . .

BYRON: I didn't say Liza was *bitter*. . . .

MISHA: Trust me, she's more bitter than you realize, if she's getting excluded like that at school. (*Typing*) Flutterseek . . . I've got seventy-two usernames. So . . . birthday?

BYRON: November eighth, 2010.

MISHA: (*Typing*) Uh . . . Sorry. No eleven-eight. Is there any other, like, number combination that would mean something to her? Probably four digits.

BYRON: Four digits . . .

MISHA: Besides birthdays, could be . . . pin number? Favorite integer sequence?

BYRON: She doesn't have a bank account. And a what-now?

MISHA: Or street address maybe? Of your house?

BYRON: . . . Our *old* house! She used to love our old house—it was *tiny,* but there was this hidden room under the stairs she used to crawl into and read. And when we lived there, Val and I were . . . things were easier, so . . . Liza threw a tantrum when we moved. Hated the new place, even though it was twice the size. The street number . . . it was 1216. Try that?

MISHA: (*Typing*) I've got . . . Flutterseek1216! Active member since December of 2020. Most recent activity was . . . March twentieth.

BYRON: . . . It's her.

BIO OF USER "FLUTTERSEEK1216"

From the Archives of TheQueendom.com

ABOUT ME: Scorpio who loves curly fries, horseback riding, villains in books, nice people in real life, my pupper Greta, good music from the 90s, and hoodies.

FAVORITE FT BOOK: Book 5 which is the one that gets the most real. I like that Ciara can be angry and not have to say sorry for it every time. I don't like it when Áine gets her wings cut but also I am hopeful they will be healed in Book 6.

WHO YOU'RE SHIPPING: Ciara and the Doggerdoth LOL

FAVORITE NON-FT BOOK: As usual right now it is the one I am CURRENTLY reading which is Mistborn by Brandon Sanderson, it is very long though.

QUOTE: "Don't tell me I'm lost when you don't even know where I'm going. And I know you don't know because I don't know either. So how could I ever be lost?"

RESUME INTERVIEW TRANSCRIPT

MISHA: Looks like she also posted some OC on here, but it's all been deleted.

BYRON: OC, meaning . . .

MISHA: Stories she wrote. Fan-fic using Annabelle's characters and world. I can see the titles in the metadata: "Gloverbeck's Gambit," "Flight of the Faun," "The Missing Doggerdoth." There were a bunch of them.

BYRON: What the hell's a Doggerdoth?

MISHA: A chimera creature. Part lion, part squid, part elephant, and a bunch more. Very powerful. Seems like this awful monster when Ciara meets it, but it becomes an ally to Ciara when she's kind to it. Which is why a lot of the fan-fic uses it as a character.

BYRON: Liza never mentioned that she was writing stories . . . can I read them?

MISHA: Sorry, she erased them all. Around the beginning of the year, it looks like.

BYRON: That was . . . she was getting bullied online by a girl from school around then. Mocking her for something, I never knew exactly what.

MISHA: I'd guess that someone found her stories and posted screen-shots. If there was anything embarrassing in there—I mean, of course there was, it was fan-fic by a twelve-year-old girl, so—it's sad, but not super shocking that she took it all down.

BYRON: What about the chats . . . these are conversations she had on here?

MISHA: Looks like there's a few people she talked to, mostly short one-offs. But there's one user—Voice of the Hidden World—she talked to pretty regularly.

BYRON: What'd she say?

MISHA: She deleted the transcripts of those too. The chats are logged, they went on for hours, but they're all empty now. . . . Well, except for the last one, here. She was probably in the habit of deleting regularly, but never got around to this one.

BYRON: Open it.

MISHA: I'd prefer not to, unless there's—

BYRON: March twentieth. That's the day she disappeared. Open it.

EXCERPT FROM DIRECT-MESSAGE USER CHAT

From the Archives of TheQueendom.com

USERNAME: FLUTTERSEEK1216   USERNAME: VOICEOFTHEHIDDENWORLD

                                                          Hi.

Hey! OK so what's your question today?

                                       Let's see. How about . . .
                                       Do you believe in fairy tales?

Lol you mean like for-real believe?
I dunno. I'm open.
Do you?

                                                  Of course.
                                   Most of my friends are fairies.
                                   And they tell me lots of tales.

Riiiiight lol.

Ok what are your favorites?

"Flight of the Faun" was good.

Omg no my stories were so cringe.

I quit doing that, I'm not a writer.

I can't even believe you remember it.

It was unforgettable.

Some of the best writing I've ever seen from a mortal.

Haha thx for the weirdest complement ever

I'm a big fan.

But I'm an even bigger fan of the ones you haven't even written yet.

The ones in the dreams you've dreamed.

And the ones in your dreams still to come.

Lol ok even weirder complement now

I'm a weird one.

It's OK. I like that.

Must be why we get along so well.

So what are you up to 2nite?

Traveling.

To and fro.

Heading back to the Hidden World soon.

Lol ok send me a postcard;)

Do you want to see it some time?

Of course.

I'll show you how to get there.

Yeah right.
You're messing with me.
Right?

I can't tell you what to believe.
But if you believe, I can show you the way.

For real?

For real.
In your dreams.

I've had plenty of dreams about it already.

No, I mean I'll show you in your dreams.
So you can go for real.
Just open your mind and invite me in.

You read my stories thats kinda the same thing.
Besides how do I know I can trust you.

You never know you can trust anyone.
You leap, and the universe catches you.
Or if not the universe, a magical friend.

You're saying you have magical powers or something.

Or something.
Where I come from there's nothing that special about them.

OK prove it. Do something magic.

I am. I'm talking to you.

I bet your full of crap.
Its ok you don't have to be magic I still talk to you.

Why don't you write something down on a piece of paper.

And I'll tell you what you wrote.

OK what did I write?

You wrote "I bet you can't read this."

Now you're kinda freaking me out.

Don't be scared.

It's only magic.

Let's try another.

Yeah.

You wrote "Are you watching me?"

But I would never do that.

I'm looking through your eyes.

This is wild.

I'm going in my closet to make sure you're not watching somehow.

OK how bout now?

You wrote "I really do want to believe you."

Whoa.

OK but like I still don't even know your name.

I have so many.

Some that are hard to pronounce.

Some that are dangerous to say.

Some that are forbidden to mortal tongues.

But you can just call me . . .

G.

Hi G. I'm Liza.

I know, Liza.

Are you ready to leave your world behind?

RESUME TRANSCRIPT OF RECORDED INTERVIEW

MISHA: What . . . the actual *fuck*?

BYRON: We found him.

MISHA: I'm so sorry . . . I had no idea there were . . . that any of this was happening on the site, that it was being used for . . .

BYRON: This is it. This is the person who lured her into running away from home.

MISHA: OK, but . . . I mean, how is he seeing what she's writing? This part here—he guesses it correctly.

BYRON: I don't know. Spying on her?

MISHA: In her closet?

BYRON: It's suggestion. The way hypnotists work, or a Ouija board. She wants to believe him, so . . . she's playing along.

MISHA: I don't think you really believe that.

BYRON: Then what do *you* think it is? Magic? Fairies?

MISHA: I think . . . We should give this to the police.

BYRON: Right. Eventually, yes, absolutely.

MISHA: *Eventually?*

BYRON: If the police get this . . . what are they gonna do?

MISHA: I mean . . . investigate!

BYRON: I've been dealing with the police, and they've been worthless. It's a cold case in their minds. Best-case scenario, they'll *eventually* track this back to the person it belongs to. Which *we* can do ourselves. You have data on this "Voice of the Hidden World" user, yes?

MISHA: (*Typing*) Their bio is blank. Email address—look, it's random letters and numbers, probably a burner too. So . . . all I have for the user is an IP address.

BYRON: Which is connected to a *real* address. Right? I've done this for a story before, it's easy. Here . . .

(*Typing*)

MISHA: Wow, yeah. 2415 Creosote Lane.

BYRON: It's in L.A. Not too far from here, right? What's that, ten miles away?

MISHA: Fancy area. That's the Hollywood Hills, right up off Bronson Canyon. Those places are *amazing*. Now we just gotta figure out who lives there.

BYRON: Come on, Misha. Who do we know that lives in an "amazing" home in the Hollywood Hills?

MISHA: You seriously think . . . ?

BYRON: Yes. I seriously think . . . *it's her.*

CHAPTER ELEVEN

EMAIL

From: bkidd@gmail.com
To: Valeriekidd@sltpartners.com

Hi Val,

Wanted to update you on my progress here. I did get access to the data I was looking for, and as a result, I turned a corner. Now, I have a meaningful and specific lead, creating a direct and verifiable connection between Annabelle Tobin and what happened to Liza. There's a lot that still doesn't make sense with this case, but the facts are starting to emerge, and I will not rest until we know what happened . . . which, I can only hope, might have the chance of bringing Liza back and restoring our family.

I know this has been incredibly painful, and the text you sent me came out of that pain. I know the ache of her absence is unbearable, and even more pointed is the twinge of guilt, the fear that we failed her. We were the authors of the story of her life, and we let the plot twist in a terrible way she never deserved before she could get hold of the narrative herself. But today, I feel empowered. To rewrite what went wrong and get the story back on track.

REPLY

Byron,

My personal emotional work has been going well, but every time I hear from you, it sends me into a spiral.

What can I say to you? Let me be a mirror and reflect a few things. When you went out to Los Angeles, it was for an article. A story. Now it's a "case," as though you were in a Raymond Chandler plot. If, God willing, Liza is ever going to return to us, it will not be the result of banging down the door of her favorite children's book author. It will not be the result of anything that WE have done at all.

In my sessions recently I've been re-examining my role as a parent, and I take exception to your analogy. We were never the AUTHORS of Liza's life. Do you honestly think you determined who she was or what she did? Do you think it's because of us that she was fixated on Ancient Egypt and the terra-cotta soldiers in China? We'd never even heard of those. And her kindness and generosity were all her own. When that Amelia girl broke Liza's thumb in PE, you wanted to murder her, and I was ready to sue her parents. But Liza forgave her and was the only one who showed up for her birthday party.

From the day I started nursing, Liza made it clear she wasn't about to let anyone tell her what to do. You taught her to read, sure, and it was beautiful, but only because the love of reading was already inside her. Remember when you tried to get her into basketball? Remember when I tried to get her to eat sushi? Everyone who said how sweet and quiet Liza was hadn't seen her when she was pushed to do something she didn't want to.

My point is, we didn't *make* her. We *met* her. We were never writing her story, we were READING it. And yes, it took a sudden tragic turn at the end, and no, I don't expect that I'll ever recover.

But I'm doing my best. And escaping into a fantasy of getting her back is no way to cope.

Warmly,
Val

INVESTIGATIVE JOURNAL OF BYRON KIDD

October 28

Just the facts: The night before Liza disappeared she talked to someone on the computer. Someone who wouldn't reveal their identity. Someone intimately familiar with the Fairy Tale stories. That someone lives in the Hollywood Hills.

I can see the Hollywood Hills from my motel. The lights glittering at night. Decadent ~~palaces~~ homes looking down on the city below. ~~Olympian gods lording their status over the teeming mass of humanity down below.~~ It's a series of canyons that the ordinary folk can intrude upon only in designated areas for hikes and picnics. Another illusion—this one of divine superiority over the mundane losers down below.

And that's where Annabelle Tobin lives. Of course.

It's her. I'm sure it's her. Question is why. What is she getting out of luring kids away from home? She has all the money in the world. Has her own child. Has everything to lose. Doesn't make sense.

Doesn't matter. Fuck why. I need to stop her. Need to get her to lead me to Liza.

But first I need to confirm. Need to get her on tape. Need to bring the police a mountain of actionable evidence. Need to get fact-checkable, on-the-record, undeniable PROOF that she's not only connected but RESPONSIBLE.

I don't even know for certain that it's her address. And Annabelle is being evasive, won't agree to a second interview. Need a new line of attack. Need someone who can help me get to her.

INTERVIEW WITH TOM CALDWELL

October 28, 4:45 P.M.

Location: Met poolside in the backyard of his Hancock Park home. Traditional English garden with hedges trimmed into irreverent shapes—exclamation mark, hand giving the middle finger, etc. Workers still cleaning the detritus of a recent party out of the pool when I arrived.

Subject: Ex-husband of Annabelle Tobin. British. Mid-40s. Stubble-beard. Work boots and designer jeans. Oxford worn open halfway down his chest, with numerous necklaces and expensive sunglasses. Egomaniac with an inferiority complex.

TRANSCRIPT OF RECORDED INTERVIEW

TOM: Annabelle and I . . . we had this connection right away. I came in on the second movie, *Bridge of Dreams,* when they wanted to take the tone in a slightly edgier direction. I was skeptical at first, I've seen how this goes. You make a cool little horror movie, and then you get brought up to the majors to direct a franchise picture, and it has the potential to just erase any shred of creativity you ever had. Plus I knew Annabelle wanted to be involved on the screenplay, and I did, too, and I was worried that would just be a disaster. But I needed some real money, and I didn't want to go back to directing commercials, so I said fuck it, let's go make a kids' movie.

It started as a bit of a one-for-them job, so I could get to the next one for myself. But then I met Annabelle and there was instantly this . . . *spark.*

BYRON: You two started dating immediately?

TOM: Yeah. There was no pretense of a professional relationship separate from a personal one. They were, literally from day one, intertwined.

BYRON: You began work on this movie in 2013 . . . this would've been while you were still married to Bridget Ley?

TOM: It was . . . I don't remember exactly *when* Annabelle and I hooked up, but . . .

BYRON: It was while you were still married.

TOM: I think we were separated then, but . . . sorry, can we leave this bit out? It's old history.

BYRON: Just trying to get the facts straight.

TOM: Sure, sure, but you can decide which facts matter, and—look, my son's gonna read this someday. You'd understand if—do you have kids?

BYRON: A daughter. But I have nothing to hide from her. I believe in brutal honesty.

TOM: Good for you, mate, but I don't believe in brutal *anything*.

BYRON: I'll write around your little "overlap" as long as you help me understand it all. Including the timeline, all right? When you and Annabelle started your relationship—you were working together and became romantically involved pretty fast, and within six months, you were living together?

TOM: Yeah, right away, we bought a house in the Hills.

BYRON: This is the one at . . . 2415 Creosote Lane?

TOM: Exactly. Loved that house. 'Course, it's all hers now, and—Hang on, how'd you get the address? Annabelle doesn't give that out to *anyone*.

BYRON: Oh, she wanted me to see where she writes.

TOM: Guess she's getting a little less paranoid. Beautiful place, isn't it?

BYRON: Incredible.

TOM: That year when we first moved in was a dream come true. Our whole life honestly felt like a fairy tale that Annabelle was magically summoning out of her pen, and I was happy to come along for the ride.

Most days, she was on set with me, and while I'm shooting *Bridge*, she's in her trailer writing Book Four, *The Crystal Palace*. We're both pitching each other ideas and putting them in. Really creatively fertile time for both of us. Making a book, and a movie—and, it turned out, a human. Gable was born just a few months after Book Four came out, and that one was a hit on a whole other level. Midnight release parties, instant bestseller. And then the second film came out, and it was a total smash. Good reviews, bananas box office, I made a deal for movies three and four together back-to-back, which *never* happens. Everything was happening all at once, and I loved it.

BYRON: Did you start to feel some ownership over Fairy Tale?

TOM: Ya know . . . I did. The books were hers, but I felt like I was having a role in shaping and sharing them with the world. Which . . . yeah, that made me feel like I might have some leeway to start making a few more creative choices. Little things, mostly. Some of it I was just trying to create a more grounded set of rules for how it all works.

BYRON: For example . . . ?

TOM: OK, in the books, when Ciara travels into the Hidden World, she gets there a different way every time. But I thought we should make it consistent, and stick to the Wishing Well that's established in the first one. Have it magically appear in different places with each new film.

Of course, we tweaked the Wishing Well from the first movie, since that one looked like dogshit. The first movie was an overload of mediocre CG, but I love doing as much as possible with old-school practical effects, so we built the well as a large prop, which felt much more believable and lived-in. Everyone was obsessed with seeing it on the studio tour. They had so many fans breaking in after hours they had to get rid of a bunch of that stuff. Sold it all in an auction. Which I didn't see a penny of, by the way, even though I designed half the bloody stuff.

But anyway—the way the Wishing Well was handled, Annabelle was pissed about it. Said the rules of our world don't apply to the Hidden World. The studio backed me on that one and we used it in all the movies, but . . . my point is, she's very protective of what she's built.

BYRON: Do you think she believes in the fictional world she's created?

TOM: I think . . . for Annabelle . . . I don't know how to say this exactly. The thing that made her so attractive to me as a creative partner was the same thing that later became such a problem. Her work is all-consuming. She disappears into it completely. And at first, it was a real joy to disappear with her. It was like getting sucked into the Hidden World yourself.

BYRON: I guess what I'm wondering is . . . does she literally believe it exists?

TOM: I don't think she "literally" believes *anything* . . . but then literally believes *everything* at the same time. She believes in fate and wishes and dreams and miracles. She believes in astrology, tai chi, tarot cards. But it's like . . . she believes those things exist only if you believe in them too. Does that make sense?

BYRON: Not one bit.

TOM: Maybe it's an artist thing, mate. Made sense to me. Even though it made us fight like hell. "Creative differences" is the preferred term. (*Laughs*)

BYRON: And those differences led to the discord in your marriage?

TOM: Some of it, yeah. She said things that were very dismissive of my work. This one time, she said she had created a whole world, and I was just there to photograph it. Please. But there were other issues too. I'm sure you saw the tabloids.

BYRON: You started another relationship. With an actress who was originally cast to appear in movie four in the role of the Wind-Witch.

TOM: Yeah. I don't mean to excuse my behavior on that one, I was being a bit laddish, but to be fair, Annabelle had become a complete . . . had become difficult to connect with, shall we say. She was a great mom, she was a great novelist, but there was no time for me. While I was shooting *The Forgotten Abyss,* she took Gable off to some remote spot in Ireland. I was lonely, and I had a bit of a lapse in judgment. I do regret it, and I apologized, but Annabelle was . . . unforgiving, to say the least. Hell hath no fury, right?

BYRON: She said in an interview, "He can have the witch. Everything else is mine."

TOM: (*Chuckles*) Oh boy, yeah . . . put me through the fuckin' ringer on that one. Worst divorce of my life.

BYRON: In the proceedings, Annabelle got majority custody of your son. But two years ago, you sued to try to obtain full custody for yourself. Can you comment on that?

TOM: Absolutely. I want to say for the record, all I want is what's best for my son. I understand why the custody decision went so strongly in her favor at first. But the situation has changed. We've all changed since then. I've grown immensely. Annabelle . . . she's not the same. But the thing that keeps me up at night is how Gable has changed.

BYRON: What do you mean?

TOM: Well . . . It was like his personality altered overnight. Couple years ago. This wasn't puberty; he was only seven at the time. One day he's a happy kid, active and imaginative and funny and outgoing . . .

then all of a sudden, he's sullen and withdrawn. Doesn't really engage. Like he's lost in his own world. And there was an incident at school. Last year. A disagreement with another kid, and . . . it escalated.

BYRON: Gable was violent?

TOM: Only in self-defense. He was getting bullied!

BYRON: Do you think the incident caused the change in him?

TOM: Other way around. His personality shifted first, and that's when he started getting bullied. Kids calling him "spaz," picking on him, stuff like that. He stopped engaging with anyone. And this other kid was pushing his buttons one day, and Gable just . . . snapped. He bit the kid, on the hand.

Personally, I feel like it got blown out of proportion, but the kid did need stitches, and you know how it is with L.A. parents. They sued and threatened to make it a whole thing with the tabloids so . . . Annabelle and I both shelled out for that one. And Annabelle pulled him out after that, started homeschooling him herself.

Naturally, I wanted to know what was going on with him. Psychologically, or whatever. But Annabelle refused to have him evaluated. She's still evasive about the whole thing. And I see him so little, every other weekend. I try to enjoy the time I have with him, but . . . the kid is suffering, and it kills me.

BYRON: What do you attribute the change to?

TOM: I'm no shrink, but it sounds like a textbook reaction to trauma.

BYRON: You think Annabelle might have been . . .

TOM: I'm not accusing anyone of anything. But Gable's mum is the biggest author on the planet. She's had more than a few stalkers and obsessives. Became reclusive and paranoid . . . I just don't think it's a safe environment, emotionally. I went over to pick him up last month, he wasn't in the house. Annabelle says, oh yes, well, it's 6:30, so he's taking his hike down to the Batcave. Like that's a perfectly normal thing for a nine-year-old kid to do every evening as it's getting dark.

BYRON: Sorry, the Batcave?

TOM: Right, you're from out of town. There's these caves over there, maybe a couple miles from the house—the Bronson Caves. It's a popular spot because they've been used as a location in so many different films. I actually shot there on *Valley of Shadows*. The scene when Ciara tries to get home through the Crossing Cave, we're using the Batcave, plussed up with a little CG of course.

Anyway, Annabelle tells me Gable is hiking down there, does so every day at 6:00. And why's she letting him wander off like that? There's mountain lions in the hills, not to mention whatever weirdos might be on the trail. She tells me to come back later, but I wait around, and finally he returns, coming out of the woods, and I'm telling you he is *filthy*, scratched-up all over, bleeding from his forehead. He won't say one word about the whole thing, and Annabelle acts like it's no big deal!

BYRON: Why do you think he does that?

TOM: No. Fucking. Idea. (*Sighs*) Honestly . . . I just want my son back.

BYRON: Yeah . . . I can imagine. (*Clears throat*) Truth be told, I think this article might be helpful in that direction.

TOM: How do you mean?

BYRON: Look, this is off the record, just one father to another . . . I think it's horseshit the way you've been railroaded here and the way Annabelle is worshipped. My article is not going to flatter her like everything else that's come out.

TOM: I appreciate that.

BYRON: I've seen this type of thing before. As soon as the article is published, it'll be a breeze for you to file for more custody. Maybe full, depending on what comes out.

TOM: What's your timeline here? How soon will you publish?

BYRON: Hard to say. I really need to get Annabelle to agree to talk to me again. Until I get a follow-up interview, my editor will never move on this. So—listen, it's not your job, but if you can help nudge that along, it would really move things forward.

TOM: I'd love to, mate, but I'm the last person in the world Annabelle's gonna be taking advice from.

BYRON: Of course, not if you come right out and say it. But maybe just . . . let her know that we spoke. Don't be threatening, just tell her that you've shared your side of the story with me—which includes the part about her withholding custody. She'll realize what's at stake for her, and she'll want to head off any perception that could go against her. I'll bet the article is back on track within the week. More important, she'll try to reverse the damage to her reputation—and I'll bet she'll become more amenable to sharing custody overnight.

EMAIL

> From: a.q.tobin@gmail.com
> To: bybyronjames@gmail.com

> Byron,

> Hope that you're well. I shudder to think of what you might write based only on our first conversation, and on my ex-husband's unbalanced, likely unhinged, account of things. But after speaking with him, I realize I may have been a bit unduly sensitive in our first meeting. Perhaps we can resume our conversation and clear the air.

> A.T.

REPLY

Hi Annabelle,

Sounds good. If you're comfortable with it, I'd love to visit your home and see where you write from. It could add significant color and texture to the article. No need for pictures or any other details that would compromise your privacy, but I want readers to feel transported into your world, and I can think of no better avenue to achieve that.

Best,
Byron

CHAPTER TWELVE

INTERVIEW WITH ANNABELLE TOBIN #2

October 29, 10:14 A.M.

Subject: At home, Annabelle seems more at ease than when I first met her, but her projected confidence feels a bit put on. Her wardrobe (vintage Rolling Stones T-shirt and jeans) and her hair (pulled back, tousled) indicate a more casual person than I believe she is, and I get the sense she tried out several variations of this look before I arrived.

Location: Annabelle's home, which, it has been impressed upon me, has never been visited by a journalist. I was told not to trust Google Maps, as the front gate is accessible only by roads that are deliberately excluded from such services.

The house is nestled in an inlet of Beachwood Canyon, a small, elite residential enclave adjoining the wider, more popular Bronson Canyon. For a century, Beachwood has been home to celebrities seeking proximity to the city coupled with privacy from it; Charlie Chaplin kept a place there for his mistresses. It makes perfect sense as both the location Annabelle moved to when her star rose and the place she's remained while retreating into obscurity.

It was an unseasonably gloomy day as I drove in, and fog hung in the hills, making it hard to navigate the twisty roads, which were light on

street signs and heavy on switchbacks. I proceeded off the main stretch
up two miles of one-lane road, wondering if I'd gotten lost before I
started to ascend the backside of a hill. Near the crest, I saw an imposing iron gate. I pulled up, searching for a call box, but the gate merely
swung open; I clocked a security camera watching me.

The house is built in the 1920s Old Hollywood mode, with a mix of
ranch-style Spanish influence and Art Deco flourishes. Feels like it's
been transported from a bygone era.

Annabelle let me inside and provided me with a tour that, no doubt,
was meant to feel comprehensive, but it was clearly uncomfortable for
her to have someone in her house. Built into the hillside, the house has
four levels, connected by several narrow wooden staircases. Annabelle
explained that its construction had originally been commissioned by an
oil magnate, who had passed it on to a film producer, upon whose death
it sat unoccupied and in disrepair for several years before she took it
over and fixed it up.

The decor is sparse, as though she hadn't bothered to refurnish after
her divorce emptied the house of half its contents. She took me through
the kitchen and dining room, which looked rarely used. She gestured
vaguely up a staircase, explaining that entire wing of the house belonged to her son, and since we agreed he was off-limits, we wouldn't be
going that way. I lingered for a moment, listening, and heard ~~a strange
sound like the labored breathing of some creature~~ heavy breathing,
which left me wondering what the young boy might get up to with such
a large space to himself.

The backyard is a terraced landscape, no lawn, all natural, with
vines and trees. One level is flat enough for a long swimming pool, but
it's been abandoned to the elements. A tall iron fence surrounds the
property, beyond which is the scrubby-pine wilderness of the Hollywood Hills.

We eventually came to her office, which is absurdly high-security.
Annabelle had a key for the handle, and there was also a high-tech bio-
metric pad that used her thumb to magnetically unlock the door. Inside, the space was sprawling, with the look and feel of an old Victorian

library, complete with tower shelves and sliding ladders. A massive writing desk was decorated with an antique globe and an astrolabe.

As we started the interview, Annabelle allowed me to peruse her collection of books while lingering over my shoulder.

TRANSCRIPT OF RECORDED INTERVIEW

BYRON: Wow. First-edition Gatsby. That's gotta be pricey.

ANNABELLE: I understand what you're doing. Trying to connect, so I'll open up.

BYRON: You got me. Busted for basic human decency. But I'm genuinely interested. What's your prized possession here?

ANNABELLE: Oh, that's like asking a mother to pick a favorite child, but . . . this one is quite special. The original print run of *The Wizard of Oz*. Look at those illustrations. . . .

BYRON: Beautiful. The story of a teenage girl who gets magically whisked off to another world . . . you're lucky he didn't come after you for ripping him off.

ANNABELLE: Lucky that he's dead, and it's public domain.

BYRON: So where are all the copies of *The Hidden World*?

ANNABELLE: Hidden, of course.

BYRON: In another library?

ANNABELLE: Another world, perhaps.

BYRON: Is that where Book Six is too?

ANNABELLE: That's where all the books begin. Writing them is more like a process of discovery than one of invention.

BYRON: So you're like Michelangelo, finding your *David* in the marble.

ANNABELLE: Don't bait me into grandiosity. I found something far bigger than myself, and have done my best to excavate it with care.

BYRON: Seems like Book Six has taken a lot longer to find than the others.

ANNABELLE: I've had to take my time, to get everything right. This is my legacy, you realize. The way I'll be remembered.

BYRON: What about your son?

ANNABELLE: We're not talking about my son.

BYRON: Sorry, I just mean . . . legacy. How you're remembered. Doesn't parenthood change your perspective on that?

ANNABELLE: If anything, being a mother only increased my desire to make the final book *perfect*. I'm sure you've experienced some of that with your own career. We all want our kids to be proud of us.

BYRON: Of course, but . . . I dunno, it all starts to matter a little less, doesn't it?

ANNABELLE: Not to me. There are *billions* of women who can have babies and raise them reasonably well. Do you know how few people can do what I've done, and am still doing, with this series? I'm sure I sound dreadfully vain, but I find false modesty to be so irritating. I chose *you* to tell my story because I hoped you might understand that and not fall into the male-writer trap of subtly shaming me for my ambition.

BYRON: I get ambition. In my twenties, I went charging into my career, determined to prove myself. It's embarrassing how much I needed the whole world to know I was a genius. But after Liza was born . . . the way *she* looked at me . . . I was everything to her, and she didn't care about journalism awards, or reputation, or my job title. She cared about whether I was there to roll the ball back to her a hundred times in a row.

ANNABELLE: That's very sweet. And yet here you are, far from home, desperately chasing a big story. And a glance at the list of stories you've reported in the last decade does not suggest you've done a lot of ball-rolling. It's nothing to be ashamed of. I'm sure you started parenthood full of epiphanies and selfless intentions. But over the years, that initial rush of purpose . . . it wears off. You cannot be anyone but who you are.

BYRON: Maybe. But I'm trying to get back to what matters.

ANNABELLE: There's nothing wrong with chasing greatness, Byron. Even though our world of self-accepting mediocrity would have you believe otherwise.

BYRON: So that's why Book Six has taken you so long? The quest for greatness?

ANNABELLE: Exactly. And now, finally . . . I'm almost there.

BYRON: But it won't be the first time you've finished the book, will it? I found some of your tweets about it from a couple years ago. They've been deleted, but a friend had them in her archive.

TWITTER POSTS

@RealAnnabelleT
Fairy fans, thank you for your patience. It will be rewarded soon . . . #BookSix #FairyTale

@RealAnnabelleT
You know the opening scene in Misery where he finishes his book and has a single cigarette and a glass of champagne? Well I don't smoke, but I'll be having that champagne very soon. #BookSix #AlmostFinished #Finally

@RealAnnabelleT
My sixfold series is a day away from being done. Only a few revisions to the manuscript remain. I'll be doing a livestream

to announce the completion and you can watch me send it to my editor tomorrow at 4PM PST. Should be in your hands by the holidays! #BookSix #FairyTale

RESUME INTERVIEW TRANSCRIPT

ANNABELLE: Yes, well . . . notice that this time, I'm staying off Twitter.

BYRON: I'm just wondering . . . what happened?

ANNABELLE: That draft was all wrong. After I read it, I had to start over.

BYRON: There's an odd word choice in that last tweet. "Sixfold."

ANNABELLE: I suppose, as a writer, I enjoy old-fashioned linguistic flourishes.

BYRON: It crops up in the *Hidden World* book, in one of the folktales. If you wouldn't mind taking a look, I'm curious . . . do you remember this story?

SHORT STORY

From *The Hidden World: On Faeries, Fauns & Other Creatures of Folklore,* by Sir Henry Raleigh. Published 1889, Oxford University Press.

THE SIXFOLD SUMMONING

This tale comes to my ears from the lips of the Visconte Marco Principella, proprietor of a vineyard in Calabria, and a nobleman well respected for his wisdom.

There once was an orphan boy named Lorenzo, a vagabond who wandered and scrounged to eat. In his hardship, Lorenzo turned to thievery and came to infamy as a brigand. He raided the town of Giovella and absconded with a sack of gold.

Living fugitive from the law, Lorenzo fled into the woods. For months, he could not show his face, or spend a single ducat of his fortune, for such was his notoriety that he knew he would be hanged if he were caught.

One day as he wandered the wood, Lorenzo chanced upon a spriggan. Since spriggans are despised by the farmers of Calabria, Lorenzo asked the creature how it managed to survive living in this wood. "I come and go," the spriggan said. "Whenever I need, I leave this world behind and return when it's safe."

Lorenzo was intrigued and demanded to know how the spriggan could accomplish such a feat. With a gleam in its eye, the spriggan beckoned him close and told him in confidence, "There is a spell that can open a door to the hidden world. *The Sixfold Summoning.*"

"I must know how this magic is accomplished!" Lorenzo demanded. But the spriggan refused, for such knowledge is forbidden to mortal men.

"I promise to keep the secret with my life," Lorenzo swore, but still the spriggan declined. The more he was refused, the more Lorenzo grew desperate. "If you share with me the secret of this magic, I will give you my entire fortune of gold!"

The spriggan's mischievous heart somersaulted with joy, for Lorenzo had fallen right into his trap. With a show of reluctance, the spriggan relented, drew a rune upon the ground, and instructed Lorenzo to mark the rune upon a tree of his choosing. "Show this mark to six people, and persuade them that the rune holds the power to open a door unto the hidden world. By the power of their belief, the door will appear."

Lorenzo set out to do as the spriggan instructed, but owing to his ungodly reputation, he knew it would be hard to find six good souls to hear him out, much less believe a tale as fantastical as that.

As he walked down the road, wondering who he might fool, he passed a farm and heard the shouts of children at play. He poked his head through the brush, and saw three boys and three girls, chasing each other through the fields. "What a fortunate discovery!" Lorenzo exclaimed.

He traipsed into the forest and made the mark the spriggan had shown him upon a tree. Then he returned to the field and whistled loudly, calling the children to his side.

"I'm looking for a magical tree with the power to open a door to the hidden world. And I'll pay a mighty reward to any who help me find one whose trunk bears this mark." Lorenzo showed them the rune, and the younger children were captivated.

But the eldest boy was skeptical. "There's no such thing as magic trees."

Lorenzo shrugged. "Very well then. I'll find another for this quest and for this gold as well." He casually showed them the sack overflowing with gold ducats. With their little eyes lit up with wonder, they went charging into the forest.

Moments later, Lorenzo heard cries of excitement and followed them to the very tree he had recently marked. The children were enchanted by the intoxicating combination of a story and the promise of gold. So when all six of them beheld the marked tree, all six believed with all their hearts the story Lorenzo had told. Thus the story was rendered true, and the tree's bark opened up with a door to another world.

"We found it!" exclaimed the children. "Now let's have our gold!"

Lorenzo, scoundrel that he was, had no intention to pay them, nor the spriggan to whom the same prize had also been promised. He laughed wickedly and ran for the door in the tree, aiming to escape into the hidden world.

But his way was blocked by another stepping forth from the

door. It was Striga, the fiery demon. For long ages had Striga been banished to the hidden world, hungering all the while for mortal flesh.

Lorenzo beseeched the demon to step aside. "I have rightly earned access to this passage and all that lies beyond."

"Indeed you have," Striga replied. "And here is your prize." Then her great clawed hand lashed out and grabbed Lorenzo. She tossed him into her gaping maw, and Lorenzo was swallowed whole.

"We are due a reward of gold!" the children exclaimed.

"Help yourself," Striga said, and she dumped Lorenzo's gold upon the ground. As the children lunged for it, the demon lashed out and grabbed them all with a single sweep of her mighty flaming arm. She gobbled them whole, and roared with delight.

Striga then set off toward the town of Giovella and would have gone on to eat many more mortals. But now that the six believers were gone, so too was the magic that had enabled her to step forth from the hidden world. Thus Striga was pulled back through the door, and it sealed shut behind her. Mercifully she has not since been seen.

Once she was gone, the spriggan dropped down from the trees, saw the carnage his mischief had caused, and was greatly delighted. He gathered up Lorenzo's gold coins and disappeared into the wood.

So by this tale are you warned, dear reader, to leave the hidden world be, and never trust a spriggan, and be most careful what stories you choose to believe.

RESUME INTERVIEW TRANSCRIPT

ANNABELLE: Quite a dark story. And a reminder that fairy tales are not only for children.

BYRON: I'm curious if it inspired you. The notion of a spell, in six parts . . . I wonder if there's a connection to your series of books. You could've written three of them, three being a much more common number in fairy tales. But you seemed to go for six.

ANNABELLE: Well, I had more story to tell than three books would allow. Twice as much, apparently.

BYRON: There's another parallel, with the missing children. Ciara disappears into another realm . . . and now, in real life, there have been kids—readers of your books—who have gone missing.

ANNABELLE: And you think maybe they're being gobbled up by Striga, the demon of rural Italian folk stories?

BYRON: No, it's just . . . You have voiced certain superstitious beliefs in the past. So with this story as part of the context—alongside the tweets, and the scrapping of the sixth book . . . I wonder at the connection.

ANNABELLE: And I wonder what you've been smoking.

BYRON: Let's take a look at the timing. I noticed that the day you sent that first tweet . . . those two girls ran away in Oakland. And the day of the last one—that was when that boy went missing in South Africa. Other stories started to pop up online too. That month was when the whole theory about the disappearances really took off. And by the end of the month, you deleted those tweets announcing that the book was finished. As far as I can tell, you scrapped that draft entirely.

ANNABELLE: Mmm. Is there a question in there?

BYRON: I'm just trying to establish some causality.

ANNABELLE: You think my tweets made two girls disappear in Oakland.

BYRON: No, no. It seems more likely that children were disappearing, and when you found out, you destroyed the novel you'd been working on for years. Perhaps connected to your feelings about this folktale . . . or a superstitious fear of finishing the sixth part.

ANNABELLE: If you have a point to make, get to it. Or an accusation?

BYRON: I'm not trying to make you look like a monster, Annabelle. Quite the opposite. I think the dots are there to be connected . . . and the line between them is actually your compassion. Did you feel bad about what was happening?

ANNABELLE: That would imply that I bore some responsibility, which is patently untrue.

BYRON: I understand you don't want to take any of it on yourself, but . . . did you feel bad for the parents? Who had lost children?

ANNABELLE: Of course I did! And I still do. You think I don't feel their pain? You think I don't know what it's like to lose a child?

BYRON: Do you?

ANNABELLE: Well . . . I'm not saying, exactly, that—

BYRON: You mean Gable. You feel like you've lost him?

ANNABELLE: . . . Sometimes, yes.

BYRON: Because of how he's changed.

ANNABELLE: Where'd you get that idea? From Tom?

BYRON: The change your son has gone through started around the same time, right? Two years ago.

ANNABELLE: You agreed—Gable is off-limits.

BYRON: I won't mention him in the article if you don't want me to. But I'm trying to understand *you*. A mother would do anything for her child.

ANNABELLE: What are you getting at?

BYRON: I'm trying to understand why you feel like you've *lost* him.

ANNABELLE: I'm saying . . . maybe it would be easier if he *was* gone, because people might see that *I'm* hurting too.

BYRON: You're hurting, because . . . ?

ANNABELLE: Listen, Byron, there are things I can't talk about, but . . . I want to try to make a few things . . . if not exactly clear, then at least *possible* for you to understand. How familiar are you with Shakespeare?

BYRON: Um . . . enough to graduate with an English degree, but that's about it. What does Shakespeare have to do with . . . any of this?

ANNABELLE: I'm not the first author to deal with magic and fairies and other worlds. And to look to them for inspiration. Shakespeare, his works were full of the fantastical.

BYRON: You're comparing yourself to Shakespeare now.

ANNABELLE: I'm not talking about talent. How do you even explain a genius like his? There are all manner of theories about how an ordinary country boy churned out the most densely beautiful stories in the English language, and at such a staggering rate. Some are classist conspiracies, some imagine a coterie of other creators. But Shakespeare practically told us how with *Midsummer Night's Dream*. A story of a magical world impinging upon the mortal one, insisting on their tales being told.

BYRON: Hang on, you're saying Shakespeare didn't just write *about* fairies, he was actually visited by them?

ANNABELLE: I'm only saying his works suggest as much. And it was not uncommon in his time to attribute inspiration to otherworldly sources.

Since you want to talk about timelines and causality, take a look at the history. *Midsummer* was written in 1595, finished early 1596. Within weeks of its completion, his son fell ill. Possibly plague. Possibly "sleeping sickness," it's written. But the source of the sickness was never determined.

BYRON: So . . . you think fairies killed William Shakespeare's son?

ANNABELLE: I'm not saying that, but—do you know what he wrote in *Comedy of Errors*, only a year later? "This is the fairy land, o spite of spites, We talk with goblins, owls, and sprites! If we obey them not, this will ensue: they'll suck our breath, and pinch us til we're black and blue."

BYRON: I'm not seeing how that's—

ANNABELLE: You're looking for connections, and I'm trying to help. Trying to expand your notion of what's possible.

BYRON: Let's come back to *your* timeline. What led to what and when.

ANNABELLE: Why don't you just get to what you really want to ask me?

BYRON: All right . . . (*Sighs*) March. How well do you remember it?

ANNABELLE: Well enough.

BYRON: Do you know where you were the night of March twentieth?

ANNABELLE: What kind of question is that?

BYRON: A straightforward one. Where were you, that night? At home?

ANNABELLE: Can you account for your whereabouts on a particular date seven months ago?

BYRON: If I had to, I could. Email, cell phone records . . .

ANNABELLE: Well . . . March twentieth, as it happens . . . I do know where I was. That's the vernal equinox, and I was in Stockholm during the vernal equinox. There's an environmental conference I'm on the board for, and I was in attendance. I even gave a talk that day.

BYRON: You have proof of this?

ANNABELLE: Let me see. I've asked that this not be posted online, but . . . yes, I can show you something on my phone, in fact . . .

EXCERPT FROM VIDEO TRANSCRIPT

Of Annabelle Tobin's Speech to the Society for Global Transformation

A. TOBIN: . . . And while I may be a fantasist, I am not deluded about the very real threat posed by man-made climate change. I am grateful for the possibility that great minds, like those gathered here today, might be able to save the world. Because there is not another one for us to escape to.

RESUME INTERVIEW TRANSCRIPT

ANNABELLE: Are you satisfied?

BYRON: I'm, uh . . . Yes. Thanks, that's very helpful.

ANNABELLE: With what? Feels like a rather aggressive line of questioning you began.

BYRON: My goal has always been to disprove the more outlandish allegations against you. And . . . this will help.

ANNABELLE: I get the sense you're not being completely honest with me, Byron.

BYRON: Likewise. Now, one last question. You say Book Six is almost complete.

ANNABELLE: Yes. Pages away.

BYRON: May I read it?

ANNABELLE: (*Laughs*) Oh, you're serious?

BYRON: It would be helpful for the article. And in proving the truth of your claim. I won't include any details you don't approve, I just need to know what's in it.

ANNABELLE: Tell you what, Byron. I'll let you sit here and read it right now. If you let me read through that notebook you carry around with you.

BYRON: That's . . . I can't do that. This is the story I'm writing.

ANNABELLE: And Book Six is the story *I'm* writing. One that many more people are clamoring to read. So why does yours—which is *about me*—deserve more secrecy?

BYRON: That's just . . . not my process.

ANNABELLE: Well, sharing a work-in-progress is contrary to *my* process. And I don't need *your* help in proving anything. I don't want to overstate the significance of anything here, but my book is going to change the world. Can you say the same about your little article?

BYRON: I don't . . . How do you imagine your book will change the world?

ANNABELLE: You'll see. Soon enough. Now . . . I think we're done here.

CHAPTER THIRTEEN

TEXT MESSAGE EXCHANGE

BYRON KIDD   MISHA PIMM

12:45 P.M.

It's not her.

                                                    You're sure?

Positive. She has a rock-solid alibi.
Video of her in Stockholm.
Recorded the same night the messages were sent to Liza.

                                                    Oh shit.
            But the address we tracked it to . . . that WAS Annabelle's house?

Yes. I did the interview there this morning.

                                                    Well shit.
                                    Guess it was a bit of a long shot.
                        Could be someone else was spoofing her IP address?
                        Or someone actually WENT there and logged on?

Those possibilities only make sense if someone is trying to frame her.
Question then is: who?

Could be a lot of people.

I know she's gotten death threats from fans.

People were PISSED she killed off Gloverbeck in Book Five.

I know people care about these books, but this is bigger than angry fandom.

Could be political maybe.

Right-wingers HATE Annabelle and would love nothing more than to take her down.

Her books don't seem political.

To a hammer, everything looks like a nail.

Check this out (LINK).

EXCERPT FROM LINKED ARTICLE

"The New Idolatry: False Gods and Pagan Revisionism in the World's Most Popular Children's Books," by Margaret Cannalin, published in *National Issues,* April 2017

. . . Since the popularity of the Fairy Tale books with young people has vastly outstripped the Bible in even the most Christian states of our Union, we ought to look critically at what, if any, spiritual beliefs might be promoted by the series. Many parents shrug off the books and films as harmless escapism, but that is how a truly insidious agenda has been smuggled into the minds and hearts of an entire generation.

How so? The Fairy Tale series presents an alternative spirituality, one that is pantheistic and essentially amoral. The books make occasional reference to the "ancient ones" who hold sway over the Hidden World where the fairies live. The laws of magic are ever-shifting, and if there is any single law that guides how they work, it is *belief.*

While that metaphysical notion may not *seem* particularly dangerous, it is the loose thread that could unravel the fabric of our entire society. Once an entire generation accepts that individual beliefs can re-shape reality, collective consciousness replaces higher authority. God is dead, the Constitution is meaningless, parents are irrelevant; *popularity* becomes the new and only coin of the realm. For a generation raised on likes and shares, it should come as no surprise that this notion holds such sway.

The primacy of belief is not a subtextual element of the books; Tobin makes explicitly clear that it is central to how her universe works. Queen Áine of the fey derives her magical abilities from the agreement of her subjects that she has said powers. The creature known as the "Doggerdoth" was brought into being by a story that faerie children started to believe as true.

The first three books of the series even make oblique reference to an all-pervasive "spirit" called the Green Man, who shapes the reality of the Hidden World. This "Green Man," while only a behind-the-scenes figure, is the actual name of an ancient Pagan god. Unsurprisingly, references to the figure were dropped entirely from the two most recent books, no doubt in an effort to conceal Tobin's true agenda.

The notion of belief as the cornerstone for a system of magic is certainly not unique to the Fairy Tale books, but Tobin has taken it beyond a cheap narrative device and turned it into a systematic and insidious attack on the cornerstones of our faith-based country. Divine authority, law and order, and any belief in objective truth are obliterated by the cosmology that Tobin presents.

It's important to note the significant way in which this inverts the paradigm of virtually every monotheistic faith. These systems presume that God exists, therefore we ought to believe in him, and act accordingly. Instead, Tobin's fantasy world is one where our belief summons various gods and magical beings into existence, placing human subjectivity at the center of the universe. There could scarcely be a more appealing cosmology for the most narcissistic generation in human history, nor could there be one more dangerous to the shared ideals that bind our society together.

There has been much debate about how Tobin's work fits into contemporary conversations about identity politics, race, sexuality and gender. But these miss the point. Tobin's true agenda is both more subtle and more treacherous: she is undermining our children's faith in a just God ruling over a sensible universe and replacing it instead with a postmodern disregard for truth in all its forms.

How, then, to combat this cultural travesty, in a political climate where the Left will scream about censorship at the slightest mention of curbing the books' availability to all ages? We need to go to the source: our children. We need to teach them the reasoning skills, beliefs and creeds that can challenge this nonsense. A child's mind can be warped and distorted, and these books are more dangerous than any videogame or social media star. We need to save our children's minds from the dangerous ideas of this abominable book series and its creator.

TEXT MESSAGE EXCHANGE

BYRON KIDD   MISHA PIMM

1:21 P.M.

Holy shit.

> I know right, this lady's off her fuckin rocker.

No no no, she's right.

> Uhhhhbout what?

"G." I get it now.

Green Man? You think that's what it stood for?

No. Children.

Kids CAN be dangerous. Twisted. Corrupted.

That's what you got from this article seriously?

Oohhhhhh fuck I get where you're going.

There IS another person who lives at Annabelle's house.

You really think it's HIM?

Only one way to find out.

INVESTIGATIVE JOURNAL OF BYRON KIDD

October 29, 2nd Entry

The events of the rest of the day have been baffling. Trying to understand, while the experience is still fresh. Needed half a glass (bourbon,
cheap) just to steady my nerves enough to confront this all—but I won't
touch another drop until I've gotten it down. ~~Any sense of certainty has
been shredded, and I'm~~

New Theory: Gable. Annabelle's son.

"G" for Gable, so simple. And the IP address. Could be possible that
this kid, tormented and isolated by the popularity of his mom's books,
started using her fictional world as a way, an excuse, to reach out, to
lure other kids. . . .

Hard to make sense of the timing—the disappearances started before Gable was even born. And the boy's age made it seem unlikely;
could a nine-year-old boy keep up an elaborate deception like the one
on the other end of the conversation Liza had on Queendom? I don't
know. But it's possible. The precocious son of an author, maybe so.

Toward what end? I don't know. Is he violent? Possibly. Psycho-
pathic? Can't say. ~~Some other sort of monster I never could've~~ I had to
find answers. Connections.

So for the second time in the same day, I drove to Annabelle's house. But as I crept up Creosote Lane, instead of turning down her imposing gated driveway, I continued up into the hills. I looped back along the one-lane access road that skirted the edge of Annabelle's property and parked, out of sight of the house. Then I hiked to a ridge, which looked down on her home, from 100 yards away.

I was aware I was crossing a line from reporter to stalker. I didn't care. I'd never been a reporter anyway, not really. I'm a dad. I'm here for Liza, and those distinctions mean nothing. ~~Trying to convince myself of that~~

I retrieved binoculars from the glove box and sat, watching the house. Might have seemed like a fool's errand, but I did have one thing to go on: Tom Caldwell's observation about Gable's behavior: every day at sunset he goes for a hike, down to the Bronson Caves, where Tom Caldwell shot scenes for the third film.

While I waited, I found the script for the film easily enough online and perused it on my phone, looking for clues as to what the meaning of those caves might be. . . .

SCRIPT EXCERPT

From FAIRY TALE: VALLEY OF SHADOWS, pages 77–78

TIGHT ON: Ciara's face, whipped by branches, as she CRASHES through the trees.

Pull back to REVEAL: Ciara rides the DOGGERDOTH through the Living Labyrinth. The untamable beast thunders across the ground before finally emerging into the light, as they come to:

EXT. THE CROSSING CAVE

The beast pulls to a halt, and Ciara nearly flies off. Then dismounts gracefully, patting the beast's neck.

                    CIARA
          You trying to kill me?

The Doggerdoth GRUMBLES in response.

The cave is a dark eye set in the stone of Amber
Mountain. A gate of GLEAMING-WHITE BONE frames the
entrance, with runic enchantments inscribed.

We hear the throbbing HUM of life from within. The
Doggerdoth WHIMPERS and backs away.

As Ciara approaches the entrance, a figure steps out
of the darkness: VERGIS, the stone troll (prod note:
full CG), 9 feet tall, with dark green skin, footlong
claws, and Tim Burton proportions. Voice dripping
with malice.

                    VERGIS
          Well, well, well. This is the child
          that the whole realm is a-titter
          about. How . . . underwhelming.

                    CIARA
          Vergis. I have no qualm with your
          kind. Step aside, I need not slay you.

Nonetheless, Ciara draws the RUBY SHARD. She means
business.

                    VERGIS
          And I'll have no need to feast on your
          entrails, if you turn back now.

                    CIARA
          If you know how badly I need to get
          home, then you should understand
          that I'm not going to do that.

                         VERGIS
          The Crossing Cave won't take you
          home. It is not what you think it is.

                         CIARA
          It's a gateway between worlds. Áine
          told me herself.

                         VERGIS
                    (shakes his head)
          It is a space that exists in *both*
          worlds. I can go inside and feed on
          children from your world that wander
          in. But I could never emerge into
          the mortal realm. Neither will you.

                         CIARA
          You're wrong. Because that is where
          I'm from. It's where I *belong*!

                         VERGIS
          Perhaps when you first came here you
          did, and you could've gotten home
          that way back then. Back when your
          heart belonged to the mortals. But
          you've stayed too long. You're one
          of us now, child.

                         CIARA
          No! My mother . . . she's dying.

                         VERGIS
          And she will die alone, wondering why
          her daughter abandoned her.

          Vergis LAUGHS wickedly.

                              CIARA

          Liar!

Ciara charges, the blade of the Ruby Shard FLASHING.
Vergis's claws extend. Purple troll blood SPATTERS
the bone-carved gates.

An epic duel for the ages ensues. Think the Bride
from *Kill Bill* taking on Grendel from *Beowulf*.

RESUME JOURNAL ENTRY

Why did a nine-year-old boy visit the caves every day? Trying to see a
troll? Attempting to be in "both worlds" at once? Or was it a way to connect with his parents' creation—the story his mother wrote, the location
his dad filmed to bring it to life?

Or maybe he was just a ~~creepy little fucker~~ troubled child, needing
to escape from a tense household.

As 6:00 approached, I put the script away and focused on the
house. There was still a layer of lingering fog, and the light was starting
to fade, long shadows stretching across the canyon. From my high
angle, it was hard to see much of the interior of the house. Occasionally caught glimpses of Annabelle, anxiously pacing inside.

Then 6:00, on the dot, exactly as predicted, a door slid open, and
Gable emerged from the back door. The boy is younger than Liza but
surprisingly tall and gangly for his age. He came out wearing black
slacks and a baggy white shirt, like a kid reluctantly dressed for church.
I felt a twinge of guilt at spying on a child but was also relieved that my
patience was rewarded.

He behaved strangely, staring off into the forest for what felt like
ages. He never had a phone or tablet that I could see, which alone was
enough to make the behavior feel odd for a kid his age. Eventually, he
stepped across the yard, to the edge of the wilderness. Then he took

off his shoes and socks. He left them in a neat pile in the yard and set off into the forest, quickly disappearing, his silhouette melting into the fog ~~like a vanishing ghost~~.

Perfect. He had left behind Annabelle's property. He was traipsing through unimproved wilderness now, but I knew where he was heading, and as soon as he joined a public hiking trail, I could approach him. These were rationalizations, of course, but they were enough for me.

I hurried into the trees so my path would intersect with his. Not wanting to startle him—not wanting to be seen either—I walked as quietly as I could, avoiding leaves and sticking to the dirt and roots. I was able to move quickly downhill but did my best to keep hidden. At the bottom of the hill, I looked around, unsure if I'd lost him. I saw the boy's dim shadow through the trees and hurried to catch up, remaining a sufficient distance behind to go undetected.

Gable moved with remarkable ease through the woods. Based on his awkward young form, I would've assumed he'd be bumbling noisily through the brush. But out here in nature, he was in his element. His torso remained erect as his legs bore him along swiftly, leaping barefoot from one fallen log to another.

I followed as quietly as I could, but leaves crackled underfoot. One step snapped a branch. Gable's shadow paused, and I ducked behind a tree as he started to turn. I held my breath, as though he could hear an exhalation from fifty feet away. Eventually, I peeked around the trunk.

Gable had moved on, and I hurried to catch up. I crested a ridge, leaving behind the intermittently residential Beachwood Canyon, moving into the larger Bronson Canyon. The Hollywood sign was visible, though only as a spectral silhouette in the fog.

As the terrain flattened out, it intersected with a well-worn hiking path, unsurprisingly empty this late in the day, especially given the chilly weather and low visibility. I turned uphill, and when I came around a corner, I saw the opening of a cave.

The Bronson Caves are, indeed, vaguely familiar, no doubt from having been photographed countless times for film and television. The entrance is impressively grand, around twenty feet high, gaping like the maw of some massive creature

I didn't see Gable nearby, so I assumed he had gone inside. I considered waiting at the entrance, so I could speak to the child when he emerged. But was he even to be called a "child"? He might be a predator or an enabler to one; he might be responsible for Liza's disappearance. He might be violent, unbalanced, a vile little

I headed inside. Perhaps it was a mistake, but I had no patience and was determined to confront him, to get whatever answers I could.

The first fifty feet of the cave were still permeated by enough light from the surface to see, up to the point where the cave came to a two-pronged fork; one direction led back to the outside, while the other progressed deeper into the hill. I took the second path, of course, uncertain how far it might go.

The cave narrowed and its height dropped quickly, forcing me to stoop, while the slope ascended into the hillside. Water trickled down the center of the tunnel, which was incredibly slick, forcing me to straddle the thin stream as I walked. As the daylight of the entrance retreated, I flipped on the flashlight of my phone; its glow was shockingly bright but didn't penetrate far.

Hearing something up ahead, I paused. A faint voice—I assumed Gable's—echoed across the rocky walls. I didn't think to record the sound, and even if I had, I suspect I would not have captured much. He was barely audible. The rhythm indicated that he was having a conversation with someone . . . and as I listened, I realized: he was talking to HIMSELF. Keeping up both sides of a dialogue, like a demented madman concocting

At that distance, the words were unclear. I heard him ask a question, too softly to ascertain what, and then answer loudly, "SOON." More was said after that, but I couldn't make out anything else. The voices faded, retreating deeper.

I continued another fifty yards or so, then paused. I could no longer see the opening of the cave at all. I was now swallowed whole by the darkness, and a premonition of horror

I continued uphill and upstream, following the faint whisper of ~~voices~~ Gable's voice. I began to hurry and took a misplaced step. My foot went down on the sludgy moss at the edge of the trickling water. I pitched forward, barely breaking my fall on the wet ground. My phone fell from my hand, clattered against the stone, and slid into the shallow water.

I fumbled for it desperately in the darkness. Then, perhaps cued by the racket I'd made, I heard a commotion deeper in the tunnel. Footsteps. Running, splashing in the water. Unnerved, I spoke into the darkness: "Hello?"

The rapid footsteps approached, and I braced myself, not sure what might be coming. Suddenly, a shape moved past—a figure, dodging nimbly around me in the narrow passage. I turned to see the figure's silhouette, barely visible in the near-darkness, rushing back toward the entrance.

Was it Gable? I couldn't tell. The height was right, and the white shirt looked like the one he'd been wearing. It had to be.

"Gable, wait!" I shouted, but the figure did not even slow or glance in my direction, running back toward the surface. I wanted to go after him but didn't want to leave my phone behind. I made another groping search of the ground and found the device, wet but still working.

I prepared to turn back, hoping I could catch up with Gable—but to my surprise, the flashlight beam, pointed into the depths of the cave, fell upon a face. Dirty skin, eyes dilating in the light, hair a ratty mess. Barely five feet away. I startled, nearly fell again, then realized . . .

THIS was Gable. Standing in the tunnel, staring at me.

Then who just ran past me? Is it possible that, in my fumbling efforts to get up, I imagined the other figure? Or had it been someone else, around the same size, fleeing this cave and ignoring me completely?

Regardless . . . the boy I was staring at in the tunnel was undeniably Annabelle's son. Only now he was filthy and shirtless, his torso caked with mud, his pants threadbare. Moss and leaves clung to his thick mop of hair. He looked out at me from sunken eyes, as though he'd gone feral.

I was shocked into silence. I could not understand how I had seen him fleeing . . . yet here he was, staring at me with preternatural calm.

As I searched for words, he asked simply, "Who are you?"

"I'm . . . Byron?" I said, uncertain how much to explain, or what he already knew. Then I told him (perhaps foolishly): "I'm Liza's father."

He nodded vaguely, noncommittal, but I saw a flash of recognition in the boy's eyes. He clicked his tongue. ~~Strangely menacing.~~ Then said, "You're not supposed to be here." He looked around. "They won't like it."

There were a thousand questions I needed to ask, perhaps none more pressing than who "they" might refer to, but as my adrenaline spiked, I had some sense that my time was limited, and I shot right to the point: "Where is she?"

"You should go" was his reply.

I stepped forward, towering over the boy as my anger rose. "What'd you do with her?"

"Nothing!" he shouted. But his defensiveness made it clear he knew who I was talking about.

I pressed him, "You know where she is. You've seen her?" The boy held perfectly still and looked away, a reluctant affirmation. "Take me there," I insisted. "Take me . . . wherever she is."

He shook his head. "I can't." He abruptly turned and ran deeper into the tunnel. As he did, I saw something strange, on the boy's bare back. A symbol nearly a foot tall running up his spine onto the back of his neck. The same symbol I'd seen on a poster in Liza's bedroom. It must have been drawn, but it looked as permanent as if it were inked into his skin. Only it was a vibrant, mossy-green color that seemed almost radiant in the dark cave.

The sight of it startled me enough that I hesitated, staring, as the boy disappeared into the darkness. I called out, "Wait!" and wanted to go after him . . . but he was gone so fast that suddenly, I wasn't sure if

I had imagined THIS Gable or had imagined the one who ran the other way a few moments earlier.

I started to follow but heard a skittering noise from deeper in the cave. The rocky walls of the tunnel seemed to vibrate, thrumming with omnidirectional energy. ~~Like some living, malevolent presence had manifested itself and permeated this entire space.~~

"Gable!" I called into the darkness . . . but the sound of my voice was swallowed up by the rising, squawking hum. I turned and fled back toward the light of the entrance. I slipped and tripped, went down hard on my knee, stumbled to my feet, kept running.

As I rushed back toward the faint glow of daylight, the sound behind me got louder, closer. Like ~~wordless whispers teeth chattering~~ beating wings in the dark.

I sprinted, stooped over in the tunnel, heart racing. Glanced back and saw movement behind me, surging shapes in the darkness. The seething sound drew closer, all-consuming.

I was almost out when suddenly the sound overtook me. It was everywhere. Like a shockwave, it knocked me to the ground, and I covered my head with my hands. Black wings on all sides whipped my skin. My eyes shut in horror and disgust. I clawed at them, writhing. There were too many, impossibly many, fluttering. My entire body shivered with revulsion as I staggered to my feet, trudged toward the entrance, still covering my face. . . .

But as I broke through to the surface, suddenly, they were gone. The deafening sound of wings was replaced by silence as I stumbled out of the tunnel and looked around—expecting to see a massive swarm of bats taking flight. But they were nowhere to be found.

I was alone, at the gaping maw. Bleeding from cuts and scrapes, but otherwise unharmed. The sky was almost completely dark now, the ground shrouded in chilly fog.

I dared a look back at the tunnel. No bats . . . nothing but an inky abyss. I worried that Gable was still inside . . . but was equally frightened that he was not.

As darkness claimed the forest, I retraced my route back toward the car. Bloodied and afraid. Navigating with the flashlight on my phone. With difficulty, I climbed the hill to where I had parked.

I looked down on Annabelle's house and considered going to tell her what I had seen. If I did, I would have to confide that I had stalked her, spied on her child, and followed him into the forest—which would mean the end of our relationship, and no hope of gaining any further information from her. But if her child was still out there, still perhaps in danger in that cave, I had no choice. To imagine learning he had been hurt, or worse, and I had done nothing was unconscionable.

I started walking downhill but then stopped. From this high vantage point, I could now see into the bright kitchen, where Gable was seated at the kitchen table, across from Annabelle. A candle burned on the table between them.

This appeared to answer my question about "which Gable" had been the real one. The one who fled the cave, clearly. He was now at home, sitting with his mother. I took out my phone, zoomed in, and snapped a photo of him, confirming it was true.

But even with the evidence in front of me, it was hard to confront what that meant. That what I'd seen in the tunnel had been . . . a hallucination?

Holding my phone steady against a tree trunk, I zoomed in on the domestic scene, noting the oddity of Gable's posture. Strangely upright, rigid, stiff. He reached into his pocket and took out a piece of paper that was rolled up like a scroll and handed it to Annabelle. It was covered in handwritten script, though at that distance I couldn't make out a word.

She read it, grave-faced, then nodded and handed it back to the boy. He promptly put the corner of the paper to the flame of the candle, and held it while it spread across the page. As it turned to ashes, he dropped it on the table, then smiled and walked away.

Annabelle stared after him as he left, and I could see tears running silently down her face. Even through her sorrow, I could tell: she was afraid.

Watching her from fifty yards away . . . I was too.

CHAPTER FOURTEEN

EMAIL

From: a.q.tobin@gmail.com
To: sg@rotterdampress.com

Hi Stan,

Hope this message finds you well. Quick question, don't think about it too hard: do you know a journalist named Byron James?

A.T.

REPLY

Annabelle,

Nice to hear from you! It's been a while. I have been quite eager to check in but have restrained myself in deference to your wishes. I've also dutifully fended off countless inquiries from both the powers that be here at Rotterdam and from the film executives desperate for the final film.

So naturally, it is puzzling to finally hear from you, and with such an apparent non-sequitur of a question. To answer plainly: no, I had never heard of the man until your email arrived. A quick google reveals that I have read one or two of his articles but never knew him by name.

Now my curiosity is piqued, so please, do tell: why do you ask? And why is this, of all things, the sole correspondence that I receive from you when you know I am waiting with bated breath for the draft?

Sincerely,
Stanley Gottheim (he/him/his)
Senior Editor, Rotterdam Press

REPLY

Stan,

That's what I was afraid of. I'm forwarding you a series of messages I thought I exchanged with you, starting a week ago. But if you take a closer look at the email address I was corresponding with, you'll see the address is actually sg@rotterdarnpress.com. That's d-a-r-n. The r-n sequence looks like an m.

In other words: someone masquerading as you persuaded me to speak to the journalist Byron James. And that someone, I'm confident, was Byron James himself.

A.T.

REPLY

Annabelle,

This is alarming! I am quite unsettled to discover my identity has been stolen, even more so given that the perpetrator appears to have mimicked the formatting and style of my correspondence.

I'm certain you are even more disturbed to have been so fla-

grantly deceived. Naturally we should contact the police or perhaps even the FBI? I would be happy to handle the matter and can
do so as discreetly as you'd like.

In relaying information to the authorities, it would be helpful
for me to understand: how did you uncover the ruse?

Sincerely,
Stanley Gottheim (he/him/his)
Senior Editor, Rotterdam Press

REPLY

I found him out because he was asking some suspicious questions,
and he inquired, out of nowhere, about the night of March 20th.
Never explained why. So after our last interview, I googled his
name plus March 20th (which initially yielded nothing), then
added the term "missing child," since that seems to be his primary
preoccupation.

What I discovered was this article: WATERTOWN PARENTS
EXPAND SEARCH FOR MISSING DAUGHTER, 12 (LINK),
which relates the story of a missing girl, whose father is Byron
Kidd (apparently James is a pen name). That's right: he's one of
the conspiracy nuts. The parent of a missing child, flailing for a
connection to my books.

That said, let's hold off on the police for now. I'm sure you'd be
discreet, but I fear the story would leak, and it's the last thing I
need publicity-wise. The man is unhinged but not a real threat in
my estimation. I'm confident that he's run into a dead end with
whatever wild theory he was pursuing, and I fear having him arrested would only draw more attention to the matter than simply
letting it lapse. I have other ways of bringing consequence to bear
upon him.

REPLY

Annabelle,

Well done on your detective work there (perhaps a mystery novel awaits in your future! Kidding, kidding, let's focus on the work at hand for now. . . .)

As you requested, I will hold off on involving legal authorities, though I would encourage you to err on the side of caution when it comes to this sort of extreme character.

I would be loath to apply any pressure at a time like this, but I would be remiss in my duties as your editor if I did not take the opportunity to gently inquire about Book Six. Any update? Nearing completion? Please know that I ask this as a fan of your work. The world is darker than ever these days and in need of some fantastical escapism.

While I've got you: FairyCon is this weekend, and I have of course made the customary gracious refusals to all the appearance requests. But if you'll recall we did agree to provide signed bookplates for a giveaway event that Rotterdam is running. Have you had a chance to sign those yet? Or could you this evening? I can have a courier pick them up as soon as they're ready.

Sincerely,
Stanley Gottheim (he/him/his)
Senior Editor, Rotterdam Press

REPLY

You know, Stan, you're right. The world does need this book. And I need to get it out there and out of my head. This troubling incident with the reporter has given me a new perspective and renewed vigor.

Regarding the draft: I am only one chapter away from completion. I've been mulling over how to conclude the story, but it's clear to me now. I'll have it done by the end of the week.

I'm glad you mentioned FairyCon. Bookplates are a little un-derwhelming, but I'm thinking . . . what if I were to make a sur-prise appearance instead? It's become apparent to me that if I don't step out to tell my own story, others will tell it their way. This might be the perfect opportunity to end my self-imposed exile and take back the narrative. Let's hop on the phone this af-ternoon to discuss details.

A.T.

TEXT MESSAGE EXCHANGE

BYRON KIDD   MISHA PIMM

10:33 A.M.

> Dude, what did you even say to Annabelle?
> You visited her yesterday, the very next morning this gets announced:
> (SCREENSHOT OF EMAIL)

EMAIL

From: community@fairycon.org
To: (Undisclosed Recipients)

FAIRY FANS!

History is being made. And you can be there to watch it happen—at this weekend's FairyCon celebration!

We have all patiently waited for years. Some of you doubted this day would ever come. But we are pleased to announce . . .

BOOK SIX is nearly finished. And Annabelle Tobin has prom-ised to announce its completion and a release date(!!!)—LIVE, in person, exclusively for our community.

She will even do a READING from the new book—your first

chance for a sneak peek of the final chapter in Ciara's journey! Followed by a moderated conversation.

PANEL: "The Future of Fairy Tale"
WHERE: LA Convention Center, Hall C
WHEN: Saturday, November 2, 2:00 PM

Tickets are available for all FairyCon passholders. Reservation LINK goes live tomorrow at 9 AM. Overflow seating will be available in Halls D, E, and F.

If you're not able to join in person, anyone with a VIRTUAL PASS can LIVESTREAM the event through the website.

Let's show our queen how we feel about her!

RESUME TEXT MESSAGE EXCHANGE

BYRON KIDD   MISHA PIMM

11:10 A.M.

                                              Helloooooooo?!

Hey. Sorry. Late night.
I certainly didn't suggest she finish the book sooner.
She was cagey about her timeline to me.

                                              It just seems crazy.
                                              You met w her . . .
Next day we find out she's about to announce completion of the book.
                                              This is huge! But why now?!

Maybe she's tired of ppl asking her about it.
Maybe she's hoping to move on already.
Or maybe she just doesn't care anymore if she summons an ancient demon.

                                              ????

We should talk.

CHAPTER FIFTEEN

3RD INTERVIEW WITH MISHA PIMM

October 30, 12:51 P.M.

Location: Misha's apartment. Surprisingly, not nearly as juvenile fangirly as her office would suggest. Decor is boho-chic; exposed brick walls, pendant lamps, hand-woven dreamcatcher on the wall. An Anthropologie catalogue brought to life. Clearly owing to the influence of her girlfriend, Shelby, who I'd guess is five years older, and a good deal more sensible than Misha.

Misha's home office seems to be the one arena where her interests reign supreme. Comic books in plastic sleeves, toys in a glass case. Numerous videogame consoles running the gamut from an original Nintendo like the one I played before Misha was born to the latest spaceship-looking devices with wireless controllers. And of course, multiple editions of every Fairy Tale book. *The Hidden World* is open on her desk.

Subject: Misha looks at me like I'm crazy. The girl with the electric-blue hair, the adult with the absurd obsession with kids' stories and toys, looks at me with pity in her eyes because I'm a fucking loon to her now. Probably because she just listened to my last interview and read my last journal entry, both of which I shared with her in a futile effort to make sense of what happened.

TRANSCRIPT OF RECORDED INTERVIEW

BYRON: So . . . What do you make of all that?

MISHA: Well, first off, thank you for letting me read from your journal. I get that you don't usually do that sort of thing, and letting anyone into your process, that's vulnerable, and—

BYRON: Strange times call for strange measures. I need someone to tell me if I'm losing it.

MISHA: You seem sane to me. But this is . . . unbelievable.

BYRON: Meaning, you don't believe me.

MISHA: I'm not saying that. I *do* believe you, even though what you're describing is . . . well, impossible.

BYRON: Two of the same person—yeah, that's . . . uncommon.

MISHA: Before we even get to that . . . Let's talk about the cave. From your description, it sounds like you must've gone a couple hundred yards in there.

BYRON: At least.

MISHA: Well . . . that whole cave is maybe two hundred feet deep, tops. Deep isn't even the right word, it's flat and straight, and then it opens to the outside. You can walk through it standing upright.

BYRON: What are you talking about? Even if I got the distances wrong, it was pitch-dark in there. You couldn't see the surface.

MISHA: Look, there are pictures online. (*Typing*) See? It doesn't go nearly as far as what you're describing. . . .

BYRON: You're telling me . . . No way. What I went in was a different cave.

MISHA: If this is what happened, then yeah, you didn't go in the Bronson Caves. Especially if you got attacked by, like, a million bats.

BYRON: I thought it was also called the Batcave.

MISHA: Yeah, because it was used in the '60s *Batman* TV show. Whenever there's a shot of the Batmobile driving out, it's filmed right there.

BYRON: Fuck. I knew it looked familiar.

MISHA: OK, so let's just say . . . you found some different cave. In the Hollywood Hills. A huge cave that I've somehow never heard of, that has been left open even though the city would obviously close that shit up before L.A. hiker idiots could kill themselves in there. Fine, we're gonna run with that and see where it gets us. We still have to talk about the bigger mystery.

BYRON: Right. The kid.

MISHA: Or kids, plural?

BYRON: What I know for certain is I saw Gable leave Annabelle's house . . . I saw him enter the cave . . . and I saw him back at Annabelle's house after. The part *in* the cave is the haziest.

MISHA: So it's possible the kid you talked to in the cave . . . maybe that was someone different?

BYRON: I mean . . . maybe. But he looked *identical*. So I guess it could've been him and he left after me but knew a faster way back, so he beat me home, and . . .

MISHA: And got cleaned up and sat down for dinner with his mother?

BYRON: (*Sighs*) I'm doing my best here, OK?

MISHA: I know, and I'm on your team. I'm just walking us through the facts. And neither of those options seems very plausible. So maybe . . . maybe we should consider . . . it could be something else.

BYRON: What kind of something else?

MISHA: Something that might not fit your usual categories of what's possible . . . Look, I've been going through the book you left with me, digging into the stories, and—there's one that you should take a look at.

SHORT STORY

From *The Hidden World: On Faeries, Fauns & Other Creatures of Folklore,* by Sir Henry Raleigh. Published 1889, Oxford University Press.

THE CHANGELING

This story comes to me from Olafur Furlson, an elder in the fishing village of Liaduur, in the northernmost reaches of Finland. It was relayed over a traditional meal of kipper fillet and a braided, half-baked sweet dough whose name is, to this Anglican ear, utterly unpronounceable.

Once there lived a young married couple, Jesper and Hildur, who settled upon a farm at the edge of the steppe. They tilled the land and called up a hearty crop of barley from rocky earth and were blessed with prosperity. Yet Hildur felt cursed, for though her land had grown fertile, she herself was barren as salted stone.

One day as Hildur gathered moss in the hills, she lamented her misfortune loudly, then heard a voice calling in return. She followed it into a cave, whereupon she encountered a troll named Løthus of the underground folk.

Løthus was tall as three men and as fat around the middle as four. He had horns upon his head and a tail that dragged in the rocks. Hildur was greatly startled and turned to flee, but Løthus blocked her way and told her he had no design on eating her that day.

Instead, he offered her a seed and told her if she would ingest it, it would grow in her belly into a child. She could keep the child as long as every year she left a gift at the edge of the cave for the underground folk: an offering of seven elk steaks, seven bushels of barley, and seven woven baskets.

Hildur eagerly accepted the terms, for there was nothing more dear to her heart than to have a family. So she promptly ingested the troll's seed and returned to her home with a spring in her step, whereupon she told her husband of the deal she had made.

Jesper was skeptical of the tale. But lo, it came to pass that Hildur's belly swelled, and the couple was greatly joyed to usher a beautiful babe into the world.

At the child's birth, Hildur told Jesper to take seven elk steaks, seven bushels of barley, and seven woven baskets from the winter stores and leave them at the edge of the hill-cave. And though Jesper did not believe her tale, he did as she said, for such was his gratitude at being a father.

On the child's birthday every year, the offering was made and vanished before the morning. Every year, the child grew in strength, and his parents grew prouder.

But in the fourth year of the child's life, he became surly and ill-tempered. No longer would he speak but would only screech like a suckling. He would consume four times the quantity of meat proper to his age, and in the middle of the night would climb the walls and crawl across the ceiling and pull down bowls and plates to the floor, creating such a racket that Jesper and Hildur never slept.

Eventually they were at such a loss that they called upon a völva, who inspected the child and proclaimed that the boy was a changeling, and their own child had been spirited away by the underground folk. The völva told them there was only one remedy: the changeling would have to be exposed by flame. Jesper protested that if she were wrong, they would burn up their own child, but the völva insisted it was the only way.

They set about stoking a mighty fire, and when it was ready the three of them together wrestled the child to the edge of the hearth and trapped him in the flame. The child sweated and screamed and pleaded for mercy, but still they held him in. At last, the changeling exposed his true form, sprouting a tail, two horns, and a forked tongue that came down to his navel.

The changeling bartered for his life and swore to return their true child, but the couple would have to resume making full payment to the underground folk, and increase the offering as punishment for failure to keep up their end of the original bargain.

Hildur insisted they had never missed a payment. But Jesper grew pale in the face and confessed that he had skimped on the offering, as food for the winter was tight, and he had long believed his wife's tale to be womanly superstition.

Hildur cursed her husband but agreed to the new terms. And so every year after that, they would leave a tribute of seven elk steaks, seven bushels of barley, seven woven baskets . . . and one human finger.

Each new birthday of their son, one of his parents would pick up their ice-ax and slice off one of their fingers, and it would be left at the edge of the cave with the rest of the offering. Every year, it was gone by morning.

Year by year their labor grew harder as their hands grew more difficult to use. But as the child came of age he was able to help his father with the harvest and the hunt, and help his mother in the home, and so all was balanced righteously.

RESUME INTERVIEW TRANSCRIPT

BYRON: OK, so, setting aside how fucked-up Scandinavian folklore is . . . what does this have to do with anything?

MISHA: I think that the story you're telling me—one way it could be explained is if . . . maybe there actually *are* two versions of Gable.

BYRON: Uh-huh. And the kid I saw in the cave was actually . . . what, a fairy, who looks exactly like him?

MISHA: Possibly. Or more likely, it could be that the one who's living at Annabelle's house—who you yourself said she seems to be afraid of—what if *that's* the changeling? And the one in the cave is the real Gable.

BYRON: I'm sorry, you're saying that the explanation for all this is . . . magic.

MISHA: Changeling stories are culturally ubiquitous.

BYRON: That doesn't make them *true*.

MISHA: Of course not, but they *are* rooted in something deep in human nature, something that you can't deny.

BYRON: She did bring up Shakespeare. *Midsummer Night's Dream* . . .

MISHA: There you go! A changeling baby is a huge part of the plot.

BYRON: But you're . . . this is ridiculous. You really believe . . .

MISHA: Forget what *I* believe for a second. Let's talk about what Annabelle believes. There was an article I read a couple years ago when I was prepping my dissertation prospectus that was . . . let me see if I can find it . . . (*Typing*)

SCHOLARLY ARTICLE EXCERPT

From "Psychological and Cultural Origins of the Changeling Myth," by Patrick McClusky, from *Jungian Journal*, January 2004.

One of the most ubiquitous elements of global myth is the story of the "changeling"—the replacement of a human baby with a familiar from another world. Similar stories crop up in cultures around the globe dating to the medieval period. In many such tales, the placement of a changeling is viewed as a punishment upon the parents, and restoration of the original child is possible only following atonement for a particular sin—often one of envy, pride, or ambition.

Most likely, the roots of the myth are in the inability of parents to psychologically cope with a child whose developmental capacities may have become stunted. It is likely that babies suffering from cognitive disabilities or who sustained illnesses that caused lasting brain damage became unruly, unresponsive, and disobedient. The guilt of the parents is sublimated through the explanation that the child they know has been replaced by a changeling, and there is hope to be found in the assertion that a rectification of wrongs will restore the child and the family unit.

Yet it is important to note that belief in changelings is not harmless. Whether it is literal or figurative, it creates a disassociation from and dehumanization of the child. In 1826, Irish mother Anne Roche, believing her four-year-old son Michael to have been replaced by a changeling, repeatedly dunked him in the River Flesk. Eventually, he drowned. Anne was acquitted of the murder on the grounds that she genuinely believed him to be possessed by a fairy spirit. Therefore, while we can recognize the psychosocial value of the fantasy, we must be careful not to indulge it to the point of harm.

RESUME INTERVIEW TRANSCRIPT

BYRON: So now you're saying, it's *not* real, it's just . . . Annabelle Tobin has some kind of delusion. There's something wrong with her son, and she's made up this changeling story to try to put the blame on something else, when in fact, she feels guilty for . . . what, exactly?

MISHA: Getting famous. Getting divorced. Screwing up his life.

BYRON: That sort of makes sense. Psychologically. Except it doesn't do *anything* to explain how I saw two of the same kid! Just come out and tell me—are you implying magic is real, or Annabelle is crazy?

MISHA: Both, maybe! I don't know, I'm trying to figure this out too! And figure out what it has to do with her suddenly being done with her book. You're the one who pointed out the connection to the Six-fold Summoning!

BYRON: Yeah, but I didn't think . . . this is so *fucked*! And none of it is getting me any closer to finding Liza!

(*Sound of a loud slam. Then moments later, a door opening, as Misha's girlfriend, Shelby, pokes her head in, concerned.*)

SHELBY: Hey. Everything OK in here?

MISHA: Yeah, babe. We're fine.

SHELBY: I'm trying to work out there.

BYRON: It's my fault. Sorry for the outburst.

SHELBY: And you are . . . ?

BYRON: Byron. I'm a friend from the university.

SHELBY: Uh-huh. You sure you're all right, Mish?

MISHA: Totally. He's just . . . rough day. We'll keep it down.

(*Door closes. Long silence.*)

MISHA: A friend, huh?

BYRON: What was I supposed to tell her, the truth?

MISHA: Maybe it is the truth. Maybe this is the beginning of a beautiful friendship.

BYRON: That's the last thing I need right now. And you are, no offense, very annoying.

MISHA: Me? You're the one yelling like a crazy person.

BYRON: Yeah, yeah. Sorry for getting you in trouble with the missus.

MISHA: It's all good, she's put up with worse. And we're not married. Maybe someday, but . . . I dunno. This whole thing we've got going on is great, but we're kind of at an impasse, ya know? Eh, you don't wanna hear about my drama.

BYRON: It's fine, I should probably think about someone else's problems for one second. I'm no expert on relationships, but—what's the holdup?

MISHA: Well, as you figured out . . . we don't have kids. And Shelby wants babies, for sure. Two at least. She's open to adopting, implantation, whatever, but the whole thing, for me, that's like a nonstarter.

BYRON: (*Laughs*) I'm sorry, *you* don't want kids?

MISHA: Hell no. I mean, someday, *maybe,* but definitely not anytime soon. I'm still out here trying to *be* a kid! I missed out on the whole happy-childhood thing, so I'm doing it now.

BYRON: I see. Well, if you're looking for advice . . .

MISHA: Open to it.

BYRON: Get over yourself. Just do it already.

MISHA: Seriously? That's not what I was expecting you to say.

BYRON: Look . . . when my wife got pregnant, we were not planning on having a baby. We weren't married, Val was still in law school, I was grinding it out at the beginning of my career. A baby did not fit into any of the plans we had. But Val decided she wanted to go ahead with it and didn't even ask for my input, which I'm grateful for.

Of course, it was hard as hell. The late nights, the crying, getting spit up on. But the thing is—you're never gonna believe me until you feel it, but it's true—you're not gonna mind. Any of it. Because . . . I'm not gonna try to sell you any of that "deeper happiness than I've ever known" shit, even though it's all true.

I'll just tell you this: If you've ever felt like, "What's it all for?" . . . if you ever got anxious about your purpose and depressed about your pointless life . . . all of that is gonna go away. Because you're gonna hold your kid and see what they need, and you're gonna *know*. For the first time in your life, you're gonna have something that it's all for.

You don't want kids today because they don't fit with your life the way it is. But you gotta realize, your life's gonna change. And the you that's on the other side of that change is gonna love kids. *Your* kid, certainly. I promise.

MISHA: But like . . . what if I'm just *bad* at it? I suck at adulting in every form.

BYRON: Oh, I don't doubt that for a second. But you'll be a great mom. Someday.

(*Long silence.*)

MISHA: We're gonna find her. I promise.

BYRON: Thanks. But right now, I've got more questions than answers. Any ideas?

MISHA: There is one thing that you mentioned in your journal . . . The kid you saw, in the cave—that symbol on his back . . .

BYRON: Yeah. I mean, it looked like a tattoo. But he was nine years old, and it was green and . . . shiny.

MISHA: That's the Fairy Rune. In the books, it appears on various gateways—like the Wishing Well—to mark passages between the two worlds. And it can be inscribed onto those from our world in order to enable passage between realms.

BYRON: So a kid who puts this on himself might think it's giving him access to fairy-land.

MISHA: Something like that. It's become a popular tattoo for fans.

BYRON: You think the symbol could be useful?

MISHA: I think there's probably someone who does *this* specific tattoo, in exactly this way. And since we know that Liza was trying to get across to the Hidden World . . . maybe this could've been on her radar, as a way to do that.

BYRON: OK. So first, we gotta find someone else who has the tattoo. Which . . . you know someone?

MISHA: Not yet.

INVESTIGATIVE JOURNAL OF BYRON KIDD

I never imagined that my investigative career would involve using Instagram. But then, I suppose I can't count this particular search as part of my "career," since I am working outside of the parameters of my job, and if anything, undermining whatever hope for continuing the career I might've had left.

Focus. No time for self-pity. Just the facts.

Misha searched "#FairyRune" on Instagram, which it turns out is a remarkably popular hashtag. The postings show the symbol on a wide array of objects—T-shirts, lunchboxes, endless products manufactured abroad and sold to fans around the world. More homemade iterations too. A rune drawn in nail polish on a middle-schooler's backpack. A VW bus with the symbol painted on the front where a peace-symbol might've gone in an earlier era, and "FairyWagon" painted on the side.

And tattoos. Hundreds of tattoos, perhaps thousands. Most of them small, found on arms, backs, necks, wrists, and more. Many were sensibly inked in black, but we found a couple that were green, and we

messaged the users they belonged to. But those looked different from
the one I'd seen in the cave—they didn't "shine" in the same way.

We were not restricting ourselves to the upper back, but then we
found one with that exact same placement—the "wings" spreading
across its owner's shoulder blades, the top rising up his neck. And
even more telling: it was the EXACT same vibrant green hue I'd seen
on the boy in the cave.

"Scott Angelik." At least, that was the name he gave online. He was
a~~boy~~ a young man in his late teens, early twenties at the oldest, with
sharp cheekbones accentuated by dramatic makeup, and glitter around
his eyes. Naked to the waist in his profile picture, with a tapered, an-
drogynous, David Bowie-ish physique. He sported a pair of feathery
black wings with straps affixing them around his torso, dramatically
spread wide. The costume appeared professional enough for a film.

RESUME INTERVIEW TRANSCRIPT

MISHA: He's a Duster.

BYRON: Excuse me?

MISHA: A Duster. In the books, the term is used for human characters who have been hit with fairy dust and transformed into half-fairy
hybrids. So there's a movement of fans who really identify with that,
and go all the way with the look. Some people dress up as Dusters for
Halloween, or conventions, but some . . . I mean, this guy, I can't find
a photo in his entire grid that's not full-glam.

BYRON: Are Dusters all guys?

MISHA: Pretty much. Plenty of women cosplay as different characters, but Dusters are more . . . it's like drag, kind of. An aesthetic and a
performance.

BYRON: OK. So it's not a kinky fetish type of thing?

MISHA: Well . . . not until it is. Like with Bronies.

BYRON: What are Bronies?

MISHA: Are you serious?

BYRON: Is that the people who dress up like mascots?

MISHA: Those are Furries. Bronies are men who are really into My Little Pony.

BYRON: Why are they—

MISHA: Look, from this guy's pictures, it seems like . . . it's his job too.

BYRON: You can get paid to be a Brony?

MISHA: A Duster. And—not exactly. But around the Kodak Theatre—that's kinda the shithole heart of Hollywood, total tourist-trap—there are people who dress up as all kinds of characters from movies and sell photos with themselves. Vader, Spider-Man, you name it, there's someone out there. It's nothing official, they're just guys who show up with suits.

BYRON: And tourists pay them . . . just to take a picture?

MISHA: Yeah. Some of them do pretty well.

BYRON: I really don't get this fucking town.

CHAPTER SIXTEEN

EXCERPT FROM FAIRY TALE BOOK TWO: *The Bridge of Dreams*

By Annabelle Tobin. Published by Rotterdam Press, 2007. Page 66.

Gloverbeck and his retinue pushed Ciara into the throne room, and she fell to the stone floor in a fit of coughing. Her throat burned, and her eyes blinked furiously. She felt like she was dying.

An ethereal voice pierced her to the core: "Stop fighting, and it will be easier."

Ciara looked up. Perched on a dais above her, seated on a majestic throne of glowing shafts of quartz, was the most beautiful thing Ciara had seen in her entire life. An elfin-featured being, both ancient and childlike at once, wearing a gold filigree crown.

Queen Áine explained to Ciara, "The Dust is thick in our air. And you are unaccustomed to it. Relax and breathe normally, you won't die. At least, not the way you fear now."

"Dust . . . you mean Fairy Dust, right?" Ciara exclaimed with excitement. "Is it magical?"

Áine darkened. "Of course. But do not presume that 'magic' is an uncomplicated good. Magic is *transformation*, which can be beneficial or destructive. Dust will awaken new corners of your soul. And while some new abilities may arise, others may be taken."

Ciara nodded, her heart beating faster. Whatever change the Dust held for her, she was committed now.

Áine continued: "Many a mortal mind has been driven mad by Dust. Indeed, if you were a year or two older, we would not even consider letting you into this space. Once mortals are adults, their minds are too rigid to tolerate its effects. Sanity can shatter, like a brittle stone struck by a powerful hammer."

Ciara suddenly felt a powerful itch on her shoulder blades, which quickly escalated into intense pain. She doubled over. "Sorry, my shoulders hurt. Like there's . . ."

"Something trying to grow out of them?" Áine finished Ciara's thought.

"Exactly!" Ciara exclaimed. Áine and Gloverbeck shared a look of concern.

INVESTIGATIVE JOURNAL OF BYRON KIDD

October 30

It seemed like a long shot that the specific guy we were looking for would be out on Hollywood Boulevard at any particular time, but Misha told me that it was the week of FairyCon, which meant there would be plenty of fan-tourists in town: the perfect time for someone like Scott Angelik.

She volunteered to come along as my "Duster-whisperer." I was hesitant to bring her with, but I had to concede there was credible evidence connecting Liza's disappearance with all of these subcultures surrounding the Fairy Tale books. I told Misha she could come as long as she agreed to do whatever I said.

She did not agree to that at all, of course, but we nonetheless headed down to the parking garage together, and I squeezed into the passenger seat of her Honda Fit.

INTERVIEW WITH "SCOTT ANGELIK"

October 30, 2:09 P.M.

Location: The "shithole heart of Hollywood," in Misha's words. The corner of Hollywood and Highland. Outside the Kodak Theatre, surrounded by T-shirt and souvenir shops, within view of the gaudy Madame Tussauds Wax Museum, and the famous Hollywood Walk of Fame, where celebrities pay for the honor of having their names engraved inside tacky stars in the sidewalk.

The plaza outside the Kodak was ground zero for the costume players that Misha had referenced. Scott Angelik was nowhere in sight when we first arrived—just a Mandalorian, a couple Avengers (I made the mistake of calling them Justice Leaguers, which Misha was not about to let slide), and a Wonder Woman (apparently *she's* a Justice Leaguer). While we searched for our target, I was treated to a lengthy discourse on the complicated gender politics of Wonder Woman's history; turns out she was dreamed up by the same man who invented the lie-detector test.

I'm having more and more trouble sticking to the facts. And yet that bothers me less and less.

The location was already filling up with tourists and costumed ~~beggars harassers~~ superheroes. Still no sign of Scott Angelik. It was sticky-hot, the crowds were getting obnoxious, I'd already rejected two different Indiana Joneses trying to get me to pay for a picture. I almost felt like I was floating out of my body, looking down in horror that a supposedly rigorous effort to find my daughter had led me to *this* particular low. I was ready to pack it in and head out.

Of course, that's when we found him.

Subject: "Scott Angelik" was pulling on a Juul at the edge of the plaza, getting a few good puffs in before making himself a worthy accessory for family photos. He was dressed identically to his Instagram photo, which was not surprising—but it was probably the first time I appreciated the full extent of the photo editing that went into images on the platform.

Scott's physique was just as lithe as we had seen—but where his skin
had appeared bronzed and youthful, here in the midday sun he looked
pale and flabby despite being skinny. Stubble was visible on his chest
and stomach. Makeup had been applied to his body as well as his face
and was most apparent on his inner arms . . . surefire evidence of hiding
track marks. Even without the evidence of his arms, the glazed shimmer of his eyes proved that he was ~~gazing out at the world through an
opiate gauze~~ high as fuck on heroin.

(I really need to watch my descriptions, I'm losing my edge. Stick to
the facts.)

The tattoo on his back was partially concealed by the wings he
wore, almost like the tattoo provided the root from which the wings
grew. It was no less striking than the version I'd glimpsed on his profile
picture—if anything, it was even more arresting in person. As though it
glowed with a life of its own, shining more vibrantly than the cheap
glitter around his eyes.

Misha told me to let her take the lead on the interview, as she would
have a better shot at getting through to him. It was hard for me to bite
my tongue through all the talk of Hidden Worlds and magical travel,
which eventually made it impossible for me to hang back.

TRANSCRIPT OF RECORDED INTERVIEW

MISHA: Hi there. Are you Scott?

SCOTT: I'm Angelik. Why?

MISHA: Sorry to bother you. We're just wondering if you could tell us
about your tattoo.

SCOTT: It's a tattoo. You want one too?

MISHA: Maybe, yeah. I've thought about it. I study Fairy Tale, aca-
demically.

SCOTT: Well, it's not for dabblers or overthinkers, it's for those who
are serious about crossing over.

MISHA: Crossing over, you mean . . . ?

SCOTT: If you have to ask, then you're not serious. Now, I'm trying to work here.

MISHA: Did you? Cross over?

SCOTT: I was crossing before it was cool. Not that anybody believes me. That's the world for you these days. You do a few hundred hallucinogens and suddenly every word you say is super sus.

MISHA: We believe you. At least, we want to.

SCOTT: Heard that before.

BYRON: Please, if there's anything that could be helpful, there's . . . a child missing. Have you . . . seen anyone like that?

SCOTT: I've *been* a child missing. And seen plenty.

BYRON: Do you have any proof?

SCOTT: If there was evidence it wouldn't be magic, now, would it?

MISHA: What was it like? The Hidden World.

SCOTT: I barely remember. The only way to get home was by leaving a lot behind, so most of my mind is still buried somewhere under the Dreamvale.

MISHA: Well, from what you *can* recall . . . was it like the books?

SCOTT: Like but not. Darker but blinding bright. You dive in, you think you're there to feast, but then you realize, you *are* the feast.

MISHA: What do you mean?

SCOTT: Have you ever been a tree? You grow and reach for the sun, but then you get cut down, again and again.

BYRON: That's not how trees work.

SCOTT: How 'bout a sheep? Sheared. Only the wool is your dreams. It's a baaaaaad time. (*Laughs*)

MISHA: Did you encounter the Green Man there?

SCOTT: Oh, he encountered me. Devoured me, really. Never saw his face. Or saw too many to say. Why?

MISHA: We're looking for someone. Someone who might've gone the same way you did.

SCOTT: Sorry to hear that. I don't know anyone else who made it back.

BYRON: This is bullshit. He's messing with us.

SCOTT: You're both welcome to fuck off and let me do my job.

MISHA: Hang on, don't just . . . Byron, do you have a picture of her?

BYRON: Of course, but I'm not showing it to this freak show.

MISHA: Come on. You've got nothing to lose.

BYRON: (*Sighs, then eventually:*) Have you seen this girl?

SCOTT: . . . Sure, yeah.

MISHA: You have? You're certain. You know where?

SCOTT: On the other side. In the graveyard.

BYRON: Wait . . . the graveyard? No . . .

SCOTT: She wasn't dead. The Dreamvale, that's where we were kept.

MISHA: It's from the books.

BYRON: He's lying. If you really saw her, what's her name?

SCOTT: She's your daughter, you don't even remember her name?

MISHA: How'd you know . . . We never said she was his daughter.

BYRON: That's a lucky guess. She looks like me.

SCOTT: She does, poor thing.

BYRON: You watch your mouth.

SCOTT: Honey, you're the one who came to me. What do I look like, the lost and found? (*Laughs*)

BYRON: You're lying. You can't even tell me her name. Or yours, for that matter.

SCOTT: We didn't have names over there. Why would we? She was done being a kid, and I was done being a baker. That's the whole reason we went. Now, kindly piss off and go get yourself a souvenir.

(*Scott walks away. Long silence.*)

MISHA: Byron? You OK?

BYRON: She was done being a kid. My last name, her last name: K-I-D-D.

MISHA: You think that's what he meant?

BYRON: If he was done being a baker, maybe that's . . .

(*Sounds of iPhone typing.*)

BYRON: Look at this. It's him . . .

NEWS ARTICLE

Originally published in the *Detroit Times,* June 14, 2005.

BAKER FAMILY NOT GIVING UP HOPE IN SEARCH FOR MISSING SON

Grieving parents Martin and Tina Baker held a press conference today in conjunction with the Detroit Police Department to declare that they are not giving up hope in the search for their son, Scott. They have asked local residents to share any details or observations that might help locate him.

Scott Baker, 17, was a student at Mumford High School who disappeared the night of prom. Baker attended the dance with a group of friends, wearing an unconventional outfit that included makeup and costume wings. Reportedly he was verbally harassed by several other students, but none of the threats escalated to physical violence.

Numerous witnesses claim to have heard him state he planned to attend a popular after-prom party, but he never showed up for it. Police have investigated over a dozen students but made no arrests in the case, and other parents have said the time has come to stop harassing their children.

Many have claimed Scott was unhappy in his community and may have run away from home. But the Bakers insist that Scott would never abandon his family. "He was a good kid, and we were a tight family," said Martin, his father. His mother, Tina, added, "We just want our baby to come home."

RESUME RECORDED TRANSCRIPT

MISHA: That *is* him! I mean, he looks a little different, but—totally him.

BYRON: Yeah. Look at the date.

MISHA: What? That's . . . eighteen years ago. About a year after the first book came out.

BYRON: He said he was crossing before it was cool. . . .

MISHA: But—forget about that part, it would mean he's . . . thirty-five now? Noooo, no way.

BYRON: I know. He looks like he's the exact same age as in this picture.

(*Sound of rapid steps, catching up.*)

BYRON: Hey . . . Scott? Scott Baker?

SCOTT: Angelik.

BYRON: OK. Angelik. Sorry if I was a little, uh . . .

SCOTT: Rude? Stubborn? Stupid?

BYRON: All that. But if you can help us, in any way . . .

SCOTT: I'm working now, I don't have time.

BYRON: Look—here's fifty bucks. That's your next ten pictures. Just to talk to us.

SCOTT: . . . Five minutes. What do you wanna know?

BYRON: I mean . . . first, is she OK? The girl. Her name's Liza.

SCOTT: I dunno, it's been ages since I left. Literally. I aged out. No dreams left to shear, you know?

BYRON: OK, but . . . When you last saw her—it had to be sometime in the last six months . . . Was she all right?

SCOTT: Oh yeah, she was doing *great* in the Dreamvale. That's where people go to live their best lives.

BYRON: Don't waste my time. Either tell me something *useful,* or—

MISHA: Hang on. Did she have a tattoo like yours? A rune?

SCOTT: Sure. How else would she have gotten there?

MISHA: OK, so the way it works . . . someone tattoos you . . .

SCOTT: Not just anyone. The Illuminator.

MISHA: The Illuminator . . . In our world?

BYRON: Who's the—

MISHA: I'll explain later. Scott, how did you find the Illuminator?

SCOTT: Doesn't matter, it's different for everyone. The answers are all in the books. Just follow the stars.

BYRON: Is this making any sense to you?

SCOTT: The rune's the easy part. Crossing the divide, that's where it gets tricky.

BYRON: Stop with this cryptic bullshit! If you've seen Liza, I need to know where she is.

SCOTT: OK, I am super done with this.

BYRON: No! Wait, just—

SCOTT: Ah-ah-ah, excuse me sir, if you do not get out of my way, I will scream, and I know that you might think my costumed friends don't look like much, but we watch out for each other, and my friend Kylo Ren over there has pepper spray and will use it. Now if you don't mind . . .

BYRON: Please, I'm sorry if—look, I'll pay you. More, lots more, if you can just—

SCOTT: Money won't buy what you need to find her.

BYRON: Which is what? An Illuminator?

SCOTT: Bye-bye, now . . .

(*Long silence.*)

MISHA: Well, that was . . .

BYRON: The Illuminator. That's a reference to the books, right?

MISHA: Yeah, the Illuminator is a sorceress in the Hidden World. She's the one who's able to cast the Fairy Rune. She puts it on trees, other characters, the Wishing Well—anything to enable passage between worlds.

BYRON: And . . . Follow the stars?

MISHA: Yeah, that's in Book One, when Ciara goes to try to look for her. Here, let me see if I can find it, I've got the ebooks on my phone. . . .

EXCERPT FROM FAIRY TALE BOOK ONE: *The Wishing Well*

By Annabelle Tobin. Published by Rotterdam Press, 2004. Page 129.

Ciara struggled up the cliff face, tightly gripping each narrow outcropping and trying not to look down at the yawning chasm beneath her. At last, she pulled herself over the ledge at the top.

From this high vantage point, she could behold an immense vista of the Hidden World, stretching westward to the Sea of Nothing and north to the Castle in the Clouds. She even glimpsed the glittering Crystal Palace of the faerie court to the east.

But when she looked around the mountaintop, her heart sank, as she found the peak empty and bare. A few boulders lay about, and the withered, stick-like remains of a tree were wind-bent and ready to snap.

The Ancient One she had been promised was nowhere in sight.

But it turned out, nowhere in sight was not a problem. The wind howled around her, and then, in the whistling, she could make out . . . a voice. "Wherefore comest thou upon my mountaintop, child? Who is it that boldly scales these heights?"

Ciara spun a full circle but still could not see who addressed her. Perhaps the Ancient One was invisible to mortal eyes. So she spoke, with all the confidence she could muster: "Greetings, Ancient One. I am Ciara from the realm of mortals. I have stumbled by accident into the world of the fey, and I wish to find my way home."

Again the voice came from no apparent source: "That will not be easy, child! Once there was a time when many Illuminators worked their magicks, many who could cast the rune and open passage between worlds."

This time Ciara was able to ascertain the voice's direction and deduced that the sound was coming from the spindly tree that grew out of the rocks.

The talking tree continued, "But the Green Man's minions killed them all off, and he stole their enchantments in his mad mission to control the borders of our realm." Ciara's focus narrowed further. She approached the tree, spotting a tiny spiderweb between its branches. Dangling from the thinnest thread was a spider, barely larger than a grain of rice yet speaking with a voice that boomed.

"You're so small . . . ," Ciara said.

"Indeed," came the voice of the Ancient One. "How else would I last so long?"

Ciara nodded, taking this to heart. For as long as she could remember, she had wanted to be *bigger*—not only in size, but in her impact upon the world and the attention she commanded. She had not considered a downside to largeness, or an upside to smallness.

The Ancient One went on: "You come seeking answers, and answers I have aplenty. If you wish to meet the one surviving Illuminator, you need only follow the stars! Start at sunset and go where they lead. When you reach the road of the King, follow it up until you meet the *original* Queen of the Fey. Then head south to the feet of the divine yarn-spinner. There, between the cracks of the world, the Illuminator awaits."

Ciara squinted at the tiny creature, puzzled by its cryptic instructions. But before she could formulate a follow-up question, the spider retracted itself up its silky strand. "Now, child, I must rest, for truth-telling takes it out of me. Good luck getting home, if that is truly where you're meant to be."

RESUME INTERVIEW RECORDING

BYRON: Ooohkay. And this is supposed to be helpful . . . how?

MISHA: I'm just telling you, this is what he was referring to.

BYRON: So in the book, does Ciara do it? Does she follow these instructions and get to . . . the Illuminator?

MISHA: Not really. She starts, but then she gets captured, and then—she sort of gets sent on a different quest, within the fairy realm, and . . . ultimately she realizes she doesn't *want* to go home. She does meet the Illuminator later, in Book Three, but not by this path.

BYRON: Right. Huh . . .

MISHA: Hey . . . Byron? You OK? What're you looking at?

BYRON: *Fuuuuck.*

MISHA: What?

BYRON: I don't even want to say it, but . . . Follow the stars. The sidewalk here . . .

MISHA: Oh my God. The Walk of Fame! That's brilliant.

BYRON: Is it though?

MISHA: YES! It can't be a coincidence! We are standing on a literal path made of stars! This is incredible.

BYRON: OK, but . . . that would imply what exactly? That Annabelle Tobin put some sort of coded reference to the Hollywood Walk of Fame in her first book? And that . . . later, people picked up on it, and . . . it doesn't make sense.

MISHA: However the connection was made, I feel like we have to follow it, because that's probably what Scott did—and it might be what Liza did too.

BYRON: Fair enough. But look, the stars go down the sidewalk in every direction. There's not one clear path. They're all over this neighborhood. Where do we even start?

MISHA: Start at Sunset! It's not the time, it's the *street*. Just a couple blocks south of here. Come on.

BYRON: OK, I'm coming, but—Sunset runs east–west. Where *on* Sunset?

MISHA: "Start at sunset, and go where it leads." The sun setting leads west? Go where . . . Gower! One of the main streets here—Sunset and Gower! It's sort of like the southeast corner of this whole area.

BYRON: This is gonna take all day.

INVESTIGATIVE JOURNAL OF BYRON KIDD

October 30 (Cont'd)

At that point, I stopped my audio recording, which seemed reasonable at the time. We were embarking on a wild-goose chase through an obnoxious and noisy neighborhood, with no one to talk to but each other.

We made our way down to the corner of Sunset and Gower, which was home to a tall building of film studio offices and a smattering of seedy businesses (like a club called Sunset Strippin') and greasy restaurants (like Roscoe's Chicken and Waffles). Misha pointed out the ghastly silhouette of Netflix's headquarters—an obnoxiously modern office building with a memorably geometric (yet unappealing) shape. She seemed to expect I would be more interested in this than I was. I was only excited to make progress toward finding Liza, and otherwise to get the hell out of that neighborhood as fast as humanly possible.

Hollywood stinks. Literally. The most tourist-trafficked corners and businesses are protected by the police, but as soon as you're ten feet off a main thoroughfare, the homeless population is staggering.

At the corner of Sunset and Gower, Misha and I debated our next move, attempting to decipher the clue "follow it up until you reach the road of the King." Misha was stumped and said the line had always been puzzling to her; in the matriarchal realm of the fey, there were no kings. There was a Kings Road in Los Angeles, but it was several miles west.

With little to offer on local geography or Fairy Tale lore, I told her the first "King" that came to mind for me was Elvis. Misha rolled her eyes, probably thinking I had been a teenager myself in the '50s, and continued going through a list of Fairy Tale characters who might metaphorically be "the King."

Bristling with indignation, I googled "Elvis Star Hollywood Walk of Fame" and showed her the result—which Maps pegged on a sidewalk DIRECTLY NORTH of our current position. Misha agreed it was worth looking into at least.

We found Elvis's star on Hollywood Boulevard, which Misha grudgingly accepted, as a working hypothesis, as the "road of the King." But we still needed to figure out where to go next. I asked Misha about the "original Queen of the Fey," and she explained that the queen of the fey was Áine, but that in the mythology of the books, Áine had replaced another who had been named Arianna, so we should be on the lookout for stars belonging to other Arianna celebrities. Grande seemed most likely, but a quick search revealed that Ariana Grande's star was nowhere near and had been installed almost a decade after the first book was published.

As Misha racked her brain for other famous Arianas, I instead asked Misha who was the actress who played the role of Queen Áine. She explained that it was Dame Judi Dench, but we quickly learned (surprisingly) that Dame Judi didn't have a Walk of Fame Star either.

Misha's eyes abruptly lit up, and she said, "But ORIGINALLY, it was Helen Mirren that was cast! Only, she had to drop out before shooting began." Another quick online search yielded the information that Helen Mirren's star was two blocks directly to the west.

As we walked, my skepticism returned. How could Annabelle Tobin have planted that clue before she had even sold the first book, much less entertained the possibility of a film adaptation?

We reached the spot we were looking for, right on the corner of the intersection with Vine, so it seemed worthwhile to nonetheless follow through on the directions and head south. As we walked, Misha mused that the "divine yarn-spinner" might refer to the Ancient One herself, the spider spinning and unraveling her web at the top of a mountain. Who had voiced the character in the movie? Misha was looking it up when I stopped her and pointed to the next star in the sidewalk.

Annabelle Tobin. "Divine yarn-spinner"? Apparently she thought rather highly of herself. Not much of a surprise.

Working Theory: Annabelle encoded her books with an elaborate puzzle spanning a mix of references to her work, L.A. geography, and Hollywood history. This puzzle attracts fans from around the world to Los Angeles, even makes them run away from home and behave secretively . . . and it exists to reward them with . . . what exactly? Some secret location perhaps. And maybe . . . someone was taking advantage of that secret location, using it to kidnap/capture/disappear children who were already vulnerable, because they were far from home and desperate to believe in something.

Still . . . it didn't make sense. Annabelle had been awarded a Walk of Fame star six years ago, after the movies had become a huge hit but before she had begun her period of reclusiveness. She hadn't even wanted one but the studio had persuaded her that it was good for the fourth film's publicity. Yet the first book, which featured this strange set of clues, was now two decades old.

I felt angry at the nonsense, the illogic. It seemed deliberately designed to torture the parts of my brain I held most dear. I was ready to storm off and forget the whole thing when Misha drew my attention across the street to a narrow alleyway. It was not exactly "between the cracks of the world," but close enough. Hanging over the alley was a small neon sign: Illuminated Ink.

I instantly walked toward the sign like a ~~spell had been cast~~ goddamn idiot—foolishly stepping into Vine Street. Misha had to pull me back before a bus could flatten me. We waited for a lull in traffic and then jaywalked, not exchanging a word. Mutually astonished that our traipse through Hollywood had led to SOMETHING.

Liza had been here. I was certain.

CHAPTER SEVENTEEN

INTERVIEW WITH "SALLY," AKA "THE ILLUMINATOR"

October 30, 3:44 p.m.

Location: Illuminated Ink. Tattoo shop in a heavily foot-trafficked neighborhood, tucked away in an alley that would make it nearly impossible to find if you weren't actively looking for it. Alley is impossibly tall and narrow, oddly empty of service entrances or trash cans, as if the two buildings had formerly been touching and only recently pulled apart to make this space. The acoustics were reverberant; as soon as Misha and I stepped into the alley, the din of Hollywood behind us sounded oddly distant, replaced by . . . music. More accurately, electric-guitar shredding, tortured through an amp.

The sound grew louder as we approached the unremarkable glass door with an Open sign flipped outward. Misha and I exchanged a look before proceeding; she was clearly freaked out but equally curious. We stepped inside and were greeted by a cramped "lobby," typical for a seedy tattoo shop, with linoleum floors, vinyl seats, a waist-high counter. But the whole room was jarring to the eyes, almost menacing, because it was soaked in blood-red neon light from another ILLUMINATED INK sign on the wall.

The walls, the counter, every available surface, was covered with sample art—not atypical for a tattoo studio, though the range of designs skewed much more esoteric than most. No flowers or hearts or barbed wire; it was mostly odd symbols I'd never seen before. Some looked tribal, others were closer to Egyptian hieroglyphics. Alphabets I'd never seen spelling out messages I couldn't read.

But many of the symbols were familiar in a way I couldn't put my finger on. I looked at one, vaguely reminiscent of an inverted ankh, and intuitively felt that it represented the concept of a healer. The one next to it, for no reason I could place, seemed to symbolize a sacrifice. The next: the ocean, but also the concept of time. Where were these guesses coming from? And why did I feel so certain?

Strangest of all, by some trick of the flickering neon light, the images in my vision's periphery constantly seemed to be moving, subtly shifting and reshaping themselves. When I'd turn toward the movement and focus on the symbols, they would stop—but I could swear that they were different from the ones I'd seen before. And movement would start back up in my periphery, causing me to look in the other direction, only to be disappointed in the same way. I must have looked a little crazy, continually glancing back and forth, trying to catch the movement dead-on, but constantly let down.

Subject: Sitting in a reclining chair, with her feet propped up on the counter, was the sole current employee. She had a Les Paul electric guitar on her lap and manipulated the strings with fierce precision.

She wore dark overalls without a shirt underneath, and a 1950s-diner-uniform name tag that said Sally. Thick-frame eyeglasses. Winged eyeliner. Her hair was dark, long down one side but partly shaved in a dramatic undercut. Gauge earrings, nose ring, and a stud under her lip. Sleeves of colorful tattoos crept up to her neck. Sized us up suspiciously as we entered.

TRANSCRIPT OF RECORDED INTERVIEW

(*Extremely loud guitar plays at the start of recording. Then cuts out.*)

SALLY: Uh . . . hey.

BYRON: This is your shop?

SALLY: I work here. You have an appointment?

BYRON: We're actually . . . we have some questions.

SALLY: Well, I got a busy afternoon. Try back another time.

BYRON: Doesn't look very busy. Looks empty.

SALLY: It won't be soon. Lotta people in town looking to get ink. So . . .

MISHA: You mean—because of FairyCon, right? Are you gonna be there?

SALLY: My band is playing, so yeah. Here, want a flyer?

MISHA: Oh my God, you're in Wings of Flame? I love you guys. I didn't know you were playing FairyCon this year. This is huge!

SALLY: Yeah, should be good. We haven't played the Navel since 2016. Too many screamy teenagers. But once it was announced that Annabelle would be there, we figured why not.

MISHA: Did you call it the Navel? I love that.

BYRON: We're here about a customer of yours. A girl who—

SALLY: Who told you about the shop?

BYRON: Scott Baker. Er, Scott Angelik, whichever you prefer.

SALLY: No shit? How's Scotty? I haven't seen him in forever.

MISHA: Uh, he's . . . good. Ish. He's working, not far from here.

SALLY: Right, right, I heard he made it back. Good for him.

MISHA: You did his rune, right? It's gorgeous. Kinda your specialty, isn't it?

SALLY: I mean, I'm the only one who can do it, so . . . I guess.

BYRON: You've done it for a lot of people, I'm sure. But I want to ask you about one in particular. (*Sound of phone swiping.*) Do you recognize this girl?

SALLY: She looks young.

BYRON: She is. She come through here? About seven months ago?

SALLY: That's protected by artist-subject confidentiality.

BYRON: OK, well, there wouldn't be any artist-subject confidentiality unless you *had* tattooed her. Which, given that she is *very* much a minor, is a crime.

SALLY: I never said that. And if that's the attitude you're gonna hit me with, time for you to go.

BYRON: I can leave, sure. I can go talk to a cop, about the fact that you are tattooing numerous underage children, which may be connected to a series of abductions and disappearances. I can have this place crawling with cops within the hour. Or would that interrupt your big rush before the convention?

SALLY: Go ahead. Good luck finding us again. Surprised you made it here once.

BYRON: All right then. The hard way.

(*Shuffling sounds, followed by a drop in Misha's voice, so only Byron can hear.*)

MISHA: Come on, Byron. Even if you did get the police to show up, what good is that gonna do?

BYRON: I want to know who she's working with. And what she's getting *paid* to mark these kids who are disappearing!

SALLY: The cops are gonna love this whole Pizzagate-horror-movie theory.

MISHA: Give him a break. He's a dad looking for his kid.

SALLY: He's still an asshole. And dude, why're you even asking me these questions when you're not gonna believe the answers anyway?

BYRON: I'm trying to *understand*. I'm trying to . . . I'm sorry. I can't do this alone.

SALLY: . . . Tell ya what. You wanna understand, you wanna find your kid . . . I can help. But you have to get inked.

BYRON: You mean . . .

SALLY: Yeah. Since you're so interested in the Fairy Rune, and who did and didn't get it. How about *you* get it. Then you might be able to hear what I have to say.

BYRON: I'm not here for a tattoo.

SALLY: Then get the fuck out. Because that's what *I'm* here for, and I've got more customers coming soon. So you can either put down two hundred bucks and come in back and get in a chair . . . or you can walk back up those stairs, and forget this place exists.

BYRON: . . . You take Visa?

INTERVIEW WITH "SALLY," AKA "THE ILLLUMINATOR" PT. 2

Location #2: The "back room" of the Illuminated Ink parlor would better be described as a basement. Or maybe a bunker. Misha stayed behind as I followed "Sally" behind the counter, where she opened a metal door and led me into a stairwell. I descended the concrete steps, past multiple landings. Back and forth, down we went, I would guess five stories below street level.

At the bottom, a long, narrow hallway led to a room that included a reclining chair, not unlike you'd find at a dentist. The room was dark, lit only by dim candles, which seemed like an awful choice for a site where art was being etched in perpetuity on people's skin. The two side walls were mirrored, creating an infinite hall-of-mirrors effect.

As I sat in the chair, Sally worked at an apothecary bench behind me, and I glanced back, catching glimpses in the reflection. She seemed to be using a mortar and pestle and beaker—grinding and mixing and titrating ingredients, one of which looked to be an impossibly long feather.

I took a deep breath as she worked, trying to persuade myself that as long as this yielded useful information, it was worth it. But I was also very much wondering if I had lost my goddamn mind.

RESUME INTERVIEW TRANSCRIPT

SALLY: All set here. You've had a tattoo before?

BYRON: My wife's name. Left arm. College.

SALLY: Didn't have you pegged for a hopeless romantic.

BYRON: Long time ago.

SALLY: Just hopeless now, huh? Well, this tattoo will be . . . a little different. I do a more traditional method. Hand-mixed ink, bone-and-mallet application.

BYRON: Artisanal tattoos . . . that the new frontier of hipsterdom?

SALLY: I've been doing it this way for a long time. And if you want it to actually *work*, this is the way. Now—shirt off, lay on your belly.

(Tink *sound as the first mark is placed. Continues through the rest of the recording.*)

BYRON: Ohhhhhh fuck, that hurts!

SALLY: The pain is in proportion to your resistance. So for you . . . yeah, it's *really* gonna hurt. You wanna keep going?

BYRON: It's fine. Ah! You can continue, but I want answers.

SALLY: Fair enough. But first I need you to tell *me* something. Because if I don't find out the answer, I'm gonna be in trouble.

BYRON: With who? What do you mean?

SALLY: Were you not listening? I just explained . . . God, you're difficult. Now, who else knows about your little investigation?

BYRON: It's just me. And Misha out there.

SALLY: I get a sense there's someone else.

BYRON: My wife knows, sort of, although—we're separated, and . . . she doesn't believe any of it. Ahh . . .

SALLY: You don't really believe it either. Grip these handles down here, it'll help with the pain.

BYRON: OK. . . . Hey! Did you . . . am I tied down? How'd you do that?

SALLY: I need you to sit still. All right?

BYRON: Let me . . . what the fuck?

SALLY: No one can hear you down here. Now, if those are the only people that know what you're doing—good. Keep it that way.

BYRON: OK . . . OW!

SALLY: Under no condition should you tell anyone else. Don't put anything online, on social, anything like that. Or you'll be in biiiiig trouble.

BYRON: With who? What're you—ahh, Jesus!

SALLY: Hold still. Now, I'm gonna tell you what you've probably heard, but haven't bothered to believe. This rune will grant you the ability to move across the divide. Obviously, others who wanted to cross the threshold have come here before.

BYRON: Liza . . .

SALLY: All that I'll say is most who cross over these days come to me first. But that doesn't mean everyone who's come to me has crossed over. Understand?

BYRON: You're a step on the way.

SALLY: Something like that. The rune is required—the rune can open your eyes—but the rune alone is not enough. You need to find a portal.

BYRON: OK. And where—ahh, Jesus!

SALLY: Don't squirm. Portals are all over if you know how to look. Now, I need to warn you: crossing over requires a complete psychic change. And once you're there—you can't come back. Not without permission.

BYRON: You mean . . . from Annabelle?

SALLY: Annabelle? Hilarious. I'm talking about a god.

BYRON: The . . . the Green Man.

SALLY: You said it, not me. He controls the borders. The only ones who come back, they do so because he wants something from them.

BYRON: Something like . . . tattoos. To bring more people to him.

SALLY: Now you're getting it.

BYRON: Or a series of books?

SALLY: He doesn't care about books. He cares about *belief.*

BYRON: And a spell, right? In six parts.

SALLY: The outline is complete, I have to switch over for the primary catalyst.

(*Sound of bottles clinking.*)

BYRON: Wait, wait, wait, no, what is *that*?

SALLY: This is what you signed up for. *Dust.*

BYRON: No! Stop it! Stop . . . Misha! Help! Fuck, what're you . . .

(*Cries of extreme pain. End of recording.*)

CHAPTER EIGHTEEN

EMAIL

From: m.pimm@ucla.eng.edu
To: bybyronjames@gmail.com

Byron,

Like you asked, I'm writing down what I saw when you got your tattoo. I understand that you want to try to have everything documented, so I'll endeavor to be as precise as possible. I know this is about more than journalistic rigor. The story has power.

After you went through the door into the back room of the parlor, I was alone in the lobby, and started studying the symbols on the wall. From my research, I recognized many of them as letters from various ancient alphabets. Gaelic, Sanskrit, etc.

While I waited, two girls came into the parlor. They were escorted by a tall, gangly older man in an old-fashioned suit. Perhaps he had considered the possibility of staying, but when he saw me, his eyes narrowed in suspicion, and he left with a bow.

The girls were both excited, wearing backpacks, carrying nearly empty Frosty cups. Teenage girls on vacation. I would've guessed their ages to be sixteen and thirteen, though they told me they were both eighteen—no doubt so I wouldn't impugn their presence at a tattoo parlor. I asked if they were here for the Fairy Rune, too, and they said yes. Apparently my "too" put them at ease, and they were suddenly more forthcoming. They had come from Baltimore with their father escorting them on a trip to attend FairyCon that weekend. They were excited to have gotten tickets to Annabelle's panel, which sold out instantly; people are scalping tickets for $500 each.

Around this point in the conversation, the door to the back opened, and Sally emerged, removing latex gloves. She let me know her work was complete, but you were rather indisposed— "Maybe not as tough as he thought," she said—and you needed help getting out. I went around the counter into the back room, where I found you passed out in the tattoo chair, eyes flitting, in and out of consciousness.

(I'll note here for clarity and in response to some of your own description that the back room immediately adjoined the front, with no travel down stairs required.)

Sally had already put your shirt back on, but I could see the top of the tattoo at the base of your neck. In the darkness, it looked radiant with greenish light. Sally informed me nonchalantly that you would be fine, you just needed to drink lots of water and rest. I helped you to your feet; it was like assisting an extremely inebriated person.

We headed out the front door. I was disturbed to leave those two girls to get a tattoo—one whose effect on you had been so extreme—but my focus was on taking care of you. I helped you down the alley, out onto Vine, where you recoiled painfully from the sun. I asked if you wanted to go to the hospital, but you declined, and we headed to the car.

Once you had collapsed into my passenger seat and drank an entire water bottle, you regained some clear-headedness. You then insisted on going back, on helping those girls, on getting answers. I tried to convince you to go home, but you wouldn't hear of it, so I looped around the block, drove slowly down Vine. . . .

But there was no Illuminated Ink.

I say this with absolute certainty. The unnaturally small alleyway was still there, but the neon sign was gone. I parked and got
out to make sure; I found a metal service door where the glass
entrance had been. I waited for it to open, but when it did, I saw
into the kitchen of a restaurant.

After that, I took you back to your motel, and you collapsed
into a deep sleep. I stayed for a while to make sure you were OK,
but once the (remarkably loud) snoring started, I headed out.

I drove back to the Westside, exhausted. I needed to get to campus for class. The whole time I was distracted, playing back the
events of the morning, wondering if I could trust my own recollections. That's when you started blowing up my phone. I stepped
out to speak with you briefly, and you were . . . agitated, to say the
least. You kept saying to me I needed to "Get it down, get it all
down."

Now that it is evening, and I have had a couple cannabis gum-
mies to settle my nerves, I have written everything under the terms
that you demanded: just the facts.

But there are other facts I ought to add to this list. Facts from
today. Like that we spoke to a young man who appears to have
aged little, if at all, in the past eighteen years. And the fact that we
found a code, hidden in Annabelle's book, that led us to a tattoo
shop, which then disappeared entirely.

If all this is not proof of *magic*—of some force or energy that
defies rational explanation—then I'd like to know what it is.

Best,
Misha

REPLY

Misha,

Thank you for your account of the day's events. I suppose it should go without saying, but I'll say it anyway—thank you for helping me get the fuck out of that tattoo parlor. Without your help, I might be lying in a heap on a sidewalk in Hollywood.

I slept through the rest of the afternoon and woke at 8 PM, which boded poorly for any hope of getting back on a normal sleeping schedule. Since waking, I've felt strange. I have an odd sense of *clarity*, as though a veil has been pierced. Perhaps the pain of the tattoo, worse than any I can remember, was purifying.

When I look at said tattoo in the mirror, it feels oddly *right* on me. I endured it in the service of getting information, and it will be worthwhile if it helps get me closer to Liza. But even if it doesn't, I take pleasure knowing it brings me into communion with her. To many, this mark symbolizes their love for a work of fiction; to me, it represents my love for my daughter. I'm OK with that.

All these things *could* make me more susceptible to wondering if something "magic" is going on. But the word "magic" is essentially a surrender. A concession that the problem is unsolvable. And I'm not about to give up like that.

Upon reflection, I think there is a reasonable, scientific explanation for everything we've witnessed: I was drugged. It would be easy to administer an IV while tattooing someone, and if some of the compound was in my skin it could even be slowly releasing into my body now. This might have colored and shaped my recollections, creating a false memory of descending deep below ground.

What did *you* see that you can't explain? As far as I can tell, it's only your inability to find the tattoo parlor again. Given that you were driving around with me passed out in the passenger seat, hurrying to get me back to the motel, feeling disoriented and exhausted by our journey all over Hollywood, your difficulty finding the place again hardly seems surprising.

REPLY

Byron,

If you think you're drugged, go to the hospital ffs!

Look, I actually care about you, dude. And I care about your wonderfully weird daughter, even though we've never met. You are not insane to be looking for her . . . but it seems clear to me that the rules of the search won't be the ones you're used to. They will not be the ones that have aided you in dozens of journalistic investigations. They are irrational rules. Imaginative ones. They are not rules at all—they are forces primal and primeval, energetic and untamable. You don't know what you're dealing with, and you apparently don't know how to say "I don't know."

In other words, maybe the "surrender" you're afraid of is exactly what you need. From the Christ narrative to Buddhist transcendence to the tenets of Islam (which literally translates as "submission"), all the great spiritual stories are united by one common theme: victory and understanding are paradoxically only possible by *giving up*.

I say all this because I want to help you find Liza. But until you are willing to embrace the existence of what you don't understand, you will only scratch the surface of this mystery. And you will never bring her back.

I would point you toward a story from *The Hidden World*, which I think might be important to your investigation.

Best,
Misha

SHORT STORY

From *The Hidden World: On Faeries, Fauns & Other Creatures of Folklore,* by Sir Henry Raleigh. Published 1889, Oxford University Press.

THE GREEN MAN

This tale was passed unto me while I ventured through the forests of central Prussia, an ancient stronghold of various Pagan peoples who see themselves as children of these verdant lands. This account can be attributed to no singular individual, for it is more Creation Myth than Fairy Tale. It is my own best amalgamation of the shreds I gathered from numerous Tellers, each willing to part with only a small morsel of narrative, as though divulging more might incur the wrath of the story's subject.

At the beginning of time, the first tribe of man lived in a state of dependence upon Mother Nature. Her seasons gave order to their days; her branches gave shelter to their homes; her fruits and animals provided the food that sustained the tribe. Nature herself was worshipped and held in esteem above all mankind.

But eventually, the tribe's Shaman grew jealous of the reverence paid to Mother Nature, for he was hungry for power and adoration. So the Shaman devised a great deceit. He told the people that his magic gave him control over Mother Nature.

At first, the tribe laughed at his claim. But he was a weaver of stories, the one to whom they listened every night around the fire. And everything that happened in the natural world, he turned into a story and explained to them as his own doing.

When the rains fell, the Shaman told a story of how various members of the tribe had shown him kindness that day, and he said the rains were a reward for their generosity. Many laughed at his claims and mocked the Shaman without mercy.

Then the rains turned to flood and two of the tribe's children were washed away, never to be seen again. The Shaman told the tribe that the flood was punishment for the mockery he had endured. Some still doubted him, but some began to wonder if he was speaking the truth.

To persuade the tribe, the Shaman challenged Mother Nature to appear and refute his claim that night. But she did not appear. So the tribe began to follow the Shaman's instructions and brought him gifts the next day.

Then a great wind blew across the land, and the flooding began to dry, and the crops began to bloom. The Shaman told the people that the wind was his own breath, dispelling the flood and delivering life. And he sang to the people:

Come hear me and heed me, come feed me your love

Your fate is my burden, your faith is my blood . . .

Thus did the tribe come to believe that the Shaman truly did control the natural world. They named him the Green Man, for his stories brought the life of spring.

But as spring turned to summer, there came a period of drought. Months passed without a rain, and crops withered on the vine. The people began to starve, and some turned their appetites upon one another.

In their fear, they beseeched the Green Man for answers. He told them he wished nothing more than to bring relief, but he could not until they recognized him for his true nature: as a god.

So the starving people did. They fell on their knees in desperation and hailed the Green Man as the holiest of holies. They begged him for relief from the drought.

And from their belief, a curious transformation unfolded. The power of their belief rendered upon the Green Man the very powers he had claimed. Thus his lie was made a truth; his deceitful claim to power was realized; he was elevated unto divinity.

That night, the rain fell mightily upon the tribe. The drought was ended. And when the morning came, the Green Man was gone—transported from the realm of mortals into the Hidden World. Never to be seen again, but forever to be worshipped. For those who honor him will be fed with rain, and those who forsake him will be drowned by flood.

And those who listen carefully at night may sometimes hear his song upon the wind . . .

Come hear me and heed me, come feed me your love
Your fate is my burden, your faith is my blood . . .

REPLY

Misha,

I appreciate that you are invested in finding Liza too. And maybe it's true that the "rules" of this investigation are not the ones that have served me before. I don't appreciate your insinuation that my methodologies are endangering my child. But one thing you said did strike a chord, because Liza used to say it too: I don't know how to say "I don't know."

Liza used to get so mad whenever she'd tried to talk to me. She'd have a problem at school, usually another kid not treating her well, and when she unloaded her issues during the car-ride home, it always SOUNDED like she was asking for advice. Naturally, I'd want to roll up my sleeves and figure out how to solve the problem, whether that meant repairing a friendship or getting righteous justice (I was always more inclined toward the latter). But she was never looking for a solution. She was looking for empathy. She didn't WANT to "know" the answer. She wanted a hug.

I'm still not inclined to explain anything by magic. But I can concede with regard to MANY aspects of this mystery, including the question that matters most (where Liza actually IS)—I DON'T HAVE A FUCKING CLUE. And maybe that's OK for today. As long as I keep finding enough to move forward.

Which brings me to the story you sent. I don't know if you believe it to be literally/historically true. I don't think that even matters. What matters is that it clearly describes an origin for the
strange, obscure deity Annabelle has referred to, and who was
mentioned in the first couple FT books. Oddly enough, it also
feels like a story about Annabelle herself—a storyteller whose creation takes on a life of its own.

But more important to me is the song here—which I've heard
before. The homeless man near my motel, who attacked me one
time and saved me another, was singing those words the night I
met him. So I decided I needed to talk to him again.

Problem was: how to find him? He had abandoned my motel
and returned to whatever corner of the city he called home. Did I
have any clue to go on? He had introduced himself as "Mr. Echo,"
and one night had said he was going back home to the "Kingdom
of Echoes."

A week ago, I wouldn't have given that a second thought. But
after our scavenger hunt through Hollywood, I was looking at
things differently. I opened Maps on my phone, scrolled around
the surrounding area. And since you know L.A. much better than
I do, you can probably guess what I found, just a couple miles
south of the shithole motel where I currently reside.

ECHO PARK.

CHAPTER NINETEEN

INTERVIEW WITH MR. ECHO

Location: Echo Park is a microcosm of Los Angeles, alternately beautiful and hideous. Ten acres of grass and paths, dominated by a large man-made lake. On one side, swan boats for tourists to enjoy by day. On the other side, a sprawling homeless encampment, with two hundred residents in an amorphous, informal community on the shore. Trash cans overflow, syringes collect in eddies, and the sunset turns the water's surface so fiery red and orange it looks almost like lava.

As I looked for parking nearby, I could see that the neighborhood was awkwardly mid-gentrification, like a werewolf halfway transformed. Hip coffee shops and artisan ice cream and converted lofts were sandwiched in among laundromats and payday lenders. A taco truck had a line down the block, as dozens of urban foodies waited an hour for the Most Authentic Taco in L.A.

I stopped in a liquor store run by a Korean family, picked up a bottle of bourbon. Made my way over to the park itself. Took a moment to read the plaque at the entrance. Learned that back in the '20s, the park had been the site of the Christian revival led by Aimee Semple McPherson, who pioneered the use of mass media to build America's first megachurch. (She also later faked her own death in an effort to run off with her secret lover and pretended to have been kidnapped when she was caught.)

I digress. But is it a digression? This is the energy that permeates this park, this lake, this city. A spirit of beautiful illusion and dangerous deception, of belief and lies and magic.

Looking for Mr. Echo, I made my way into the homeless encampment, astonished by the breadth and diversity of life there. There were a few people shooting up or sprawled out unconscious, as I expected. But there was also a handful of young residents playing instruments and dancing. A few loners gathered near the brightest streetlights to read books from the library as the sun went down. Old women gossiped and handed out food.

I made my way among an Escher-esque amalgamation of tents augmented with plywood boards, tarps, ladders, shopping carts, and extension cords to create a multi-tiered housing complex with no clear boundaries. Plenty of joy alongside the hardship. I felt a strange mix of curiosity and compassion and shame for how I usually averted my gaze from such communities, such people, such realities. (All right, enough indulgence, back to the facts.)

As darkness fell, I asked around about Mr. Echo, and everyone seemed to know who I was talking about, though they differed on where to find him. Eventually I was pointed to a location south of the main encampment, and I left behind the little city of tents, striding down into the quieter part of the park. I found him on a bench near the water's edge, in front of a large restroom building, its walls entirely covered in layers of graffiti. A scattering of incandescent lights provided intermittent pools of visibility.

Subject: Mr. Echo was wearing worn-out UGG boots two sizes too small for him, with his toes poking out of holes he'd cut in the ends. He had on a trench coat, no shirt, and a pair of baggy black slacks. His beard touched the middle of his chest and contained bits of his last several meals.

Beside him sat an empty bottle of gin. His eyes were glassy, but he smiled at me in recognition as I approached, and when I showed him the bourbon, he indicated for me to join him. I started the recording.

TRANSCRIPT OF RECORDED INTERVIEW

MR. ECHO: Well, look who it is. What brings you down here?

BYRON: I was hoping I could ask you a couple questions.

MR. ECHO: You provide the drinks, you can ask anything you'd like.

BYRON: OK, first off, I guess I'll just come right out and ask . . . are you the Green Man?

(*Mr. Echo laughs uproariously.*)

MR. ECHO: Oh, that's good. I wish! Where'd you get that idea?

(*Sound of pages flipping.*)

BYRON: It's this book. In the story "The Green Man" . . . he sings a song that I've heard you singing. Are you familiar with the story at all?

MR. ECHO: Oh, I know it inside and out. I wrote the damn thing!

BYRON: I'm sorry . . . you wrote that song?

MR. ECHO: No, no, the song is ancient. But that story. All of 'em actually. I wrote that book.

BYRON: Ahhh. I . . . think you're mistaken.

MR. ECHO: I mean only that I put together the words in the right order to tell the tale. In truth, no one writes anything on their own. A book like that is written in magic and bound in dreams. It's all inspiration, beamed into your brain! Stories are the light that starts at the dawn of time, a great Big Bang burst blown outward, reflected off of cultures, refracted through individual minds, so we can see the colors. Understand? Stories are *interpreted,* not created. And never never, *never* destroyed.

BYRON: Right. Well, this book is over a century old. It's written by a man named Sir Henry Raleigh.

MR. ECHO: Yeah. That's me! At least, it was.

BYRON: . . . I don't understand. That's not possible.

MR. ECHO: Yet here we are. You didn't really think my name was Echo, did you?

BYRON: No, but . . . it doesn't make sense. That you, or any living person, could've written this.

MR. ECHO: Like I said, I *transcribed* the story. It was around well before I came along.

BYRON: So you are . . . how old?

MR. ECHO: Five or six decades, I'd guess.

BYRON: And yet you claim to be the author of something more than twice that age.

MR. ECHO: I skipped some time. Time on the other side, you don't age, it barely goes by. Like an unlit candle, you know?

BYRON: Not really.

MR. ECHO: Listen—you came and found me. You are entitled to your skepticism, but if you intend to cling to it until the bitter end, why bother with the questions?

BYRON: (*Sighs*) Because . . . my daughter. I'm lost.

MR. ECHO: Ah, yes of course. I had a daughter once. Constance.

BYRON: That . . . huh. Yes. I heard that, about Sir Henry.

MR. ECHO: You seem impressed that I remember her name. I'm not *that* old. Do you tend to forget the name of your own?

BYRON: OK, if you're who you say you are, this daughter of yours—she's the one responsible for this volume, right? The manuscript was pieced together and submitted for publication by Sir Henry's daughter after he vanished.

MR. ECHO: And I wish she hadn't! That book has wrought nothing but trouble. But the fault is my own. I was off gallivanting about the world, collecting tales, when I should've been home reading to her.

BYRON: I never did much gallivanting, but . . . I can relate.

MR. ECHO: For you there's still hope, though, isn't there? If you're willing enough.

BYRON: I'd do anything.

MR. ECHO: You'd die for her, sure. But would you suspend your disbelief? Would you believe the words of a gin-soaked trash-clad troubadour?

BYRON: If it would help, of course.

MR. ECHO: You don't get to know the outcome before you take the risk. And what's at risk is not your life but your *mind*. I ask this because to tell you my tale will cost me, and I'll not pay the price of the telling in vain.

(*Sound of a shirt being pulled up.*)

BYRON: How's this for proof of my dedication?

MR. ECHO: (*Chuckles*) My, my, my. The rune looks good on you. Well, not exactly *good,* but I've seen worse. Want to see mine?

(*More clothes ruffling.*)

BYRON: Oh, Jesus. Is that a burn?

MR. ECHO: Such was the way, back in my day. Pain is a rite of passage.

BYRON: The tattoo wasn't a walk in the park.

MR. ECHO: I'll say that counts for something in the way of bona fides. Drink with me then.

BYRON: Thanks, but I'll pass. Trying to lay off.

MR. ECHO: Suit yourself. Get comfortable, and I'll unfold for you a tale.

BYRON: One from the book?

MR. ECHO: One that didn't make it. I had planned to include this story as an introduction to *The Hidden World,* but never got around to it for reasons that will become clear. Still, it is vital to understanding who I am, and how everything came to pass.

THE TRUE TALE OF SIR HENRY RALEIGH

In Devonshire in my youth, my father, Lord Raleigh the Senior, was the Steward of lands that encompassed much of the Fellwood Forest. As a growing lad endowed with an imaginative nature, I often traipsed into those woods, making boyhood mischief.

My mother, the Lady Raleigh, being of a nervous temperament, implored me not to tarry far from sight of our manor home, and to stay away from the untamed wild of the forest. No doubt in a well-intended effort to impress upon me the danger therein, she warned me of the fey that lived on our lands, who were greatly angered by any mortal intrusion upon their territory. Yet my mind was stirred by the possibility of making the acquaintance of a fairy, and so my mother relayed to me . . .

The Terrible and Tragic Story of George Calloway: Once there was a curious lad who lived in the nearby village of Barnaby, and who defied common sense and went into the Fellwood in search of joy and mischief, and thus was kidnapped by the fey and taken captive in their realm. For sixty days they held him there and then released him home—but in that time, sixty years had passed in the mortal world, so he returned to find his parents long dead and his brothers aged into old men. None in the village knew him, and they foreswore his tale for vile treachery and drove him into exile.

I was entranced by this fable, yet its warning fell upon deaf ears. It so played upon my boyhood dreams that I was even more possessed by the curiosity that drove me into the trees in search of the fey, even if they might spirit me away. The most immense sadness of my youth may have been never coming upon a single fairy in that wood.

Yet there came a day after some years when my father saw fit to call upon his brother in Cardinham, and our entire household uprooted for the two-days' journey to pass an August in the more temperate lands nearer the sea. There I met my cousins and was quickly taken into their confidence. Not far from their estate was the dark and dense Westingwood, a forest that called to my imagination even more than the one near our own home had done. I thrilled with delight at the chance to visit it—but my cousins sat me down and did thus unfold:

The Terrible and Tragic Story of Alan Gregory: Once there lived a troublemaking youth who dwelt in the nearby hamlet of Isgrove and who defied common sense and went into the wood in search of joy and mischief. Thus was he kidnapped by the fey and taken captive in their realm. He was held there for one hundred days, at which point the fey took pity and freed him to go home. But as he staggered back into Isgrove, he discovered that one hundred years had passed in his village. He wept over the graves of his parents, and his name had been long since forgotten. When he tried to tell his tale to the descendants of his brothers, they accused him of devilry, and banished him for all time.

The tale was nearly identical to the one I'd heard at home! And to many, this similarity might be taken as proof that it was merely a cautionary falsehood, crafted for the prevention of mischief and the protection of adventuresome children. Yet to me the similarity had the opposite effect, instead serving to verify its deepest truth. Such is my nature that it did not seem impossible for both tales to be equally valid and real.

I thus ventured deep into the Westingwood, and there encountered a unique and intriguing being, whose precise nature I shall not name but whose personage was winged and whose provenance was that Other World that adjoins but evades our own. He informed me that his own world was in fearful retreat, as the Age of Reason drove back its edges and encroached upon its boundaries. When I implored him for advice on how to find his realm, he told me to seek out a lake of pure swirling silver, then look up and see the castle in the clouds, then climb up to meet it and look down on the world with new eyes.

The seed was thus planted in my soul that would one day grow into my calling, though it was many a year before I was able to heed it in full. I became a collector of stories, and sought out great volumes from around the world. I filled our manor's study with written treasures in many tongues. Yet to my father, these trifles were merely a waste of my allowance, and he endeavored mightily to drive those passions from my heart.

At that, he failed. When my father passed from consumption, rest his soul, I was liberated to enlarge the scope of my study. Leaving my wife and young daughter at home, I took to the sea in search of noble truth, like many a gentleman-scholar of my age But instead of seeking out truth in the natural world, I endeavored to discover it in the narrative one. Instead of collecting specimens, I went out to collect stories.

Many of them I found, from the lips of many a great teller, and I endeavored to do justice to the depths and rhythms that animate them all. And when I had found enough and gained enough insight and saw the world anew, at last the great heart of all stories revealed itself to me, and through it I moved across the void and entered that Hidden World from whence the stories came.

(*Long silence.*)

BYRON: OK. So . . . wow. Let me get this straight. You went looking for stories . . . because you wanted to get over to the Hidden World.

MR. ECHO: Yes! That's what people call it here, where it seems to be hidden, but then you're there, and it's this world that's hidden, and oh lord do you miss it. Couple decades without certain essentials like food, daylight, and reliable physical laws, and you get a little squirrelly.

BYRON: You're saying . . . you found it. You went there.

MR. ECHO: Indeed. Little by little, each new tale provided another piece of the puzzle. I wrote them all down until the tales started writing themselves. That's what "The Djinn Within" was all about. Did you read that one yet?

BYRON: Sorry, I sort of gave the book to someone else who's helping me.

MR. ECHO: Ah, Mr. Quixote, I'm glad to hear you've found a Sancho Panza of your own! I never could. I was doomed to solo-seek the truth, and it took me quite some time to find my way.

BYRON: But . . . how did you do it?

MR. ECHO: By following the instructions I was given in the Westingwood!

BYRON: That stuff about a lake and a castle in the clouds—you call those instructions?

MR. ECHO: I followed them to the best of my ability and caught my first glimpse. It was still many years and many stories before I was able to get over there.

BYRON: I don't have many years, I need to get there now. And even if I somehow do "cross over" . . . I need to be able to get back. And bring Liza. Now, can you help, or not?

MR. ECHO: Getting back is both much harder and much simpler. For the Hidden World belongs to the Green Man, and the only way you'll ever come back is with his permission. But he rarely grants it, since the human imagination is the resource upon which he feeds. He is more likely to suck at your mind until all that's left is a shell of misery and despair.

BYRON: But he let *you* leave.

MR. ECHO: Yes, well, I made him a deal. That's the only way: to offer something more valuable than the energy of your spirit. I was a ripe resource, apparently, and afforded him a century of dreams to consume.

When I was reaching the end of my usefulness, he proposed an alternative. He informed me that my collection of tales had not merely languished in my library but in fact, had been published, thanks to my daughter. She was long dead, sadly, but the book remained in limited circulation. And the Green Man told me that he'd send me home—send me *here* anyway—if I'd do a little job. Get my old book into the hands of a certain young dreamer.

BYRON: Annabelle . . .

MR. ECHO: That's how he works. He sees the lines of fate and plucks the strings from over in his world. He knew Annabelle was special and somehow saw that with the right little nudge he could get her to change the world.

So, I hopped over to be the nudger. I tracked down a manuscript of my book and donated it to a little bookstore in North Hollywood. Just the tiniest intervention, so that it would be there for her. That was all it took. And in exchange—freedom! Seemed to me like a good deal at the time. But looking back, I'd rather have been drunk to the lees of my soul than have played such a part in what happened.

BYRON: So he honored his half of the deal.

MR. ECHO: He cannot do otherwise. It's the laws of his magic, the way he works. The terms are clear and binding. Of course, he always gets the better end.

BYRON: Suppose he were to make it over to our world . . .

MR. ECHO: I'd rather not!

BYRON: What might happen, if he could?

MR. ECHO: Same thing that happened to the Hidden World. The end of one story, and the beginning of another. *His* story. He is a god now, you understand? If he came over here, with all the power he's built up . . . people here would believe in him, and the world would be his.

BYRON: If he's that powerful, then why'd he let you out, and let you tell this story to anyone who will hear it?

MR. ECHO: Oh, he didn't "let me" do anything. Part of the terms are that if I tell anyone the truth about what happened to me, tell anyone who I really am and where I've been, that's the end for me! Hasn't been the easiest. Every night I go to sleep with nightmares from another world, and I can't tell anyone about them, or I'll pay with my life!

BYRON: But look—you're telling me now. And you're OK.

MR. ECHO: Oh, not for long. You should probably be going.

BYRON: I'm not about to—

MR. ECHO: *Go,* Byron. You can't do me any good. But your daughter . . . maybe it's not too late for her.

(*Soft rippling and splashing sounds can be heard on the recording.*)

BYRON: What was that?

MR. ECHO: That, friend, was the sound of my time coming.

EMAIL

From: bybyronjames@gmail.com
To: m.pimm@ucla.eng.edu

Misha,

I'm entrusting you with this recording, in part because I fear more than ever that I won't be able to finish this. I don't want to burden you with that responsibility, but I need someone to know what happened. I'm also writing to you because getting it all down is the only way I know to wrap my mind around what's happened.

As you'll notice, the recording after Mr. Echo/Sir Henry said, "The sound of my time coming," is a jumbled chaotic mess, so I will instead try to describe what happened. Upon uttering those words, Henry pointed at the lake in front of us. The green algae that rippled on the water seemed to be drifting together, like a congealing island of pond scum forming the image of . . . a man? The surface *slished* with eddying currents, as if something were moving through the depths.

Henry glanced over his shoulder at the restroom building behind us. I followed his gaze to see a message spray-painted on the wall:

The oath is broken. The price is paid.

And underneath it, almost like a signature, was the symbol tattooed on my back. The Fairy Rune.

I was certain the message and symbol had not been there when I arrived. But they looked caked-on and grimy, as though they'd been written ages ago.

As I stared in disbelief, I heard a cry of surprise, followed by a splash. I turned—and saw Henry, now thrashing in the lake. How had he managed to fall in? A simple drunken stumble? Or something else entirely?

Didn't matter. He churned the water furiously, then disappeared under the surface. Within seconds, he surged upward, fighting for air, for his life.

Roused from my stupor, I went to him, pulling off my jacket and wading into the chilly water, trying to do what I could to help. He thrashed and kicked and shouted, desperately battling for breath.

It became clear that Henry was tangled in thick reeds. But it was impossible how thoroughly his body was encircled. As I came over and attempted to help, he looked half-mummified by the slippery, slimy tendrils.

Panic is a surefire way to drown faster, so I shouted at Henry to calm down, which of course had the opposite effect. I trudged closer but paused when I saw a silvery shape gleaming in the moonlight. It was Henry's knife, the same impossibly sharp one he'd used to break into my motel room. And it whistled through the air.

I pulled up short, inches from getting sliced. Henry was cutting through the reeds wrapped around him, but in the churning chaos of the water, he was barely making progress.

I shouted at Henry to stop, but he could barely even grunt through the pain and terror. His head dropped below the surface, and he gurgled each time he bobbed up. I circled around, trying to stay clear of the weapon.

Swimming up from behind, I grabbed Henry around the midsection and heaved backward, floating him toward shore. But even as I kept his head above water, I heard awful gurgling sounds from his throat and realized he was choking. A thick reed was stretched taut around his neck while another seemed to be sliding *into* his mouth, as though crawling down his throat.

Whatever was happening to him . . . it was alive.

Henry became increasingly desperate, thrashing. I tugged at the reed that was suffocating him, pulled at it in vain, but its scum-slicked surface resisted my grip.

Henry wriggled his knife up to slash at the reed—and I could swear, I felt it go soft before he even struck it. All the tendrils that were holding his body *relaxed* at the very moment he moved the knife. As a result, Henry's blade easily cut through the reed.

But that was not all it cut through. As Henry was freed and I extracted the slimy mass from his neck, he let loose a horrible groan. Deep crimson swirled in the water. In cutting himself free, he had also stabbed himself in the throat. He gave a sputtering cough of surprise, followed, incredibly, by a chuckle, as though amused at how he had been fooled.

I dragged him up onto the shore. He was clutching his neck, but the blood was erupting through his fingers and darkening his beard. He must've hit an artery. I told him he'd be all right, though I knew it was a lie. I fumbled for my cellphone to call 911. Henry shook his head, with a strange measure of equanimity, and pushed the cellphone away. "Finished," he told me. "Doesn't matter."

I knew he was right and put the phone away. He didn't want an ambulance. He wanted someone to witness his final moments.

Henry pushed his massive knife into my hands. "You'll need it," he told me. "The Ruby Shard." The blade was still slick and dark from his "self-inflicted" wound.

My mind recoiled at the prospect of leaving with this weapon in my possession, but I knew he was right. Whatever was ahead, I would need any small advantage I could get, and I started to suspect there really was something special about the blade. Who was I to refuse a man's dying wish?

I accepted the knife, awkwardly pushing it into the large inner pocket of my jacket. Henry used the last of his strength to spit out one final blood-flecked syllable. "*Go.*" He collapsed to the grass. Dying.

As I turned back, a crowd of onlookers was gathering. Four or five inhabitants of the park's encampment had converged, their jaws dropped in shock and horror. They saw me, no doubt, standing beside a man who was crumpled and bleeding at the side of the lake. I had no time to address them. Even if I did, what would I say? The police would be on the scene soon, and my search for Liza would be over. So I fled, rushing past their stares, and eventually made it to my car.

By the time I was back at the motel, my heart was still thumping, and I felt a twinge of guilt and regret at having left Mr. Echo like that—particularly knowing that he had decided to give his life for the purpose of telling me the truth.

As I write these words, I can almost hear your voice asking if I believe that the impossible story Mr. Echo told me is, in fact, THE TRUTH?

I'm not sure. I can feel my mind seesawing in and out of accepting all that I've seen and heard tonight. Perhaps Mr. Echo spray-painted that message on the side of the restroom wall himself before I arrived. Perhaps he stumbled drunkenly into the lake and accidentally stabbed himself. Perhaps the story he told was a strange mix of mental illness (on his part) and suggestion (on my own).

But such explanations, piled on top of one another, feel woefully inadequate. There must be something in between the hard and fast rules of logic, facts, and data, and the soft squishy surrender to your insistence on "magic." Or maybe magic *is* the in-between.

Ultimately, I realize, I can either reject what Sir Henry said, which would leave me with nothing but bewilderment . . . or accept it, and believe him, which presents me with a way forward toward finding Liza, and more important, some shred of hope.

So yes. To my great surprise . . . I believe him. And as a result, already, I feel like I am *closer*. Closer to the source that Sir Henry had been seeking. Closer to the Hidden World, whatever that might be. Closer to the Green Man, if that is indeed an actual person. Closer to answers.

Most important . . . closer to Liza.

CHAPTER TWENTY

REPLY

From: m.pimm@ucla.eng.edu
To: bybyronjames@gmail.com

Whoa.

First off, I am so sorry to hear of the loss of Sir Henry/Mr. Echo. I can hardly imagine the shock you must be in.

Yet I just want to point out that you're now writing with more clarity than ever. The email you sent me is less focused on "the facts," but I think it's not "indulgent," if anything it's more revealing of what's really going on here. You ARE getting closer. And I want to do whatever I can.

Obviously, I am freaking tf out about what this means. Um, a Victorian writer slipped into the alternate dimension that he was writing about? And emerged back into our world a century later to deliver his book to Annabelle Tobin? WUT. I'm sure you have your doubts, but it does square with all we've seen.

NOW—here's where I can be helpful. Because while you were pursuing him last night, I may have found something useful. What I'm about to tell you, I'm sure you would've laughed off a couple days ago—but something tells me enough has happened that you might see it differently now.

To back up—we know that the Hidden World of the Fairy Tale books is an analog for the one referred to in Sir Henry's book of mythology. But what IS the Hidden World? WHERE is it? What does it look like? And as you asked—how do you GET there?

Many fantasy books would give us something to go on because they come with a map. One of the defining features of the genre (ever since Tolkien) is a hand-drawn map (or several) on the first or last pages of the book. It can orient the reader in complex stories, but more than anything serves to inspire confidence. It says, *Don't worry, I've thought this all through.*

As a child fantasy fan, I always loved a good map and was disappointed when I picked up the first Fairy Tale and didn't see one. You could infer that Annabelle was creating something more lyrical than literal. Lewis Carroll certainly never drew a map of Wonderland. But I've always wanted one. And now . . . oh boy.

OK, first, let's go back to what you figured out: the Kingdom of Echoes = Echo Park. That caught my eye, because the Kingdom of Echoes is a feature of the Fairy Tale Hidden World—it's the location where Ciara meets and battles her evil doppelgänger.

By itself, that wouldn't have been much to go on. But I started to see hints of a larger pattern.

When we were at Illuminated Ink, Sally mentioned that her band was playing at FairyCon. Only, the way she said it is that they were playing at "the Navel." The Navel of the Universe is also a location that's described in the books—an ancient arena that serves as a gathering spot for the great spectacles of the fairy kingdom. In *Forgotten Abyss,* it's where Ciara is pitted against Gloverbeck in gladiatorial combat.

FairyCon is taking place at the L.A. Convention Center, which is downtown. It's just like any convention center, no big deal. But she called it the Navel so effortlessly, which made me realize: maybe the Convention Center IS the Navel. Maybe there's some *correspondence* between them.

That's another dot on the map. The trickier part is to give them some order. To figure out where the Navel is relative to other parts of the Hidden World. I looked through the books for any reference that could help. Bear with me here. This is a sentence from Book Five, page 402:

From the Pits of the Dead, Ciara and her companions traveled east, and even with their packs heavy with supplies, they reached the Navel of the World by mid-morning with energy to spare.

OK, so—the Pits of the Dead are a burial site where magical bodies are decomposed and reabsorbed into the world. Ciara is tossed in, alive, and has to fight her way out. In terms of real-world corollaries, I've only considered it in literary terms; Dante's *Inferno,* stuff like that. But thinking about this passage in terms of real-world geography—how long is it from sunrise to "mid-morning"? A couple hours? And how far could you march in that time? Twenty minutes of walking per mile, so about six miles.

So what is roughly six miles west of the Convention Center? Scrolling through Maps, following the main thoroughfare of Wilshire Blvd., led straight to–THE LA BREA TAR PITS! Distance: 5.7 miles.

That means the Pits of the Dead in the books correspond to the La Brea Tar Pits in real-life L.A.! Actual pits where dead, ancient creatures are being unearthed.

Could be a coincidence? Maaaaaybe. I combed the books for other references to geography that might help. Some general descriptions included:

"... they were trapped in the hills, since any travel farther north would drop them directly into the Hollow Valley, where skeletal predators and blistering heat would kill them faster than Áine's soldiers."
—*Book Two: The Bridge of Dreams,* Chapter Nine

"Ervever flitted easily from branch to branch; he had descended from the densely forested mountains to the northeast and was at home among the trees."

—*Book Five: The Forgotten Abyss,* Chapter Two

"And so they set out southwest toward the sea at the end of the world."

—*Book Four: The Crystal Palace,* Chapter Eighteen

Now, look at a wide regional map of L.A. Thick forests to the northeast—that matches with the Angeles National Forest. A vast ocean to the southwest—the Pacific, obviously. And a sprawling valley to the northwest . . . that's the San Fernando Valley!

In order to test my theory, I posted this morning on a Queendom forum that I was looking for ANY geographical references in the books that suggested DISTANCE between two specific locations. (A perk of creating a beloved fan site is fans are eager to help you in any way they can.) The clearest useful reply I got was this one—

u/Periwinkle614: Check out this passage from B3 Ch4 P79: "The Selkies helped to provision the craft in the marina, and Ciara and her crew embarked at dawn, hugging the western-curving shoreline for fear of the kraken, but still hoping to reach the Bay of Doom at the edge of the realm before nightfall."

OK, how far could you sail in a day, while hugging a coast? About thirty miles. Now, guess what you hit if you sail up the western edge of L.A. into Malibu. Point Dume! That's the Bay of Doom! And Marina del Rey is the marina!

THE HIDDEN WORLD IS LOS ANGELES!

And based on these findings, I would venture to say that virtually EVERY locale from the books has a corollary in our world. Even if you want to try to skeptic me on the magic here, you have to admit, at the very least—Annabelle built her fictional world with these assumptions in mind.

REPLY

Misha,

Interesting. You are exactly right that I would've laughed at you a couple days ago, but considering . . . well, everything . . . I'm not about to dismiss any connection I can find.

I'm trying to see things more like you. The most I have to go on, from Henry, is a series of hopelessly vague instructions, which begin with "a lake of purest, swirling silver" and include "a castle in the clouds."

They certainly seem nonsensical, but I'm willing to try anything—so this morning, I returned to the lake at Echo Park, where I had met with Henry last night. A section of the park is crime-scene taped off, and a few cops were interviewing some of the homeless residents. The lake hadn't seemed particularly silvery last night, and in the light of midday was even less so. Its surface was greenish-brown, punctuated by oily rainbows.

I'll have to try another lake. Or perhaps not an *actual* lake; perhaps the description refers to something else entirely. Or perhaps I am truly losing it.

REPLY

Byron,

You're not crazy, you're just a little more open-minded. And given everything we've encountered, you'd be crazy not to be. Plus, in terms of making sense of the clue, I can help with some L.A. geography basics, because we have an actual lake called Silver Lake! (It's technically a reservoir, but whatever.)

I dunno about any castles in the clouds, but that's gotta be a good place to start!

INVESTIGATIVE JOURNAL OF BYRON KIDD

October 31

Get it down, get it down. It will be TRUE if it's down on paper. It will be true no matter what, right? Hard to say. I feel like it could slip away. Like the day's events could yet be unwound and taken from me. And while there is much I'd like to forget, there is so much I would do anything to protect.

(What is happening to my writing? My old editor would murder me for the way my syntax is becoming elliptical and vague.)

Just the facts. Who what where when why.

Start with where. Silver Lake. A man-made reservoir, enclosed by chain-link fence, surrounded by walking paths and several-million-dollar homes. The area is home to hip young creative types, all dressed in '90s-style sweatshirts and puffy sneakers, each one accompanied by a rescue mutt in a Halloween costume.

Oh yeah, it's Halloween. And I fucking hate Halloween. Especially when I find myself in a place where the mostly childless population has not realized that this is not a holiday for them. The number of grown adults in costumes I've seen today is absurd. It's not even a weekend. What self-respecting forty-year-olds dress up as his-and-hers Mario and Luigi at 10 AM?

But I digress, perhaps drifting from the point because to tackle it head-on tears my heart. Perhaps the tattoo needle ripped me open. The mark on my back has been throbbing. Different from the usual pain of a tattoo. Almost like I can feel my heartbeat in it. Still wonder if I was drugged, especially after everything today.

There's a small park area on the east side of the lake called the Silver Lake Meadows. So I went there and sat on a bench and looked out toward the water, experiencing nothing the least bit mystical. But it seemed like the best place to try to make sense of the next direction that Sir Henry gave: "Then look up, and see the castle in the clouds!"

I did. It was a piercingly bright L.A. day, without a wisp of cloud in the sky. Literally the only thing resembling "clouds" are the layers of thick smog that hang over the city in every direction, this hazy brown-gray mass that hovers at the horizon line. It's awful. But I realized, the smog-mass only rises up a couple hundred feet . . . and as a result, from this angle, the tops of the Hollywood Hills poke up over it. I scanned them, and on top of one of the highest hills, I glimpsed . . . a castle.

Not a CASTLE, exactly, but a large structure that was familiar to me—gleaming white, with a curving dome and a pair of spires. It really did have a fantastical, medieval quality.

I pulled out my phone, consulted the map, and quickly deduced that the landmark I was studying was Griffith Observatory. That rang a bell of familiarity . . . even though I'd never seen it, I felt like I had (probably because, it turns out, it's been featured in so many films). But after I pocketed my phone, I started to doubt myself, and the castleishness of the structure began to fade.

I decided that if I was going to undertake this quest in the spirit that Sir Henry once had, perhaps instant access to all the information in the world was an obstacle more than an asset. I put my phone in the glove box of the rental car, locked it, and set off on foot toward the Observatory, in service of the next instruction: "Climb up to meet it, if you can."

As I approached, feeling naked without a phone or car, the Observatory moved in and out of my vision—and it did once again start to resemble a castle over the clouds, a shining white beacon on top of a hill, out of place and time, so seeing it was like peeking through a window into . . . well, I hate to say it, some other world.

Drawing closer, I felt the still-fresh rune tattoo on my back start to throb more intensely, as though some power in it was awakening, stirring. Hope it's not infected.

I navigated the streets by my best guess, always tacking vaguely in the direction of the Observatory. I found myself walking up Glendower Ave, which initially seemed to point in the right direction but then curved parallel to my destination. Suddenly, the path up the hill was blocked by a series of fancy houses, all with gated drives and high fences.

I felt embarrassed by my decision to leave my phone behind and feared getting lost in these streets. I was about to double back when I saw a narrow staircase, rising between two houses' fences, creating a steep alleyway up the hill. It looked strange, even mythic, like a secret passageway dropped into a modern neighborhood.

As I climbed the stairs, I passed a small plaque that identified this as one of the "Hidden Stairways of Hollywood." Energized by my find, I climbed up quickly, emerging onto another residential street full of Teslas and G-Wagons. I looked both directions—and three houses to the west, I spotted the narrow alley-opening of another staircase.

With mounting excitement, I went from one staircase to the next, finding and climbing up five of them in total. Each one felt like it was constructed for my own private ascent. A few homeowners eyed me warily from their exposed backyards, which only added to my flush of pleasure at the stolen passage.

At last, winded and dehydrated and exhausted, I climbed a final paved stretch and emerged onto the lawn in front of Griffith Observatory. A placard explained that it was an astronomical observatory that opened in the 1930s and has always doubled as a science museum and tourist attraction. The site has been used numerous times as a filming location—most iconically in Rebel Without a Cause, more recently in La La Land.

This last detail would have seemed like senseless trivia to me a few days ago, but today it took on monumental importance. The caves I visited had been a popular filming location as well. These places were conduits for collective dreaming. And whether the Hidden World was an actual place or merely a dangerous idea, it was drawing power from these dreams.

I found a busker with an acoustic guitar and a case open in front of him, playing a grimy cover of "When the Man Comes Around." I'm not one to hand out money, as I've generally regarded buskers as a public nuisance, but without much thought I opened my wallet and dropped him what I had, which was two twenties. I don't think it was out of kindness so much as some sense of tribute.

I turned away, but the busker stopped playing and said, "Your change." I looked back and he was holding out a single quarter. I wasn't sure if that was meant as a joke, but I accepted the coin from him and he resumed the song.

I then approached the view and turned my thoughts to Sir Henry's final instruction: "Look down on the world with new eyes."

OBSERVATORY. Of course. The telescope. Should I have come at night? A bit of quick investigation revealed that the telescope is a historical object, and even the area where it's contained is closed for long-term remodeling. I tried talking to a security guard, wondering if I could finagle a way into the chamber to see if there was some other clue there. No luck.

I started to despair, wondering if this whole excursion had been a waste of time. The lines I was connecting were so tenuous. My own mind was so desperate for any link it could find. And the person I had enlisted to help me, Misha, wanted just as badly as I did to make an earth-shaking discovery. How could I be so stupid?

But there was plenty I couldn't deny. The tattoo parlor . . . the photos in the museum . . . hell, I saw a man murdered by a lake last night.

These thoughts swirled in my head as I wandered around the periphery of the Observatory, watching tourists taking pictures, posing for engagement photos and pregnancy announcements, everyone laughing and smiling from up high with the smog-choked hellscape of Los Angeles below. I kept walking around the terrace that encircled the structure, trying to escape the fatuous, fake happiness, as sour bitterness encroached on my mind.

That's when I saw it. An ancient set of mounted viewing binoculars, fixed in place. An old-timey attraction. Drop in a quarter and see the city up close. Useless in the age of phones with zoom lenses, but nonetheless, apparently kept up here as a historical curiosity.

I walked up to the binoculars, pointed southwest. My body was drawn toward them, my soul tugged to the darkness of the viewing piece. Once again, the tattoo tingled with recognition.

I put my face to the viewer and looked. Nothing but blackness.

Of course. I pulled away, thwarted. Who carries change these days?

But then I remembered: the quarter the busker returned to me. My change. I popped it in the slot, turned a knob, and heard it clink into the machine. I pressed my eyes to the glass, expecting to see some corner of Hollywood—maybe one of the film studios, maybe some other landmark, maybe nothing at all.

I saw the Hidden World.

The view of the binoculars was firmly fixed in place, and from this height encompassed an area perhaps a quarter of a mile on each side. Not a small stretch by any means, but close enough from this perspective to afford some sense of detail.

What did I see? There were structures growing up from the ground, like tall pillars—but they were not made of stone. They were made of vines, intertwining and rising in serpentine mutual support. And these living columns were spaced with *perfect* regularity, planted with the precision of a vineyard, creating little avenues between and among them. At the edges of the space, thick forest rose up, dense and foreboding.

The quality of light was different, as though it were twilight in the place I was looking, with a greenish tint along with the gold. I could see strands of bioluminescence on nearly every living thing; the ground was made up of spongy-looking moss that emanated a glow from within, and the vines pulsed with bluish energy, adding a black-light surreality to the whole scene.

And I saw people. Not many, just a few walking among the vine-columns listlessly, as though each were directed toward some goal but having trouble remembering what it was. The people were unhurried. And they were small. Not only by feature of the distance but from the shapes of their limbs, their gaits, I could see . . .

They were children. I believe I saw a girl as young as eight, perhaps a boy as old as eighteen, but they were all kids. Not that many—four or five, perhaps.

The children did not seem to be restrained by any wall or bars that

I could see . . . but as I watched, I realized the trees at the edge of the clearing were keeping them there. The trees moved slightly, and at first glance I thought it was simply wind rippling their branches. But the wind would have to be blowing in numerous directions at once (and not at all in some places) to produce the seething effect of what I saw.

One girl walked down an avenue of vine structures near the edge of the visible space, heading off into the thick forest. But as she reached the tree line, suddenly the branches of two trees on either side of her descended like massive arms, sweeping down from above. They intertwined, forming a barrier, and then whooshed forward, walloping the little girl and hurling her back ten feet.

She rolled to the ground, unperturbed by the violence. And as she climbed to her feet and dusted herself off, something struck me as familiar about both her outfit and her shape, small as it was from this distance. While a red hoodie and jeans is hardly a distinctive look for a girl her age, the way she wore them—with her shoulders slumped and her dark hair pulled aside—was seared already into my memory.

My stomach tumbled and squeezed inside my torso with a combination of shock (it was her!) and pain (she was hurt!) and longing (she was so far away!).

But underneath it all—hope. She's alive.

With this recognition, a curious change happened with the binoculars. They zoomed in on her, as if the device not only magnified the image but actually moved closer. My point of view seemed to soar through the air and come to a rest fifty feet above her.

I could see her in vibrant detail. My horror was matched only by my joy. Because though she was undeniably alive, she looked like she had been through hell. Her hair was a tangled mass, feral. She was filthy. Her clothes were tattered and threadbare. Scratches were visible on her skin.

Worst of all were her eyes. They were vacant, glassy, turning milky-white all the way through. She got up, recovering from the blow by the trees with grim acceptance, and turned away, marching back the direction she had come. I watched her every step—desperate to go to her but terrified to tear my eyes away from the binoculars, afraid that this sight would be gone forever.

Liza stopped midway down the avenue of vine columns as if frozen in place. She stayed there, motionless, obedient . . . as seething vines emerged from the mossy ground beneath her. The vines grew fast, like a nature documentary in super-time-lapse. They wound around her body, tightening around her legs and torso to fully enclose her in a living cocoon.

I stared, slack-jawed and mesmerized, as Liza disappeared from view within a matter of seconds. Only then did I realize that the other vine columns were not merely some feature of the landscape. They were prison cells. All of them. Each holding a living child, encased just like Liza was now. Apparently each child was permitted to step out and stretch their legs periodically but never allowed to leave.

I stared helplessly as the vine column that held Liza sealed up, obscuring her completely. Moments later, the faint threads of bioluminescence up and down the tree's bark brightly glowed, pulsing with feverish light, and I almost felt I could hear a HUM as it . . . well, I cannot say what happened inside the impenetrable darkness of that structure, but the sickening dread in the pit of my stomach told me it was awful.

The words of Scott Angelik came back to me then: "You dive in, you think you're there to feast, but then you realize, you ARE the feast."

It was feeding on her. On her soul. Her dreams.

I might have stayed and waited all day for her to emerge from that parasitic trap, but the viewing machine clicked, and my vision was plunged into darkness. My time had run out. My tiny sliver of connection with her was severed. I pulled away and looked out over the vista of the city below, greeted only by the bright sight of grimy L.A. sprawling before me. None of it seemed to have anything in common with the world I'd just beheld.

I needed another quarter. Nothing in my pockets. I started desperately asking passersby if they had one to spare. I clearly irritated and perhaps frightened some tourists, but I didn't care, and eventually, an older Chinese man indulged me. I popped the quarter into the machine, put my eyes to the binoculars, and saw . . .

Our world. A view of a large green hill, sporting just a few trees, and dotted with whitish monuments. Gravestones? Near the bottom of my view, a few large buildings were visible. Utterly mundane.

Whatever transformative power this object had held moments ago . . . it was gone.

I tried again, moving my eyes to and from the viewer, as though I might reawaken the magic the device whatever had shown me that other world. But I could not recapture the enchanted perspective from moments earlier.

I slumped in defeat. Stepped away from the viewing device, fearing I might have just seen the last of her—might have been momentarily teased by a glimmer of hope only to have it stomped out entirely.

But then I saw a plaque on the side of the viewing machine:

"From this vantage point, see the historic Hollywood Forever Cemetery, incorporated in 1899, and home to the final resting place of stars including Marion Davies, Burt Reynolds, Judy Garland, Douglas Fairbanks, and Rudolph Valentino. Adjoining the eastern edge of the property, you can see the studio lot of Paramount Pictures—which was formerly part of the cemetery, until the land was purchased in 1920."

A graveyard. One steeped in mythology. The pieces were coming into focus . . . I just needed to figure out how they fit together.

But first, I needed to share this with the person to whom it would matter most.

EMAIL

From: bkidd@gmail.com
To: Valeriekidd@sltpartners.com

Val,

I've been in L.A. for a week now, and my investigation has been
a strange and twisting process. But I am now at a point where I
know one thing with certainty: Liza is alive. And Annabelle Tobin
is involved. I can't pinpoint *exactly* how, but I will find out.

I know this will sound far-fetched and maybe even crazy. But I
know if you had learned anything related to her disappearance,
I'd want to hear it no matter what. So I'm sharing the truth, even
though the particulars of it, at this juncture, must remain a secret.

Our baby girl is out there. She's frightened, and she's hurt, and
she's lost . . . but she still can come home to us. I'm sure of it.
Don't give up hope.

Love,
Byron

REPLY

Byron,

Your email has been causing me extreme emotional distress,
and if this persists, I may need to cut off contact for the sake of my
own well-being.

Over the course of the past few months, I've shared most of
what you've sent me with Martin, my therapist. He's helped me
make sense of it and figure out how to respond. As I'm going
through this period of transition and grief, it's been very helpful.
But I had my appointment with him a few hours ago, and while
your latest email was very much on my mind, I didn't mention it.

Why? Because I want it to be true, of course. But at the same
time, I am terrified. I want with every fiber of my being to believe
that you're right. But if you ARE right, then everything that I have
done to move on—including the memorial service I organized and

that you refused to attend—it is all recklessly irresponsible and damaging to our daughter's prospects of coming home.

If you find her, I will be forever in your debt. But with the information and evidence I have at hand . . . I have to believe that she is gone. So send me some proof, if you discover any. But until then, I don't want to hear anything else from you.

Best,
Val

TEXT MESSAGE CONVERSATION

BYRON KIDD   MISHA PIMM

I think I just saw the Hidden World.

                                      What do you mean?
                                      What did it look like?!

I saw my daughter.

                                      Ohmygod.
                                      Byron that's amazing!
                                      Did you go to the Dreamvale?!
                                      That's where Angelik said Liza was.

I didn't go but I think I looked into it.
I was at Griffith Observatory.
But where she was, I think, is a place called Hollywood Forever Cemetery.
Or I guess the Dreamvale is connected to the Cemetery?
I'm still figuring out how this works.

                                      OF COURSE!
                                      That makes total sense.

I have to go there.

I feel like if I'm there I can do something.

I'm not sure what but I have to try.

It's usually closed to the public, but there's an event there tonight.

For Halloween.

?

I'm on their mailing list.

You're on the mailing list of a cemetery?

FORWARDED EMAIL

Subject: Halloween in Hollywood Forever!

From: Events@Cinespiascreenings.org

To: <Undisclosed recipients>

Hey Film Fans!

What better way to celebrate the night of spirits than among them?!

Cinespia will screen NIGHT OF THE LIVING DEAD on the Douglas Fairbanks Lawn.

Come dressed in your best undead duds!

Gates at 6.

Costume Contest at 7.

Film at 8.

Brain-eating all night long!

RESUME TEXT MESSAGE CONVERSATION

BYRON KIDD   MISHA PIMM

I don't understand. They're showing a movie in a graveyard?
WTF is wrong with this city?
Who would go to something like that?

> I mean, I've been to several of them.
> Last year it was Beetlejuice.

Of course.

> I think this one is sold out but I know someone who works at Cinespia.
> I was gonna take Shelby to a party w some other grad students
> but she'd be thrilled to have an excuse NOT to go, sooooo. . . .
> Wanna go see a movie?

CHAPTER TWENTY-ONE

INVESTIGATIVE JOURNAL OF BYRON KIDD

October 31 (Cont'd)

Misha and I arrived at the cemetery around 7 and found a line around the block of "grown-ups" in zombie costumes, ranging from the simple and off-the-shelf to truly grotesque film-worthy decaying flesh and oozing wounds. At least Misha had the decency not to dress up, but she did wear a Dawn of the Dead T-shirt.

As we waited in line, Misha peppered me with questions about what I had seen, and I tried to fill her in on the geographical correspondences I had discovered. But when it came to relating the story of what I'd glimpsed through the viewer, I was vague, afraid to speak aloud the details. If there was anyone who would be eager to believe me, it was her—but I felt like spelling it out might make me question it more myself. And I was trying desperately to hold on to some shred of possibility that it was real.

At the gates, I felt a momentary panic, as I realized that I still had Henry's footlong knife in the inner pocket of my jacket. There was no time to dispose of it discreetly before I found myself walking through a metal-detector archway. But whether owing to lax security or some remarkable property of the weapon, we were waved through.

Once inside, I was floored by the size of the event. At least two thousand people were gathered (and paying $25 each) to watch a schlocky fifty-year-old film. Even after waiting forever to get in the front gates, many of them were queuing up for another hour to get their picture snapped at an instagrammy photo-booth setup.

Hollywood Forever is a massive cemetery, and entering it is akin to entering another world; the city outside is dense with gas stations, strip malls, apartments, and traffic—but once you're inside its high-walled interior, the urban reality vanishes, replaced by sprawling, grassy grounds dotted with antiquated headstones. The sun was setting as we entered, and twilight added to the sense of unreality, as the entire space was bathed in shadow.

The grave markers tended toward the ostentatious—numerous large statues and mausoleums seemed to compete for attention—which was hardly surprising given the cemetery's famous and wealthy clientele. In contrast with the solemn and imposing structures, the crowd was raucous and lively; numerous zombie-dressed twentysome-things leaped out at their friends, who screamed and laughed in response.

Flashing cones created a pathway from the entrance, through the winding roads of the sprawling grounds, keeping attendees off the lawns and directing us toward the eastern edge of the park, where the festivities were set up—mercifully away from the actual grave-stones, though the film was projected on the large flat white wall of the crematorium, which seemed in poor taste to me. But then, good taste was not the guiding principle for an occasion like this.

My goal was to get away from the crowd, out toward the western end of the cemetery grounds, which seemed to correspond with where I had glimpsed Liza through the binoculars. Did I expect to find her there? Not exactly. I did not know WHAT to expect. But I needed to get to where she was—even if I was removed by an entire layer of reality.

As we followed the crowd, drawn toward the sound of a DJ remixing "Thriller" with some aggressive electronica, I saw a few girls sneak into a roped-off section, which Misha informed me was the site of Marilyn

Monroe's final resting place. But a pair of security guards with flashlights were on them quickly, ordering them back to the prescribed path and threatening them with ejection if they did it again.

Misha told me that once the sun had set, there might be more of an opportunity to slip away into the portions of the cemetery farther from the film screening. We settled into a spot on the lawn near the back and waited. Other people were spread out on picnic blankets with remarkably elaborate wine-and-cheese setups, while we looked sorely out of place without even folding chairs.

I was quiet with my thoughts and appreciated that Misha seemed to sense the gravity of what was happening for me. Even though she was visibly interested in the Halloween-party madness around us, she didn't regale me with any history of zombie movies or geek out over face paint.

Eventually the film began, well after the advertised 8:00 start time. The vibe was still festive and getting rowdier with the addition of alcohol. Misha and I headed to the rear of the partitioned area, where people waited in lines for beer and snacks and porta-potties. There were security guards strategically spaced, creating a protected border so that the audience couldn't venture into the rest of the cemetery. Which was a problem.

But Misha provided a solution. She cut to the front of the sizable porta-potty line, affecting a stagger and slur as she elbowed her way through, insisting that she needed to get in quicker than anyone else. This prompted a series of angry shouts from the others queuing behind her—toward whom Misha then unleashed a profanity-laced tirade I never would've imagined her capable of.

I was pretty entertained, watching my fiery, blue-haired, five-foot-two ~~partner~~ ~~friend~~ helper getting in the face of a six-foot-plus guy who looked like an advertisement for CrossFit. She promised to burn down his house and salt his fields. But there wasn't time to linger and enjoy the show because a pair of nearby security guards were moving in to defuse the situation before anyone got hurt. Her antics created the opportunity for me to slip past.

I walked nonchalantly into the darkness, making my way among the graves. I must've succeeded at evading detection because soon the sounds of the film and the occasional roar of the audience were distantly behind me. Of course, now I was wandering through a graveyard in the dark. On Halloween. And this is what I had been TRYING to achieve.

There were trees scattered around the property, but none with the geometrical regularity I had glimpsed on the other side. Instead, I realized it was the gravestones that mirrored the pattern of the vine structures I had seen. I was as close to where I was trying to get as I could be.

For several minutes, I wandered aimlessly, looking for any landmark or sign that might trigger some inspiration. Nothing. I stumbled upon the gravestone of director Cecil B. DeMille. Nearly fell into a small man-made pond, it was so pitch-black.

But I didn't find anything to hang on to. So I started to call out into the darkness. "Liza?!" As if hoping that she might be just around a corner.

Silence. Wind. The distant thrum of traffic, the murmur of the movie playing at the opposite end of the property.

I started to feel ridiculous, traipsing among the graves. I had looked down on all those people who had come to this graveyard for entertainment, but I was here for . . . what, exactly? Hoping to find a door to another world?

I might have given up at that moment. I felt a shiver of fear run down my spine as the shadows around me seemed to shift. Some barely perceptible movement in the periphery of my vision signaled an encroaching force and reminded me of the shadow-being that Echo/Henry had fought inside my motel room.

On a gut level, I was terrified. But I also knew that if there was anything to be afraid of, then I was getting closer to what I was seeking. I could not say how, but I sensed some thinning of the veil between worlds, some bleed-over of another reality.

The wind picked up, blowing in my face, as though pushing me back the way I came. But in its rising and falling, I could hear . . . a voice.

I called out for Liza again, to no avail. Spun around, desperate now, afraid I had already missed the message.

Then I found myself standing before a massive mausoleum. The marble was a gleaming abyss, blacker than black. The sheen of moonlight on its surface warned against the impenetrable infinity behind. Its entrance was a giant wrought-iron door that looked like it had been sealed shut for decades, but when I touched it, to my surprise, it opened easily.

I could see nothing inside the tomb. I brought up my phone and turned on the flashlight, but the light did not penetrate the inky dark.

I knew, somehow, that this was an in-between place.

On my phone, I opened the recording app and started it up, surprised that it worked. With the recording running, I put the phone back in my pocket.

Then I took a deep breath and stepped into the abyss.

INTERVIEW ~~WITH LIZA KIDD?~~

Location: A mausoleum—though given the fact that no light at all penetrated the space, it was a void. My feet were on solid ground, but as I stepped inside, I closed my eyes, letting myself get lost in the silence so that I could listen more closely.

The only sound I heard was the wind blowing across the threshold of the door. But after I stood there for a few minutes, the sound took shape. Instantly, goosebumps rose on the backs of my arms.

Subject: A voice in the wind, scratchy and indistinct, rising and falling. I am grateful that I captured it on the recording, because otherwise I might've feared it was only in my mind. As I listen back after the fact, it's hard to gauge any sense of distance; she oscillates from sounding incredibly far-off one moment and inches away from the microphone the next.

To say that the voice is "familiar" would be an understatement. It's the sound I know better than any, etched in my neurons and written on my heart. At the same time, that makes me question myself, and whether identifying Liza as the speaker is accurate or wishful thinking. All I can think is . . .

~~It has to be~~

~~I know it's~~

I hope it's really her.

TRANSCRIPT OF RECORDED INTERVIEW

(Sound of wind.)

BYRON: Liza?

VOICE: . . . I'm here.

BYRON: I'm here, too, sweetheart. I'm . . . my God, it's really you?

LIZA: I think so.

BYRON: You *think* . . . OK. We need to . . . Is there any way I can know it's you?

VOICE: You don't believe.

BYRON: Why don't you tell me something, Liza. Something only I would know.

VOICE: You'll never believe.

BYRON: I'm trying to, OK? Tell me your birthday.

VOICE: You forgot my birthday last year.

BYRON: I missed it, I didn't *forget*.

VOICE: You won't have to worry about that anymore.

BYRON: Worry? I will never—

VOICE: I know.

BYRON: I am so sorry, sweetheart. About your birthday. And the costume.

VOICE: It's OK.

BYRON: I'm sorry I didn't really *see* you.

VOICE: I didn't want to be seen.

BYRON: It's my job to protect you, and . . . are you scared?

VOICE: I'm just tired. I'm ready to go to sleep. We never sleep here.

BYRON: But you dream . . .

VOICE: He feeds on our dreams. But there's no rest.

BYRON: That's awful.

VOICE: I would do anything just to get some real sleep.

BYRON: I'm gonna bring you home, and then . . . you can go in your bed, and you can get in your fluffy pajamas. You can sleep in as late as you want. I'll never wake you up early again if you come back to me, and there will be pancakes every day, and—

VOICE: I can't.

BYRON: I need to figure out how to get you home. But first, you have to tell me how you got there.

VOICE: Same as Ciara.

BYRON: OK. But those are stories. In real life, you talked to someone online. . . .

VOICE: I thought he was my friend.

BYRON: He convinced you to leave home.

VOICE: I just wanted people to like my stories.

BYRON: You got to Los Angeles, somehow. And then how'd you get . . . over there?

VOICE: It's all mixed-up now, I'm sorry.

BYRON: You don't need to be sorry. Whatever it takes, I'm gonna bring you back.

VOICE: Too late.

BYRON: No. I don't accept that. I've come so far. . . .

VOICE: That's good. But for me it's too late. There are others who need your help now.

BYRON: Others, you mean . . . ?

VOICE: We can never go back. But there's so many more over there. And he's coming for them when it's finished.

BYRON: You mean when the last book comes out . . . the spell?

VOICE: Yes.

BYRON: He . . . the Green Man. He wants to bring more kids over?

VOICE: This world isn't enough for him. He wants your world too. You have to stop the Summoning.

BYRON: I will if I can, but first—

VOICE: Shhh . . .

BYRON: . . . Liza? Are you still there?

VOICE: He sees me now. I'm in trouble.

BYRON: He . . . where is he? Are you OK?

VOICE: Get out of here.

BYRON: I'm not going anywhere until I—

VOICE: GO!

BYRON: Liza? *Liza?!* What the . . . ?

(*Deep, metallic slamming sound. Followed by pounding.*)

BYRON: Help! Can anyone . . . Liza? Are you still there?

(*Sounds of coughing.*)

INVESTIGATIVE JOURNAL OF BYRON KIDD

As my conversation with Liza was forced to a premature conclusion, the door of the mausoleum slammed shut, plunging me into a darkness so complete I felt like I was lost in outer space. I heard a deep clang of metal as a lock turned. I fumbled for the handle, but it was totally immobile, as though melted into position.

I banged on the door of the mausoleum, yelling for help. But I was a couple hundred yards away from another soul, and the sound of the film and the crowd were too loud to be heard over even if I were much closer.

I felt the air around me start to thin, and my dread turned to panic. It didn't make sense—even if the tomb were perfectly airtight, I should be able to breathe for a long time before I started running out of oxygen.

The ice-chill of terror saturated my bones. I was going to suffocate. I threw my shoulder into the door uselessly. Clawed at the handle, the sliding bolt lock. Neither one budged. My breathing grew shallower, and my strength waned. I was going to die in here, already entombed, perhaps discovered days later, no doubt dismissed as a drunken filmgoer who'd wandered off into the cemetery and gotten himself trapped.

Despair filled me. Hot tears rose to my eyes. I had come so far, I had been teased by the possibility of saving her, and SHE had been teased by a false promise of rescue. My inability to save her would be another failure, another disappointment.

I slumped against the door in defeat. But in doing so, I felt a weight inside my jacket, pressing against my chest.

The knife. Sir Henry's weapon.

I got up, fumbling it out of my pocket. Ordinarily, I would not consider it a viable option for getting through a thick metal door . . . but I had seen the way it had effortlessly sliced through the lock at my motel, and I wondered what it might be capable of.

In the darkness, my hand found the iron latch that had closed me inside. With my strength evaporating, I didn't think I could manage much of a swing, but perhaps I didn't need to. I held the blade out before me, finding the target . . . and then, to my surprise, didn't even need to apply much pressure.

It went straight through, shinking the thick metal bar in two without a whisper of effort.

I pushed. The door opened. And I stumbled out into the night, gasping for air.

Free. Alive. Thoroughly confused. And horrified by the prospect of what Liza might be facing on the other side of the metaphysical divide between us.

Nonetheless, I felt reinvigorated. As my strength returned, it was fused with a newfound sense of RAGE. I looked around, gripping the knife tightly, wishing more than anything that this being, this entity, this creature that had taken her from me would reveal himself, so I could shred every inch of his form as I had carved through the iron door.

I knew that finding him would not be easy. But I was more determined than ever—even as I was starting to come around to the reality that I was dealing with something more powerful than I'd ever imagined possible.

EMAIL

From: bkidd@gmail.com
To: Valeriekidd@sltpartners.com

Val,

You asked me for proof. I have it now. Listen to the attached audio file. This is different from the picture, I promise. This is something I experienced live, in person, and when I play back the recording, it's faint, but it is undeniably HER.

It's hard to explain what's going on here. Think of it like I was able to talk to Liza on the phone. That's not exactly the case, but it's close enough. I could talk to her, even though I wasn't with her, and I don't know exactly where she was. But I'll find out. I'll bring her home. I promise.

Love,
Byron

REPLY

Byron,

I've listened to this several times. I'm speechless. More than speechless, I'm gutted.

I got this in the middle of my workday, and I had to go home. I wasn't sure how to explain it to my boss. I spent an hour pacing the house, playing it again and again. I've memorized it, even as I've struggled to find some explanation.

It does sound like her. And I desperately want to believe that it's real. But with no visual evidence—and a conversation that is utterly opaque and nonsensical—it's hard to take this as definitive proof of anything other than the fact that someone wants us to believe she's alive. Which is alarming. I was so distraught that I reached out to Martin, and he agreed to an emergency appointment, and helped me come to a decision about how to proceed.

So it's only fair that I let you know, I've shared this recording with the police, both here and in L.A. Both cities still have open case files for her disappearance, even though they've been inactive for several months. The detectives I spoke with were receptive, though they had a lot of questions I didn't have answers to. But you do, and I expect they'll be in touch.

I know this isn't what you want. I know you want to continue heroically on your quixotic quest to find her on your own. But as much as I'm impressed that you've gotten anywhere, I can't risk letting you endanger her. It's time to leave this to the professionals. And if your search is employing legal means, there's no reason you should have a problem with the police re-engaging with the case.

Warmly,
Val

REPLY

You are unbelievable. You never believed in me, and you never learn. You never thought I could make it as a writer but I did, you worried I wouldn't be a good dad but I was, I've been trying to PROVE MYSELF to you every single step of our relationship and I made the mistake of trying to do it again. Now it blew up in my face and you might fuck up the most important thing I've ever tried to do.

RECORDED CONVERSATION WITH MISHA PIMM

MISHA: Sorry about . . . your wife.

BYRON: Me too. I'm sure you've had some of that kind of thing.

MISHA: I mean . . . yeah, I've been with a couple other people in the past where it was an uphill battle to get them to understand what I was about. But Shelby . . . she's been great. She doesn't give a flying fuck about old myths or intersectional cultural studies. But she's stayed with me through some lean years and is pretty much paying our rent now so that I can become, in her words, "a Fairy Doctor." 'Cause she believes in me.

BYRON: Sounds like it might be worth locking that down.

MISHA: OK dude, cool it with the life advice. We've still got a mystery to solve. And now the police are involved.

BYRON: Yeah, I already got a call from a detective here in L.A. Just ignored it.

MISHA: Is that illegal?

BYRON: Not really. If they threaten an obstruction charge, they can compel me to talk, but otherwise I don't have to share anything with them. Which is good, because . . . telling the truth about the shit I've seen won't help anything. If I'm gonna bring Liza home, I have to do it on my own.

MISHA: Not *entirely* on your own. I got you.

BYRON: I know. But I can't expect you to come with me when I go after her.

MISHA: You think it might be possible to cross over? To the other side?

BYRON: It has to be. Whatever the "other side" is.

MISHA: I guess the question is . . . how? You've got the rune, that's a start.

BYRON: What Liza told me, when I asked how she crossed, was the "same as Ciara." So let's start there.

MISHA: OK, well, Ciara fell into the Wishing Well. She was running away from home, got to the edge of her village, and found an old well in a field where she knew it had never been before. She leaned over to make a wish—she wished for adventure and escape—and she was so consumed with wishing, she fell in. Splashed down into the water at the bottom, and when she swam to the surface, she was on the other side.

BYRON: All right. Wishing Well. Is there anything about the geography of L.A. that might help us find something like that?

MISHA: Ciara surfaced in a lake somewhere in the Living Labyrinth. That's a forest full of trees that walk and talk. She gets grabbed and brought before Áine. But we don't have any sense of distance or direction, so . . . that first location could be anywhere.

BYRON: Some body of water, then. We've already been to two different lakes. We need something *like* a well, in Los Angeles.

MISHA: A fountain maybe?

BYRON: Or a sewer?

MISHA: It has to be something more magical. The Wishing Well was the first magical element Annabelle came up with.

BYRON: Maybe she hadn't even figured out the whole idea of mapping L.A. onto her fantasy world yet.

MISHA: That's true. Oh my God. Wait . . . Check this out.

BYRON: What am I looking at?

MISHA: This is the cover of the film tie-in edition of the first book. That image of the Wishing Well—that's the one in the movie.

BYRON: OK . . .

MISHA: What if the Wishing Well you're looking for . . . is *that one*?

BYRON: The movie one? I thought they filmed those in England.

MISHA: Scotland, actually, for the exteriors. But the well wasn't located in that spot. It's a prop that was brought in.

BYRON: Ahhh. And the prop is in L.A., I'm guessing? Or it was, at least. Annabelle's ex-husband said the studio had to get rid of all the standing sets because people kept breaking in to see them.

MISHA: Yeah, there was a big auction. They sold off a bunch of costumes and props. The prices were bananas, I couldn't compete. But I'm sure there are records. You can probably do your investigator thing with the studio, right? Try to figure out who got that one?

BYRON: We could, sure. But that would take forever, and I bet we would just find out it was an anonymous buyer.

MISHA: It's worth a shot though, right?

BYRON: Not when I already have a good idea who got it.

MISHA: . . . Ohhhh. Seriously? You think she'd want it?

BYRON: If she knew how powerful it was, definitely. She's already bought up all the copies of *The Hidden World* she could get her hands on. Whatever this other world is that she's created or discovered . . . she's trying to control it.

MISHA: So what are we gonna do?

BYRON: *We* aren't going to do anything. But I am going there to find it. You . . . are going to hang on to my notebook.

MISHA: That's it?

BYRON: That's a lot. Because this binder contains every single bit of documentation from my investigation. If anything happens to me—

and there's a pretty decent chance of that—then I need you to get this out into the world. Understood?

MISHA: Got it. To be clear, I prefer it doesn't come to that. But this whole thing *would* make one hell of an entry to the "Sightings" section of the website.

CHAPTER TWENTY-TWO

LAPD ARREST REPORT

Detained Individual: Byron James Kidd

Arresting Officer: Sgt. Angelica Chua

Date of Incident: Nov. 2

Time: 2:15 AM

Location of Incident: 2415 Creosote Lane, Los Angeles, CA 92011 (home of victim)

Victim/s: Annabelle Tobin (Female, 46)

Circumstances of Arrest: Dispatch was notified approx 1:50 AM of a possible break-in of victim's home with intent to burgle. Victim was advised not to confront suspect.

Charge/s:

Homicide
Breaking and entering
Possession of a deadly weapon
Threatening grievous bodily harm

Confiscated Property:

1 Wallet (contents: 2 credit cards, ID, insurance card, no cash)
1 Knife (unknown make, 14-in. blade, recovered from hillside)
1 Cellphone
1 Audio recording device

Apprehension Notes: When police arrived on scene, suspect fled into surrounding hills. Search helicopter was summoned, and additional units were dispatched throughout surrounding neighborhood and public lands. Suspect surrendered near Mulholland Drive.

Subsequent to apprehension, suspect was matched with visual description from a separate crime, the homicide of John Doe vagrant found in Echo Park. Knife in subject's possession consistent with fatal wounds to John Doe. Witnesses being brought in for lineup. DNA testing in process.

Condition of Suspect: Suspect sustained bloody wounds to left leg during confrontation with victim and additional minor scrapes from falling while fleeing into public lands. Suspect was treated at Cedars-Sinai Hospital and released into police custody.

Detention: Suspect is currently being held in LAPD Metropolitan Detention Facility, pending formal charges. Suspect declined offer of counsel and offered to provide written confession on the condition that he be given pen and paper with which to write in his cell. Capt. Marco Velez approved the request on the condition that satisfactory confession be drafted immediately. Written confession to be reviewed by DA's Office, after which suspect will be formally charged.

THE CONFESSION OF BYRON KIDD

November 2, 5:30 AM

I, Byron Kidd, make this confession in good faith, and in full possession of my mental faculties. The following is a truthful account of the events of the early morning of November 2nd.

OK, now that I'm done with the legal boilerplate, I'm gonna do this my way. Because that's the only way it's going to work.

If someone wanted to break into MY home, it would not be very difficult, especially in the last seven months, since I've stopped bothering to lock the doors. It hardly seemed worthwhile after Liza was gone; what was I protecting, a 4-year-old MacBook? Carte blanche, burglars.

What's not so easy is breaking into the home of a celebrity who has spent years in paranoid seclusion, trying to avoid overzealous fans and detractors. A famous author who can afford banks of cameras, motion sensors, and an alarm system wired to every door and window on the property.

The one thing I had going for me was the fact that there was no on-site security personnel. Annabelle could afford them but was so protective of her privacy that she wouldn't allow anyone to witness what was happening with Gable, her son. Or rather, the otherworldly entity that was masquerading as her son. (I'm aware that last bit might engender some questions, but I won't belabor an explanation for an audience that won't believe it.)

I drove to Annabelle's home around 1:00 AM and parked my car in the same place I'd parked the previous day when I had followed her son into the woods. The canyons are pitch-dark at night. There are no streetlights, nothing but the glow of the houses—a few tasteful exterior lanterns, the occasional flickering blue of a TV set.

Annabelle's house looked completely dark. I surveyed the property from above, formulating my plan. Simplicity was the goal. And patience. I clocked two cars parked out in the gravel turnaround driveway—a vintage '60s BMW, and a newish Audi SUV.

A plan took shape.

I made my way down the hillside toward the house, stepping carefully in the darkness. Some part of me rebelled against this mission; the modernist castle loomed menacingly and seemed to exert an awful gravity. Descending toward it was like being pulled into a pit from which I did not know if I'd emerge. Not only a pit of danger but one of MADNESS. If I were stopped at this juncture and asked to explain my intentions, I would be hard-pressed to do so without sounding delusional.

I kept my focus simple: This is the best lead I have. It's the only way to get to Liza.

I picked up a handful of decent-sized rocks on my way down the hill, then I slowly approached the house itself. I came toward a side door, and once I got within fifty feet, a motion-sensor caught my movement. A floodlight clicked on, hitting me with a bright light. If anyone had been looking out the window, they would've seen me plainly, and no doubt the system was intended as a deterrent. But I kept hurrying forward until I was up against the house. I leaned on the wall, hoping no one came out to investigate. I was confident there wouldn't be any noisy alarm triggered by such a detection, since the homeowner would be awakened multiple times a night by wildlife passing through the yard.

After five minutes of standing stock-still against the house, the light finally clicked off, returning the obscurity of darkness.

I was within sight of the cars, perhaps forty or fifty feet away. I palmed one of the rocks I'd collected on my way down and gave my best baseball throw at the Audi. It missed by an embarrassing margin, and I wondered if I had overestimated my abilities. But I couldn't move closer, or I risked setting off the floodlight again. I threw and missed again, but my third attempt, thankfully, hit the Audi squarely on the hood, and the impact set off the car alarm.

The noisy WOOP-WOOP-WOOP cut through the silence of the canyon. My adrenaline spiked, and it was physically painful to stay rooted in place. But after twenty seconds or so, a light came on in the house. I crouched, at the ready. Another thirty seconds, and the front door opened. Annabelle came out, a flowing nightgown over sweatpants, muttering curses. She clicked the keyfob of the Audi from the threshold, but wasn't close enough, so she strode out toward the vehicle.

That was my chance. Pressed against the house, I moved in, my footsteps helpfully concealed by the alarm. I stepped inside the darkened front door behind her back.

BEE-BEEP. She got the alarm off, turned, started heading back inside.

I was in the darkened foyer. Needed to hide, as she was coming soon. I moved, and my foot caught the lip of a step. I nearly fell but caught myself. Stepped quietly as I could over the hardwood—and just as she stepped through the door, I moved into the darkness of a guest bathroom.

I stood barely out of sight, hoping desperately she couldn't see or hear me. I heard her go to the kitchen, get herself a glass of water, and put back the car keys. Then her footsteps faded off toward her bedroom. Oblivious.

I was in. I stood still for a few minutes, catching my breath and letting my eyes adjust to the darkness while, hopefully, Annabelle got back to sleep. After fifteen minutes had passed in silence, I emerged from hiding, pulled off my shoes, and started to tiptoe across the hardwood.

During my brief tour of the house, I had already seen several rooms, so I made my way over to the section Annabelle had referred to as "Gable's wing," which she had discouraged me from going into.

I stopped at various doors, peering inside. There was a room dominated by toys of all shapes and sizes, a living room with a massive television and numerous videogame consoles, a high-ceilinged chamber with a large trampoline and Ping-Pong table and punching bag. Everything a young boy could want—all looking utterly unused. Since apparently the actual CHILD was far away from here.

The door to the boy's bedroom was open just a crack. I paused at the entrance, peering inside. I doubted that a massive film prop like the Wishing Well could be in there, but I had to be sure. I pushed the door open ever so slightly, revealing book-shelves, a couch, posters, toys, and finally, a bed, with race-car sheets. Neatly made. No child to be seen. Which was troubling, to say the least.

It was possible that he (or it?) was away from the house. But it was equally possible that the changeling was here, somewhere, in the house.

There was also no Wishing Well—and since this was the last room in this wing, I started to fear that this entire hunch might be wrong. I made my way back toward the center of the house and briefly considered going into Annabelle's wing. I hadn't seen her actual BEDROOM, after all, and didn't know how many other rooms might be in that direction.

But I equally considered cutting my losses and heading out. I looked out the windows, back the way I'd come. Saw Annabelle's two vehicles. And something clicked. The house had a massive attached garage . . . but nothing about Annabelle suggested an affinity for cars. Would she really have so many that her garage space overflowed, leaving the two I'd seen to sit outside? Hardly.

It wasn't hard to find my way to the garage from the kitchen. When I opened the door, it elicited a painfully sharp creak, and I quickly stepped through into the pitch-dark space and fumbled for a light switch.

The hazy yellow glow revealed a rarely visited storage space. Dust hung thick in the air and a kingdom of cobwebs overtook the corners. There were no cars, only silhouettes—large objects of varying shapes and sizes, draped with sheets, creating a mysterious menagerie. One resembled a horse, another looked to be a pinball machine, and there were a few that COULD be the Wishing Well.

I got to work and pulled off one that looked promising—revealing a crystalline throne (actually molded plastic) with elaborate inlaid designs of trees, fairies, and intertwining vines. It was seven feet tall but with a seat suited for someone half my size. The throne of Áine, the Fairy Queen, no doubt.

I pulled down another sheet. This one hid a clothing rack, full of costumes ranging from chain-mail armor to full-body skintight mermaid scales. I shook my head in disbelief. Based on what I'd gleaned from Misha, this small space was filled with several hundred thousand dollars' worth of Fairy Tale collectibles, all hidden away from sight for years.

Then I heard a scurrying sound. I froze, listening closely. Wouldn't surprise me if there were rodents here, but obviously, I was on high alert. The door hadn't budged; I would've heard the creak for sure. Which meant that any sound was coming from something that had been here already when I arrived.

I moved on, pulling the sheet off another object, and jumped back in fear as a monstrous creature underneath lunged out at me, fangs bared, tentacles whipping. But no, it was only another plastic-mold creation. A Doggerdoth, I now understood—a chimera-like combination of squid and tiger and bear, eight feet tall. A product of Tom Caldwell's penchant for practical effects.

Another sound. I whipped around—and this time, caught the edge of a sheet dancing in the breeze. Perhaps wind coming into the space. Perhaps not. I peered around, looking for the source of the disturbance, but . . . nothing.

The next sheet revealed exactly what I'd been looking for. A large replica of an old-fashioned water well. Stone base, wooden roof, bucket attached to a rope. It looked ancient . . . though in the light, I could see that the distressing was manufactured; the lichen growing over the brick was artificial, the dirt and soot were caked on like makeup.

The Wishing Well.

I stepped forward, peering over the edge of the base. Of course, I saw the bottom—nothing but a rubber mat, no deeper than the floor. The whole thing was a prop, probably carried out to the location where they had filmed; any cavernous depths had been a calculated camera trick.

Nonetheless, I felt a pang of disappointment. I was not sure what I had expected. A churning, glowing magical portal? Of course not. But . . . SOMETHING.

I was struck by the insanity of this trip. But insanity was the one thing that had brought me closer to Liza. It was the one thing in these last seven excruciating months that had afforded me the possibility of a conversation with her. Insanity, for me, was synonymous with HOPE. So I would choose insanity today. Would embrace it. I had no choice.

As I stared into that well, I thought of the pages of the book where Liza had left her goodbye note. If this well had meant something to Liza, then it would mean something to me.

I tried to visualize this well as it had been seen by Ciara in the books . . . and perhaps by Liza too. Imagined it in the middle of a field, utterly out of place, surrounded by knee-high wildflowers. I saw it catching a ray of sunlight that broke through the clouds, spotlit by nature, impossible to ignore. I tried to imagine the lichen on its surface crawling and shifting in the light, tried to submerge myself in this vision of the well as a living thing. And I tried, in the deepest part of me, to connect with this object in the way my daughter might have. To touch the wonder.

It wasn't easy. There was part of me that knew the well was a manufactured fake, meant to be photographed from a particular angle to sell an illusion. I sought to kill that part. There was part of me that knew it had only been preserved in a callous effort to capitalize on the success of the films. I sought to drive away that thought as well.

Instead, I tried to locate some source of wonder from my OWN childhood, when I had seen things for the first time— a dragonfly, a card trick, a pile of presents on Christmas morning. Things that once made me believe in magic.

I felt a tingle down my spine. The space where my back had been marked . . . something was alive there, radiating through me. A spreading warmth. A glow from within.

Again, I peered over the edge of the well . . . and this time, it ran deeper. This time there was no rubber bottom close enough to touch. There was an expanse, a hundred feet or more, plunging into the ground. Vertigo electrified my entire body as my fear of heights took over, making me desperate to recoil. But I forced myself to lean in, absorbed by the vision.

Down below, I could see water lapping gently against the curved walls, and I could see the wet stone shimmering with silvery moonlight.

I gazed deeper, overtaken by the spectacle. Through it, faintly, I could even see . . . shapes. The moonlight coming through from the other side was brighter than any our world has ever known. Beyond the gauzy rippling water I could even see the outline of trees, swaying—not in the wind, but of their own volition.

The surface of the water was the portal. And from the perspective of the other world, I was down below the bottom of the water's surface. I could swim through, and up into the lake, just as Ciara had done.

I leaned forward, over the edge. Was I really going to dive? Was I ready to plunge? My fear of heights took on new shape in my mind—it was not only the drop, it was the loss of control. I could feel the dogs of doubt nipping at my heels, insisting that I was foolish, desperate, self-deluded, that I would forever be a gullible sucker if I indulged this fantasy.

I didn't care. There was another world, calling to me. The world where Liza was. I would get her and bring her back.

I crawled up on the stone lip, preparing to dive. I was ready.

But then—searing pain tore through my right leg, and I was jolted back to reality. I recoiled, pushed myself back from the edge of the fake well and rolled away, kicking at whatever had attacked me.

It was Gable. Annabelle's son. He must have crept down into the garage after me, and there was now blood dripping from his mouth. I glanced at my leg and saw that he had BITTEN me, that his teeth had torn through the thick fabric of my jeans and into my calf. It was streaming blood down into my left shoe, and holy hell, even through the shock, the pain was FIERCE.

The child stared at me, and I reminded myself he was not, in fact, a child at all. The Gable I had seen in the cave was the real one, and this was some awful denizen of another world. He hissed, lips curling back to bare his teeth—which were sharpened points with protruding fangs.

For fuck's sake, this was not what I signed up for.

The boy approached me slowly, hands up as if ready to grapple. I scooted away, smearing blood across the concrete, and told him, "Stay back," but he didn't even seem to recognize the words. I tried to get to my feet, but I was weak and my leg buckled.

The changeling boy leaped at me, jaws wide. He grabbed on and attempted to take another bite from my forearm. I whipped around and flung him off, and he flew several feet, knocking into another object draped in a sheet, pulling it down and revealing a large black cauldron.

I retreated while he scrambled back, pulling down the sheet, which now obscured his form . . . and then suddenly, all was still.

Was he under the pile of cloth that had been pulled down? Had he escaped behind it, into the labyrinth of props and memorabilia?

I drew the knife I'd been given by Sir Henry. On guard against

danger from any direction, though not particularly inclined to
shank a nine-year-old.

I heard a skittering behind me. Whipped around. Wincing at
the pain in my leg. Couldn't see anything. I was being stalked.

Time to get the hell out of here. I tried calling out: "I'm going
to leave now. Let me be, and I won't hurt you."

Silence. I crept toward the door, eyes darting in every direction.

I was almost there when a blur of motion in my periphery
startled me. I turned, trying to shield myself, as the boy came at
me from above, leaping down and clinging to my back as I spun,
trying to get him off. He shrieked with rage, an inhuman sound,
and his teeth snapped, ready to tear into my neck.

I wriggled, got hold of him, and dropped heavily, pinning him
to the ground. He fought me with every fiber of his being, and
goddamn he was STRONG, impossibly strong for his size—but
physics being what it was, I still managed to press him down into
the cement, subduing his churning limbs.

"Stop! Stop!" I shouted, brandishing the knife with my one
free hand. Gable ignored the threat, perhaps able to see that I
was not about to slash at anything that resembled a child.

The changeling's screams of fury only escalated, and I wasn't
sure how I was going to get out of this untenable stalemate—
until finally, an icy voice cut through the noisy din: "ENOUGH!"

The boy stopped fighting then, and I glanced up to see Annabelle standing at the door, drawn by the commotion. She surveyed the scene with a sense of detachment rather than the alarm
a mother would ordinarily feel upon seeing her child threatened.

At least we were done pretending, I thought. But the next
thing she said to him was, "Gable, go to your room." The
changeling-child hissed at her, more petulant than defiant, and
she followed with "NOW." I released him, and he scooted away,
making nonverbal noises of frustration.

The child walked up to Annabelle, stopped before her, and let out another hiss of fury. She stood her ground, staring him down, and he stared back at her contemptuously as though weighing whether or not to attack HER . . . then he moved on, pausing briefly at the door to shoot a nasty sneer in my direction before he headed inside.

I sprawled out on the garage floor. Bloody. Clutching my blade.

Thankfully, during the brief confrontation between mother and not-son, I had the sense to surreptitiously fumble my hand into my pocket and activate my voice recorder.

If everything was to be out in the open now, I hoped to catch the truth from Annabelle's lips. Assuming she didn't simply kill me herself. I will not attempt to reproduce the specifics of my conversation with her since I know a complete recording of it is in possession of the police department.

TRANSCRIPT OF 3RD "INTERVIEW" WITH ANNABELLE TOBIN

ANNABELLE: Byron Kidd.

BYRON: Annabelle.

ANNABELLE: Kidd. Not James.

BYRON: Yes. It's not uncommon, in my profession. To protect your identity.

ANNABELLE: Not uncommon in mine either. But I chose not to hide behind a pseudonym.

BYRON: Hardly a noble choice when you're hungry for fame.

ANNABELLE: You think fame is what I'm after? Fame has been the great curse of my life.

BYRON: I think you *were* after fame when you started. Fame and love and recognition. And when you got it, you found yourself stuck with a different curse. One that's a lot worse than getting recognized at Starbucks.

ANNABELLE: Maybe so.

BYRON: I wasn't going to kill him, you know.

ANNABELLE: Good.

BYRON: Even though I know what he is. And on some level, I bet you wish I had.

ANNABELLE: Not at all. That would create significant problems for me.

BYRON: Problems with the Green Man?

ANNABELLE: What were you hoping to do here, exactly? Cross over?

BYRON: I was almost there. I could see it.

ANNABELLE: But you hesitated.

BYRON: Just tell me the truth. Was she here?

ANNABELLE: Your daughter? Lord no. You think that dozens of children have gone missing after sneaking into my garage? You have this all wrong.

BYRON: Then explain it to me.

ANNABELLE: I'm tired of telling the truth to people who won't listen.

BYRON: I'm ready now. See?

ANNABELLE: (*Laughs*) You might be the first non-fan to get the rune permanently inked on their body.

BYRON: I've come so far. I just need to know what happened to her. Please.

ANNABELLE: (*Sighs*) Objects have no power except what we give them. Whether we're talking about ritual vessels or movie memorabilia, it's the same phenomenon. They're junk, in and of themselves. Any power they possess is conferred upon them by belief.

The objects in this room, I have acquired in an effort to take them out of circulation, because of the power they have been given. It was an attempt to prevent more people from getting hurt—but it has been a fool's errand.

People who are truly equipped to cross over . . . they don't need a specific item, or place, or anything. They only need to believe, completely and thoroughly—yet also, at the same time, know that what they're believing in is only a story. They need to know magic is not real and still put faith in it. That double-consciousness—truly believing, even while rationally acknowledging the artifice—that requires a special kind of mind. The littlest children can't manage it because they are too gullible. Adults can rarely achieve it because they're too credulous. But children on a certain cusp—their minds are rational enough to comprehend but still brimming with imagination, alive with wonder. They're able to suspend their disbelief.

BYRON: You managed it. As an adult.

ANNABELLE: When I was younger, yes. When my mind was more flexible, and my dreams were still alive. But I can't anymore.

BYRON: You *created* this whole goddamn mess.

ANNABELLE: That is . . . not entirely accurate.

BYRON: Then help me understand. My daughter . . . and your son . . . and all these other kids . . . where did they *go*? They must've been taken *somewhere*. If it really is another world, alternate dimension, whatever you want to call it, it's a real *place*. And that place is somehow parallel to Los Angeles. Right?

ANNABELLE: My, my, you *have* been busy.

BYRON: What came first? What caused what? Was this "Hidden

World" out there, and you wrote about it? Or did you write it, and somehow summon it into existence?

ANNABELLE: Perhaps it was both.

BYRON: That's not how cause and effect works.

ANNABELLE: The Hidden World preceded me by a long time. A realm that existed concurrently with our world. Fueled by our belief and imagination. Those energies come from beyond us, and they also *feed* the world we draw them from. Our world is in a symbiotic relationship with the hidden one.

For a long time, that relationship ebbed and flowed. Different regions of the Hidden World grew out of the dreams and stories of different cultures. The realm was peopled with all manner of gods for a time—Anubis alongside Zeus—as well as all manner of magical creatures. Dragons and harpies and sea monsters and more. Rising and falling in strength as they rose and fell in popularity.

But as time progressed, and the Age of Reason dawned, people stopped believing in all those things. The stories became nothing more than stories. Starved of the power of belief, the Hidden World withered into a shell of its former self.

That's when the Green Man came to power. You've read his tale, I hope, in Sir Henry's book? Good. Then you know that he started his existence as a human. A shaman. A storyteller. And through the power of his stories, he *became* something more. A god who dwelt in the Hidden World, feeding on the faith of his followers. Never the most popular god of course, so never the most powerful . . .

But when the Hidden World was in decline, he saw an opportunity. He sought a way to restore the crumbling empire of imagination. But it was not easy for him to affect our world, and getting harder every year. Human attention was shifting, human reverence was diminishing, and human connection was dwindling. But eventually, he found someone who still desperately, *desperately* wanted to believe.

BYRON: You.

ANNABELLE: Yes. A young dreamer, hungry for purpose, searching for her path. He revealed himself to me. I wasn't sure if I was losing my mind . . . or finding my calling. I chose to believe the latter, though the truth was a bit of both.

BYRON: And you made a deal with him. You cast his spell, in exchange for . . . what, success beyond your wildest dreams?

ANNABELLE: I didn't understand the nature of what I had agreed to. I only agreed to tell stories for him. And what he offered me was not fame or riches . . . it was *inspiration*. He brought me to the Hidden World, and I was introduced to the fey. I don't much expect you to believe me, but it's true. I had counsel with Áine and others of her race.

BYRON: OK, but . . . supposing this is all true . . . why *fairies*? Out of all the mythical creatures . . .

ANNABELLE: Fairies are the most culturally ubiquitous. They've been described by different names in cultures around the world for thousands of years. Local superstitions persist to this day. They are so popular that our term for a magical story for children is, of course, a fairy tale.

So that became the title for my book—and those otherworldly encounters became the inspiration for what I wrote. Much of the plot was my own invention. But I was overflowing with inspiration. The first book poured out of me, and the others close behind.

What I didn't realize, as I wrote those words, was the *power* they had. As I described those places and characters and rules of magic—and as people around the world read them, cherished them, even *believed* them . . . the Hidden World was reshaping in their image so that it could harness the energy of the faith and imagination they evoked.

BYRON: And the Green Man . . . he was at the center of it all.

ANNABELLE: He fed on it, yes. I even made the Green Man a part of the early books. Not as a character, per se, but as a force of nature, a part of the mythology, which I imagined might play into the ending of the series.

But when the first movie came out, the books reached another level of popularity. I was working on Book Four at the time, and I could feel things were changing. Not just in terms of the popularity. I could sense . . . a darkness. Genuine danger. So while I continued the story of Ciara, I left the Green Man out of the world.

Still, things got worse, and I could tell he was getting stronger. That's when I realized that fans were starting to . . . disappear. I tried to abandon the series altogether. But he wouldn't let me.

BYRON: He took your son. . . .

ANNABELLE: Exactly. And I have to finish what I started, and uphold my end of the bargain—because there's nothing else I can do to bring him back.

BYRON: But you tried. That's why you were at the End of the World Museum a few months ago.

ANNABELLE: I've attempted everything that you have and more. But I can't cross. Even though I *know* the Hidden World is real, I can't *feel* it anymore.

BYRON: I can help you, Annabelle.

ANNABELLE: It's too late. The last message I received from the Green Man . . . it was a threat.

BYRON: Three days ago. The meeting in the cave . . .

ANNABELLE: He has grown impatient. If I don't complete the series soon, Gable will be gone. Forever. You of all people ought to understand, that is unacceptable.

BYRON: If everything you're saying is true, if it's all real, then so is the spell. You complete the book, it will open a portal, and he'll come over here. Into *our* world.

ANNABELLE: Perhaps that wouldn't be so terrible. We've certainly made a mess of it on our own. An ancient god couldn't muck it up much worse.

BYRON: That's bullshit. How many more children will suffer, just so you can have your son back?

ANNABELLE: If I had another choice, I would take it.

BYRON: Look . . . I don't think that you're a bad person for writing those books. Or even for accepting whatever deal he offered you.

ANNABELLE: I appreciate that.

BYRON: But I do think you're a coward. For keeping the secret. For burying your head in the sand.

ANNABELLE: It is hilarious to me what a pot-and-kettle *that* is. You act like your daughter's disappearance were some lightning strike out of the blue. Please. Try telling me she wasn't retreating from you for months, probably *years,* before that happened. Tell me you could name her true friends, or even knew if she had any.

   I have no doubt that you loved your daughter, Byron, and that it was painful to lose her. But you were losing her for a long time before she left, and my books are not the source of the problem, they were merely a conduit for her escape.

(*Silence. Then, sirens approaching in the distance.*)

BYRON: You called the police?

ANNABELLE: You broke into my house. You *lied* to me.

BYRON: For good reason.

ANNABELLE: Maybe so. But you're trying to stop me from what I need to do for my son. And I can't let that happen.

BYRON: . . . I'll see you around, Annabelle.

ANNABELLE: Only if I visit you in prison.

CONFESSION OF BYRON KIDD (RESUME)

The events after that conversation need little further explanation,
I imagine. I did attempt to escape once I knew the police were on
their way. I raced through the house and out a side door, just as
red-and-blue light flooded the gravel driveway. If there had been
any hope of getting to tree cover before I was spotted, that dissolved when the motion lights triggered.

I was spotlit like I was standing center stage—and at that moment, I became acutely aware that I was still holding Sir Henry's
knife in my hand. Not a good look, from a law-enforcement perspective. The officers on scene drew their weapons and shouted
at me to freeze and drop the weapon.

I bolted. I'm grateful that I wasn't shot in the back but suspect
that might owe as much to the surprise of the officers as anything
else. I made it quickly across the manicured yard and into the
dark cover of the trees.

Why did I flee? I need to find my daughter. And apparently, I
also need to save the world. Once Annabelle debuts her final
book, the spell will be complete. The portal will open. An ancient god will come devour our dreams.

I know that to those of you in the LAPD reading this document, this will come across as deluded self-righteous ranting. But
I need to write it nonetheless. And I hope that, coupled with the
recording of my conversation with Annabelle, it at least gives
pause to a few investigators and might engender an inkling of
curiosity about what truth might be found in these words.

Once I made it into the wilderness, I could hear the officers
giving chase. I ditched the knife, tossed it randomly into the
brush. I didn't expect it would never be recovered, but I wanted it
as far from me as possible. I understand that it was found, and
its connection to Sir Henry is the reason I'm being charged with
homicide, so let me try to set the record straight:

I did not kill Sir Henry. In fact, I would regard him as a friend. His wound was self-inflicted, though it was really caused by someone else (or perhaps some-THING). For the sake of simplicity, I'll just say that I don't know who it was, and I hope very much that the killing will be avenged.

Once I got away from Annabelle's house, I headed downhill toward the Bronson Caves, which I imagined would be an avenue for escape—not only from the police but from the world.

I didn't make it. Once the police helicopter arrived, it spotlit my position. Officers on the ground moved in from farther down the hill, cutting me off. I'd like to express my gratitude to the officers who brought me in without any serious harm. Given the circumstances, I'm lucky.

I am also grateful to the department for giving me the opportunity to provide this confession in written form—even though, when you read it, you will probably regret doing so. Because the writing of it will also be, I hope, the means of my escape.

As Annabelle made clear . . . portals to cross over are not limited to objects or places. They are limited only by the consciousness of the individual. And my consciousness is opening.

But first it must be purged. And to do that, I must confess. Not to murder, of which I am not guilty, or to breaking and entering, of which I am quite guilty, though I feel no remorse for that.

I must confess to failing her. To failing Liza.

I confess that when she was five years old and had an imaginary friend, a talking ten-foot-tall monkey named Terry, I told her that Terry wasn't real, and she was too old for make-believe. I made her feel foolish and small.

I confess that when she was six years old she came to me crying in the middle of the night from a nightmare, and I sent her back to her room and told her it was just a dream. I was impatient and rough and dismissive.

I confess that when she was eight and said she liked horseback lessons but wanted to someday ride a unicorn, I told her there's no such thing as unicorns, and she needed to stop talking about imaginary things or she couldn't continue her lessons. I was cold and belittling and harsh.

And I confess that when she wanted to dress up as a Fairy Tale character in March, I told her that was a waste of money, and she should stop wasting her time on such frivolous things, and try reading REAL stories about REAL things. I was so consumed with "just the facts" that I missed the most important fact of all—that I was driving her away, one day at a time, by denying what she loved. And if I'd been open to sharing in a little of that magic, I might not have lost her.

Now, to top it all off, I'm losing my mind. I don't know where I am anymore. Not really.

I might be inside a jail cell in downtown Los Angeles. Or I might be in the Hidden World.

All around me the walls are blank, white, sterile. Metal toilet, metal bed, stiff sheets, all too real. But I can feel the contours of another space at the same time. The Crystal Palace.

I look at the walls, and they're shifting. The transparent six-inch-thick plastic in the door is a prism, breaking open the light into a rainbow, and the rainbow scatters and diffuses across the floor.

The pen is the key. Can't stop writing. Imagining brings it forward. Writing makes it real. Maybe that's giving over to madness, but I don't have any reason left to fight it.

The crystal chamber is filling with light now, and out of the radiant swirling convergence, a form is materializing. It's me, taking shape, and I can see it from outside and feel it from within, my body nothing but energy and light that ebbs and flows.

I'm in-between now. I know it's not real and try to forget, but the thing that is real is Liza, and the only thing I can cling to is hope that I can save her, she has to be alive because if not, then nothing is worth anything. My faith in HER is the anchor I drop on the other side of the divide.

Going now, untethered by sanity, propelled by love, I can feel mys

(End of written confession)

LAPD METROPOLITAN DETENTION CENTER— INCIDENT REPORT

Date: November 2

Time: 7:03 AM

Personnel: Officer Leann Kleinman

Description: During morning bed check, cell was empty and unoccupied. No damage to cell bars or structure was observed. Complete facility lockdown was initiated, and full search conducted. Search yielded no evidence of inmate on premises. Current whereabouts unknown.

Video surveillance from hallway outside cell includes visual documentation of inmate entering cell escorted by Officers Brinks and Chua at 5:15 AM. Officer Chua completes visual check at 5:45 AM. No other activity observed in hallway until Officer Kleinman starts shift and conducts her own visual inspection, which discovered suspect's absence at 6:40 AM.

Suspect's written confession was the only object left behind in vacant cell. Additionally, suspect's knife is now missing from Evidence. Suspect at large, presumed armed and dangerous.

CHAPTER TWENTY-THREE

Once upon a time, there was a man who did not believe. He didn't believe in the world beyond worlds. He didn't even believe in himself. He didn't believe in anything—until he was confronted with the loss of everything he loved. Even then, he tried desperately to cling to his non-belief.

But fate conspired to *make* him believe. So it came to pass that one day he found himself in another world, waking up on a floor as smooth as glass, surrounded by the endlessly refracting walls of the Crystal Palace.

From his high perch, out through the gauzy walls that surrounded him, he beheld the Hidden World. The place he had denied for so long now lay before him—a landscape of sweeping and relentless *presence*. The twilit air glimmered with golden dust, and low-hanging clouds undulated rapidly through different colors and shapes. Rising over them on a towering mountain, he beheld the Castle in the Clouds, and far below it, a lake of purest silver gleamed in the light.

The non-believer thus woke to a sight that would stitch itself into his mind for the rest of his days. He was confronted by wonders upon wonders and would have done well to reflect upon the infinite error of his short-sighted ways.

But he didn't do any of that. Because he had a total mindfuck of a hangover.

And I should know, because the non-believer . . . that's me. And if I'm going to tell the truth about what happened, as impossible as it will sound, I need to be up front about the fact that I'm telling my own story.

The thing is, it wasn't exactly a *hangover;* I hadn't had a drink in a couple days. But it sure felt like the worst hangover I'd ever experienced times a thousand. My head throbbed, my eyes narrowed to slits in the face of unrelentingly bright light, and my muscles ached. All of them. All of which was probably the result of my not-particularly-fit body making the leap from one reality to another.

This didn't happen for the Narnia kids, did it? Or to Alice tumbling into Wonderland? It hadn't been mentioned in Annabelle's Fairy Tale books.

Maybe kids make the transition more seamlessly. But for me, it felt like I'd been worked over by a roided-up rugby team for a couple hours. Goddamn.

It was hard to gauge how much time had passed or to judge distances down below. First step was to get out of this cell. I ran my hands over the three inner walls, finding them completely seamless. No door anywhere. Then I touched my fingers to the glassy, crystalline surface of the outer wall—like a floor-to-ceiling window—and it effortlessly rotated about the middle, exposing me to the open air.

OK, so—that was the way out. But as I looked down, I was greeted by an incredible drop, a thousand feet or more, to a series of stone steps. My vision swam, and I felt as though I would tumble over the edge. I stepped back, nausea bubbling up, afraid I might barf on the immaculate glass floor.

I took a few deep breaths, trying to calm myself. No reason to panic. I was in another world, yes, but that was exactly what I'd been *trying* to do. It was like a lucid dream. Regardless of how fantastical my surroundings might be, I knew *I* was real, and that made the experience real. I closed my eyes, centering myself. . . .

Then the silence was interrupted by a rising, subtle hum, and I dared another look out the open wall to see a bird, winging its way up from below. Only, as it approached, it became apparent that it was no bird at all. It was a humanoid creature with a pair of rapidly flapping wings that steadily propelled him upward through the air, hummingbird-style. He came to a stop directly outside my cell, hovering.

I mean, I hate to say it, given how adamantly I'd been denying their existence up to this point, but . . . it was a fairy.

And not the spritely, slight form I might have imagined. Rather, he was taller than I was, sported a pointed beard, and was outfitted head-to-toe in plate armor with articulated joints. A golden helmet obscured most of his face, but through the slits for his eyes and mouth, I could see that his skin was a frosty blue. His likeness was alien, but at the same time, vaguely familiar. He carried a hefty spear, its tip pointed and barbed, which he wielded with deadly grace.

"Uh . . . hey." That was the first thing I said to a magical being from another world. "I'm Byron." I pointed at myself, not certain if he could understand my language. "By-ron," I said again emphatically.

He rolled his eyes. "I know," he replied. "We've been aware of you for some time."

I squinted, not sure if this information should disturb me or give me hope. My new companion then added, "I'm Gloverbeck, by the way."

Suddenly it clicked, and I realized why I recognized him. Liza's drawing. She had drawn me as this particular character from the books. But the creature before me did not resemble me in the least. I considered offering my hand to shake, but I wasn't coming anywhere near the ledge, and he continued to hover a few feet beyond the threshold. His wings were an effortless motion-blur in the air that kept him in place.

I nodded thoughtfully, remembering what I'd learned from

Misha, and asked: "Aren't you supposed to be dead? Ever since Book Five?"

He frowned. "You have a very *mortal* view of time. But that's not how it works here." But before I could ask him how it *did* work, he gruffly informed me, "Queen Áine will see you now." It wasn't a question. I nodded in dumb agreement.

He sheathed the spear on his back, directly between his wings, and beckoned me toward the edge. I realized what he had in mind and violently shook my head, backing away.

"Do not make this difficult. You will come in my arms or impaled on my spear. Up to you."

I nodded, not interested in testing how serious the threat was. I crept closer to the edge, feeling the cold wind lick my face. I was still probably a few feet from the threshold when full-on panic set in, my fear of heights rearing its head more strongly than it had in years. I hesitated, about to back away—but Gloverbeck lunged forward, grabbed me, and pulled me out.

Terror roared through my body as I was dragged over the abyss. Gloverbeck handled me effortlessly, flipping me around and working his hands under my armpits while my legs dangled below.

I would like to say that I shouted in alarm, but the word "scream" is more accurate. The entire landscape of this world was foreign to me, and I was soaring out over it, unsupported by anything except the strength of a being I would've sworn yesterday was entirely fictional. He banked through the sky, swooping down in a steep drop and a wide turn. My heart lurched, my stomach heaved, my adrenaline spiked, and I was grateful to have an empty bladder.

We leveled off, and as we turned, I got a look at the Crystal Palace from the outside: a towering spire, its walls curving glass ridges, reminiscent of a seashell. It looked like a seamless whole, but I could see that there were inlets along its grooved edges— tunnels leading into the structure. Its surface was radiant, shimmering with such vibrancy that it appeared to glow from within.

Gloverbeck zoomed us into one of the tunnels midway up the

structure. I saw other armored fairy guards just like my escort, though their armor was silver instead of gold, a sign of rank, I assumed; they nodded and stood down as we passed.

Gloverbeck brought me into a central chamber of pure white crystal, as tall as the palace, like the spine of the building. I could see other fairy creatures flitting about from perch to perch, conferring in dozens of small groups. As we entered, every eye in the room was upon me, and a murmur of interest rippled through the cavernous space.

The center of the chamber was a dais supported by a thin thread of marble, totally unreachable on foot; it could only be flown to. Gloverbeck hovered over it, still dangling me. Down below, I saw a throne of intricately carved crystal—similar to the one I'd seen in Annabelle's garage, only constructed on a scale that dwarfed the meager prop.

And seated there was another fairy. If she were a human, I would've guessed she was in her forties, with high cheekbones and regal features. There was something familiar about her. She was draped in a series of flowing, colorful cloaks that elegantly hung off her wings, which were tucked neatly behind her. Upon her head was a simple woven-wood crown, an organic contrast to the smooth stone that dominated the space.

Everything in this world was amazing; the very fact that it existed was shocking. But Queen Áine herself filled me with awe more than any of the grandiosity I had witnessed. She looked so delicate and so strong at the same time, and perhaps most shocking of all, so very . . . *alive*. My mouth hung open in wonder.

She regarded me with curious amusement, then nodded. Gloverbeck descended slowly and dropped me on the crystal floor.

"Welcome to the Hidden World," she said.

"Thank you," I replied. "It's, uh . . . really nice."

She looked me over, appraising. "What is your business here?"

I told her, "I'm here for my daughter. Her name is Liza. She came to this place, and . . . she's stuck. I need to bring her home."

Queen Áine nodded, not surprised. "Many children share her

fate, and I understand your desire to rescue her. She is, after all, your creation. But what you would attempt is not possible. We do not have your daughter; the Green Man does. And he does not part with them."

I shook my head, refusing to accept that. "Then tell me how to get her. I don't understand, what's your part in this world? You're a fictional character, brought to life!" She glowered at me, and I apologized. "I'm sorry, this is all just overwhelming."

Queen Áine's gaze pierced me—then abruptly, to my surprise, she laughed. "A fictional character indeed." She settled in, as she began to tell me her story.

"I have been alive as long as people in your world have dreamed. But I have only had a name since one was given to me . . . oh, a few thousand years ago. The Celts of your world. Their stories gave me shape, and more important, power. But that power waned as other stories took root. Such is the way of things. Like the rest of the fairy folk, I faded away. It is not unpleasant to wane, as long as you don't fight it. It is simply like . . . sleep.

"But in time, to my great surprise, we were brought back. In new ways, in new stories. At first, I was delighted, seeing my world flourish and transform. New places were born, new beings, wondrous new horizons. I saw that fairy folk would speak to a new age of dreamers. One hungry for wonder and starved for connection with nature.

"Then I realized *why* we had been revived. We were being used. We were a lure for the Green Man to bring dreamers from your realm into ours. No longer would he content himself to be nourished from afar. He had to possess the dreamers he fed on, devour them whole. By the time we realized what he was doing, it was too late. We opposed him—and were nearly wiped out in the process. He subdued us and only kept us alive so he could keep using us to draw a steady supply of victims.

"But even that was not enough. For him, there is no such thing as 'enough.' So he plotted to employ an ancient magic to bridge himself into *your* reality. Soon, his enchantment will be complete, and he will gorge himself on the hopes and dreams of your world."

I nodded, seeing how her narrative tied together the disparate threads, but not sure of her place within it. "And you're OK with that?"

Queen Áine sighed and shook her head. "We do not find it within our power to stop him. We are confined here, to the Crystal Palace. The rest of our world now belongs to him."

I heard the resignation in her voice, and it awakened anger in my chest. "That's bullshit. You've given up?"

"I have accepted a more limited role in this world, in order to protect the fey," Queen Áine replied, tempering her anger. "The Green Man is an ancient entity at the height of his powers. We do not stand a chance against him in battle. And in case it was not clear—neither do you."

I puffed myself up as defiantly as I could manage. "I've gotten this far . . . I'm gonna find my daughter and bring her home. I even know where she is. I just need to know how to get there."

Queen Áine nodded. "The Dreamvale is not far. A half-day's travel on foot to the west. But finding it will not be easy."

I glanced around at the many winged fairy folk about the chamber and tried my luck. "You could fly me there, I bet."

Queen Áine chuckled, probably at my audacity, before a sadness settled over her. "Alas, if we are seen aiding you against the Green Man, our fragile truce with him will be undone. So we cannot fly you there. But I can wish you well—and return to you that which is already yours, and which you will most certainly need."

At that, she nodded to Gloverbeck, who hovered down to my level, holding before him a strange weapon: a sword whose blade was a blood-red gem, over a foot long. Its faceted sides made a sharp edge with a gleaming, pointed tip. The sword refracted the light, and I realized from the dimensions that this was Sir Henry's knife. Returned to this world . . . and in the process, restored to its original form.

"The Ruby Shard," Queen Áine informed me. "Summoned back into our world at the same time as you. I gifted it long ago to a worthy man from your world, and it served him well. I hope it will serve you too."

Gloverbeck then gave me a sheath as well, which I clipped to my waist. The queen said nothing further; my audience with her was apparently complete. I attempted to bow, in a show of respect and gratitude, but it was clear from her puzzled expression that the gesture meant nothing in this world. She merely looked to Gloverbeck, who lifted me up and flew me out of the throne room.

I was dropped off just outside the Crystal Palace, where marble steps descended from the structure. Gloverbeck pointed me in the direction of a trail that led west into a thick sea of trees.

"This path will take me to the Dreamvale?" I asked.

Gloverbeck shrugged. "If it feels like doing so, it might." And without a word, he flew back into the Crystal Palace.

It wasn't much to go on, but it was a start. And given the distance I had to cover, there was no time to waste. So I set off on foot into the vast forest of the Living Labyrinth.

CHAPTER TWENTY-FOUR

The Living Labyrinth lived up to its name.

First, in the *living* part, because every inch of the place was alive. The canopy was crisscrossed by various creatures I glimpsed only fleetingly. There were humming wings, which always flitted out of sight as soon as I turned my gaze, like when you spot a shooting star in the sky. Furry little lemur-like critters dangled from branches over the path; they looked cute enough that I might have ventured to pet one, except that I could see that their jaws were massive—and indeed, when I came within five feet, one snapped at me, revealing razor-sharp teeth.

On another tree trunk, I saw a snake, slithering circles around the bark—and when its head came into view, I realized that it was devouring its own body. An ouroboros.

But the most "living" thing of all were the trees themselves, which were responsible for the "labyrinth." Their movement was subtle when I'd viewed it from afar, but up close, it was clear they were in constant motion, shuffling and reaching out their limbs, stroking and swatting at one another, occasionally lifting their lumbering roots out of the soil to step into a new position.

As a result, the path before me was merely the current one the trees had given shape to, but at any given moment they were redirecting the way. Whether this was deliberate or accidental, I could not say. But anytime I attempted to venture from the path, I was brushed back by powerful swinging limbs.

At first, the way through the forest seemed straightforward, curving slightly but generally headed in the direction I needed to go. When I reached a fork, I looked around, hoping for some landmark to help me navigate. Through the trees back the way I came, I briefly glimpsed a tall stone building—the Los Angeles Municipal Center, where I had been detained. But as I moved, peering through a different gap in the trees, it had become the impossible spire of the Crystal Palace.

I thought I might have imagined it, but as I turned, looking to the north, I saw the rounded dome of Griffith Observatory peeking over the tree line. Again, I shifted for a better look, and it became a medieval castle, resting atop a bank of clouds.

The reality I had come from was bleeding into this one—at least, in my perception. This filled me with hope that I could successfully navigate based on what I knew of Los Angeles . . . but when I contemplated *why* that bleed-over might be happening, my hope quickly turned to dread.

The Sixfold Summoning was nearly finished. The Green Man's bridge between worlds was almost complete.

I turned back to the fork in the path, and based on what I had seen, I concluded that the fork to the right would correspond with "north." If the Dreamvale was an analogue for the Hollywood Forever Cemetery, that would be my best bet.

The next split in the path presented similar options, but this time the trees were too tall for any landmark on the horizon to be visible. As I considered which option to pursue, my gaze drifted across the path. Etched in the dirt in one direction, I could make out faint geometric shapes formed by the moss on the ground at regular intervals.

Stars. The Walk of Fame, leaking over into this world. Showing me the way.

This was all guesswork, of course, but intuition told me that I was moving in the right direction. There stirred within me . . . not confidence, exactly, so much as profound bewilderment at how far I'd come.

After a while longer, though, I started to feel like I was too far north. I worried that I should go back to the last fork and try the other path.

That's when I started to hear a sound from deep in the forest. A low rumbling, coupled with trampling steps that crushed branches and leaves and shook the earth. I squinted, looking for the source of the sound. . . .

A shape moved through the trees. Massive, but surprisingly agile. It was up ahead and to my left . . . and lumbering toward the path. It let out a low growl that I could only interpret as angry, or hungry, or a combination of the two.

I turned around and proceeded quickly in the other direction. I heard motion in the forest, but no more massive footfalls, so I hoped it might not be chasing me, even as my heart thudded with certainty that it was.

But then, up ahead, in the direction I was fleeing, I caught sight of a shape moving through the canopy—the same one I was trying to escape. It was propelling itself like a monkey from branch to branch, only instead of arms, it was grabbing on with ten-foot-long *tentacles* that shot through the air, gripped powerfully, and swung it forward. It grabbed a tree trunk in that way, whipped around it, and landed in my path.

My jaw dropped. Fight-or-flight instincts were overridden in favor of *freeze*.

The creature was fear incarnate. A dozen terrifying predators mixed and matched into one abomination. The mane and jaws of a lion, tusks like an elephant, tentacles coming out of its back like a giant squid, and the shifting camouflage coloration of a chameleon.

The Doggerdoth.

Compared to the model I'd seen in Annabelle's garage, the real thing was two to three times as large, and indescribably more frightening. Aggressive energy coursed through its body. It pawed the ground with hooves like a rhino's, a deep growl emanating from its throat.

Finally coming to my senses, I turned to flee, only to find that I
was ten feet away from a dead end. The trees in that direction were
knitted together into a tight wall of wood, conspiring with the
creature to force a confrontation.

The Living Labyrinth, I decided, was a real asshole.

I turned back to the monstrosity lumbering toward me, savor-
ing my helplessness. I drew the Ruby Shard then; the blade looked
needle-thin and insignificant in the face of this beast, but I knew
the weapon's power to slice through anything.

The Doggerdoth grew enraged when I brought out the sword.
It dropped its massive head, tusks lowered, and charged, its tentacles whipping the air above it. I waited in the face of this runaway train . . . then, at the last moment, leaped to the side and
slashed blindly at the creature. The Doggerdoth's head struck me
obliquely, and it felt like being hit by a car, but at least I dodged its
tusks, and my weapon opened a slice up the side of its face.

It turned quickly, shaking its head in fury, spattering blood
onto the path. Then it came at me again, jaws snapping. Not a full
charge, but a slower approach, cornering me in the dead end. Its
tentacles surrounded me from both sides, and I sliced at them.
Suddenly, one tentacle seized my leg. The world turned upside
down, and I found myself being fed into the abyss of the creature's
wide-open maw.

I bent sharply at the waist and swung my weapon blindly. The
world spun as I was abruptly dropped. I hit the ground hard, right
alongside the severed, still-flopping end of the tentacle that had
grabbed me.

The Doggerdoth roared in pain and retreated. It felt like a victory, but it was only a brief reprieve. The creature's tentacle grew
back, regenerating effortlessly before my eyes. The cut on its face
was already gone.

Well, shit. Given that I couldn't outrun it, or even damage it . . .
this wasn't looking good.

Even worse, I saw that the living trees were crowding in, restricting the path to a narrow alley, so there wasn't even room to dodge or escape.

The Doggerdoth pawed the earth, eyes gleaming with rage. I stared death in the face, unable to believe I was about to be gored by a creature that an author had invented in her imagination. Every awful trait of this beast was just a detail that Annabelle had made up, but that wasn't going to stop the thing from killing me.

Unless . . . what could I remember about it? Liza had mentioned it in her profile and . . . What was it that Misha had said? The Doggerdoth was not a malicious creature; it was a wild animal, one that had been first obstacle and then ally to Ciara in the books. It wasn't *evil*; it responded to kindness.

The creature that reared up twenty yards away did not betray the slightest hint of gentleness. It bellowed and charged again, tusks leveled, dead set on impaling me into the trees. I raised the Ruby Shard up in front of me . . . then drove the blade into the ground, and instead of fighting, held out my open palm.

The Doggerdoth didn't slow. I closed my eyes, wondering briefly what would become of me when I died in another world. The thunder of its hooves and the wild roar were closing in, on top of me now, and I braced myself—

But then . . . silence. I didn't dare open my eyes. But I felt a slimy wetness on my palm. And when I finally managed to look, I found the creature was licking my hand. The rage in its eyes was replaced with friendly curiosity.

I did not recoil, despite my disgust. I met its gaze and offered the warmest smile I could muster given that I'd been certain of my imminent demise moments before. I took a step forward, touching its leonine face and rubbing its fur, which earned a deep rumble of contentment from its throat.

"You know the way to the Dreamvale?" I asked. I wasn't sure the creature would understand my language, but from the way it looked away and the dark fear that came over its eyes, its comprehension was undeniable.

I gently turned its head toward me (as best as I could, given that its head was as large as my entire body). "I need to go there. I need you to take me."

The Doggerdoth shook its head. But I moved in closer, telling it, "Please. It is very important. My daughter . . ." I couldn't finish the thought; in my overwhelmed fatigue, the emotion of my longing stabbed out quickly, took me by surprise, trembled in my voice.

The creature appeared to understand not only my intention now but the gravity of my feeling. With a resigned whimper, it lowered its head to the ground, lying down on its belly. At first, I took the gesture to be a sign of resignation and defeat. . . .

But then I realized that the back of its neck was now level with my shoulder. It was offering itself. And without hesitation, I swung up onto it, like getting on a horse.

I would have liked a moment or two to acquaint myself with how best to brace myself, but the Doggerdoth did not offer any safety instructions. The second my legs dug in and gripped both sides of its shoulders, it was on its feet and launched itself into the trees. My hands desperately grabbed its mane as the beast accelerated like a rocket into the trees, which allowed us passage.

Branches whipped my face, drawing blood. The churning motion of the creature's body was like a bucking bronco without a reliable rhythm. I was jostled and jolted, bruised and battered, and probably would've dismounted if not for our breakneck speed. It was painful and terrifying and . . . something else that I couldn't put my finger on at first, but slowly dawned on me.

God, I hate to say it, but it was also *fun*.

It was a roller coaster and a safari all at once. We surged across an alien landscape with glowing moss blurring by and strange creatures calling out from the dark, uttering noises never heard by human ears. The Doggerdoth bounded off tree trunks and leaped over boulders bigger than cars. I was probably on a hopeless suicide mission—but I couldn't deny that some long-buried part of me was tapped by the exhilaration of the ride.

Getting to the Dreamvale would have taken me many hours on foot, and I might have *never* gotten there on my own. But riding the Doggerdoth wasn't only fast; the forest seemed more cooperative, making room and herding us *toward* our destination rather than away from it.

It felt like only a matter of minutes before the Living Labyrinth opened up to reveal a huge, sprawling hillside, barren of trees. The ground was overgrown with a thick bed of moss, and dotted with columns of vines, roughly resembling the pattern of the graves in the Hollywood Forever Cemetery.

I knew what those were. I could now see that there were *hundreds* of them already in place . . . and rolling hills with space for many thousands more to grow.

The Doggerdoth stopped at the edge of the Dreamvale, and its body shivered. I urged it onward, digging in my heels as if it were a horse, but it only backed away. I couldn't blame it. I slid off its back and told the creature, "Thank you," and it was soon traipsing back into the Living Labyrinth.

Moments after it departed, the path it had traveled down was gone, the trees pulling up their roots and closing rank. There was no way back.

Not that I wanted one. This was the place where I had seen Liza. The place where I'd spoken with her across the divide.

Rationally, this was the time for hope. But I certainly didn't *feel* hopeful. A cold wind whistled over the hill. Low clouds knitted themselves overhead, obscuring the sun. Dread knotted in the pit of my stomach.

I gulped as I stepped forward, approaching the first of the viny columns. I almost didn't want to look, but I needed to see. Through the thick tangle, I caught glimpses of fabric and skin, and when I came close enough, I saw part of a face.

A child. He was perhaps only eight years old, with brown skin, delicate features, short hair. Nearly completely encased by the vines. His eyes were open but rolled back, twitching with REM.

Up close, the vines *pulsed* with energy, glowing from within. The glow appeared to move within the vines, like a circulatory system—filling up with the energy of the child's dreams, drawing them into the ground below.

It was hard to believe this was real. It *wasn't,* in one sense. This whole place was built on imagination and fantasy. Yet this was happening to a real child, draining him of real life. I felt horror like I'd never known, and a shiver ran through my body.

I pulled myself away from the boy, looking about the eerie landscape. I was not here for him. Guilt bubbled up inside me at turning away from him, but I pushed it aside. I needed to find Liza.

There were a few children milling about aimlessly, as there had been when I first came over. None of them was Liza, I could see—but I did register a face that I knew. It was a boy, stumbling across the spongy ground without a shirt on, a green pulsing tattoo across his upper back. *Gable.*

I ran to Annabelle's son and tried to get his attention, but his eyes, half-lidded, didn't even register my presence. He ambled on, pushing past me, continuing the hopeless meandering walk that must have been his brief daily respite from enforced stasis.

I moved on. I had to find her. I ran from one viny column to the next, calling out, "LIZA!" at each one. The children inside remained mostly unresponsive as I peered at their partially obscured faces through the thick tangle of plant matter, though I saw occasional flickers of dim awareness.

I needed to hurry. I glanced toward the tree line, certain some monstrous threat would arrive soon—one that could not be tamed by a simple act of submission.

I kept searching, growing more and more desperate and hardening my heart against the plight of all the children I beheld. My breath grew ragged as I ran and peered and moved on, trying to suppress the despair in the pit of my stomach, until at last I caught sight of a familiar red hooded sweatshirt through a tangle of thorny vines.

Liza.

It was her. It could only be her. She was all I had come for, exactly what I had expected, yet startling to behold. She had loomed
so large in my mind that it was shocking how very *small* she was—
barely five feet tall, and not aged a day in the months since she had
disappeared.

My heart soared. She was alive—and against all odds, I had
found her. Euphoria surged through me, and I felt a lump in my
throat and a warmth in my cheeks as the tears I had kept down for
so long welled up close to the surface. I wanted to weep for joy at
the very fact of her existence.

But in the next moment, as I took in the conditions of her un-
natural imprisonment, my heart sank and my stomach dropped.
The gravity of all she had endured walloped me with a force I
could hardly comprehend, and I felt I might collapse. Tears that
might've been joyful seconds earlier now burned with despair.

There was no time to sort through these reactions. I needed to
act; I could process all this later. Coming in close, I whispered to
her fiercely, "Liza!" Her eyes flickered with recognition. "I'm here
for you, honey, I'm here, just hold on." I brought the Ruby Shard
up to cut through a vine. . . .

But abruptly, a chilly voice pierced me to the core: "*Stop.*" The
sound came from Liza's throat and superficially sounded like her,
but the tone was utterly alien.

"Liza? Honey, it's me . . . it's Dad." I waited, hoping that recognizing my voice would open her eyes and bring her back.

"*Byron,*" she said slowly, milking the word with decadent men-
ace.

I shivered. And I knew it was not my daughter talking to me
now. It was her throat, her mouth, her body that spoke, but the
words were not her own.

At that point, I should not have been surprised by any strange-
ness I encountered, but this magic nonetheless shocked me to the
core. The arrogant, thoughtless *violation* of it all offended me

deeply, as the long-sought reunion with my daughter was hijacked by this creature, and Liza's autonomy was stolen in a way I had never imagined possible.

I could feel blood rushing to my head, like a churning cloud behind my eyes, as rage overtook me. It vibrated through my entire nervous system, leaving me feeling hollowed out yet energized to the point of restlessness. My throat tightened and my voice quavered as I snarled, "Let her go."

Liza's mouth curled into a nasty grin, one that my real daughter was incapable of. A grin full of malice and spite, taking pleasure in the suffering that this was evidently causing me. A grin that could only belong to the Green Man, taunting me for my useless demand.

My muscles twitched, eager to lash out and strike, but I knew I had to keep myself under control to avoid hurting Liza. I grabbed one of the vines imprisoning her and slid the Ruby Shard under it, then fiercely tugged it back, slicing clean through. The cut was easy, but there were dozens more to be made.

As I prepared to make my second slice, Liza spoke again, coldly commanding: "*Stop.*" I hesitated, and Liza added, "*Or she will be . . . no longer.*" The instant the threat was voiced, the whole column tightened around Liza, and a leafy vine encircled her throat. The vine I'd just severed regrew, with ropy tendrils reaching out from both ends and knitting back together. Regenerating as quickly and easily as the Doggerdoth.

How could I possibly free her from a living prison and a jailor who could control her so completely? My mind raced, searching for a strategy.

I tried goading: "Why are you hiding if you're so powerful? Why don't you show yourself instead of talking through a helpless child?"

"*If you want to see me, look around,*" came the reply through my daughter's mouth. I did, casting a gaze in every direction— but no new form emerged from the gloom. Liza went on, "*That*

is all me. *For I am not in this world, or of this world. I am* this
world."

At that moment, I felt pressure on my legs, squeezing painfully
where my calf had been bitten the night before, and looked down
to find a lattice of vines was growing up out of the squishy lichen
ground, grabbing me. I reacted quickly, swiping at the vines, but
the instant I did, one whipped up lightning-quick and captured
my wrist, stopping my attack and bending me awkwardly. I tried
to run, but my feet were bolted in place, and the shackles were
expanding, overtaking my body.

My efforts to fight it quickly became the useless thrashing of a
trapped animal, and I felt the sinking, burning sensation of *hu-
miliation.* I desperately hoped that Liza herself could not witness
any of this, as I was so easily defeated at the end of such a long
quest. Exposed as a ridiculous fool, bumbling and utterly unpre-
pared, unable to help.

As the vines overtook me, Liza spoke again. *"It has been some
time since I have tasted the dreams of one as old as yourself. What
a pleasure it will be to suck the marrow from your soul, while you
are face-to-face with your doomed progeny."*

I could feel the viny tendrils snaking up inside my shirt now,
constricting my ribs, reaching up toward my mouth—and as I
verged on total envelopment, I spat out the words: "Wait! I have a
proposal."

The vines did not *stop* exactly, but their progress subtly de-
murred, avoiding my mouth and climbing the back of my head
instead. *"Your first day here, and already you wish to barter?"* A
mirthless laugh escaped Liza's lips.

Despite the apparent rebuke, I saw an opening. "Yes. You make
deals, I know that. And I want you to let her go."

Liza sneered, *"I know what* you *want. The question is what a
mortal—a full-grown one, at that—could ever offer me."*

I took a breath. "The Summoning. The spell. Annabelle's final
book, the one she's been holding back . . . I can get her to finish it."

Liza's face sneered: "*You offer me something that is already mine. The storyteller is finishing the book as we speak. My changeling has compelled her cooperation.*"

With one plan thwarted, my mind raced for another—and I saw it in the ego of my enemy. "That's true, the book will be out in the world soon. But don't you think *you* should be a character in it?"

There was a long silence before the reply came slowly: "*It is true that far too much of her fable has been consumed with trivial nonsense.*"

"Why do you think she cut you out of the story after the third book?" I said. "She's trying to take away your power. Because she knows that you feed on belief."

"*It matters not whether the mortals of your world know my name. They will believe in me when they witness my power.*"

"The stories matter," I pressed. "And Annabelle's not only leaving you out of the final book . . . she's denying your existence. Making a mockery of the whole *idea* of the Green Man." This, of course, was total fabrication, and a dangerous provocation. . . .

But it worked. Apparently even an ancient god is not all-seeing and can be deceived. Liza flinched, and her lip curled with the Green Man's bitter rage. "*She wouldn't dare. . . .*"

"She hates you every bit as much as she loves her son," I said. "She intends to honor the letter of your agreement, but the ending she's crafted will undermine everything you're working for."

There was another long silence as the Green Man weighed this. "*And you propose . . . a solution?*"

"I can get her to change the ending," I insisted. "I can compel her to rewrite the final chapter so it makes *you* the true hero of the story."

"*I don't need to be seen as a hero. I need to be worshipped. As a god!*"

"Then you haven't given much thought to the way stories work," I said. "People don't want any more gods. They want *he-*

roes." I studied Liza's expression, which betrayed nothing, but the Green Man's silence suggested that my argument was getting through. I barreled on, "But it's not too late. I can make her change it."

Liza licked her lips; then the reply came, thoughtful and languid. "*It is not my habit to visit physical harm upon the children who come here. Pain damages the quality of the dreams. Hope bleeds out quickly. But I will make an exception for your daughter here . . . if you do not make good on your word and succeed in this task.*"

The vines tightened around Liza again, showing how easily he could harm her. Fury crackled through my body like an electric pulse. But I was helpless, and I knew any threat would only undermine my petition. "I will succeed," I promised. "I will make Annabelle deliver an ending that includes you and demonstrates your power. And in return, you swear to let my daughter free."

"*You have one day to complete the task,*" said the ancient god through Liza's mouth.

One day? That was impossible. But the vines were continuing to constrict around Liza, and I knew that negotiation was useless. "Agreed!" I shouted quickly.

"*Then we are so bound,*" came the answer from Liza's mouth. The vines around my body slithered across my skin, and rough thorns sliced open lines on my forearms. Blood welled to the surface and was instantly absorbed by the plant. A blood oath. The consecration of the magic.

"Now, let me go," I snapped, a tiny fraction of the anger burning inside me coming through in the words. A part of me desperately wanted to uncork the rage completely, to unleash curses and screams of primal fury. But I knew the deal we had struck was a delicate balance I could not afford to upset.

When the Green Man finally replied from Liza's mouth, the voice dripped with hatred: "*Do not test my patience. Or forget for an instant that both of your lives are in my hands.*"

With that, the mossy ground beneath me opened up like quicksand, and I was jerked downward by the vines, pulling me into the earth. Panic gripped my body as the sight of Liza retreated from view. I fought viciously but helplessly. I was dragged down, down, down, until my vision was obscured entirely amid the dirt, and the opening above me closed.

I was buried alive. Every primal fear imaginable overtook me at once—fear of darkness, of death, of confinement. And when I opened my mouth to scream, wet dirt filled my mouth, and my body was wracked with spasmodic coughs.

But my hands, outstretched above me, were now free. I clawed at the soil, pushed through desperately, until at last the feeling of open air touched my fingertips. My arms wriggled through the earth and my body churned, and I climbed and crawled until finally, exhausted and hacking and spitting mud, I dragged myself out into the sun.

I was alive. With that knowledge came a hollow feeling of relief as the extreme adrenaline flush slowly subsided, and I looked around me. Puzzled.

The harsh quality of the light had changed. The spongy lichen ground was now replaced by well-manicured lawn. As my eyes adjusted, I saw that I was not alone. Half a dozen solemn mourners, wearing black and bearing flowers, were gathered before a gravestone nearby.

They stared at me in horror. A reasonable response, given that they'd come to pay respects to their dearly departed grandpa or whatever and did not expect to see a half-crazed man claw his way out of the ground.

I waved at them. "Just . . . paying my respects." I spat out a clod of dirt and started walking as calmly as possible toward the gates of the Hollywood Forever Cemetery.

What more could I say? That my daughter was in another realm, being tortured by an evil being with godlike powers, who was planning an apocalyptic invasion of our world? The moment

I even contemplated the full reality of the situation, panic and despair overwhelmed me.

I needed to focus on the positive. I had visited the Hidden World and made it back alive. I'd gotten the Green Man to agree to a deal of sorts; even if it seemed impossible to live up to it, that was a victory.

But it had taken a toll. I felt like I'd been scraped raw. I had failed to bring Liza home, even after coming so tantalizingly close. Walking through the cemetery, I felt like she was simultaneously within reach and more elusive than ever. I *missed* her, and my heart ached in the most palpable, visceral way.

Even so, there was a glimmer of hope. And that was enough.

CHAPTER TWENTY-FIVE

INTERVIEW #WHO-EVEN-KNOWS-NOW
WITH MISHA PIMM

Subject: Who else? Misha answered the door in pajamas decorated with a phone booth all over them (a TARDIS, I was corrected, whatever that means), looking alternately relieved and enraged to see me on her doorstep.

Location: Misha's apartment yet again. Well, Misha *and Shelby's* apartment, to be more precise, and if the whispered argument from the next room was any indication, Shelby did *not* want Misha letting me in. Or ever talking to me again. But I found myself in Misha's study, waiting patiently for her to join me, which eventually she did, and she even agreed to let me record our conversation. I told her it was important.

TRANSCRIPT OF INTERVIEW

MISHA: Wonderful—now I'm aiding and abetting. That's a real crime, right, not just a *Law & Order* thing?

BYRON: Sorry, I don't mean to put you in a bad spot.

MISHA: You're like a full-on fugitive now! There's an article online, and the police put out a wanted poster. Nice mugshot, by the way, you look like a nutjob.

BYRON: I know. But this is too important to—

MISHA: You broke into Annabelle's house! You busted out of jail! How the fuck did you bust out of jail?

BYRON: I didn't *exactly*—

MISHA: What was it like anyway?

BYRON: Jail?

MISHA: Annabelle's house! Did you find the Wishing Well?

BYRON: Sort of. Listen, do you still have the notebook I left with you?

MISHA: Yeah, and just for the record, I'm not super happy about that. It's one thing to hold on to your shit while you take a trip out of town, it's another thing entirely to hide evidence from the cops while you're off on some citywide crime spree. You realize you're wanted for *murder* now?

BYRON: I didn't kill anyone.

MISHA: But the police think you did! And your notebook is obviously some serious evidence they'd wanna get their hands on.

BYRON: So why didn't you turn it in?

MISHA: 'Cause I'm not a narc. And I was worried it would implicate me as your accomplice. And against my better judgment, I still care about you and want to help you get Liza back.

BYRON: Thank you. Now, can I assume that you read the contents?

MISHA: Uh, *yeah*. Right away. You didn't say not to.

BYRON: It's fine, I'm glad. I want you to look at it now. I think . . .

MISHA: You think what?

BYRON: Just look at it. Look at where it ends.

(*Silence, sounds of papers shuffling. Eventually . . .*)

MISHA: I don't understand. There's . . . *more.*

BYRON: That's what I thought.

MISHA: (*Reading aloud*) Chapter Twenty, LAPD Arrest Report. When did you write this?

BYRON: I didn't. How could I?

MISHA: (*Reading*) The Confession of Byron Kidd . . .

BYRON: I did write that. But not in that notebook.

MISHA: Then how'd it get in here?

BYRON: (*Sighs*) A smart person once told me, any great story eventually takes on a life of its own.

MISHA: This is not what I meant.

BYRON: OK, then . . . magic?

MISHA: So all these pages . . . this is what happened to you. How you escaped . . .

BYRON: I think you should read it now. We need to get on the same page. Literally.

MISHA: No shit . . .

(*Several minutes of silence.*)

MISHA: Ha! The Doggerdoth?! You're *serious* about this?

BYRON: Yup.

(*More silence.*)

MISHA: Hang on. All of this . . . How long were you gone for?

BYRON: It felt like a day or so. But when I came back, in the grave-yard, only a few hours had passed. Like Sir Henry said . . . time works differently over there.

(*More silence.*)

MISHA: OK. Whew. Got it.

BYRON: Got it?

MISHA: I mean, the information is received. What to do with it . . . first, just to be clear, you're saying that all of this actually happened, right?

BYRON: Yeah. And normally I might entertain the possibility that I was drugged in my prison cell and had some wild hallucination—but that would also mean I was pulled out of my cell and buried alive in the Hollywood Forever Cemetery. And that wouldn't explain how those words got onto that page.

MISHA: How is this possible?

BYRON: The answers are in *The Hidden World*. The book, not the place. There's a story Sir Henry referenced that I think might help explain.

SHORT STORY

From *The Hidden World: On Faeries, Fauns & Other Creatures of Folklore*, by Sir Henry Raleigh. Published 1889, Oxford University Press.

THE DJINN WITHIN

This story comes to this page from my lips, uttered and trans-muted here amid the shifting sands of Persia.

There once was a wandering bard who roamed the land in search of tales that might unfold the secrets of the universe. Low and high, he sought out such narratives as might lead the way back to the great original Source of all such stories.

Many he found, each one a new facet of the gem through which he might catch a glimpse of the Hidden World that lay concealed behind the veil of time and space.

The stories brought him far, to campfires and ruling huts, to castle parapets and fishing boats and secret coves. They came to him in tongues both known and unknown to him.

As the tales fell upon his ears and flowed into his mind and emerged through the stroke of his quill, they settled into his bones. The tales took on a life of their own, and he came to believe in the Impossible. Some tales seemed to write themselves, so effortlessly were they transcribed. Others he could not even recall writing down, for when he went to his book to set them in ink, already were they there, perfectly inscribed in his own penmanship.

Thus did he come to suspect that magic was not merely the subject of the tales; the magic was in the telling itself, and he was becoming merely its vessel.

His journey took him even farther, in search of an ancient force he'd heard whispers about: the djinn, the powerful spirits that permeated the oldest stories. Some were wish-granters, some demonic. They were housed in lamps or jars, rubbed into freedom or summoned into service. The bard went in search of the truest original djinn tale.

His quest catapulted him from one great capital to another, from Constantinople to Jerusalem to Babylon—but none he met would share the story he sought.

In time, his journey brought him to Persia, where he trekked deep into the desert in pursuit of an imam who might tell the tale. But every tent that danced across the horizon proved to be a mirage, and he wondered if ever he would make it back.

At last the bard chanced upon a humble trader on camelback,

bearing spice and linens to Mecca. The bard waved down the trader, who gave him water.

But the bard spoke none of the trader's tongue; even the words he had learned in the city were useless to this desert-crosser. At last, the bard found a single word that they both knew: "djinn." The trader's eyes lit with recognition. "Djinn!" the bard cried, again and again, and the trader nodded.

Digging into his pack, the trader fished out a brass oil-lamp, tossed it to the bard, and made a motion suggestive of rubbing across its surface. Without uttering a syllable, the trader confirmed the legend the bard had sought.

Then the trader left, trudging his camel eastward across the dunes. The bard, alone with his dubious prize, stared at its clouded bronze surface. He rubbed it, both fearing and hoping that a billowing cloud of smoke might emerge to herald forth a powerful spirit. But no such being came.

Again and again, the bard rubbed with all his might to summon the mighty djinn. But in little time, the bard found himself merely staring at a shined-clean reflection of his own face. His mouth gaped open, such was his shock at the revelation unfolded before him.

He *was* the djinn. The wishes of his heart were his own to grant. And the magic lay within his storytelling power.

So, he spoke these very same words, and this time watched them inscribe themselves upon his page. Never again would he need to lift his quill, for his heart was illuminated by faith, and his page would ever obey his will.

Now the stories pass through him like a clear vessel, and he calls upon them all to show the way. He pleads for passage into that netherworld from whence they all sprang; he entreats them to open the way to their secret realm. . . .

And the stories oblige.

RESUME TRANSCRIPT

MISHA: OK, cool. The bard in that story, that's Henry . . . and he's saying . . . this is how he got to the Hidden World.

BYRON: Yes. He stopped having to *write* the stories.

MISHA: And you think . . . that's what's happening with your notebook.

BYRON: Turn the page. Look. It's the conversation we're having right now. . . .

MISHA: Holy shit. How'd that happen? Right when I said it . . . it's doing it now!

BYRON: Now you believe me?

MISHA: I could just say anything and it . . . Kangaroo! Damn. Bangkok! Un-fucking-believable . . .

BYRON: It's real, Misha.

MISHA: Pillsbury Doughboy. How does it know how to do that?

BYRON: I mean, as much as it pains me to say this, to you of all people . . . *magic.*

MISHA: Yeesh. Hoo boy. Oh jeez.

BYRON: You OK?

MISHA: This is really fucking with my anxiety.

(*Sound of the notebook being slammed shut.*)

BYRON: Deep breaths, Misha. If there is anyone prepared to handle this, it's you.

MISHA: No! No, it's not. Because I'm not studying all this stuff so I can get caught up in some cross-dimensional child-trafficking plot.

BYRON: This is your chance to do some real good.

MISHA: I never asked for this. I never wanted to be responsible for anyone. And now—I've got a great job, and somebody who loves me, and that's enough for me.

BYRON: I'm sorry. It's not fair that I'm asking. But Liza needs you.

MISHA: And what about all the other kids? What about all those children you found out there, trapped and getting the life drained out of them?

BYRON: They need you too. Because if what I'm trying to do *works*, then maybe I can bring them home too.

MISHA: . . . Really?

BYRON: Yes. But I'm gonna need your help.

CHAPTER TWENTY-SIX

EMAIL

From: bkidd@gmail.com
To: Valeriekidd@sltpartners.com

Val,

First off—as soon as I send this message I'm going to toss my phone, so don't worry about replying. I don't think I can handle hearing any more secondhand psychobabble from Martin anyway.

I'm writing to say I'm sorry. Sorry my last email was so harsh. Sorry I said you never believed in me, when the truth, I can see now, is that I didn't believe in myself. I chose the path I thought was safest—the path of logic and reason and just the facts—because I thought it was the only way to live in reality and take care of you and Liza.

But it wasn't. It drove you both away.

It might be too late now, but I'm ready to believe. Even though what I'm about to attempt is, to put it mildly, impossible. It is likely I'll lose my life in the process. But it is the only way I can conceive of to bring our daughter home.

I love you and wish you all the best,
Byron

INVESTIGATIVE JOURNAL OF BYRON KIDD

November 2

FairyCon is a strange phenomenon. A weekend-long celebration of the Fairy Tale series in all its forms. It's not the biggest gathering of its kind, of course; it's dwarfed by ComicCon and Disney's Marvel-and-Star-Wars extravaganza. But according to Misha, it is notable for the fevered devotion of its attendees, resulting in the highest cosplay rate of any fandom celebration—meaning the greatest percentage of festival-goers who dress up in character.

A few weeks ago, I would have regarded the packed throngs of ten-to-sixty-year-olds in attendance with disdain. But now, that feeling was replaced by a sense of bemusement, tinged with wonder. All these people were dressed up in tribute to fictional characters, having no idea that those beings actually EXISTED in another realm adjacent to our own. And I had seen them! I had walked among and talked with these otherworldly creatures and returned to tell the tale.

Perhaps strangest of all: I was not only attending FairyCon willingly but in costume.

Misha suggested it as the best way to conceal my identity since I was now a wanted fugitive. She showed me news stories about the "deranged stalker" who had been arrested near the home of Annabelle Tobin; an escaped suspect in the recent homicide of a homeless man. My mugshot accompanied the story, which was being widely circulated.

But my legal problems hardly even registered, except insofar as they might prevent me from finding Annabelle and quickly convincing her to change her ending so I could bring Liza home. Then save the world. Somehow.

So as much as I recoiled from the notion of playing dress-up at a time like this, I had to concede it made sense. Misha showed me an entire closet jam-packed with costume pieces, face paint, and accessories, and asked if there was a character I could see myself as.

My immediate reaction was to say I had no idea. But after a moment of reflection, I realized that I now knew several characters by name. I felt an absurd pride at the fact . . . or perhaps it was merely a sense that Liza would be pleased.

"Gloverbeck," I told Misha. That was who Liza had drawn me as. And it didn't hurt that I'd met him in person the previous day. (Did "in person" apply to fairies?)

The plate armor was plastic and lightweight but nonetheless remarkably hot. It didn't breathe at all. The fake beard that came down to my chest was itchy; the blue face paint was thick and flaked easily, so I had to keep my facial muscles as still as possible to prevent it from coming off. The helmet, crafted from Styrofoam, was too small, but mercifully Misha was able to buff out the interior and enlarge it to fit me, which was good, since that was the element that most concealed my identity.

"You look awesome," Misha told me, and when I looked at myself in the mirror, I didn't feel as embarrassed as I expected. Instead, I felt a ripple of energy through the skin of my back, as though the tattoo I'd gotten were electrified and hypersensitized.

I felt a twinge of sadness that Liza could not see me. The last time I had spoken to my daughter, I denied her a hundred bucks to help build her own fairy costume. Yet here I was wearing a world-class one myself. And if I had indulged her hobby, even shared in it along with her, perhaps she would not have felt the need to run away from home. The guilt and shame of my own role in her disappearance bubbled to the surface. . . .

But there was no time to wallow in self-pity. The best I could do now was try to make things right.

Getting into the passenger seat of Misha's Honda Fit was challenging, but I appreciated how thorough the transformation was. I could hardly imagine anyone recognizing me unless they looked very closely and expected to see me.

We parked in a massive structure where we passed dozens of other convention-goers who were getting into costume at their cars—affixing wings, applying face paint, gluing on details. I glimpsed one woman with a full sewing machine set up on the blacktop.

Misha applied finishing touches to her own costume, which cast her as a fairy with a slightly gothic bent—dark wings, swirling red face paint, and an angular, corset-like bodysuit. "I'm Flutterseek," she informed me, and it was not lost on me that her choice was Liza's favorite.

As we made our way down the stairwell of the parking garage, I had my first inkling that we were not alone.

Obviously this was a crowded event, but the nagging feeling I had was about something more than that. Maybe it was just the sleeplessness of the last few days, but I felt like my intuition had come online more than it had in years; I was attuned to the world in a new way, and I sensed that we were being watched, even followed.

We walked down several flights of stairs, and the yellow industrial lighting cast our shadows starkly on the cement walls . . . but as we passed, I had the sense that our shadows were shifting unnaturally, lagging and moving out of sync with our bodies.

Even after all I'd seen, my instinct was to chalk up anything unexplainable to my own paranoia, or a trick of the eye. But if my experience the past week had taught me anything, it was that I couldn't disregard my perceptions, even when they were at odds with what I logically expected. ESPECIALLY then.

I quickened my pace down the stairwell, out into the bright sun of downtown L.A. The street was thronged with Fairy Tale superfans, converging on the massive dome of the Convention Center.

As we pushed through the crowd, I kept glancing at the ground, certain that our shadows were misbehaving. The ongoing sense was of some subtle *wrongness,* but it was never specific or concrete enough to draw Misha's attention.

We got into line under an awning, mercifully set up to shade people waiting to get inside. The moody score from the Fairy Tale films wafted out from the open doors, along with the blast of cold AC. There were no more shadows that we cast, so I relaxed, hoping to stop worrying about shadow creatures. There was a safety among this massive crowd; everything I'd seen told me I didn't need to fear attack out in the open, as the Green Man's power depended on maintaining a measure of secrecy. But he was becoming bolder . . . and a shiver went up my spine as I felt an alien presence behind me.

I turned. Directly behind us in line were two . . . not people, but human shapes. One whose silhouette was physically identical to my own, the other identical to Misha. But they were utterly featureless, as if they were made of infinite darkness. It was hard to believe they were there, taking up three-dimensional space. Every inch of their bodies was completely black, as though they were both clad in seamless head-to-toe fabric that absorbed any light. Two person-shaped holes in the universe. Both seemed unfazed by the crowd around them.

. I had now been to another realm and met several magical entities. But this was different. These were otherworldly creatures walking casually through our own. Standing in line like it was no big deal. My heart quickened with a mix of fear and excitement.

Misha was flipping through a pamphlet when I tapped her insistently on the shoulder. She turned around, saying, "Yeah, what do you want me to—" Then I felt her body stiffen as she saw them, and she stammered, trying to find words: "Oh, fuck me . . . those are . . . those're REAL . . ."

She couldn't say the word "Hollowbodies," but she didn't have to. I realized this was what I'd encountered in my motel room last week, when Mr. Echo/Sir Henry came to my rescue. This is what had tried to kill me.

For a second, I wondered if we were the only ones who could see them. But a teenage girl in line behind the strange creatures ran forward, shouting, "Oh my God, those are the literal BEST Hollowbody costumes I have ever seen. Seriously, amazing. How'd you even manage that?"

The two creatures of darkness did not reply or acknowledge her. She giggled, "I love the commitment, you guys are rad. Mind if I get a pic?" Without waiting for permission, the girl posed and took a selfie, standing in front of these supernatural entities.

I was numb, frozen by the sheer absurdity of the situation. Given that the creatures didn't have eyes, I could not even guess what they were thinking. Did they know this was the one place they could show themselves and no one would blink? Or was the Green Man simply past the point of caring about secrecy? And more important—were they going to kill me?

At least I could answer the last question. NO. If they had intended to attack us, they would have done so in the stairwell, where there would have been no witnesses. I realized they must have been sent by the Green Man to keep an eye on me.

But I couldn't have that. If the Green Man learned what I was attempting, the Hollowbodies would go from being observers to being . . . well, what they'd almost been in my motel room a few days earlier. Killers. That meant I had to get rid of them.

My attention was so fixated on the Hollowbodies, I wasn't paying attention to what was ahead—and as we stepped through the doors of the Convention Center, I realized I had a serious problem. The security checkpoint.

Misha had procured a pair of "STAFF" badges for us, which would help expedite our entrance, but we still had to clear the checkpoint— which included metal detectors, armed security guards, and a half dozen police officers overseeing the process. This all seemed rather intense for a gathering of fantasy fans, but perhaps the police presence had been stepped up in light of the fact that Annabelle was planning to be here, and her dangerous stalker was now a fugitive at large.

I tried to keep my blue-painted face turned toward the floor, knowing the helm provided some additional coverage. But the metal detector was still going to present a problem, since the Ruby Shard (back in its rusty-looking knife form) was in its sheath at my waist. It had gotten through at the cemetery film screening, but that may have simply been due to the laxness of their security, which was far from the case here.

Up ahead, I saw other cosplayers presenting weapons to the staff, who were examining them to make sure they were harmless. I saw a four-foot-long faux battle ax get approved, along with a longbow and its quiver of Styrofoam arrows.

Misha and I were almost to the security check. If I got out of line and ran off at this point, I'd arouse the suspicion of the cops on duty and would have to pass right by another one on the way out. If I hurried over to a trash can and tossed my knife, that would be an even bigger red flag.

My best bet was to try to pass through and play dumb. As we stepped up to the metal detector, I flashed my "STAFF" badge, put my keys in the bowl, and unclipped the sheath on my belt, handing the knife over to the security guard. I caught Misha staring in disbelief at the weapon.

I walked as casually as I could manage through the metal detector, which didn't beep. My body tensed as I turned toward the security guard, trying to play this off as low-key as possible, ready to give up my weapon and blame it all on a harmless mistake.

But to my surprise, as he examined the blade—which had been strong and sharp enough to slice through solid metal at the cemetery—it easily bent to the side as if it were made of rubber. The security guard wiggled it, took a close look, admiring the craftsmanship, then passed it right back to me with a smile.

My jaw dropped. I tested the blade out in my hand, wondering if it had somehow been replaced—and discovered that now that it was back in my possession, it appeared to be restored to its hard, sharp, deadly form. I hoped the security guard hadn't witnessed my disbelief as I hastily sheathed it once again.

Misha quickly grabbed my arm and pulled me away, hoping to escape the Hollowbodies, who were now stepping up to proceed through the checkpoint behind us. At a brisk pace, we disappeared into the crowd.

Inside the LACC, FairyCon surged with irrepressible enthusiasm. Various booths were set up throughout the convention floor. One served food that was mentioned in the books. Another sold foreign-language editions. There were cosplay traders, photo ops in a movie-set version of the Living Labyrinth, marketplaces for people trading pins and collectible cards and memorabilia and more.

All of this effort and energy and commitment to make-believe was

ridiculous. And yet, moving through this space with blue skin, I understood it in a new way. Cosplayers passing would salute me or brandish
their weapons menacingly, play-acting the parts of the characters they
represented. I was embarrassed at first but did my best to mirror their
attitudes, mostly to maintain my disguise. But in doing so, I did feel
some measure of my resistance slipping. . . .

I remembered all the times Liza had asked me to bring her to this
event. Flying out from Boston and staying at a hotel was prohibitively
expensive, and that had been reason enough to refuse. But I had to
admit, I probably would have indulged her if it had been traveling for a
sport, or some academic activity I deemed constructive. Anything other
than THIS.

But now, witnessing the joy on the faces of the participants, losing
themselves in their strange, shared love of this fantasy, I was filled with
sadness that I had been so resistant. I silently vowed that if I got her
back, Liza would attend every goddamn FairyCon she wanted for the
rest of her life.

It was also astonishing to find that, in this small world, Misha was
practically a celebrity. People kept coming up and greeting her warmly;
a few thanked her for what she had created. She tried to be warm and
kind with everyone, but I also saw that she was extricating herself from
every interaction—no doubt for my benefit.

We worked our way over toward the admin booth, where Misha said
she would talk to her friends among the staff to try to find out when
Annabelle would arrive and where she would be held before her event.

As we got there, I glanced behind and saw that the Hollowbody
creatures were still trailing us. Occasionally an excited fan would run
over and try to talk to them or get a picture, but most people gave them
a wide berth, staring from a safe distance—creeped out not only by
their costumes but by their joyless demeanor.

"You work on finding Annabelle," I told Misha. "I'll try to get rid of
them."

Misha nodded and I broke off, heading for an exit at the back of the
hall. The Hollowbodies followed, as I both hoped and feared.

I went through the doors and into a service corridor, where I intently marched past a few rooms set aside for festival admin and a food-prep station. Down a flight of stairs, losing myself in the labyrinth of the facility until I was confident that no one else was nearby.

I went through a service door into a long concrete corridor and locked the door behind me. This was the place where I would make my stand. I drew the knife that Sir Henry had given me, holding it at my side. Ready.

Moments later, the Hollowbodies caught up. I heard them bang against the door. It was locked, but they didn't miss a beat.

Seconds later, two shadows slid through the crack underneath. I felt a moment of awestruck horror, witnessing how easily they changed form, becoming two-dimensional manifestations of darkness gliding across the linoleum. But I quickly launched myself at them, sinking the knife into the floor, attempting to destroy them while they were in shadow form, flat on the ground.

They were too fast. The shadows flitted away in either direction, bolting across the floor. I frantically tried to follow one of them, chasing it toward the wall, and raised my weapon to stab it—but suddenly, its leg extended out of the concrete, taking solid form, and kicked me in the solar plexus.

The air exploded from my lungs. I wheezed and doubled over as pain shot through my body. My vision swam and I staggered backward, out of its range, reeling. . . .

A pair of hands grabbed me from behind, encircling my neck. The other Hollowbody had been flat on the ceiling, but now had partially emerged. Its arms descended from above and seized my throat, strangling me and pulling me up off my feet. I choked, gasping and wildly kicking.

The knife clattered to the floor as my hands instinctively went to the fingers tight around my neck, trying in vain to pull them free.

The world blurred. My throat burned. I clawed uselessly at my spectral attacker as I was choked in midair. Fight-or-flight instincts turned me into a writhing, helpless victim.

I needed a way to get free. My feet were close enough to the wall that I could swing them up, and I pressed them into the concrete—then pushed off with all my might, like a swimmer kicking off the wall, desperately trying to free myself.

I didn't—but I did manage to pull the Hollowbody back with me, dragging it out of the ceiling. I hit the tile at a bad angle, pain surging through my neck and back as I rolled to the ground, with the creature tangled up in a heap along with me.

Momentarily free, I gasped a single ragged inhale that burned all the way down into my lungs. The creature was recovering, and it rose to its feet, towering over me. . . .

I saw the knife on the floor, only a few feet away, and scrambled to get it. The Hollowbody stomped my hand reaching for the weapon, and lightning exploded up my arm as I heard the pop of at least one broken finger. But as the creature bent to pick up the knife, I surged forward with my other hand and grabbed it first.

I slashed wildly and the weapon pierced the thing's leg. The Hollowbody bellowed an inhuman screech of agony and fell forward to its knees. Before it could recover, I drove the blade straight into its chest— and the creature instantly burst apart, bits of shadow-remains flying in every direction. The shards of darkness lingered for a moment where they struck the floor and walls, then melted away in the light, dispelled like ordinary shadows.

One down. But where was the other?

The floor beneath me. The Hollowbody burst forth from below, grabbed my shirt, and pulled me down. My head hit the tile hard and the world spun. It wrapped me in a chokehold with one arm, suffocating me against the floor while its other arm grabbed my wrist that held the knife, smashing the weapon on the ground. I lost my grip on the knife, and the Hollowbody hand got hold of it.

I was pinned to the floor and I could feel the skin of its arm, cold and clammy and impossibly smooth, pressed against my neck . . . while its other hand flipped the knife around and attempted to stab it downward into my face.

I grabbed the creature's wrist, stopping the blade inches from my eye. It hovered there, wavering . . . but it was a battle of strength I couldn't win. I was losing oxygen quickly, and the Hollowbody had leverage. The weapon sank closer and closer toward my face. I turned aside, desperately trying to escape.

The arm that was choking me shifted, attempting to keep my head steady for the fatal blow, and I felt its cold not-flesh against my chin.

Desperately, savagely, I bit the fucking thing. My teeth sank into the strange bloodless nothingness of its body, and it roared in anger and pain.

The bite was enough to buy me a momentary advantage. I wriggled loose, twisted away, and at the same time released my grip on the creature's arm holding the weapon, which sank into the floor—and into its own shadow-body.

The creature's screech was a half second of agony and pure rage before it burst apart like the other, its arms melting away even as its shadow form dissolved across the floor.

I lay there for a moment, recovering my breath. As my adrenaline subsided, the pain of the encounter roared to the surface. The middle finger of my left hand was swollen and bent and useless. I spat repeatedly on the tile, trying to clear the taste of the creature's flesh.

But there was also a cold satisfaction in my gut. These creatures were what the Green Man had deemed sufficient to keep me in line. And now they were gone.

When I made it back up to the main floor of the convention, my wings had been torn away and my costume armor was spattered with dark shadow-blood. I didn't bother cleaning it; if anything, it added to the look.

Unfortunately, the centerpiece of my helmet had been broken, and my blue face-paint was smeared, so I was no longer as well concealed. I didn't realize it until I was striding across the convention floor, catching looks. I saw a woman pointing at me and whispering to her boyfriend. A man working a booth held up his phone, taking a photo.

I'd been spotted. Fuck. But there weren't yet police closing in . . . I had to do what I came for, and quickly.

I met back up with Misha, who had learned where Annabelle's green room would be prior to her appearance at "The Future of Fairy Tale" panel at 2:00. Luckily, Misha knew the ins and outs of the convention center well, and she kept me out of public view as we navigated the service tunnels behind the scenes. She knew exactly how to walk briskly and flash the staff badge with irritation to get past security guards quickly.

The security officers stationed outside Annabelle's green room were not so willing to simply wave us through, but Misha ripped into them: "Did Paula not get us cleared already? For fuck's sake, I'm the one interviewing Annabelle in front of two thousand people, and I'm gonna have ten minutes MAX to prep her. If you want to be the reason she gets sent out there with no prep, fine, call Paula and let her know that's on YOU."

A minute later, Misha and I were seated inside Annabelle's green room. Misha nibbled nervously at a cheese spread; I stood beside the door, taking deep breaths. Waiting.

When Annabelle finally entered, carrying a bag slung over one shoulder, she saw Misha first and greeted her with curiosity. As Annabelle came farther into the room, I closed the door behind her, and she turned to find me blocking the way out, resting my hand on the weapon at my belt. Annabelle seemed more amused than truly frightened.

TRANSCRIPT OF RECORDED CONVERSATION

BYRON: Sit, please. I just want to talk.

ANNABELLE: Well, you are certainly . . . *persistent*.

MISHA: We're really sorry about this whole thing. I would never do something like this. I'm, like, your biggest fan, and—

ANNABELLE: It's all right, dear. I know better than to be afraid of Byron here. If he was going to kill me, he would've done so a while ago.

BYRON: And if you wanted the police to come, you would've screamed for help already.

ANNABELLE: It's beneath my dignity to scream. And I'm curious about how you managed to escape from that jail cell.

BYRON: We're a little short on time here, so let's save that story for another day. I'm here because—

MISHA: Tell her, Byron. She needs to know.

BYRON: (*Sighs*) I crossed over.

ANNABELLE: . . . No.

BYRON: I did. I was . . . not even trying, exactly. It was like I had given up, and then . . . I was there. It worked.

ANNABELLE: And you saw . . . ?

BYRON: The Crystal Palace. The Living Labyrinth.

ANNABELLE: I don't care about all that. Did you—

BYRON: Yes, I saw him. I saw Gable.

ANNABELLE: (*Sobs*) And he's . . .

BYRON: He's alive. And so is Liza. So are dozens more. Maybe hundreds.

ANNABELLE: I am . . . glad they're alive. But I'm sure if it had been possible, you would have brought them back. So I hope you do not intend to stop me from trying to save my son.

BYRON: Is it in that bag? Book Six?

ANNABELLE: Yes. I put the finishing touches on the manuscript just this morning, and my editor will be here to receive it. I'm sure there will be tweaks before it goes to print, but once I publicly declare the book to be finished and turn it in, the spell should be complete. This whole event is happening so I can honor my end of the bargain.

BYRON: You can't do that.

ANNABELLE: We've been over this, Byron. I don't have a choice.

BYRON: I get that you need to complete the spell. But the version you wrote . . . you can't just leave him out of the story you've been building this whole time.

ANNABELLE: I'm sorry, your issue is with me cutting the Green Man from the narrative?

BYRON: The book needs to include him in order to *expose* him. Diminish him. Show the world the truth of who and what he is.

ANNABELLE: So you want me to . . . what, exactly? Write a different book? I don't have time for that, Byron. If I don't do this now, he's going to kill my son!

MISHA: We think there might be another way.

ANNABELLE: What are you talking about?

BYRON: I can bring back your son. And my daughter. I just need you to believe me. Believe *in* me.

(*Heavy knocking. Followed by the voice of a security officer.*)

OFFICER: Ms. Tobin?

MISHA: You can trust us, Ms. Tobin. I swear on everything that matters to me, this will work. At least, I think it could, if everything goes right.

(*Doorknob jiggling.*)

ANNABELLE: I don't understand.

BYRON: Please, there's no time. Liza needs me.

(*Keys turn. Sound of a door opening.*)

OFFICER: You! (*Into radio*) This is Walker, I've got him! Green Room for Hall C!

BYRON: Listen, I'm sure we can—

OFFICER: Sir, put your hands on your head. Now.

BYRON: Ah, fuck.

OFFICER: Do not move. Get down on the ground.

BYRON: Annabelle, sorry, but this is my cue. Misha will take it from here. Do everything she tells you.

MISHA: No, wait, Byron—what are you doing?

BYRON: I need to get back, or this won't work. You know what to do.

ANNABELLE: Officer, I'm sure he's—

OFFICER: Sir, get down, now!

INVESTIGATIVE JOURNAL OF BYRON KIDD

Until that week, I'd never had a gun drawn on me. But there I was, staring down a barrel for the second time in as many days.

Perhaps my arrest the previous night had dimmed my fear, especially since it had involved so many MORE guns. Or perhaps I had simply lost my mind—and with it any ability to think through consequences.

I raised my hands as if to surrender. That bought me the slightest opportunity. As the officer reached for his restraints and moved in, I charged at him full-tilt and hit him like a football player trying to break through the line. The officer was bigger than me, but I had the element of surprise in my favor and caught him off-guard.

We both sprawled to the ground, and it was a mad scramble to get up. He grabbed my leg and I kicked at him, caught him in the shoulder. It was enough to get free and take off down the slippery tile floor. He was up quickly and chasing me, but slowed down as he used his radio to notify law enforcement that I was on the run.

As I left the concrete tunnels of the backstage area and emerged into the main convention lobby, I stumbled over the threshold and fell down, panting and out of breath—and an entire crowd of Fairy Tale fans turned toward me in sync.

To my surprise, I was hit with a sudden wave of embarrassment. A heat in my cheeks, as though I had committed some faux pas at a party, and I wanted, irrationally, to apologize to everyone for the disruption I was creating. I had never been "that guy," the one people shook their heads about.

It wasn't so much that I feared what people might think of me. It was a sense of doubt creeping back in. I was so far out on a limb, it was hard to even believe my own memory of the past twenty-four hours. And it was harder still to put much stock in the plan I was pursuing—the one that would require Annabelle's total cooperation based on a two-minute interaction that had probably frightened her more than persuaded her.

And the doubt inside my mind was exacerbated by dozens of pairs of eyes suddenly fixated on me, obviously wondering: What the hell is that guy's problem?

But there wasn't time to contemplate, much less come up with any alternative. I steeled my resolve and committed myself completely. Even if I was going to jail or going to die, I would do so knowing I had given everything to the effort. All the uncomfortable feelings were shoved down, buried beneath the adrenaline rush of fear—numbing me and giving me the strength to push onward.

I got up quickly and rushed back out onto the convention floor, where the crowd offered a chance to disappear. But other security guards were already rushing toward the scene and caught sight of me. I wove between booths and people. Everyone was confused by the commotion, and a startled murmur rippled through the hall.

I tried to make it out the way I'd come in but more security forces were mustering there, blocking the exits. Panic reared its head, and with it a momentary desire to surrender, but I fought through it. Gotta keep moving.

I cut across the floor instead, and was getting out ahead of my pursuers—until a good citizen in goblin-shaman regalia saw a chance to be a hero and hit me with a linebacker-worthy body-block that knocked the wind out of me and sent me sprawling to the floor.

Officers closed in. I rolled into a pop-up Instagram photo-op that cheaply mimicked the Crystal Palace and tore through the back wall (a flimsy cellophane prop), making it out to the edge of the convention floor.

There: a fire exit. I hit the door full speed, charged into a stairwell, and thundered down a flight with footsteps echoing behind me and repeated shouts to stop. I was past the point of listening, past the point of contemplating any rational alternatives. A singular focus overtook my thoughts, and every decision was pure instinct now.

I barreled through another door, out into the blinding sun of downtown L.A. gleaming off the high-rises nearby. I raced down the street, no idea how I was ever going to lose so many of them tailing so close.

The question became moot when I saw the cops converging on me. Numerous cars with lights flashing were zooming down South Figueroa toward the Convention Center. I ran right out into the street in front of an entire parade of police. A fugitive served up on a silver platter.

Any rational assessment of the situation would conclude that I was finished. But I didn't even slow down. It felt like I was watching one of those impossibly long police chases, with swarms of cars and helicopters, where the idiotic perpetrator keeps going long past the point where his fate is inevitable. Except this time, the idiot was me.

Even so, I didn't stop. I ran in the one direction that was open, which took me directly across the street, through a pair of glass doors, into the lobby of a luxury-condo development.

I rushed past the faux-gold decor and oversized potted plants, past a very confused concierge, straight into the closing doors of an elevator, occupied by a professional-looking woman who was mid–cellphone call. She fell silent as I barely made it into her elevator. No doubt she clocked the flurry of police activity outside and regretted missing her chance to step off and escape.

The doors closed behind us. The woman was too startled to do anything but end her phone call and look away from me. The seventh-floor button was illuminated. I pressed another, for the penthouse, and up we went.

After several minutes of full-sprint fleeing, it was jarring to suddenly find myself perfectly still in the elevator, fighting to catch my beath. I could feel my pulse pounding in my neck and a layer of sweat cooling all over my body in the air-conditioning as soothing jazz played softly through a speaker overhead.

The walls of the elevator were mirrored, so I could see myself—and my fellow passenger—from six different angles. She looked appropri-ately freaked out, given that she was suddenly trapped in a six-by-six confined space with a man wearing the half-busted armor of a fairy knight, his face a wild smear of blue paint. I looked utterly insane. Which was only exacerbated by the fact that, upon seeing the woman's perfectly understandable terror, I could not help but laugh. An involun-tary release of the tension, but one that added to her impression of me as a maniac.

Ding! We hit the seventh floor, and she was through the doors, nearly tripping over herself to get away from me.

I was still half chuckling when the doors closed . . . and to my sur-prise, once I was alone, the release afforded by the laughter became a half-choked sob. Tears welled in my eyes. From where? I realized that my hands were shaking. Was I badly injured?

No. I realized, then, that I was terrified. Far more so than the woman beside me had been. More so than I had ever been in my life. I wasn't cut out for any of this. I had almost been killed in the hallway below the LACC. I had nearly been arrested, repeatedly—and if I went into cus-tody, this time I wasn't coming out. Now the police had seen me go in-side this high-rise; no doubt they were blocking all the entrances, surrounding the building completely. I wasn't getting out of here unless it was in cuffs or on a stretcher.

But those possibilities, terrible though they might be, were not what really scared me. More than anything, I was scared that I was WRONG. That all of this was every bit as delusional as it looked from the outside.

That I had gotten here by connecting red threads on a conspiracy-theory corkboard in my mind. That I was indulging an impossible fantasy, wanting so badly to believe I was on a path toward Liza that I was hallucinating a whole mad adventure in the hope it might lead to her salvation.

As I rode up toward the penthouse, I considered that, even if I wasn't wrong, the plan that I had made placed the life of my daughter (and countless others) in Misha's hands. And assumed that she would be able, in just a few minutes, to change Annabelle's mind and earn her cooperation, which was no small feat. What had I had been thinking?

The elevator ride afforded my rational mind a few moments back in the driver's seat—and it instantly rebelled against what I was intending to do, trying to present logical alternatives. Maybe I could find an apartment, break in, hide, wait for the police to give up their search . . . then slip off, run away, cross the border, live as a fugitive. . . .

Or perhaps I could surrender, fight to clear my name, try to explain the truth about Mr. Echo's death, convince Annabelle to drop the charges. . . .

Of course not. These options were not only implausible, they wouldn't get me back to Liza. There was no chance of going back to my old life. I had to finish what I'd started.

Ding! The penthouse floor presented a short hallway with keypad doors to two lavish condos, and, more important, an off-limits service door with roof access. I was through it, pulling down a service ladder, climbing up to a porthole, and soon made my way out onto the sunbaked asphalt of the rooftop.

I stepped up on the ledge at the edge of the roof, buffeted by the wind. Even without looking straight down, the electric shock of vertigo twinged through my abdomen. My chest tightened, my stomach dropped, and my phobia roared. My body sent primal signals to my brain: Stop this! Get down!

But there was no going back now.

Down below, witnesses spotted me and started to cry out in alarm.

Police officers scrambled to the base of the building. Panic churned my belly. To fight it, I looked outward rather than down.

The view was astonishing. I could see the city in a new light. This place I had hated with such fury since I arrived was garish and sprawling and filthy, self-satisfied and self-deluded, filled with self-importance and self-loathing in equal measure. . . . But it was beautiful too. It was not only traffic and money that coursed through its veins; it was DREAMS. Not only greed and gluttony animated its purpose; it was HOPE. If cities could tilt at windmills, this one would never stop.

Everything shifted. The pinpricks of cars below, glinting in the sun, were like living diamonds. The miasma of smog hanging over the skyline was a shimmering haze of fairy dust. A little squint rendered it all magical.

I felt the mark on my back begin to throb again in a familiar way. It was hot now, and it was almost as though I could direct my energy to it—and in response, I could feel it feeding my imagination in a symbiotic cycle.

In my mind's eye, I began to overlay the city of L.A. below with the incredible vista of the Hidden World I had beheld from the Crystal Palace. And I could believe, on some level, that they were one and the same, because for Liza they had been equally real, and I needed to be in the same world as her.

The rune opened up. The pain was purifying. Blood ran down my back. The transformation was starting. Only one way forward now.

I leaped.

CHAPTER TWENTY-SEVEN

TRANSCRIPT OF VIDEO

From FairyCon Panel: "The Future of Fairy Tale"
Recorded in Hall C of Los Angeles Convention Center
Posted to YouTube by user WingsandCrowns

(*Crowd milling around. Background chatter. Then, lights shift. Applause. A young woman with blue hair steps out onstage.*)

MISHA: Hello, Fairy Fans! Hi. I know I'm not your regularly scheduled moderator, but there's been a little change of plans today. I'm Misha Pimm, a UCLA doctoral scholar in narrative studies. But you might know me better as the founder of TheQueendom.com.

(*Cheering.*)

MISHA: Oh, thank you. Wow. Got a couple users in the house. Sorry, I'm not usually the type of person who says "in the house." I'm just a little nervous. It's been a few years since I've been onstage at FairyCon, and I wasn't expecting to be today, but . . . there's been a little change, so, here I am.

Thank you all for being here. I understand there was, uh, an incident a few minutes ago, and some portions of the convention are being . . . postponed, maybe. But I appreciate you coming, and we'll make sure to keep you all safe. All right?

This is a super-huge honor for me. Because today . . . I got to meet my hero. Only, she's . . . not everything I thought she was. And that's OK.

See, when I was younger, I fought against growing up, tooth and nail. I didn't want to be anything like the adults I knew. But that's because I thought being a grown-up would mean closing my heart. I didn't realize that growing up would actually tear it wide open. And it turns out, that's a good thing. Because you can't accomplish anything that matters until you do.

Of course, you're not here to hear about me. You're here to hear about the future of the Fairy Tale series. Straight from the horse's mouth. Not that she's a horse. Maybe a workhorse, the way she's labored over . . . I'm babbling, sorry. I know that all of us have been wondering and dreaming and speculating about the conclusion of the series. But I can promise you, what's coming . . . is not what you expected.

There's only one person who can shed light on what it will be. So without further ado, I'm delighted to present to you . . . appearing at FairyCon for the first time in six years . . . Annabelle. Fucking. Tobin!

(*Wild applause. Annabelle comes out onstage, waving to the crowd.*)

THE BATTLE FOR THE HIDDEN WORLD

What did people down on the ground see?

Many claim that they saw a crazed man up on the ledge of the building's roof. Some would even say they saw him jump. But on second thought, maybe they weren't so sure. One or two claim to have seen him in the air . . . but not dropping. No, it didn't quite make sense.

No one saw him "disappear" per se . . . it's just that they lost track. They looked away in horror. Only, there was no landing. No grisly mess on the sidewalk. Only confusion.

Then there was a manhunt, of course. Cordoning off the condo building. Barricading the Convention Center. The search went on for hours before the police gave up. The fugitive was gone.

Meanwhile, on the other side of the divide, it was a different story entirely.

No one in the Hidden World was looking up at the sky near the Navel of the World, so no one observed a man erupting into reality three hundred feet up in the air. No one caught sight of a pair of wings sprouting rapidly from his back, and even if someone had, in a land of winged creatures, it would've hardly been a remarkable sight. At most, it might have been mildly amusing for more experienced flyers to witness the mortal man's confused efforts to gain control of the newfound limbs that had erupted from his body.

He hurtled downward, spinning and rolling, out of control. The ground rose to meet him, but just before he was dashed upon the stone, he flexed a muscle he never knew he had and extended his wings, and they caught a mighty updraft, and he pulled up—taking flight.

TRANSCRIPT OF VIDEO

From Panel: "The Future of Fairy Tale"

ANNABELLE: Thank you, Misha. Hi, everyone. I am indeed "Annabelle Effing Tobin."

MISHA: Sorry about the F-bomb, family viewers! I swear when I get nervous.

ANNABELLE: And I *sweat* when I'm nervous, so if I look a little shiny up here . . . it's been a while since I appeared in public.

VOICE: We love you, Annabelle!

ANNABELLE: Oh, I love you too. All of you. God, I've missed this.

MISHA: When you signed up to be a reclusive genius, I bet nobody warned you how lonely it would be.

ANNABELLE: I suppose that's true.

MISHA: Do you think that's why you've struggled with the final book?

ANNABELLE: That was part of it. As many of you are aware, it's taken me quite some time to figure out how to end Fairy Tale. I wrote an entire draft, which I buried forever. I stared at blank pages for months on end. I agonized over whether to write the book at all. It felt as if the world depended on it, which may not have been *entirely* delusional. But eventually . . . I found my groove again.

(*Cheering.*)

ANNABELLE: In fact, I am writing Book Six even now, as I speak. In ways that you will all understand when you read it.

It has taken me considerable time to write this book, because . . . well, it's not easy, to tell the truth. When I started the series, I didn't worry about that. Words poured out of me, thousands of words a day. Hundreds of pages every year with spare hours to engage with fans and consult on scripts and write a daily blog. But over time, the words stopped coming. The Wishing Well dried up, and with it . . . my heart.

MISHA: And why do you think that happened?

ANNABELLE: Because I was scared. You see, my books are fantastical, but nonetheless, they are powerful. They're not only stories *about* magic; they *are* magic.

VOICE: Hell yeah they are!

(*More cheers.*)

MISHA: I think that's a fascinating idea, and one I'd like to dig into. And I suspect you don't only mean *your* books are magic. All stories are, right? I mean, what is magic if not a way to transform the world through the power of our thoughts? What are books if not spells? What are stories if not the most powerful and mysterious force known to man?

ANNABELLE: Exactly right. Stories send us to war and heal our pain. The story of money, the story of one nation or another, the story of your god and their god and my god—all fighting it out in the minds of people around the world. Everyone silently voting with their faith, putting marbles in the jars of the stories that resonate with them most strongly. And the stories that get the most votes take on the most power, and the world bends around them.

As storytellers, we are tempted to tell any story that works. That commands money, attention, followers, likes, whatever. As *humans,* we are desperate to be seen. But if we're not careful, we can warp the world in ways we might not like. Which means we ought to be more mindful about which stories we tell.

THE BATTLE FOR THE HIDDEN WORLD

The man flew. And in that moment, perhaps it was not right to call him a man any longer. He was a mortal, certainly, but unlike any other in history, for he was no longer bound to the earth. Yet he would never be one of the fey. He was something new, and as a result, his old name hardly suited him any longer. What to call him, then?

Whatever he was, he was still a father. So let us call him that.

The father flew, arcing high over the landscape of the Hidden World, riding the clouds and defying the winds. He zoomed and wheeled and soared, testing his new ability. Exhilaration swelled within him so intensely that he nearly forgot to breathe.

As the father beheld the landscape below, his jaw dropped in wonder. The full glory of the Hidden World unfolded, so varied and colorful he could scarcely take it all in at once. The Crystal Palace gleamed. The Living Labyrinth shifted and rippled, a thousand shades of green at once, undulating in the light. Far to the west, the Sea of Nothing was an abyss stretching to the horizon, midnight blue at the edge of black. The sky burned reddish orange, dotted with clouds of shining silver. It was glorious.

The doubt that had burdened the father was now a world away. His heart beat faster, but the terror that had quickened it shifted toward a fragile feeling that, for a moment, he couldn't quite name. Then it came to him. It was *joy*. He had simply forgotten what it felt like.

But there was no time to enjoy himself. He had returned for a purpose, and that purpose was calling him. His attention shifted toward the ground, where a single structure glowed so brightly in the sun, it seemed to be in a spotlight.

The Navel of the World was an outdoor amphitheater, a massive open-air arena. Hundreds of rows of benches were filled by an enormous audience, for *all* the denizens of the Hidden World had been assembled. The fairy folk sat obediently in stony silence in the upper decks. Below them, hundreds of strange creatures filled the stands—horned minotaurs, incorporeal spirits, armored trolls, elves and gnomes and sprites and more.

The arena at the center was a round hill covered in spongy, greenish-blue lichen, which grew in ornate patterns, forming runic characters in a language more ancient than speech. At the center of it all, at the top of the hill, grew a single tree. The Navel Tree.

The father swooped downward, and as he approached the arena, more detail came into focus. In the branches of the tree were countless small figures, each seated in a nest of sorts, a pocket of leaves and sticks that cradled them. The children from the other world. Their eyes were open but drooping, faces slack—drained of their life force, seemingly indifferent to their fate.

The father's emotions roiled—a mixture of hope and horror in equal measure as he scanned the young faces, desperately seeking his daughter. But before he could discover her among the crowd, his attention shifted to the base of the tree, and his heart hardened with cold fury. For seated there, taking on his recognizable human form for the first time in ages, sat the one known as the Green Man.

TRANSCRIPT

From Panel: "The Future of Fairy Tale"

MISHA: Before we get to the final book, I wonder if you could talk to us about the writing process a bit, since it has been a considerably protracted one. You mentioned false starts. Was it a case of writer's block?

ANNABELLE: Oh, I don't believe in writer's block. It was not a lack of ideas. It was a paralyzing fear of my ideas and their consequences. And if it were not for you, Misha, I would have produced a very different final book. You see, everyone, the reason I wanted Misha to do the panel with me is that she unlocked something. How to release a final volume I could stand behind. I was extremely resistant to the idea at first, but I could see that Misha's love for Fairy Tale was nearly equal to my own, and . . . I was convinced. So Misha, why don't *you* explain what you proposed.

MISHA: Sure, I mean, I can't take much credit, but my suggestion was that maybe what you needed was . . . a co-author.

(*Murmurs of shock.*)

ANNABELLE: Yes, you all heard right. For this final book, I was unable to finish alone. I used to always view writing as a solitary endeavor. But stories were never meant to be individual. And collaboration was thrust upon me by necessity. By the need to tell the truth. So, to my great chagrin, I found myself working with, of all people . . . a journalist.

THE BATTLE FOR THE HIDDEN WORLD

The father glided down into the Navel and made his first stumbling landing on the hill inside the arena, coming face-to-face for the first time with the ancient god who ruled the Hidden World.

The Green Man's skin was weathered and tan, and he was completely bald. His eyes and robe matched the color of his name, and so did his beard—a thick, verdant tangle of curls, which was the one feature that distinguished his appearance now from the way he had looked as a mortal man. His age was impossible to guess, as his appearance seemed to vacillate; from one angle, you might have guessed he was a young man yet surprisingly wise for his years, but another look might have you believe he was ancient yet remarkably strong.

As the father approached, the Green Man sang an ancient song with a resonant voice that carried on the wind, so it was heard by all in attendance: "*Come hear me and heed me, come feed me your love. Your fate is my burden, your faith is my blood . . .*"

The father cast his eyes around the immense amphitheater. Never before had he stood before such a crowd and felt so many stares upon him at once. His gaze drifted down from the fairy folk up top, past the throngs of strange creatures . . . up into the branches of the tree, taking in the captive children there. Searching the faces until, at last, he saw her.

His daughter. The girl he had sought for so long. Still unharmed, but looking so forlorn and drained, she appeared to be asleep even with her eyes wide open. The father's heart leaped, and it took every bit of his strength not to fly to her, to seize her and spirit her away. But he knew that such a rescue attempt would be doomed to failure. And he had a plan that needed to be seen through.

"Quite a crowd," the father said.

The Green Man grinned. "I have ordered them all here to witness the moment of my triumph. But I fear they may also witness the agony of your daughter, since you have returned without completing your quest."

"I did what I set out to do," said the father. "Annabelle is in possession of a completed final book, which includes *you* as part of the ending. And some time yet remains to solidify our agreement."

"The spell is not complete until she declares it," said the Green Man. "As soon as she does, the portal will open. Your daughter may go home then . . . but your world will be mine."

"Not if you're dead before then," said the father.

The Green Man's expression darkened—and subtly, so did the shade of his eyes, his robe, and his beard all at once. "Are you threatening me?" He rose from his seat and walked slowly down the hill. "I have patiently waited through eons. Watched my power ebb and flow with the rise and fall of cultures in your world. I've pulled strings from afar, whispered in the ears of a thousand poets, and always watched as others took credit for my power. But now, finally, I will be *known,* and rightly glorified, and I will live forever."

The father smirked. "The book that Annabelle is completing the spell with—it's not the one you had in mind." The Green Man's expression twisted, uncertain what the father meant. "I upheld my end of the bargain. You are in the book—in fact, you're making an appearance *right now.* But you're not going to be glorified. You'll be exposed as the pathetic, narcissistic piece of shit you are."

"Do not test my temper. I had intended to keep you alive to watch your child suffer if you failed. But now I grow weary of your insolence."

Witnessing the ancient god's arrogance, the father felt a burning rage, a desperate desire to bring low this creature who had so
callously hurt so many children. He drew himself up and summoned his strength, searching for an eloquent reply. But he came
up short, and settled upon: "Yeah, well . . . fuck you."

TRANSCRIPT

From Panel: "The Future of Fairy Tale"

MISHA: I know it would be hard to explain the nature of the book
that you and the journalist have been creating together. But I understand that you brought it with you. That old notebook you're carrying
around . . .

ANNABELLE: Indeed. Right now, this notebook is the only copy of
the book that exists. And it is still evolving, because our words, even
as we speak them, are part of the book. You all are part of it too.

MISHA: So it is a departure from the style of your previous Fairy Tale
books, I take it. And from the epic story that so many of us got invested in.

ANNABELLE: Yes. But it is, to my mind, the only suitable way to
bring the series to a close. I will not be concluding Ciara's story in a
conventional narrative sense, and I am sorry about that . . . but I trust
that a small army of fan-fic writers on your website will offer their
versions of the tale, which will be every bit as imaginative as what I
might have come up with.

MISHA: Hear that, lawyers? Explicit authorial approval. So quit
cease-and-desisting me. Sorry, just had to get that in. Now, I believe
you have a real treat for us today. A reading from the new book.

ANNABELLE: That's right. I know my promise that the book is done
might reasonably be met with skepticism, after so many delays. But it's

important that people here believe in this book. You all will be the first to hear it.

(*Cheering.*)

THE BATTLE FOR THE HIDDEN WORLD

The Green Man was incensed and called upon the fullness of his magic to destroy the father. Vines sprang forth from the ground, wrapping around his waist, attempting to drag him down and bury him. But the father drew the Ruby Shard and slashed the vines away as quickly as they grew.

The Green Man bellowed in rage, calling forth an army larger than any that the Hidden World had ever seen—for every living thing in that amphitheater cast a shadow, and every shadow separated from its owner.

Thousands of Hollowbodies slithered along the ground, down toward the Green Man below, converging upon the father they were sent to kill. The father saw the waves of slinking darkness descending from every direction and looked at the weapon in his hand; enchanted or not, it was useless against an entire army. He beat his great wings, fleeing into the sky.

Once the Hollowbodies reached the arena, they erupted into shape, taking form in the image of the shadow-casters from which they were birthed. Those that were made from the shadows of the fey sprouted great black wings. At a gesture of command from the Green Man, the winged Hollowbodies surged into the sky.

The father thus looked down and found an entire army of death-bringers hurtling up toward him. He banked and rolled through the air, pursued relentlessly by those blacker-than-night monstrosities. He sought to hide among the low-hanging clouds, but a Hollowbody caught his ankle and tugged him downward; another grabbed him and wrapped its hands about his throat.

The father's resolve gave way to panic as the creatures enveloped him, intent on tearing him limb from limb in midair. The creatures here were even stronger than those he had battled in the mortal realm. Their power overwhelmed him; he felt foolish for thinking he could defeat them here.

But suddenly, another wave of bodies surged upward. Another flying army. The fey. Led by Queen Áine, they defied the long-standing orders of the Green Man and took flight, forever breaking the truce they had sworn to him as they came to the aid of the father.

The great soldier Gloverbeck soared in, shield and spear outstretched before him, striking at the horrors. The dark creatures turned upon their new adversary; one was instantly met by a hurled spearpoint and atomized into nothingness. The next was obliterated by a fierce backhand from the shield. A third was pierced by the Ruby Shard as the father, freed from their grip, sprang into action.

Liberated from the Hollowbodies and afforded a moment of respite, the father hovered in the sky. But before he could give thanks to his savior, Gloverbeck was already continuing on and seeking out new foes. The father marveled at the fearlessness of the fairy knight. He felt a sense of noble responsibility, knowing that was how his daughter saw him; it was a lot to live up to, but he would do his best.

The father beat his wings, hovering in place and marveling at the immense skybound conflict raging on all sides. In that eye of the storm, Queen Áine flew to him, her pearl armor glowing with power. "I hope you are not as foolish as you look, mortal, for I have committed my forces to your aid unreservedly."

He was stunned by her support. "You broke your truce with the Green Man. Won't he destroy your entire kingdom now?"

"Not if he dies," she said, and flitted off, sword high, battle-cry erupting from her throat.

TRANSCRIPT

From Panel: The "Future of Fairy Tale"

ANNABELLE: I'm doing this reading to get it out into the world. To commit publicly to the fact that this is the story I want to tell. (*Clears throat.*) So. A reading from Fairy Tale Book Six: *The Hidden World.* By Annabelle Tobin and Byron James Kidd.

(*Pages turning. Deep breath.*)
    Dedication: For Gable. And Liza.

(*Page turns.*)
    Chapter One. Dear Mom and Dad. If you're reading this, I've already left. I'm going to the end of the world and beyond. I won't say anything more, because you won't believe me and I already know what you'll say. Dad, you'll say that I should live more in reality, and Mom, you'll say that I should take deep breaths and not make hasty decisions, but I have no choice. I have to go.
    Maybe this comes as a surprise to you because you think that on the surface I seem fine. But surfaces can be deceiving. I feel like I am meant for something more. I'm sorry because I know this will be scary, but I don't belong here. I promise I'll try to come back in the future. Maybe then I can make it better for all of us. Sincerely, Liza.
    This note was found on the morning of March 20, tucked between pages 11 and 12 of a well-worn copy of Fairy Tale Book One: *The Wishing Well.*

THE BATTLE FOR THE HIDDEN WORLD

The troops of the fey locked in combat with their own faceless doppelgängers, and the sky above the Navel of the World darkened with the ferocity of a great seething mortal struggle, punctuated by bodies tumbling from the sky.

Down below, a mighty roar echoed through the amphitheater as a large creature, inspired by the rebellious flight of the fey, lowered its head and came charging down from the stands, its fearsome tentacles waving and its leonine jaws wide.

The Doggerdoth attacked. He tore through his enemies with teeth and claws, a tornado-path of destruction, unstoppable even as the Hollowbodies piled on from all sides.

Emboldened by his assault, the other denizens of the Hidden World joined the fray. Descending from the stands into the arena, they crashed down upon the dark army that surrounded the Green Man.

The ancient god was forced to retreat, climbing up into the branches of the Navel Tree alongside the children. He raised his arms and the tree began to grow, sprouting to an impossible height and conveying him safely out of the melee below. The tree's trunk expanded and its roots quaked the ground.

The father saw the Green Man standing upon a limb of the tree. His eyes hardened with fierce purpose. The father plunged downward from the sky, hurtling into the arena on a kamikaze path. He outstretched his weapon before him, seeking to impale the Green Man against the trunk.

But at the last second, the Green Man vanished, and the Ruby Shard was buried to the hilt in the tree trunk. The father tried to withdraw his weapon, but the tree sealed shut around it, refusing to budge. The legendary blade was trapped.

The Green Man laughed. He was now perched on a branch high above the father, peering down mockingly. "It is impossible for you to defeat me here," he said. "My power over this world is complete."

With that, the Green Man flicked his wrist, and a branch of the tree swung forth like a great battering ram and knocked the father from his perch. He tumbled through the air and his wings spread wide, barely in time to catch the wind.

As the father circled around the tree, he began to wonder if the Green Man might be right. This was a world of stories and dreams, and the Green Man had spent centuries honing his power here, while the father was an interloper, attempting to turn everything on its head. His courage stalled, and his certainty faltered.

But as he flew, he caught sight of a familiar face among the children watching him. Her eyes were still glassy with the Green Man's hypnotic spell, her will not her own. Even so, a recognition passed between her and her father, a silent familial tribute, and something stirred within the girl.

Her father saw it, whatever it was, and knew that she was alive. Below the cold surface of the enchantment, his daughter was still very much herself, and still very much in need of him. Nothing could have steeled his resolve more fiercely.

The father flew toward the Green Man once again, his tone defiant. "I don't need to defeat you in this world. Only in the minds and hearts of those who believe in you."

"At that, you will fail too," the Green Man roared. "For they are gathered here to witness your weakness, and my strength."

The Green Man flicked his wrist again and the tree's branches swung from above and below. The father ducked and dodged the massive blows with a tumbling series of aerobatic maneuvers. As he did, he saw his daughter flinching at the attacks, yet clenching her fist in silent support. His heart quickened with the knowledge that she was with him, pumping bravery through his veins. He alighted on a branch and shouted to the Green Man: "They do not believe in power! They believe in *stories*."

A swooping vine knocked the father from his perch, but he caught himself on another branch and swung back up to standing, his eyes meeting the Green Man's gaze. "They came here seduced by *your* story. But I will give them a better one."

The branch below the father suddenly split into two, and he dropped straight down. Instantly the two branches whipped back together, catching the father and gripping him tightly about the middle like a crab's pincer, pinning his wings. His arms were free but ineffectual; he pushed and pried at the tree uselessly.

The Green Man grinned as the magically animated branch held the father suspended in the air before him. "And what story is that? Yours is the tale of a fool's errand. A man who gave everything, even his life, with no hope of success."

The tree squeezed the father so tightly he could scarcely breathe, but he fought through the pain and choked out a single word: "Exactly."

"You think yourself a hero?" sneered the Green Man.

The father shook his head. His ribs were cracking, and he felt near to passing out from the tree's suffocating grip. His lungs could no longer open enough to even utter a response.

In search of strength, he turned his gaze up toward his daughter's face. She was still frozen by the Green Man's magic, but her eyes were fiery with recognition. She looked at him directly, in a way she had not looked at him in ages. In a way that the father had wanted, had *ached*, to be seen by her for a very long time. She looked on him as the one person in the world who could protect her, and as a result he became that very thing, for her look stoked the fading ember of her father's heart and gave him the strength to pull a single painful breath into his chest. With it, he answered the ancient god: "Not a hero. Just a dad."

When the girl heard those words, it unlocked something in her soul, and a tear slid down her cheek. But the response enraged the Green Man. He bellowed incoherently and thrust his hand forward. Another branch swung down from above, its tip sharpened into a deadly spearpoint, and pierced the father through the chest with all the primal power of the entire Hidden World.

The father slumped in the tree's tight grip and his body went limp as the Green Man delivered the fatal blow.

All the children in the tree beheld his defeat. The Green Man exulted, turning his attention then to the warring creatures all around, prepared to lead his troops into decisive victory.

But there was a curious shift of the wind, and the tide of both battles turned. Down below, Hollowbodies were gored and trampled, melting away into nothingness on the ground. Up above, the fey soldiers felled one shadow creature after another, and their dark shapes rained down.

In the tree, one by one, the children began to stir. Waking as if from a dream. A new awareness and sense of purpose dawned within them. Some crept from their nests, peering down angrily at the Green Man.

He could sense the change, and for the first time, fear entered his eyes. He bellowed with savage anger: "What is wrong with you? Have you not seen how easily I killed him? Any who defy me will suffer the same fate!"

Children hopped down from above. Others climbed up from below. All converged upon the branch of the Green Man. He backed away toward the tree trunk in terror . . . then, in shock, he froze, and looked down upon his belly, where he discovered that a ruby-red blade, dripping crimson, had been thrust clean through him. As his life force emptied, he had enough time to turn and discover who had run him through.

It was the daughter. Still stirring from a half year's magical slumber, still reeling from the horror of her father's death just moments before—she had nonetheless been strengthened by his courage. She had plucked his weapon from the tree and driven it into his foe.

The Green Man's body instantly began to wither, drying up into a barren husk. The deathblow was not merely the one that pierced his abdomen. The fear he had fed on for so long had been overcome, and his powers were gone.

He toppled from the branch but never even hit the ground, for he was blown away like dust in the breeze.

TRANSCRIPT

From Panel: "The Future of Fairy Tale"

ANNABELLE: (*Reading*) "I'll tell you who I am. I'm the guy who can't sleep, wondering what I did wrong. Wondering how I could have possibly prevented this. Wondering if I made a mistake by teaching her to *read*, or giving her those stupid, dangerous books.

"But I'm also the guy who's gonna find her. Because it's crystal clear that you're not gonna do it. Whoever or whatever took her away, I'm gonna find the truth. If I have to go to the end of the fucking world . . . I'm gonna bring her home."

So—that's Chapter One.

(*Annabelle closes the notebook and sets it aside. Applause.*)

MISHA: Wow. Obviously quite a departure from what we all expected, but *very* intriguing. For the rest of the story, we'll have to read the book when it comes out. Which brings me to my last question: *When?* When will Fairy Tale finally be finished?

ANNABELLE: Well, actually, I believe my editor is here. Stand up, Stanley . . .

(*Applause.*)

ANNABELLE: Stanley, I hope you can join me today in committing, for the sake of the fans, to a spring release. Because I'm thrilled to let you all be the very first ones to know . . . the story is now complete. The last Fairy Tale book is finished. And with it, the entire series.

(*Wild applause.*)

THE BATTLE FOR THE HIDDEN WORLD

At that moment, in another world, the Sixfold Summoning was completed—and the Hidden World rippled with a mighty disturbance. The Navel Tree rattled, and the ground below it quaked and split open with giant fissures erupting through the spongy, blue-green ground. Denizens of the Hidden World scrambled free of the arena, many narrowly escaping as chasms broke open. Fairy folk swooped down and rescued stragglers from being pulled into the widening abyss.

But the children in the tree could see the opening for what it was: a portal to another world. The one from which they had come. The gleaming light shining from deep within the ground was the sun of the world they had left behind, a world they all yearned to return to. One by one, they leaped from the branches of the Navel Tree, plummeted through the air, and disappeared into the glowing light below.

Only one girl made no motion to leave. She strode down the wide branch where she had slain the Green Man and approached her father.

As she neared, he stirred, his eyes flitting with dim awareness. He coughed, spitting flecks of blood as he spoke. "Liza . . ."

"Dad . . . ," she said, her voice cracking. "You came for me."

"Always," he replied, feebly reaching for her.

She squeezed his hand, then stepped back, examining the manner in which he was trapped by the tree. A large branch still squeezed tight around his midsection, and a smaller one had pierced his chest. "I can cut you free," the daughter said.

The father shook his head. Blood still poured from his wound, but keeping the branch in place slowed it enough to buy him some time. Not as much time as he would've liked, but it would have to do. "Just let me rest a minute," he said.

Children continued to leap from the tree. The entire Hidden World rumbled.

But for the father and daughter, there was nothing except the air between the two of them. It was like time stopped as she knelt before him. Tears of worry sprang from her eyes, and her lower lip trembled in fear as she struggled to find words.

The father did his best to compose himself, fighting to hide the pain. He looked at her with a twinkle in his eye. "So . . . you like my outfit?"

She laughed and cried at the same time, and fought to match his playful tone. "You look good with wings." Her eyes opened wide with the realization of where he had gotten the idea. "You found my drawings?"

He nodded weakly. "Sorry for going through your things, but . . . I couldn't *find* you, until I *knew* you." He looked away, pained by the reflection. "You'd been turning into your own person for a long time, and I couldn't bear to watch it. So at some point, I lost you. And . . . I'm sorry."

She nodded. "I think maybe . . . I was afraid of you seeing me. Because I knew . . . I wasn't how you wanted me to be."

He squeezed her hand, pulling her even closer. "You are always *exactly* how I want you to be, because you're you." She looked down, embarrassed by his intensity, but he touched her cheek and looked in her eyes. "I love you, Liza . . . and I am so, so proud of you."

She hugged him tightly then, and her tears streamed down onto his shoulder. He winced at the pain but hid it from her well. "I'm sorry I ran away," she sobbed. "I'll never do that again, I promise."

"I know . . ." He took a short breath, groaning slightly at the pull in his ribs. "But the only thing you have to promise me . . . is that you'll go back to writing stories."

She sniffled. "Promise."

The tree shuddered. Down below, the crevasses that had split open the ground reversed course and began to close.

Time was running out. The father felt stung by the absurd injustice of it all. To come so far, to fight and suffer through so much . . . just to get to this point and have only a minute or two with her . . .

But he hadn't come for himself. It was for her. And she would have all the time in the world.

He sighed heavily, his victory bittersweet, and tried to look as peaceful and certain as he could manage with the life draining out of him. He knew that he still had to face one last great challenge: convincing her to leave him behind.

"It's time to go home, sweetheart."

She shook her head. "I can't leave you! Not after . . ." She trailed off, unable to even imagine all that had brought him here.

"This is where I belong now." He squeezed her hand and looked into her eyes. "And I will always be with you."

She looked at the cracks in the ground of the arena, closing up rapidly. "I can't . . ."

"You can," the father insisted. "You can do anything. And I need you to do this, for me." The girl nodded, squeezed her father's hand one last time, and with great difficulty, released him. "Now, *go*," he said, and with the last ounce of strength he had, he smiled at her, a smile that beamed out more love than she could even comprehend.

She smiled back, and it was everything he had dreamed it would be.

Then the girl jumped off the branch, tumbled through the air, and vanished into another world.

CHAPTER TWENTY-EIGHT

NEWS ARTICLE

"MISSING GIRL RECOVERED DURING FAIRYCON"
Published in the *L.A. Times,* November 3

12-year-old Liza Kidd, who was reported missing earlier this year, was found yesterday during a large gathering at the downtown Los Angeles Convention Center. She appeared to be wandering, confused and disoriented, through the crowd at "FairyCon," an annual event celebrating the popular Fairy Tale book series.

Misha Pimm, a culture writer in attendance, spotted the girl and brought her to a security desk. "I must've remembered her face from a poster or something, and I could tell she needed help," Misha explained. "I'm just glad I could be a friendly face and get her home."

The circumstances of Liza Kidd's return remain mysterious. Only an hour earlier, her father, Byron, had been pursued by police as a wanted fugitive. As of this writing, Byron Kidd remains at large, and the connection between his escape and his daughter's reappearance remains unclear.

LAPD officers on the scene notified Liza's mother, Valerie, who promptly arranged travel from Boston to reunite with her daughter. In a tearful interview by phone, Valerie Kidd told reporters, "I don't care how it happened, all that matters is that she's back."

Perhaps strangest of all, Liza Kidd's reappearance does not seem to be an isolated incident. In Mexico City, Veena Cruz, 11, was reported missing nearly three years ago. Yesterday, she approached a clerk at a shopping mall, visibly distressed. Local police arrived and confirmed her identity, and she was reunited with her parents within hours.

Multiple similar "reappearances" have been documented around the world, with children simply wandering home after prolonged absences. Smitta Agarwal, 15, walked into her London flat, shocking her parents, who were preparing dinner for her siblings. Yet according to her mother, "Smitta acted like it was no big deal at all."

Meanwhile in Nigeria, 13-year-old Chibundi Musa flagged down a healthcare worker on the road outside the village of Bende, saying he was trying to get home. Musa was over 200 miles from his family's residence on the outskirts of Abuja, and unable to explain how he had gotten there—or what had transpired in the two years he had been gone.

Teenager Miriam Yorin, 19, vanished from outside her Florida high school five years ago when she was 14 years old. She had not been seen or heard from since, and her parents had maintained a missing-persons search. But yesterday she was found wandering the halls of the school, where a former teacher recognized her. Yorin agreed to an interview but was not forthcoming about her whereabouts. "I ran away," she said. "And then I wanted to get back, and eventually, I guess, I found my way."

More stories are emerging from around the globe, all united by a strange commonality: the missing children are fans of the popular Fairy Tale series of books and films. These reappearances give credence to various theories that have circulated for years, but the exact nature of the connection remains mysterious. Officer Bethany Marks of the LAPD said, "We are investigating the possibilities of kidnapping or trafficking here, but at this point, we do not have any suspects or actionable evidence. We will continue to pursue all leads."

The FairyCon event where Liza Kidd returned was also attended by author Annabelle Tobin, who has rarely appeared in public over the past few years. Sitting with her son, Gable, Annabelle wept openly at news of the recovered children. "I'm just so glad it's all over. I can only imagine the hell those parents were going through."

Police have set up a tip line and website for the investigation. Parents of missing children may reach out directly, and anyone with pertinent information is encouraged to come forward immediately.

EMAIL

From: sg@rotterdampress.com
To: a.q.tobin@gmail.com

Annabelle,

I have never awaited a manuscript with nearly as much anticipation as that with which I viewed the arrival of your sixth and final installment in the Fairy Tale series. And I have never been so flummoxed by anything as I was by this strange document. I almost feel like I flew across the country for a practical joke. But the announcement was made in such an aggressively public manner that your sincerity appears undeniable.

All of which leaves me with many questions, but the one that most prominently bubbles to my mind is also the most direct: What are you thinking?

First off—you really want to claim Byron Kidd as your co-author? This is quite a PR headache, given that he would be in prison for murder if he were not missing and presumed dead. Even if you don't care about figuring out a royalty split with his estate, I doubt you'll enjoy having your press tour dominated by questions about this lunatic.

As for the book itself, I do not understand the intention here. Let us set aside the fact that you have abandoned the narrative that you set out in the first five (very successful!) books. The quasi-epistolary approach is a strange stylistic choice on top of that . . . but most confusing is how you are folding in real news stories and interviews that Byron Kidd conducted, then combining them with fantastical episodes. Do you mean for this book to be marketed and read as a work of nonfiction? I honestly could not have manufactured a more vexing literary conundrum if I tried.

I have not yet passed the manuscript along to anyone else at Rotterdam, in the hope that you might reconsider your submission; I believe they could find you in breach of contract over this and refuse to print the book at all. Moreover, the film studio will be infuriated by the draft.

As a final personal note . . . I don't appreciate that you've included *our* email exchanges, verbatim, much less those you had with the counterfeit account claiming to be mine. At the very least, those ought to be stricken.

Please write back and tell me that (A) you've reconsidered this reckless strategy, or (B) it was all a joke in the first place, a most elaborate trolling of an old friend. Or if neither of those things, then please explain yourself. You owe me that at the very least.

Yours,
Stanley Gottheim
Senior Editor (he/him/his)
Rotterdam Press

REPLY

Stan,

I do not owe you an explanation. I owe you a book—and I've delivered it. It may not be what you expected or what you were hoping for, but it is absolutely what I want the book to be. Nonetheless, owing to our years of friendship and your patience in waiting for this manuscript, I will attempt to answer your questions.

First, regarding the co-authorship situation: yes, I've thought this through and intend to give half the proceeds to his daughter. I know that this issue would dominate the press tour, but I've decided not to do one (and in case you don't recall since it's been so long, I have complete contractual control over my appearances or lack thereof). Look on the bright side: hopefully speculation around this unique situation will be good for drumming up media attention, right?

Regarding the factual material of the book, including the interviews: I don't think people can object to having their on-the-record words printed. They said those things; I have audio files in my possession that will verify every syllable. The fact that their interviews (and my own) stand alongside elements of a more fantastical nature . . . well, who cares? It's certainly not grounds for a lawsuit. If anyone tries, I have the resources to fight them in court.

Regarding Rotterdam: this is not breach of contract. I've consulted with my lawyers and am satisfied I've upheld every condition of my most recent deal. If your bosses refuse to print it, that is their prerogative. But contractually, all rights will revert to me, and I've already lined up an alternative publisher—my new friend Misha Pimm, who is prepared to release the book through her website.

Regarding the film studio . . . why should they be furious? I happen to think *this* story would make a fine film. If they really want to make a sixth Fairy Tale movie that is more about Ciara and Queen Áine, and that delivers exactly what the audience is expecting, I won't stand in the way. The same army of hacks that birthed the other five scripts can surely come up with one for this situation.

Finally, regarding our email exchanges: yes, they are included, and I intend to include this one as well. I hope that you'll grant your permission because they are part of the story. And why would you refuse me on this? You come off as competent and thoughtful and sane. If anyone is maligned by the content of the book, it is *me*. Yet I am content to bare myself here truthfully because I know it is the right thing to do.

In the meantime, I am leaving Los Angeles. Gable and I both need a change of scenery and a change of pace. There's a lovely spot in the Irish countryside we visited once and will return to soon. I'm not sure if I will ever write again. If I do, it will be under a pseudonym and never another fantasy. And you'll be the first to know.

Stanley, you have been a delight at times, a pain in the ass at others, and a consummate professional always. I know this is not the way you expected your work on this series to conclude, but I hope you will embrace it for what it is: the most important thing I will ever write in my life. Thank you for your friendship.

A.T.

HANDWRITTEN LETTER

Postmarked from Los Angeles, CA, to Watertown, MA

December 4

Dear Liza,

Hope you're well! Glad that we got to meet at FairyCon, though I know that was brief and probably very confusing. You don't really know me, but I kind of feel like I know you. Not in a weird way, just in the sense that we have a lot in common.

First, we have a connection because of my website, TheQueen-dom, which I know you've used for several years. I hope you'll go back to writing fan-fic. I'm sure you could also produce a hell of a "Sightings" entry.

Second, I know you've felt like you're different from other people a lot of the time, and I'm sure that feeling has only gotten more extreme with everything that's happened lately and all the attention on you and your mom. I saw the "60 Minutes" piece and the interview you gave. You looked great and you're so well spoken on camera! But I'm sure it sucks being scrutinized, especially when you should be given time and space to grieve.

Third thing we have in common, I'm sure: we both miss your dad. I mean, I can hardly even begin to compare because I only knew him for, like, a week. I just want you to know someone else out there is thinking about him. When I first met him, I did NOT think we would be friends. I thought he was stubborn and rigid and kind of a dick. Which, basically, was all true. But he was also pretty fun to be around. And a bona fide capital-H Hero.

I'm sure I don't have to tell you, but he loved you like a fucking force of nature. Seeing the way he loved you, in fact—it kinda changed my life. I realized that all the things I loved, I wasn't giving them my all. Including my work. So I finally committed to a dissertation subject that my committee approved ("Magic Words: A Multicultural, Trans-Historical Analysis of Narrative as a Vehicle for Transformation"). With a little luck and hard work, I'll be a Fairy Doctor next spring.

More important . . . I got engaged last week, which was something I was dragging my feet on. Did it up in style: roses, music, the whole nine yards. If you're ever out in L.A. again, you should meet up with me and my fiancée, Shelby. She's rad, I think you'll like her. No BS, just like your dad. And I know she's gonna be an amazing mom. As for ME becoming a parent . . . I'll do my best. We're looking into surrogacy. After the wedding though. One step at a time!

Anyway—back to the real reason I wrote. The package. I'm not sure how much you know about HOW your dad saved you, but pretty soon, the whole world's gonna know the story because it gets told in the final Fairy Tale book. It'll be in bookstores all over the world. The publisher almost wouldn't print the book, but Annabelle basically bullied them into it. She's kind of a badass like that.

Of course, before a few million people gobble this story up—you should read it first and have your own experience. I mean, it is kind of all about you. And there will be lots of people who doubt it. Hell, YOU might even doubt it. But I promise it's true. Every word. Your dad wouldn't have it any other way.

So that's why I'm sending you this notebook. This is the original manuscript—your dad's investigative journal, including the text of all the interviews he did, plus articles and stories he discovered—all edited together by Annabelle the way she's going to put it out. I even got to help a bit; she's not an easy personality, for sure, but it was still kind of a dream come true.

It's all been copied over to a computer and formatted better for the print run, but this notebook is the original document. Annabelle gave it to me as a gift, which was super sweet, and honestly, a month ago I would've basically built a shrine around it and declared my life complete. But now . . . I dunno, it doesn't seem quite as major as it once did. And more important, I know that it will mean even more to you.

So here it is. Bet you never imagined your dad would be the co-author of a Fairy Tale book. But it's all for you, so . . . feel free to add your own ending. The story belongs to you. And who knows—there might even be some magic in these pages.

Sincerely,
Misha Pimm

EPILOGUE

FAN-FIC: "THE REBIRTH OF THE HIDDEN WORLD"
By Liza Kidd

After the old god died, the life force of the Hidden World was gone. Dust settled over the arena. Everyone looked for the father who had killed the Green Man, but his body was nowhere to be found. Like it had been absorbed into the ground.

The great Navel Tree that had once been so tall and mighty was nearly dead. It shrank down to a withered sapling. It was damaged and beaten up from the immense battle and earthquake and chaos. It was not clear if it would survive.

Every day, Queen Áine came and visited the tree. She ordered Gloverbeck to stand guard over it with three of his best men.

Nourished by the love and support of all the faeriefolk, the tree started to grow back. It reached its branches toward the warm sun. New leaves bloomed. As the Navel Tree regenerated, so did the feeling of hope in the Hidden World. Hope that they might survive. With new stories.

One day Queen Áine visited the Navel Tree and found it was back to its full height once again, and it bore its first fruit in a long time: a man. The father. He gazed around in wonder at the Hidden World. Because the belief and energy that had sustained the Green Man were not *gone*. They had moved. Onto someone more deserving.

The father accepted his new role as a leader of the Hidden World. He wouldn't be called a god, though. Just a dad.

So now it was his job to keep peace among all the magical inhabitants. Which was not easy, because there were so many different creatures, and the Doggerdoth was running wild.

The father's first act was to tell Queen Áine her people were now free. This was very smart because then she promised him the fey would help. Gloverbeck was put in charge of maintaining order, and he and the father turned out to be very good friends. They went on many adventures together. They subdued the Doggerdoth and rode him into the Living Labyrinth, and they got the trees to be more cooperative so travelers could get where they needed to go.

But the most important thing he did to hold the Hidden World together was he invited everyone to gather around the campfire. And he told stories, and some of them were true but some of them were made up, and he didn't care so much as he used to. The faerie children loved it, and soon they all started telling stories too.

The father enjoyed watching the Hidden World flourish. But he could not stop thinking about his daughter. It seemed unfair that he had freed her from this world only to be stuck there without her.

The father could no longer cross back over because he was no longer just *in* this world. He *was* the Hidden World. Same as the Green Man used to be. This place, whose existence the father had once denied, was not only his home. It was *him*. Its landscape was his body. Its winds were his breath. The life force and faith of its inhabitants were the blood coursing through his veins.

He wondered if his daughter might someday come back to him. Maybe just to visit. He wondered if she might be able to move between worlds, the way he had learned to during his mortal life. He hoped she would be someone who could believe in a story, even while knowing it was a story.

To help her find her way, he built a door. He placed the doorframe in the middle of a field. On its surface, he painted an image: The Wishing Well.

At the same time he was doing this, in the other world, his little girl was thinking of him too. She had read the notebook he had left behind. She was writing her own story in its pages.

And she was looking at her bedroom door, with the image of the Wishing Well that her dad painted a long time ago. She was looking at the crack underneath it and starting to think that she could see a light flickering there—a greenish-gold light like she'd only ever seen in another place that still felt like a dream. She was starting to believe that on the other side, there might be magic. That it might be possible to cross over again, to visit safely and return.

She believed, with all her heart, that she would see her dad again. That the force of his love was strong enough to bridge worlds. That even though he was infinitely far away, he was also right on the other side of her door.

So she put down her pen and walked through.

ACKNOWLEDGMENTS

This book is a love letter to stories, and a story is nothing without an audience. So I would like to first thank you, reader, for giving it your time and attention.

I would also like to extend thanks to the many individuals who helped me bring it into the world . . .

To my editor, Sarah Peed, without whom this book would have been something very different; thank you for encouraging me to make it more personal and guiding the process with a gentle hand.

To my agent, Zoe Sandler, for her unflappable belief in my ideas, no matter how weird they might be.

To my community of early readers, for their invaluable feedback and support along the way. Sarah Schuessler, Jenny Frey, James Hillmer, Kevin Oeser, Ariel Heller, Zach Toporek, Nicole Wachell, and the esteemed minds of Deez Notes.

To my parents, for encouraging me to read and make up stories.

To my daughter, Demi, for reconnecting me with my imagination.

And to my closest collaborator, my wife, Casey. For reading drafts, encouraging perseverance, and enabling all the time in which the work was completed. This book would not exist without you.

ABOUT THE AUTHOR

Dan Frey is a professional screenwriter and the author of *The Future Is Yours* and *The Retreat*. He lives in Los Angeles.

wordsbydanfrey.com
Twitter: @wordsbyDanFrey

ABOUT THE TYPE

This book was set in Sabon, a typeface designed by the well-known German typographer Jan Tschichold (1902–74). Sabon's design is based upon the original letterforms of sixteenth-century French type designer Claude Garamond and was created specifically to be used for three sources: foundry type for hand composition, Linotype, and Monotype. Tschichold named his typeface for the famous Frankfurt typefounder Jacques Sabon (c. 1520–80).